Running out of time

A novel by

Rachael Elizabeth Conisbee
(Shorty)

© Copyright 2004 Rachael Elizabeth Conisbee. All rights reserved.

No part of this publication may be reproduced, stored in a retrieval system, or transmitted, in any form or by any means, electronic, mechanical, photocopying, recording, or otherwise, without the written prior permission of the author.

Note for Librarians: a cataloguing record for this book that includes Dewey Classification and US Library of Congress numbers is available from the National Library of Canada. The complete cataloguing record can be obtained from the National Library's online database at:
www.nlc-bnc.ca/amicus/index-e.html
ISBN 1-4120-2417-X

TRAFFORD

This book was published on-demand in cooperation with Trafford Publishing. On-demand publishing is a unique process and service of making a book available for retail sale to the public taking advantage of on-demand manufacturing and Internet marketing. On-demand publishing includes promotions, retail sales, manufacturing, order fulfilment, accounting and collecting royalties on behalf of the author.

Suite 6E, 2333 Government St., Victoria, B.C. V8T 4P4, CANADA
Phone 250-383-6864   Toll-free 1-888-232-4444 (Canada & US)
Fax 250-383-6804   E-mail sales@trafford.com   Web site www.trafford.com
TRAFFORD PUBLISHING IS A DIVISION OF TRAFFORD HOLDINGS LTD.
Trafford Catalogue #04-0245   www.trafford.com/robots/04-0245.html

10   9   8   7   6   5   4   3   2   1

For Florrie, OG and Yamee
(Mum, Dad and Becca...my reasons for being here)

And for Nana Lil, I miss you every day

And for Unkie, Georgie and Vicki 'Slick' Raymond, Granny and Granddad Jim...see you again some day

I hope I make you proud

Special thanks to everyone who has provided unwavering support and encouragement since I began this journey into writing. In particular, I would like to thank the following people; my best friend always Lee 'Lee' Calladine, Lizzie 'Mad Bird' Christie and hubby Bob, Glenny 'Blurd' Shepheard, Auntie Pat Ludden and the rest of the Ludden's, Steve McParland and Catherine, Zoë 'Norv' Holland, Michelle 'Muppet' Zudeck, Philip and Susan Margolis, Ginger Perkins, Flo Johnson, Laura 'Woody' Wood, Fran 'Eddie', Nicola Harrison, Jim Gray, Debs and Stevie, Kimmie and Drob, Wendy Fitzgerald, Hugh Whittaker, John Rawlinson, Dave Purdy, Anthea Morton Saner, Tony Lacey, Jackie, Mary and The Sportsman posse, my MEIN roomies, especially DCW, Leader of the Pack and Haro.
Also thanks to my Harry Potter and the Chamber of Secrets mates, especially Mr Russell Lodge and the PR girls, Niki, Eloise, Vanessa and Amy. Pete 'Mr Elusive' Lewinson, thanks for recording the demo of 'Nina's song at your studio, and Tony Broadstock you guitar genius, thanks for collaborating on the song. More recently I have gained great support from my new neighbours here at the moorings. Special hello to Joan and Ray, Jan, Maria, Lydia and Ian, Chris and Simon, Ali and Paulie, Laurence and Olivia (life savers!) and lastly my favourite boy, Bertie! Finally thanks to Christine 'OM' Henwood and family, and Simon (mine's bigger than yours) Mills! When times were tough, you were all instrumental in helping me get through. I will never forget...

Feel free to let me know what you think of my first novel. Please send your comments to: rachaelconisbee@yahoo.co.uk or you can visit my webpage at www.trafford.com

From the day that we arrive on the planet
To the moment that we take our leave,
We are all born to struggle through this life
We are born to endure the strife.
We live to do our very best,
We live to keep up with the rest.
And yet, the only thing that is for sure,
Is that for the inevitable, there is no cure.
For we are all born to laugh and cry
…We are all born to live and die.

Sunday 2nd August...The Calm before the Storm

Why is it that every woman on this lousy planet is completely obsessed with her weight and figure, or has been at some stage in her life? Supposedly intelligent pillars of the community, fitness fanatics promoting the feel good factor, are in fact ramming their fingers down their scrawny little throats at civic functions and Masonic dinner dances. All furtively dabbling in illegal metabolic substances, in the vain attempt to obtain or retain the perfect figure. Of course, all the while assuring their friends and work colleagues that they have been a perfect size ten since their teens. No, really!

I myself, Jennifer Constance Evans have to raise my hand and admit to this. Not the bit involving the ramming of fingers down one's throat or taking drugs. Oh God no, I can't stand being sick. Never could stomach it. Or the bit about trying to convince my friends that I'm a perfect size ten...yeah right, maybe after I've been buried for six months. No, I mean the bit about being completely obsessed with my weight. Here I am a 29 year old successful, intelligent (well that's open to debate) woman standing completely starkers in front of a full-length mirror, tentatively popping my toes one by one onto the electronic scales. As if by doing so it's going to make me lighter. Convincing myself that by emptying my bowels of last nights Four Seasons Pizza, with extra cheese, removing my earrings and not painting my toenails until after I've weighed myself, really will make a difference.

I tie my shoulder length non-descript mousey blonde hair back into a scrunchie. It's still damp from the shower but no doubt it will dry in due course. Anyway, if I try to dry it with a hair dryer, it will only go frizzy. Then I'll end up looking like Crystal Tips for the rest of the evening.

I look down past the two nipples that in the loosest of terms I refer to as my breasts, over the rounded belly that I convinced myself just last week looks Rubenesque, down past the wild forest of pubic hair to the display on the scales. Oh God, not again. What more can a girl do? I've put on three pounds. Maybe if I dry my hair? I know why. It has to be my period. A quick mental calculation proves my pathetic clutch for an acceptable excuse, factually flawed. The reds aren't due to play away from home for another three weeks. Oh bugger.

This self-depreciating, masochistic ritual that I've put myself through virtually every day of my life really is proving to be a bind. As a teenager, to my utmost despair, my puppy fat had never actually gone away as it was supposed to. Saturday morning shopping treks to Ealing Broadway with the gang became a time to dread. Whilst my friends enjoyed the pleasures of fitting into Barbie sized clothes, I feigned interest in the way I looked, and settled for rummaging through the SALE items in HMV. I'd felt obliged to buy something, just so that I had a bag to swing, as we made our way home. Needless to say, I now have some serious crap in my Record cum CD collection, from that particular time of my life. B.A Robertson's s Bang Bang…who?…exactly…need I say more?

I kick the scales into the corner of the bathroom cursing like a trooper, and head for the bedroom. Oh bloody hell, I hate it when that happens. Why wasn't I born a size ten? Why is it that I'm always the lardy arse in a crowd? Why for once, just for once, couldn't the bloody scales indicate that I've actually lost some weight? Not too much to ask is it? In the bedroom I fling my dressing gown over the only other full-length mirror in my flat, which is propped up between the dressing table and window. There's only so much torture a girl can take in any one night.

I'm going to be late again. I'm always late. I'll probably be late for my own funeral. Beck is going to kill me. I pull the new little black number I bought from Marks and Spencer last Friday, over my head and smooth the virgin material into the contours of my body. Reluctantly and purely out of necessity, I push my dressing gown to the floor. I turn slightly and check for those telltale lines. Satisfied that my V.P.L is non-existent, I pull the dress back into line. On second thoughts, maybe I should wear some knickers. I make an executive decision and decide to go commando for the evening.

What the hell is that? It's bloody sore too. I hitch up my once perfectly aligned dress to take a closer look. There's something on my back. It feels like a little lump under my skin. On closer inspection the skin is discoloured and looks bruised. Come to think of it, I've had backache for about a month now, but haven't done anything about it. I'd been moving the furniture around in the lounge one afternoon and inadvertently backed onto the door. At the time it really hurt. It had looked a bit red too. But that was probably from where I was trying to rub it better, far too hard. After a couple of days, I didn't really pay much attention to it. According to my Father, I am forever the hypochondriac, so I'd dismissed it. Instead of my usual immediate diagnosis of "Oh my God, it has to be a tumour," I'd gone for the, "Yep, probably a kidney or wee infection, and that's just a swollen kidney." Well I don't know do I! Do I look like a doctor?

Each evening, I'd religiously applied the obligatory hot water bottle to the offending area, and averaged a family-sized tub of Brown's Organic Strawberry Bio Yoghurt per week. It had been a week and a half before anyone had had the decency to tell me that the yoghurt was supposed to be of the plain, natural variety. My nether regions had been a proverbial fruit bowl for days. Simon my recent ex of four days, seven hours, thirteen minutes and counting had thought I'd been attempting to keep our dwindling love candle alight. It hadn't worked. You can't light a damp squib with an empty box of Swan Vesta's. There were to be no more fireworks for Simon and me.

The evening he finished with me, as he stormed out of the flat, he left me with one of his little nuggets of advice... "Get help Jen. You're bloody barking, fucking crazy." With that he'd grabbed his keys from the hall table and slammed the flat door behind him. I'm sure he was laughing at me. So I'd shut my eyes and willed him to fall down the stairs. But my telekinesis powers must have been on the blink that night. He exited the building safely in one piece and sped off in the loosest sense of the word in his dodgy Fiat Punto, never to be seen again. I had spent the rest of the evening picking bits of re-hydrated strawberry out of my pubes.

I can get it checked tomorrow. I have an appointment booked for my smear. I have to go every year now, which is a bit of a pain. I know, normally you only have to go every 3-5 years depending on the local authority and their budgetary restraints, right? Well this is my third yearly test. You see, exactly three years and nine months ago I had a scare. And to say scare would be understating the event. I was, to put it bluntly, shitting a brick.

I'd popped along for my routine smear, and suffered yet again for the second time in my life, the humiliation that I'm sure most women feel when they have it done. To have another person and not their loved one, crouched over their fanny and being probed with something other than a dumb stick or vibrating confidante is very disconcerting. Yet again Doctor Singh did the do and that was it. Then it was straight home for the, oh so necessary, hot bath and soak of the cervix.

Two weeks later, I'd returned to the surgery to pick up the results. Unlike the previous time, the receptionist asked me to wait because Doctor Singh wanted to see me. So just a little apprehensive but not unduly worried, I waited.

My results had come back as being abnormal. He'd come out with, "Jennifer my dear, the results show that you have stage 2 cervical intraepithelial neoplasia." Well that was easy for him to say. He went on to explain that abnormal cells had been detected but there was really nothing to worry about. And with a little laser treatment I would be fine. HANG ON...laser treatment? "Bloody hell...I've got cervical cancer haven't I?" I'd blurted out. I can be such a drama queen at times.

After much reassurance and then a final impatient, "Listen Jennifer, you are NOT dying, my dear," he'd booked an appointment for me at the Outpatients Clinic at the Hammersmith Hospital. Two weeks later Beck went with me to hold my hand. She didn't actually come into the room with me though, thank God. It was bad enough with the doctor and the nurse being there. The doctor explained what he was about to do and got on with it. The smell of burning tissue was disgusting. It was uncomfortable and totally intrusive. When he'd done he just pulled his gloves off and said, "Take it easy for a few days and you will be fine. If you feel that you need some painkillers, see the pharmacist on your way out." With that he shoved a slip of paper, which on closer inspection proved to be a prescription, into my hand and left. Beck had to help me into the cab. I could hardly walk.

I'd had period type pains for a day or so, and then light bleeding for nearly three weeks after that. The worst part was the feeling that I had been violated. It was so much more impersonal and intimidating than a smear had ever been. I still involuntarily shudder at the thought of it. Anyway, I am getting to the point here honestly. I'd had to go back after six months and then every year for the next five. Hence, I go yearly at the moment. Fingers crossed, everything has been all clear so far.

Oh no, look at the time. I'm really late now, and Beck is going to be breathing fire. I realign my dress and slurp the last dregs of a large Jamesons down my throat. Just a quick glance in the mirror by the front door... mmm... not bad at all, though I say so myself. I remember, just in time, not to slam the door shut behind me. Mrs Gladstone, my neighbour in the flat downstairs, always goes to bed early on a Sunday. I tiptoe down the stairs, past her door and pull the street door gently too behind me.

Beck is my best friend and has been since primary school. The first day we met, the school bully Abigail 'Psycho' Bentley was beating her to a pulp in the corner of the playground, by the bike racks. I'd of course, dived in headfirst. I always enjoyed a good bout of fisty-cuffs and we eventually got the upper hand. The arrival of Miss Comerford, dinner lady from hell, probably had something to do with it too.

We had sat down and shared my Dairylea and Marmite sandwiches. Beck explained that Abigail had been picking on her because of the way she was dressed, and that she hated her parents for dressing her in this way. I hadn't noticed anything different about her. When I looked, I saw that she was dressed from head to toe in full hippie regalia. I thought she looked cool. And I told her she was dead trendy. She has green eyes too. I'd always wanted green eyes. Blue is so common, don't you think? So our friendship was forged and set in stone from that day to this. She'd sealed our friendship in her own 'special' way by giving me her first boyfriend Rupert Wade, two weeks later. You never really forget a gesture like that. In return, I'd given her a quarter of floral gums, and lent her my prized copy of Five go to Smugglers Top by Enid Blyton. Hey, it was the best I could do at the time! Those were the days.

Beck now works for a prestigious Production Company in Soho, just off Dean Street. As teenagers we'd both dreamt about working in the entertainment industry. Now Beck was living the dream for the both of us. I tried to get in too but failed, so settled for second best and set up a small secretarial business services company. It had proven to be virtually impossible to penetrate the barriers surrounding the film industry. Unless you know someone who already works in the business, you can forget it. Mind you, Beck hadn't known anyone, yet she had the persistence of a mosquito and eventually cajoled an acquaintance of an acquaintance to get her into a production company. Once in, she worked her arse off and was now reaping the rewards. Most nights she calls and tells me about her day, about the stars she's met and where she's been. She doesn't brag, she just knows that it had been my dream too and wants to share her excitement with me. She really is the best.

Look at the time! I'm supposed to be at the K Bar by 9.30pm and it's now 9.25pm. I hail a cab and climb in. "K Bar please mate, and don't spare the horses," I pant, somewhat out of breath. A grunt from the general direction of the cabbie is the best response he can muster. Why is it that I always pick the ones with a bad attitude and acrid body odour that burns the back of your throat? I suppose I'm just lucky, I guess. I open the cab window, lean forward and sit like a dog with my nose poking out of the window until we reach the bar.

We eventually arrive at 10.00pm. I jump out of the cab and in my haste, catch my heel in the hem of my little black number and fall arse over tit. Shit, that didn't hurt much did it. Momentarily the cabbie regains some level of consciousness just in time to see me fall, and has a good laugh at my expense. Damn, no knickers either! I straighten up, give him one of my award-winning smiles and follow it up with a crisp one-fingered salute. Arsehole.

I manage to hold the winning smile for the Neanderthal bouncer at the door, but he has to be gay or something. He just looks me up and down, which doesn't take him long, murmurs something to his colleague then proceeds to wave two skinny tarts past me into the bar. I manage to keep calm, make an effort to suck in my tummy and queue for another 15 minutes until they finally allow me in. The bar is full to bursting. I have to raise myself up to my full 5' 2" to see anything and scan the room.

There perched on a barstool like a radiant light surrounded by male moths, is Beck. She has to do nothing to attract both male and female attention, no matter where she is. A career woman and P.A. to a director, Rebecca Moonshine Monroe, earth child and offspring born to Chastity and Troy Monroe, hippies of the Sixties, is a sexual magnet. My best friend is a babe. I wave to attract her attention. I try to catch her eye. Then she sees me. Her face is like thunder. I am in deep shit now. I think for a split second about maybe trying the award-winning smile again. But she knows me too well. I have to fight my way through the testosterone veil that has engulfed her, and squeeze her arm.

"Sorry Beck. Been waiting long?" I squeak, already in defensive mode. "Oh, you have. I know I'm a bit late, aren't I. You see I couldn't get a cab. Well, I ordered one but it didn't show so…then it did, then I fell out of it." Her look stops me dead in my tracks. I'm obviously not going to get anywhere like this. So I concede, "No you're right, I am a lousy liar and a complete shit. You know I can't lie to save my life. I'm really sorry Beck. But I did fall out of the cab, honest. That bit's true. Look at my knees if you don't believe me," I whinge pathetically.

I scrabble for the sympathy vote, but I've got more chance of getting through to the Who Wants To Be A Millionaire hotline, than getting the vote on this occasion. So, I change tack. "What would you like to drink? A large Jamie's on the rocks? Oh, of course no problem. Back in a mo'…and listen, I'm sorry okay?" Her facial expression indicates that nope it's really not okay. Oh boy, it's going to be a long night.

I turn, draw my imaginary machete from my imaginary belt and slice my way through the heavy veil of smoke, elbowing my way into the human vegetation surrounding the bar. I climb up onto the footrest and jostle myself into an advantageous spot. After five minutes of waving my monetary beer tokens in the face of each passing bar person, I finally get served. I get us both a triple Jamie's on the rocks. There's no way I'll be attempting a further expedition to the bar, so I throw back another large one before I head back. When I get back, Beck's face is still contorted into her drop-dead look. I prepare myself for the onslaught.

She takes her drink and has a sip. Only then does she unleash her most lethal weapon, her tongue. "You complete bitch. I have been here for an hour now. I have been approached by no less than seven blokes, three lesbians, and two characters that I cannot be gender specific about!" I successfully suppress a giggle. "Where the bloody hell have you been?" She demands. "And why have you got you hair tied up in a scrunchie?" she adds sarcastically. Bugger, I forgot to take it out. "It looks crap." I'm about to explain to her when she holds her hand up in front of my face. "Save the excuses, let's get the fuck out of here."

With those few choice words, we down our drinks and are out of there within ten minutes flat. She always walks fast when she's angry, so I have to run to keep up with her. That's the price you have to pay when you have a 26" inside leg. Fortunately, Beck never stays in a mood for very long. She's fierce when crossed but soon mellows when plied with alcohol. Within the hour we would be boogying our little behinds on down at the Disco Inferno Club, just off Oxford Street. We'd be thrusting, bumping and grinding with every Afro wig-wearing male within a three-meter radius. I would eventually be forgiven but would have to buy the drinks and relinquish all rights to any top totty, should I be lucky to attract any, for the rest of the evening.

Monday 3rd August

After what must have been a debauch evening with Beck, I wake up in my own bedroom with a steaming hangover and jungle drum's pounding in my head. Or is that the pounding of Michael Flatley, River Dancing his merry little leprechaun way, through my dehydrated yet perfectly pickled brain? I don't exactly remember getting home, or for that matter, how I got home. But if the size of my hangover is anything to go by, it must have been a good night...I think.

Our Sunday evening jaunts to the Disco Inferno had become a bit of a habit recently. Now every Monday morning began in the same way. First into the bathroom, throw up, then flush toilet. I'll never get used to this being sick business! Struggle to focus eyes and stop the world from spinning round so fast. Wander in to the kitchen and switch on kettle, ensuring that there's enough water in the kettle first. It had taken two burnt out kettles, before I had managed to programme myself to fill it whilst still semi-conscious. Next, place three Paracetamol ready, next to mug. Two just isn't enough anymore. Finally, make coffee...extra strong, and sit down at the kitchen table. Pop the pills, then cradle head in shaky hands ready to start piecing back together the events of the previous night. I'd never learn. Boy, my back aches. The reality of the previous evening's discovery brings me back down to earth with a hefty bump. I'd found a lump.

Blurred images of the K Bar and unthinkable carnal carry ons at the Disco Inferno, are shoved to the back of the cranial orifice that contains my brain. I slowly walk into the bedroom to check. It's still there. With a quick proverbial flick of the flannel, I pull on a pair of joggers and a sweat top and set off for the surgery. I don't want to be late. It had been instilled in me at an early age that being late was rude and inconsiderate. I did try to adhere to this moral stance but have to admit that I'm a little scatty when it comes to time and managing it successfully. Let's face it, I'm crap. And my head is killing me.

I arrive at the doctor's surgery with moments to spare. The waiting room is packed out. Of course, it's the school holidays. Screaming kids swarm around the toys that are heaped in the corner of the room. Why do they always have to shout at the top of their voices? I can't stand the waiting bit. There is nothing worse than sitting in a doctor's surgery surrounded by ill people. You never know what you are going to catch. It's as if every cough is directed at you, with each sneeze providing an impromptu shower of meningitis or some other life threatening disease. I cover my mouth, tuck my head down, and just as an extra precaution hold up an old copy of Woman's Own in front of my face. Fortunately, I don't have to wait long.

"Jennifer Evans. Doctor Singh will see you now." The voice belongs to the receptionist. I haven't seen her before. She must be new. Seems quite nice, has a pleasant smile and appears to be human. I'll give her six months. This surgery goes through good receptionists like a dose of laxatives. I think that perhaps it's because the surgery's manager isn't the most amicable of people. I think she may have been a cab driver at some time in her past. With my head still buried into my chest, I push through the swarm of children, out of the waiting room into the corridor. Gasping for clean air, I knock on the door and enter the doctor's room.

Doctor Singh is sitting behind his desk peering intensely at his computer screen. He is a tall, thin gentleman originally from Delhi in India. He moved to England back in the sixties when he was only fifteen years old. He'd left India to escape the sickness and poverty and to make his fortune. And he had done just that. He studied hard to become a doctor and was now a partner in the practice. He was as honest as the day was long and usually dressed in a two piece suit, sporting an expertly created, starched black turban. Unless it was Dewali and he'd have an orange one on. He was always so patient with me.

Without looking away from his screen he chirps, "Morning Jennifer my dear, and how are we? We seem a little out of breath? Still smoking too many cigarettes?" he says accusingly.

"Oh no, I'm fine thanks Doctor Singh, couldn't be better," I say. "Well, actually..." I am about to tell him but before I can finish, he's off again.

"Good that's what we like to hear. So, I see it's time for your check up again my dear. Hasn't it come round quickly? Now pop your pants off, and assume the usual position for me my dear." I always have to stifle a giggle at this point. Doctor Singh says it every time without fail but never appears to go visual like I do. Trying to blank out the image in my head that vaguely resembles The Yawning position of the Karma Sutra, I pop myself onto the bed and knees bent, feet together, drop knees to the side and wait. Not that I'm an expert in the fine art of the Karma Sutra or anything. They all look roughly the same to me. The positions I mean. Well apart from one. That Curving Knot is bloody impossible, unless you've got double jointed hips. You'd need an Origami expert to straighten you out after that one.

"How's your Mother these days, Jennifer my dear?" he says, pulling on a pair of surgical gloves, making polite conversation. "And how's your little sister Elizabeth? Is she well?" Doctor Singh has been the family doctor since we were kids.

"Oh they're both fine thank you Doctor," I say. He asks the same questions every time I see him. And always when his face is roughly three inches from my love zone, and he has the bloody speculum inserted way too deeply. Why he has to get that close I don't know. Pushing aside my impatience I casually throw in, "Actually I wanted to talk to you about something else."

"Oh really? You want to change your method of contraception, the pill not working for you Jennifer my dear? Feeling a bit bloated, are we? What about the coil?" he inquires, looking up from between my legs. What's he saying? Does he think I've put on weight? But I'm lying down. I always look thinner when I'm lying down.

"Uh no, that's fine thanks," I assure him, trying to avert the blushing that threatens to rampage across my face at any moment. "No, I've actually found a small lump on my back. I'm sure it's nothing, but you know I thought I'd check with you, just to make sure. I think it's just a wee infection again, like I had before. Remember?"

"Oh right. OK, well we're all done down here my dear," he says patting my knee as he straightens up. "Pop your panties back on, slip your top off and let's have a look shall we?" He peels off the gloves and places them in the bin at the end of the bed. I pull on my joggers and take off my sweat top.

"So, let's have a look then. Mmm, does that hurt? Yes? It looks a little swollen. It feels very warm to the touch too. How long have you had it, my dear?" he asks frowning. I tell him about backing onto the door and describe the backache and discomfort that I've been experiencing. "Is there any blood in your urine?" I tell him no. Well not often anyway.

The next few hours pass by as if in slow motion. Doctor Hansen, Doctor Singh's practice partner, comes into the room, introduces himself and then does the frowning bit too. I sit there like a spare part, whilst they discuss their findings. I look down at the Pirelli spare tyre I have hanging around my waist. I wish my tummy didn't hang over my joggers like that. I try wrapping my arms round it in a vain attempt to pull it into a more womanly shape. But it doesn't work.

"You say you have had a sore back for several weeks now Ms Evans," inquires Doctor Hansen. "Any other symptoms, sickness, diarrhoea, any stiffness, sore abdomen? How do you feel in general? Tired?" He quizzes me in depth then huddles back down again with Doctor Singh. I pull my jumper back on. I've had enough of staring down at my flab for one day, thanks very much.

Dr Singh makes a phone call. He tells me I have to go to Hammersmith Hospital today and see a Doctor Gibson, some sort of cancer specialist. "Under the circumstances I think we'll have that checked out properly. Purely a precautionary measure you understand, my dear" adds Doctor Singh. "Doctor Hansen is going to call a cab for you." The cab arrives and I climb in. He closes the door behind me. I wind the window down.

"Now don't you worry young Jennifer. This is just a precautionary measure, you know. Better to be safe than sorry," he says again. He leans through the passenger side window and speaks to the cabbie. I stare blankly out of the window as the cab pulls out of the surgery car park. I've got this strange feeling inside. It's a mixture of fear, attempted bravado and sickness deep in the pit of my stomach. The streets pass by in a blur. The colours and images melt into one long journey of apprehension.

I know we've arrived because a raised voice interrupts my descent into my safe place, where nothing and nobody can ever reach or harm me. As a child, I had created this state of mind, following several emotionally charged traumas. Like my Grandad dying, and then being bullied at school. I think we all create a safe place as children, but as we grow older, most of us forget how to get to that special place. My safe place is still intact, and tucked away in the furthest recess of my subconscious. For some reason, I could never let it go. On hearing the voice, I turn and start the ascent back up the stairs to reality.

The voice belongs to the driver. But he's not talking to me. He's stopped and is asking someone for directions. "S'cuse me luv, which way is it to the cancer unit?" He whispers the word cancer, as if it's a dirty word.

The woman looks through his window and smiles, her eyes full of pity. Hang on a minute this is just a precautionary measure, that's all. It's only a check up for God's sake. I'm just about to tell her when the cabbie pulls away.

I close my eyes again. Moments later I am interrupted again. "I said, that's £8.50 luv," he says impatiently. We've stopped again. True to form he smells.

"Oh sorry, I was miles away." At this particular moment in time, I wish I was miles away. I give him a tenner and slam the door shut behind me.

"Hey, what about your change?" The cab driver shouts out after me, through the open passenger side window.

"Keep it..." I mutter.

"Thanks! Thanks a lot, luv. You have a nice day now." He doesn't think I can hear him, as he mumbles under his breath, "Poor fucking bitch." What does he know anyway.

The sun shines on the main entrance to the hospital. I walk into the reception area in a daze. The air conditioning fans are working overtime, but only stir the already hot air, providing no relief at all to the awaiting patients. The waiting area is scattered with people. It smells of disinfectant and faintly of sweat. An elderly gentleman is leaning up against the drink's machine, while a handful of kids run amok, screaming, seeking that all-important elusive parental attention. They in turn, are all looking anywhere but at their offspring, disowning them, as they become increasingly hyper in the heat. The cabbie has dropped me at the wrong entrance. Bastard! And I tipped him. The receptionist points me in the direction of the cancer unit. I numbly follow the signs.

On arrival a nurse meets me from the ward. Her badge reads, Staff Nurse Vera Swain. She assures me that it is better to be safe than sorry, and to get the lump checked out. I thought I was safe, and what is there to be sorry about? She guides me towards the lifts. We get out at the third floor. My mouth feels dry. I just nod as she tries to make polite conversation. I really have nothing to say. My mind is racing. With a jolt, the doors open. Momentarily, I feel myself swaying. She reaches out to steady me. I shrug her off and mumble "I'm fine thanks." I can't stop my hands from shaking.

Without delay, I am ushered into an examination room. Then I'm to take off my clothes and put on a gown. What on earth is going on here? Can somebody please tell me? The bloke with the stethoscope around his neck introduces himself as Doctor Gibson. He prods me and asks the same questions as Doctor Singh had asked. He asks about the treatment I've had for the abnormal cells in my cervix. He mutters something about a biopsy. "When did you last eat Ms Evans?" he asks.

I have to think for a moment, "Last night," I say. I'm not one for breakfast in the mornings. I reckon the extra half-hour in bed truly compensates for the lack of nutrition at that time of the day.

"Good that's fine. Right Nurse, please admit Miss Evans." He looks at me as if I've just won a prize at the fair. "Lucky for you, there's been a cancellation. Patient stuck in traffic on the M25. So we can do you after lunch so to speak. Right, carry on Nurse," he says and turns towards the door. "Soon as you are ready," he calls back over his shoulder and walks briskly out of the room.

"Okay love, do you need me to let anybody know that you are here?" she asks. I shake my head. There's no need to panic anybody. I can handle this. I'm an adult. "Right, I'll just get the consent forms. Won't be a minute," she assures me. She's back in fifteen minutes. She apologises for taking so long. She says she had to go to the main reception desk, as the unit's one had run out. I sign the forms and she's off again.

Moments later she's back. "Right then, pop yourself on the bed for me. That's it, lie down and try to relax." Nurse Swain swabs the back of my hand with an antiseptic wipe. "Now you'll just feel a little scratch, Jennifer love. There, that's just the pre-med. There we are, all done." She pats my other hand reassuringly. She pulls up the safety rail on each side of the bed, kicks off the brake and indicates to the waiting porter to carry on. It's weird I know, but I feel quite calm. It can't be cancer because I've been having regular checks for the last two years. So this has to be just a formality, right.

I can't help but notice the hideously patterned curtains hanging around the beds in the wards that we pass. They've got big blue flowers and green vegetation on them, with a red border surround. The designer must have been colour blind, pissed or on something when he designed them. They really are that bad. Then it's through two sets of double doors, and we're in. The operating room smells weird, a bit like the waiting room without the body odour smell. Wow, now THAT is a BIG needle you have there my friend. I'm not good with needles. I have a real aversion to them. I protest weakly, but the pre-med. kicks in…and…sleep…

Within roughly four hours, I've gone from routine smear, to a check up and now a biopsy. In any hypochondriac's handbook, that is going some. Dad would be so proud. I vaguely remember Nurse Swain coming over to my bed afterwards, and she yet again reassured me that, "All this is just procedure love," and that I should just shut my eyes and get a good night's sleep. "All being well, you'll be out of here tomorrow afternoon." With another motherly pat, this time on the arm, Vera turns my bedside light off and whispers a good night. Boy, do I feel sick and I've still got a thumping hangover headache.

Tuesday 4th August...Who wants to live forever? Well I do actually

There's nothing quite like being woken up by the aroma of a freshly squeezed bladder, or the produce from a strained sphincter muscle. I am aroused from my slumber by a cornucopia of nasal stimulants. I try not to breathe through my nose or I'll be sick. A nurse is doing her rounds, collecting the bedpans from last night. A rumble alerts me to oncoming traffic. A rather large Jamaican lady expertly manhandles the rogue tea trolley to a halt at the end of my deluxe NHS bed. "Well good morning my dear, tea, coffee or how about a nice cool glass of milk?" Her name badge introduces her as Eartha May.

"Tea please, milk no sugar thanks. Mmm, that's great, thanks very much." It is actually quite good. My mouth is as dry as a Saharan sandstorm. Eartha May gives me a hearty "You're welcome love, god bless you now," kick-starts the trolley into gear and sets off to cheer up the next willing victim. Bless her.

Out of the corner of my eye I spot a vision of beauty. Oh my god, it's the bloke who saw me yesterday. I notice for the first time that he is in fact quite tasty. I must have been really distracted yesterday not to have noticed. It's Doctor Andrew Gibson, the specialist. Picture a cross between George Clooney and Nicholas Lyndhurst. A quirky combination I know, but in my eyes oh so sexy. Tall, dark and handsome with smouldering grey eyes. He has to be a good six-foot tall, and I just know he has to have a stomach like a wash board. Oh baby! I feel a moist moment coming on, but quickly go visual imagining myself entangled in an erotic embrace with Sarah Bernhardt. A sure-fire way of catapulting anyone right back into the here and now at speed, and then some.

He's coming over. Here we go, let's get this over with and then get the hell out of here. I do have a life to lead you know. "Hi there Doctor, lovely morning isn't it? So, all clear then? I'll get dressed and be out of your hair in no time. I've got so much to do today." Hardly an award-winning attempt at nonchalance, but it'll have to do.

"Morning Ms Evans, sleep well?" he inquires rhetorically. "Good. Um, yes I have the results of your biopsy here. I'd like to discuss them and talk through a few things with you in a little more depth, if that's alright with you?" He shuffles from one foot to another and fiddles with his tie. I don't like the sound of this. "Please come this way will you?" he says. From the tone of his voice I take it that it's not a request, it's an order.

"Why, what's the matter? Is there something wrong?" I ask. I have to jog to keep up with him. Something doesn't feel right here. My hands have gone cold and clammy. My heart is beating at a ridiculous rate of knots. Vera, Nurse Swain joins us to complete our cosy little menage a trois.

He waves me into a side room and gently guides me over to a chair by the window. He perches on the corner of the desk facing me. "I have received the results from the exploratory surgery that I carried out yesterday. The results show that the lump was benign. They are the harmless variety. So that's all fine, nothing to worry about at all."

"Well, that's fantastic Doctor. How can I ever thank you?" I gush. I think I over-do the show of gratitude. I shouldn't have snogged him. But hey any excuse! I feel sick with relief. For a moment there, I thought he was going to say it was cancer. He gently peels my arms away from around his neck. He's not smiling.

"Please sit back down," he says firmly. "Jennifer, I'd like to ask you a few more questions." He reaches behind him and picks up a file from the desk. "I've been looking through your recent medical history. How are you feeling in yourself at the moment? Nurse said that you asked for headache tablets when you arrived yesterday morning."

So what's he on about now? Build me up to a complete state of panic. Then tell me I'm okay. And now more questions? Thanks very much. A little irritated, I tell him that I have been having a few headaches recently. But then, I think that's because Beck and I have been living life in the fast lane for some time now. I don't tell him that bit. Don't want him to think I abuse my body. My body is a temple. Well, perhaps the size of one of those small monastic retreats, anyway.

"Jennifer, would you say that since your little accident, let me see, nine weeks ago, that your headaches have become more frequent?" he asks, tilting his head to one side, as if he is really concerned.

Great! He would have to bring that into the conversation wouldn't he. "Well actually yes they have," I tell him. Come to think of it, they have become a pretty regular occurrence since the fall.

"Can you tell me exactly what happened nine weeks ago Jennifer?" he says with a serious expression on his face. He folds his arms across his, bound to be a perfectly honed, six-pack stomach.

Oh marvellous, I have to rake it all up again. I take a deep breath and explain. Basically, on one of the not so rare occasions of Beck and I going out on the razzle, let's just say I tripped? No, that's not true. I was pissed and fell over absolutely nothing. My legs got tangled up and I went down like a sack of spuds. Apparently, I was only out for a second or a minute or two. Then I was fine, sort of. Beck took me home and stayed with me. I remember being sick when we got back, but then after that, I have no idea what happened. I seem to have lost five hours or more. I have no recollection. I woke up alone. Apparently I had convinced Beck that I was feeling better, and she'd gone home.

When I woke up, I thought I'd been burgled. The flat was completely trashed. I woke up on the sofa in the lounge, with a bath towel over me. At first I didn't know where the fuck I was. It was only when I recognised the video time display blinking in the corner of the room that I knew I was in my flat. Relief was immediately replaced by terror. I was convinced that somebody else was in the flat with me. I'd crept from room to room, heart racing, expecting to be jumped on at any moment. Needless to say, there was nobody there. In hysterics I'd phoned Beck. She was back with me in twenty minutes.

The next morning, as soon as the surgery was open, she'd marched me down there. Within 48 hours I was at the Queens Square Imaging Centre in London for an MRI (Magnetic Resonance Image) scan. Doctor Singh's concern was that because such a vast expanse of time could not be accounted for and my somewhat irrational behaviour, that maybe I had caused some damage when I'd fallen.

Fortunately, the scan was clear. Mind you, it had taken a large dose of Diazepam, a type of Valium, to even get me into that machine to have the scan in the first place. It was like a big metal box, with a thin bed that slides right into the middle of it. I hate enclosed spaces, hence the need for the hefty drug intake. First, I'd had to take off all of my jewellery. Something to do with the strong magnetic forces used inside the thing, they'd said. Then my head was strapped down so I couldn't move it, and a grid placed over my face. There was only maybe six inches between my face and the top of the tunnel. My arms were laid flat against my sides. Please put your hands together and welcome…claustrophobia!

The other scary thing about it all was the sounds it made. One minute the radiologist was telling me what was going to happen, and then it was the deafening bleeps and blips, as the images were being taken. I was in there for thirty-five minutes. When I came out of the damned contraption I swore that I would change my life style, cut down on the smoking and drinking, get some exercise and just be grateful that I was healthy.

The intention was there, and I did join a gym and cut out the drinking and fags. This new lifestyle lasted approximately three weeks and then it was back to partying. Come on, I never said I was perfect. You only live once.

I pause for breath. The Doctor looks at me, then back down at my notes. He strokes his chin. He's got one of those really pathetic lines of stubble running from his bottom lip to his chin…uh attractive…I really don't think so. But he's still a commendable eight out of ten on the Evan's Totty-o-meter. "Jennifer, you say you are still having the headaches. Experiencing any dizziness? Do you find it hard to focus your eyes at times? What about sickness, been feeling nauseous recently? Have you noticed whether you've been more forgetful in the past few weeks?" he says staring intensely into my eyes.

I look at him and try to keep a straight face and ask, "I'm sorry but who are you again?" I laugh. He's not. Mmm…bad timing huh.

"Jennifer please, these are serious questions" he snaps sharply. "I want to understand what has been happening to you and want to know that when you leave here today, that you will be fine," he says dropping the attitude momentarily. His fake concern is not a bad attempt at it at all.

He looks back at the notes again. Then he asks me to stand on one leg. "Now shut your eyes, and touch your nose." So now he's a Yoga teacher? I'm a bit wobbly but that's understandable. It's not been an easy few days that's for sure. He excuses himself and leaves me with the Nurse. I ask her what is going on.

She looks towards the door, leans forward then whispers conspiratorially, "Between you and me love, he's out to impress Mr Anthony Darius. He's the Head Consultant here. Doctor Gibson has been trying to get on his team for months now. Every case he deals with, he covers every angle and makes sure that Mr Darius knows about it." She sighs and shakes her head, "Sad really, the lengths that some people will go to, to get on in this world." She smiles and asks if I fancy a cuppa.

"Yes please," I say. She goes to get the tea. I can't wait to get home. Yet again I have had a scare and it has to be time to re-evaluate my life again. But this time, seriously. How many chances is a person given, in their lifetime? I'm thinking about the gym, when the doctor opens the door. He has a smug and satisfied smile on his face. Moments later the nurse re-appears with a tray.

"Right Jennifer," he says. "I have spoken to my colleague." I sneak a look towards the nurse. She smiles and winks knowingly.

"He agrees with me," he says ever so smugly. Agrees with what? "I'd like you to have another MRI scan. I'm a little concerned that you are still suffering from headaches and having periods of dizziness and short term memory loss."

"Yeah but," I'm about to say that, well so would you if you lead the kind of lifestyle I lead. But he cuts me dead with a gesture of the hand.

"It's purely a precautionary measure you understand," he adds reassuringly. Where have I heard that before? He turns towards the nurse. "Nurse, please make an appointment for Jennifer as soon as possible. And we will have a follow up consultation, oh let's say a week after that." Staff Nurse Swain nods her head to acknowledge him. "Great!" He looks as if he has just worked out the formula for world peace. He's obviously impressed this Anthony Darius bloke too. Two cups of tea and an hour later, I have my appointment for the scan. It's in two days time.

Thursday 6th August...Queens Square Imaging Centre

I'm going on my own. I've done it before. I can do it again. It's not so bad and they have promised me something to calm me down again. So I'll be fine. I leave the flat early because I have to catch the tube into town. The last thing you feel like doing after a scan is driving through a busy London. I didn't realise last time or even for a moment think about not driving. So I'd ended up driving like a woman possessed, semi-conscious due to my introduction and subsequent reaction to Diazepam. I was lucky not to have been pulled over by the police.

It takes half an hour to get to Tottenham Court Road. Straight down the Central line. I get off there and walk the rest of the way. It's a nice day and I need to pull myself together before I go in. My appointment is at ten thirty. So I dawdle along 'til I reach my destination. The Imaging Centre is opposite the main hospital, in the square. Once inside, I follow the signs to the basement, where the MRI unit is based. I recognise the receptionist. She smiles. I don't think she recognises me, but then she sees loads of people every day. "Hi, I'm Jennifer Evans. I have an appointment at ten thirty," I tell her.

"Oh of course Miss Evans. I remember you now. Please take a seat. Tea or coffee?" she asks. I bet she says that to everybody.

"Tea please. And I'm supposed to have some Diazepam before I go in?" A pathetic embarrassed laugh escapes me. I hate being claustrophobic. I know it's all in my head. But you tell that to the rest of my body when it's in a tight spot. There is no reasoning with it. Minutes later she's back. I whack the pills down and will them to kick in a.s.a.p.

I was quite surprised last time I was here. It's really quite a tranquil place, not really scary at all. And the best part is you don't have to get naked, wear one of those back-less gowns, and wander around with your arse hanging out. They scan you fully clothed. Oh, the wonders of modern technology. "Jennifer, they're ready for you now." Out of the ether, the receptionist has materialised and is standing in front of me.

"Right, OK. Let's do it," I say way too loudly, clapping my hands together. A pathetic show of bravado I have to say, from the Evans contingent. Still feeling surprisingly calm and relaxed. She introduces me to Giles the radiologist. Mmm...at a push he's a seven on the Totty-o-meter. He holds out a sweaty palm and shakes my hand. Well, that instils bucket loads of confidence in me. He seems nervous. Stepping back, he trips over his chair. "OOPS...sorry about that, he mumbles, hastily pushing his bifocals back into place on the bridge of his nose. "This is my first day. Just moved back to London you know. But don't worry, I do actually know what I am doing." He chuckles nervously. He helps me onto the bed and presses the emergency button into my hand and says, "If you need a break push the button Jennifer and I'll be right with you."

"Oh I'm fine thanks Giles," I say, taking a deep breath. "Bit sleepy though. Wake me up when it's all over will you?" There's no chance I'll get to fall asleep in the damned machine. It's so bloody noisy in here. Even with the mandatory earplugs that I have to put in, the sound is deafening.

The bed slides into the man-made tomb. Okay, deep breaths and start singing every song by Dido. I try to keep them in album order. It makes me concentrate more. Half way through the album I lose track of where I am, so I start again.

"Are you alright in there Jenny?" asks the voice over the intercom. I can't move my head but if I roll my eyes and look down, I can just see my toes and just past them, through a glass window, is Giles.

"Fine thanks. Is it nearly over?" I ask. Starting to feel a little closed in now. My fingers start to tap the side of my body. And I can feel the surge of panic lapping at my synthetic shore of calm.

"OK, all done Jenny. I'm going to slide you out of the scanner now." He instructs me to, "Stay still until I get in there with you."

I go to nod my head but its fixed fast into the same position. Quick now Giles, I'm starting to get edgy here. Ten minutes later when I am re-orientated, I wave bye bye to him and the receptionist. She tells me that the results will be with Doctor Gibson within the week. In a daze, I don the shades and head for the nearest pub for a swift one. Then home for a bacon buttie and sleep. What a horrible day. Still the worst is over now. I get to go home and spend the rest of the day deep sea duvet diving.

Monday 10th August

What happened to the, 'I am going to change my lifestyle, give up smoking and get a grip'? Yet again, true to current form, Beck and I hit the town last night. I didn't tell her about the scan. I decided against it. Don't want her fussing unnecessarily because she will, if she knows. For a change we didn't go to the Disco Inferno. We ended up at some bar in Soho, with two blokes who said they were officers in the Queen's Home Guard. Beck found them and pulled them and I had her cast off. Charming! Mind you he was all right actually...I think. God I can't remember what he looked like.

I'm waiting for the kettle to boil in my usual post-night out hangover position, when the phone rings. Why does it have to ring so loud? Mustering up the dregs from my reserve tank of strength, I stumble into the hall and grab the phone. "Hello" is all I can manage. Obviously must have used up the reserve some time during the night. But can I remember...?

"Good morning. Is that Miss Evans?" inquires the polite voice at the other end of the line.

"Huh, speaking." I think I'm going to faint. It has to be said that I am not good in the mornings, especially with a hangover of this size and magnitude.

"It's Doctor Gibson's secretary, Amy speaking," she says. "The Doctor has asked me to give you call. He has the results back from your MRI scan. Would it be at all possible for you to come in and see him today?" she asks.

Suddenly I am awake. "I thought the results weren't due back for a week. My appointment is for Thursday," I probe warily. "Why does he want to see me today?"

"I really don't know Miss Evans. The doctor has just asked me to ask you to come in today if you can," she adds lamely.

"Fine well I'd better come in then hadn't I," I snap. Why I am snapping? I don't know. I suppose it's a fair enough request if he has the results back early. Anyway, it's not as if I'm really that worried. They're all purely precautionary measures. I just hope his thoroughness gets him his place on Mr Whatever-your-name-is's team. Hang on, what if there is something wrong? No she would say surely. I'd be able to tell by the tone of her voice.

"Miss Evans are you still there?" she interrupts my attempt at rationalising the conversation.

"Huh, yes, sorry about that. What time did you say, eleven forty-five? Okay, bye." I put the phone back onto the cradle and head for the bathroom. I feel sick again. Did I have a kebab and chilli sauce last night on the way home? Oh look, deep joy, yes I think I did.

Eleven forty-five

Still feeling decidedly dodgy, I've made it to the hospital with time to spare. I only have to wait five minutes, and then a nurse shows me to one of the consultation rooms. Knocking on the door before I enter, I take a breath and dismiss the butterflies in my stomach as being post kebab momentary stress disorder. If in doubt blame it on the kebab. Usually works for me.

"Come in," shouts the voice from behind the door. I recognise it as Doctor Gibson's dulcet tones. He is sitting at a rather untidy desk. He looks up from his paperwork and is on his feet in seconds. "Miss Evans, thanks for coming in. Please take a seat." He gestures towards the vacant chair in front of the desk. Only when I am seated, do I notice a pale-faced gentleman standing by the examination couch. I smile. He smiles back.

"Oh forgive me," blurts Doctor Gibson. "This is my colleague Mr Darius. He is the Head Consultant here at the hospital." The pale-faced man takes a step forward and shakes my hand. It's a firm strong handshake.

"Good morning Ms Evans," he says quietly.

I nod my head to acknowledge him and turn back to Doctor Gibson. "So what's the problem then?" I ask. I just want to get this over and done with, once and for all.

"Well Ms Evans...Jennifer, the results from your MRI scan are back with us. And due to their findings, I thought it best that we have you in sooner rather than later." He's burbling, and talking way too fast. There are sweat stains on his shirt, under his arms. Okay, you're making me nervous now.

"The thing is..." Before he can continue, pale-face has stepped forward into the fray.

"Jennifer." It's pale-face. I'm getting dizzy looking from one to the other. I try concentrating just on him. "Jennifer, the results that we have had back from the Imaging Centre are not what we had hoped for or indeed expected," he says gently.

"Oh?" comes out as a whisper.

"Did you bring anyone with you today Jennifer?" he inquires, nodding his head towards the door. "Perhaps you would like them to come in and sit with you now?"

"I'm on my own," is all I can string together. They never said I should bring somebody with me. Why would they say that? Why would I need somebody with me?

"Oh right, well would you like to call someone then, perhaps your Mum? I'm more than happy to wait for them to arrive before I explain our findings," he adds.

"No," I snap, surprised at the sudden strength of my voice. "Just tell me what's going on here."

"Right then." He continues. "Here let me show you." He reaches back towards the examination couch and picks up a large brown envelope from on top of the bed. He flicks a switch on the wall, and a large white panel illuminates. He pins up two sheets that I know are scans. They'd showed me them before, the first time I'd had it done.

"This image on the left is of the scan you had nearly three months ago. As you can see it is totally clear. And this," he points to the one on the right, "Is the image taken last Thursday."

I don't have to be Einstein to spot the difference. The one on the right has a large dark patch on it. I feel uncomfortable and shift in my seat. I clasp my hands together. They are shaking.

He points to the dark patch. "This large patch here is what is known as an Astrocytoma."

"And what's that in English?" I demand. Fear drives my voice to an unusually high pitch.

He takes a breath, "It's a Grade 4 Glioma. In layman's terms…it's a malignant tumour."

I let out a giggle, "Okay, you're joking right? Now I know you have to be joking. These things don't just suddenly appear over night." Looking at their faces, Christ, they're not joking are they?

"I'm sorry, Jennifer," they say in perfect unison.

I can only manage an "Oh." That's bad right? Oh fuck that's really bad isn't it?

Pale-face's shaking his head and scratches his nose before saying softly, "Due to its positioning in the brain and its rapid growth rate…to get to that size in three months…as I said, I don't feel that any treatment will be beneficial to you at this time."

"So what can you do? I mean there has to be something you can do to help me right?" I again look from one to the other. Doctor Gibson fiddles with his pen and won't look at me. So I look to pale-face for answers. "Well?"

He looks at his watch and mumbles something under his breath, suddenly excusing himself. The sweat stains beneath Doctor Gibson's arms seem to get bigger the more I stare at him. My hands shake uncontrollably and the sound of my heart beating thuds in my ears. He stands up, walks round the desk and squats down. He takes my hands in his and tries to stop them shaking by squeezing them in his. "I'm going to die aren't I?" It comes out as a whisper.

"Well, we're all going to die at some point in the future Jennifer," he says quietly.

"How long do I have?" I blurt out, hysterically. My mind is racing. It's out of control.

He clears his throat. "Jennifer, It's not really the sort of thing we like to put a time scale on."

"Just tell me, are we talking months, weeks? Am I going to see Christmas?" I ask, praying for him to tell me yes. From the look on his face, I guess not.

"It's hard to say. Let's just wait 'til Mr Darius comes back shall we." Beads of sweat start to form on his forehead and under his nose. "He can address any of your questions then," he adds, patting me on the arm.

I'm not listening, my mind is racing, "Well what about Bonfire Night? And it's Lizzie's birthday in October. Lizzie's my younger sister you know. What about the 24th of October? Please tell me I'll be here for that? I've never missed Lizzie's birthday. Oh God, I'll still be here, won't I?" I plead desperately.

"As I said, let's wait for Mr Darius," he stammers helplessly. The door suddenly opens its Mr Darius. He has a woman with him. She looks like

Anita Roddick but her hair is flaming red. Looking slightly embarrassed, Doctor Gibson jumps to his feet and returns to his chair.

Apologising, pale-face speaks, "Sorry about that Jennifer." He waves towards the woman, who has a sickly smile on her face. "This is Drusilla Mackenzie, she is a special care nurse. She will be spending some time with you over the next few days. To make sure that you do not suffer any unnecessary pain and help you manage your medication levels."

"Hi Jennifer, I'm really sorry I am late," she says and holds out her hand to shake mine. I ignore it.

"Oh no," is all I can muster. I rest my head on the table. It's cool to the touch, soothing my burning head. Oh dear, this is not good. Everything has gone wrong. This can't be happening to me. I take a deep breath and manage a whisper, "Please, just tell me. I have to know. I'm going to die aren't I? How long do I have?" It's an effort to get the last few words out.

"Well as I said Jennifer..." Doctor Gibson starts to say but is cut dead in his tracks. I look up in time to see pale face giving him a savage look.

Overwhelmed by emotions I can't stand it any longer. I'm on my feet and in Darius's face, only because he is the nearest one to me out of the three of them. "For fucks sake...Just tell me I have a right to know. Please just tell me...tell me, tell me when? I have to know." My stomach clenches into a ball. The tightness in my chest restricts my breathing. Fear threatens to encroach upon my fragile state of so called sanity.

"Jennifer, I'm sorry," he sighs. "At the rate that the tumour is growing, there is no way we can stop it. It's inaccessible. We cannot operate. Any treatment would not be beneficial to you now. How long? It's hard to say at this point...but a week maybe two. I really am so very sorry." He gently releases my grip from his jacket.

But that's ridiculous. That's not enough time. Oh no, downward spiral, out of control. The room's going hazy. Not good, not good at all. Mayday, mayday...

"Jennifer, Jennifer love, can you hear me, Jennifer? ..."

I wake up on a bed in an empty ward. Those bloody disgusting curtains again. I must have passed out. God, my head is sore. I reach up to find a small bump on my forehead. I must have banged it when I collapsed. I don't remember. All I know is that I have to get out of here right now. I focus my eyes. Drusilla Mackenzie is sitting by the bed. I notice that she has a hold of my hand and I immediately extract it from her grip. By doing so, I send my bag flying. As it hits the floor it spills its contents.

"How are you feeling?" she asks me. Well ask a bloody silly question. I tell her I feel fine and that I just want to go home now please.

"Jennifer, we have to talk about the medication that you need to start taking. And I need you to know that I am available at any time of the day or night, should you need anything. Even if you just need someone to talk to, I am going to be at the end of the phone for you." I look at her willing myself to hate her. But I can't hate her. It's her job right. She is paid to care. I feel a sob rising in my throat, but swallow it down angrily. She pretends not to notice and starts to pick up the bits that have fallen out of my bag. "I can do that myself," I snap.

She stops what she is doing, looks up at me and says, "I know you can, I'm just trying to help."

"I don't need your help!" I shout at her. "I said leave it," and snatch the bag away. I stumble. My legs are like jelly and I crash to the floor. She immediately pulls the curtain around the bed, shooing away a passing posse of inquisitive nurses.

"It's all right Jenny," she whispers softly, kneeling down beside me. Don't call me that. Only Mum calls me Jenny.

Grabbing my head in my hands and covering my face I choke back, "It's not all right though is it." All the fear that I have inside, bubbles to the surface. "Oh God…oh no…" I allow myself to be comforted by the total stranger.

When I catch my breath I ask her, is it because I smoke and drink too much? Is that why it's there? Have I done something to make it grow? Why can't they stop it? She shakes her head. "Sometimes even the medical world is stumped and cannot put any reasoning to what or why something happens Jenny." Gently she pulls on my arm to encourage me to stand up. Shakily I do so. She sits me back into the chair, and continues to pick up the contents of my bag.

When I get my balance back, we walk in silence to the pharmacy. I have nothing to say. Fortunately, she doesn't push to make conversation. I wait while she discusses the doctor's recommendations with the pharmacist. A child of no more than maybe five years old sits on his Mum's lap next to me. Her face is drawn and the bags under her eyes give away the pain that she is obviously feeling. The child has no hair, has a tube coming out of his nose and his skin is a faint yellow colour. He looks at me and gives me a big toothy smile. I force a smile back. The mother notices and tries to smile too then looks down at her baby. She has tears collecting in the corners of her eyes.

Drusilla turns back towards me and on seeing the child her face lights up. "Hey there Ben, how you doing?" she says in a really bad American gangster accent.

On hearing her voice, the little boy seems to come to life. The smile that he'd so generously bestowed upon me, he now beams up at Drusilla. "Hey Silla, I'm doin' OK aren't I Mummy?" His attempt at a gangster accent is so cute.

She gently strokes his head and whispers "You sure are Benji." She kisses his pale head.

Drusilla turns her attentions to the mother. She notices the tears and gently wipes one away, before it can drop onto the little boy's head. "Hey Mandy, come on now be strong. Keep smiling love. You need me, you call me, you hear?" she says. Mandy nods her head. She doesn't say anything or more to the point looks as though she can't. An invisible vice-like grip reaches out and crushes my chest. How am I going to tell Mum?

Drusilla beckons for me to follow her into an empty consultation room. I am speechless. I am numb. We sit at a table and she runs through the initial medication that I am to take. "Jenny, I'm sure that you have heard of Morphine before. Well, this tablet here is Diamorphine. It's the same thing but Diamorphine is the correct medical term for it. It will control the headaches that you have been experiencing and keep the pain to a manageable level. We'll start you on 5mg every six hours. We can up the dosage as and when you feel that it's necessary." She looks up to see if I am listening.

I nod once to acknowledge that I have heard her. So she continues, "This one is called Pethedine. It's a quick hit pain reliever. They give it to pregnant women during labour. It's a small dosage 10mg, and is only to be taken as a last resort. So, those two will manage the pain. Now unfortunately most drugs have side effects. Diamorphine will initially make you feel nauseous. This tablet here is called Maxalon and is a basic anti-sickness drug. Take one of these as and when you feel nauseous, but no more than three a day. These too have a side effect. They may well make you constipated. If so, just give me a call and I'll bring something round to ease that." The table between us is peppered with different coloured and sized tablets. "It all depends how many you take really," she adds.

She takes a breath, "And finally, these ones are Diazepam, a type of Valium. I think you have had these before?" I nod my head again. "Good, well you know what they do. Stick to the dosage. These are 5mg each. So, no more than three at any one time." She folds her arms and sits back into her chair. "We will up the dosage of Diamorphine when the time is right." For a moment she looks sad. But immediately snaps back to efficient nurse mode. "So, do you have any questions Jenny?" she asks professionally.

My face must be a mixture of confusion and sheer terror, because that's what I feel inside. I am frightened. I am so frightened. What is there left to say? I don't know what to do. She can tell because she says, "You're not alone Jenny," trying to reassure me. "Plus I can drop by on a daily basis if you want me to?"

I shake my head. "No," I respond sharply. I don't want a daily reminder that I am going to die thanks all the same.

"Well I am a phone call away, so whenever you're ready. If you need to talk that's what I am here for too," she says not taking any notice of my abruptness.

"Can I go now," I ask, praying that she'll say yes.

"Of course you can Jenny. Go home have some rest. And you know, just go out and do whatever you want to do. Make the most of your time," she adds. "I can help you deal with the physical pain. And if you let me, maybe I can help you sort out how you feel inside. The medication at the moment won't inhibit your daily routine. As I said we will probably have to up the dosage in seven to ten days, depending on how the tumour is beginning to affect you."

"What? How do you mean effect my daily routine?" I don't want to know, but I have to know. I need to know what to expect.

She reaches over the table to me, takes a deep breath and says, "Well, in about ten days you will possibly experience some difficulty in co-ordinating your hand to eye movement. That is to say that you will notice some change in your motor and sensory functions. You will become increasingly forgetful and have trouble finishing your sentences. But you will not experience any pain Jenny," she adds, patting my hand. "There is a chance that you won't even be aware that it's happening."

"Oh God." A shiver runs through me. Memories of Grandpa a week or so before he'd died invade my rationale. He'd spent his last few days on this planet completely away with the fairies. They'd assured us, the nurses, that he didn't know anything about it. But at times when I was cuddling him, I'd look into his eyes. Never have a saner pair of eyes gazed back at me. He knew...I'm sure he knew. He was simply trapped inside a failing shell of a body.

"And remember if you want me to, I can help you cope with this. I can't imagine what you are thinking or feeling, unless you tell me." Her voice brings me back to now.

Getting up out of my chair I hastily shove the assortment of doctor's sweeties in to my bag. I turn to leave, "Sorry you know, about earlier," I mumble, barely audible above the sound of my heart beating ten to the dozen.

"No problem Jenny," she says. There's that smile again. Christ, how does she do it? "Do you want me to walk out with you and get you a cab?" she asks.

"No I'm fine," again snapping. "No I'm fine thank you," I force myself to re-phrase. It's not her fault is it?

I briskly walk back through the Accident and Emergency Department, and out of Hammersmith Hospital. The sun is shining and the birds are singing a heavenly chorus. The leaves on the trees look so green today. It's such a beautiful day for a Monday. Even the Scrub's looks enchanting, if a prison can ever look enchanting. I feel cold and yet the sun is burning my face.

I grab a cab into town and for the next God knows how long, wander through Soho in a daze. I go there when I want to contemplate life or to be alone. Sounds crazy I know. One of the busiest parts of London and yet I can still feel alone there. I somehow lose myself in the hustle and bustle of it all. I usually just sit outside one of the cafés, have a hot chocolate with extra white chocolate shavings, and watch the world go by. But not today, I kept walking. The plaster covering the stitches in my back kept catching on my blouse. I'm not sure what else I did or where I went during the afternoon.

The next time I look at my watch, it is nearly six o'clock. Subconsciously I've got on to the Northern Line to Finsbury Park. Beck lives in Finsbury Park. She'll know what to do. On the tube I shove my hands deep into my pockets to try and stop them from trembling. God, this is really happening? But I'm too young. I have to catch my breath, so as not to allow my rising fears and anxiety get the better of me. I bite my lip for the rest of the journey to stop myself from crying.

Beck's flat is a five-minute walk away from the tube station. I stop off at the Wine Merchants next to the Sri Lankan grocers. Laden with three bottles of Chateau Neuf du Pape, the customary tube of Pringles, and a family sized bag of chocolate covered raisins, I arrive at the flats. I press Beck's buzzer on the intercom system.

Click... "Who is it?" asks my best friend.

"S'me," I manage to mumble.

"Who's me?" she snaps impatiently. She must be tired.

"Jen..."

"Oh, it's you." Her voice softens. "No sorry, I don't mean, oh it's YOU, I mean...oh... oh shit...just come on up"...Buzz. I push the door open, and take the lift to the third floor.

Beck opens the door, her usual radiant self. She has a big green towel wrapped round her and explains that she is just about to soak her bits and take a bath with Barry White, a large scotch and Hello magazine. She sees the wine and ushers me into the kitchen, urging me to get a move on, or her bath will be cold. I have a quick shot of her scotch to try and quash the shaky hand syndrome, and walk back into the bathroom. I hand her a glass of wine, and sit myself down on the toilet seat.

"Cheers mate," she purrs, from her reclining position. She really does enjoy the simple things in life. "So how was the Doc's then the other day? Sorry I forgot to ask?"

I find I cannot speak. The lump in my throat makes it hard to swallow. Beck hasn't noticed. She is up to her neck in bubbles, sipping her wine. She is in her own special kind of paradise.

She continues. "Did he rummage through your jumble and tickle your fancy?" she chuckles and smiles up at me, "Check your lips for sores and I don't mean the ones on your face!" Giggling, she chokes momentarily on another mouthful of Chateau Neuf du Pape. I look up from the floor and into her eyes. Her expression changes mid-choke. A frown replaces her smile. "What's wrong?" she demands. "Did he touch you, you know in, 'that way'? Jesus Jen, what's happened?" No longer smiling, Beck reaches out and grabs my hand. "Jen tell me, what is it?"

I feel the hot salty tears running down my cheeks and finally allow myself to stop chewing on my lip. I try a smile but my mouth doesn't want to co-operate. What do I say? It's been hard enough listening to those words being spoken to me, let alone having to repeat them out loud to somebody else. I take a deep breath, a slug on my whisky and whisper, "I have a brain tumour..." I can't look at her anymore. I stare back down at the floor.

The silence seems to last forever. "You have a what? Hang on a minute I thought we were talking about your smear, weren't we?" In a flash Beck is out of the bath, pulling on her dressing gown and leading me into the lounge. With her foot she launches Dustin her one eared tomcat off the sofa and into touch. "Now calm down," she says softly. "Start from the beginning, slowly. Tell me what's been going on?" As the sobbing subsides, I tell her what's been happening.

"Oh Beck, what am I going to do? I don't want to die." She holds me close, rocking me gently until I stop crying. Only then does she stand up and nip back into the kitchen. Moments later, she returns with another large whisky for me, and the bottle of wine. "Thanks" I say, taking the glass from her. I notice her hand is shaking. "I just don't know what to do Beck. I feel so helpless. It's real this time."

All Beck can manage is "Oh Jen." Her face has gone a ghostly white. She hands me the box of tissues. "Why didn't you call me? I could have come with you." I tell her I hadn't wanted her to worry or fuss. There is silence for some time. We both take long gulps of alcohol, nether too sure what to say next.

Beck breaks the silence. "How long...?" she starts to ask, but cannot finish the sentence. The remaining colour leaves her cheeks. She knows me so well. "Oh Jen."

Three bottles of Chateau Neuf du Pape, the rest of the Scotch, several Tequila slammers, the contents of a box of man-sized Kleenex and a prawn Jalfrezi later, the reality of the day's events seem to sink in at a more acceptable rate. No, that's not true. I can't even see straight let alone contemplate the day's events. Fuck, I feel buggered. I feel like calling Sam.

The following morning the hangover is intense but oh so very justified. Oh why do I do this? Beck's making the coffee when I wake up. I can smell it. I pad into the kitchen and mumble, "Hey." Beck manages a grunt to acknowledge my presence.

We sit down across the kitchen table from each other in silence for several minutes, not quite sure what to say. Eventually I look up. "You know I feel fine. No really...I don't feel ill at all. Well apart from a sore back, and my nose is a bit sunburnt from yesterday. And I have a bitching hangover again." But now we know that it's not just a bitching hangover is it. It's a fucking tumour plus an upset stomach. I ask her again why me? I look into her eyes searching for answers that I know she can't possibly have. Nobody has.

She reaches out a hand and wipes a stray tear from my cheek. "Shhh…Come on now mate. Here dry your eyes," she says handing me yet another tissue from her unending supply. I look up at her through my veil of tears. She gets up, puts her arms round me and hugs me again. I try to stop crying, really I do. But it's no good. She dabs the tears from my eyes, just like Mum used to do when I was a child, whenever I fell over or was scared. In a couple of minutes I regain some level of self-control, but not much.

"So, what are we going to do about it then?" she says defiantly. Is this fighting talk? "Are you just going to give up on me Jen? Going to give up without a fight?" Her voice quivers and falters for a spilt second.

"What can I do Beck?" I sigh. "I just want all this to be a horrible nightmare, and I get to wake up any minute now. I just want it all to end now." The words sound so hollow and echo around inside my head.

Beck is staring hard at me, I can tell. Her eyes are like lasers, burning through my closed eyelids. I squeeze them shut even tighter. I can't bring myself to look at her. Then she lets rip, "You selfish bitch, Jennifer Evans. So, you're just going to give in then, are you? Well fine! Wallow in self-pity, make it hard for everyone around you? Make them suffer too? Go on, be the victim. Well don't expect me to watch you give up. You give up and…you're on your own, my friend. Do you hear me? You're on your own," she shouts. With that she kicks her chair away from under her and storms out of the kitchen into the bathroom, slamming the door behind her.

Well that's fine then. So I'm on my own then. Fine! I wipe my snotty sunburnt nose on an already soggy cuff and sip at my coffee. How can she say such things? Christ, I'm supposed to be her best friend. I light a cigarette and sit in silence for probably ten minutes before I hear the toilet flush and Beck's footsteps coming back towards the kitchen.

She places her hand on my shoulder and says, "I'm sorry Jen. I just can't bear this, you know. It's not fair. Maybe if you hadn't fallen over that time in that damned shitty bar. If only I'd looked after you better…if…I'd…"

I hold my hand up to silence her. "Beck the last thing I need is for you to start blaming yourself. It's just one of those things. Shit happens." I attempt to make it all right for her to be sad, but point out that it's not all right to blame herself. "Look on the bright side, at least I know. In most cases these things go undetected and the person just drops dead and never sees it coming." I add, "At least I can live the last days of my life relatively pain free and not have to suffer, not knowing what's going on or why I am in pain." I rest my head on my hand. "I know what to expect."

"You won't give up on me will you Jen? We still have time to settle a few scores and there's still time left to achieve… stuff." Her voice brims with emotion. She's crying. I can't face her.

"Yeah, like what?" I ask wearily. I'm not convinced.

"Mmm? I don't know…anything you want. Hey I know, maybe we could get you a few more notches on your bedpost?" She tries to laugh but it's not quite a laugh, if you know what I mean. I open one eye and look at my best friend. Her sad smile says it all. She's really going to miss me. I can't let her down, can I? I can't fail her. More importantly, I can't fail myself.

Beck picks up her chair and sits back down at the table. On the table in front of her, she slams down a pad and a pen. "Right okay, what do you want to do you know over the next let's say, ten days?" she demands. "Listen Jen, this is your license to do what the fuck you want and get away with it. And I'll be here for you, and you know that, if you need me." Beck picks up the pen and turns to a clean page.

I notice that her hands are still shaking too. I see the look in Beck's eyes. I think I get it. The clock is ticking yet I still have time to do things, and time to say whatever needs to be said. I have time to say goodbye. This is my time. This is my time to achieve as much as is both physically and mentally possible. This is my chance to make peace with myself. And I know that my best friend will be here to help me and save me should I slip into the pit of despair that I now find myself teetering on the edge of.

And so the wish list was born. The next few hours were to determine my every move for the next ten, of the last few remaining days of my life. From a totally crazy twisted perspective, it promises to be some trip.

Wednesday 12th August... A cash withdrawal on the glorious 12th

This is going to be a bad day. I can feel it in my water. My head feels as though the contents are being whizzed up in a blender. I find myself back at the flat. I'm on the floor next to my bed, wrapped up like a papoose in the duvet. I can't actually remember the last part of yesterday. It's all a bit of a blur. I vaguely remember making a list of things to do with Beck, but after that, the small details like how I got home eludes me. The sharp, spasmodic, stabbing pains in my head, and a mouth that tastes as though it's been used as an ashtray for the night, adds to the already upset stomach and overall feeling of unwell-being. I really should give up smoking. Those things will be the death of me. I manage to manoeuvre myself into a sitting position, still cocooned in my duvet.

Then it happens. From the murky depths of my post-alcoholic stupor, reality rears its ugly head. Sharp pains rack my chest. They feel like no other pains I have ever felt or experienced before. I can't breathe. I feel sick, dizzy, and unsteady. Shit...I really can't breathe. Panicking, I fight to get free of the duvet. I'm only young. Christ, I'm not even thirty. There has to be a mistake. After several minutes of sweaty palms, dizziness, irrational behaviour and sheer panic, my irregular breathing calms. Finally free from the constraints of my duvet, I sit with my head between my legs, and allow the tears to flow like a spring tide. I'm not going to get old. In a matter of weeks I am going to die.

There, I've said it. I make a dash to the bathroom and am physically sick. The remnants of Château Neuf du Pape, Jamesons and a Prawn Jalfrezi arrive in a hot, bubbling torrent. There is nothing written anywhere to say how one should act or react to such news. Nothing can prepare you for something like this. Why me? My eyes already sore from last night, for the time being, leak the last of their tears. It all sounds so final, too much. Hiccups erupt from my already over worked lungs.

Slumped against the toilet bowl, I'm unable to move. With sick all down my Laura Ashley night-shirt, I realise that, oh God I've wet myself too. I haven't wet myself since the third year at primary school. Then there had been a just reason. Vanessa Montgomery my best mate at the time, had told me a particularly adult joke, for a nine year old anyway, whilst carrying the tuck table into the playground one playtime. It went something like, "What's the difference between a hormone and a vitamin?" "You can't hear a vitamin!" I'd laughed at the time, but hadn't quite understood the meaning behind the hormone bit until some years later. At the time it had been the way Vanessa had said it, not its content that had made me laugh so hard with such dire consequences.

Well that particular day, I had to relinquish my position at the front of the queue to David Benson, one of the fourth years. Then I'd had to make the humiliating trek across the playground with wet socks, to the headmaster's secretary for the regulation 'blue knickers' and little plastic bag for the wet ones. It all seems a world away now.

The dull ache in my lower back adds to the menagerie of pain and the self-disgust I am feeling. I close my eyes, exhausted. I come around sometime later, cold yet sweaty at the same time. It must be around 8.30am. Disgusted with my lack of self-control, I throw my night-shirt into the bin and have a long hot shower. The droplets help to wash away some of the anguish and despair. I don't want anyone else to feel sorry for me. After I'd burdened Beck with my news last night and saw the sadness in her eyes, it'd made me feel all the more desperate and scared.

I've decided that if I don't tell anyone else, then no one else will have to go through the suffering that I'm now putting myself through. They will just have to deal with...with the end. This experience is for me and for me alone. And that's how I feel right at this moment in time, alone. There is nothing anyone can say or do to make it right. The facts speak for themselves. I have a malignant tumour and I am going to die. The words sound hollow inside my head. I have to make the most of the time that's left. I take my first Diamorphine.

I climb out of the shower and subconsciously pull the scales into the middle of the floor and weigh myself. I don't believe it. I've lost three pounds. I sit down on the edge of the bath. Sod's law that's what it is. I've been trying to lose weight for as long as I can remember. And now I have. Well, big deal let's put out the flags. I've wasted so much time worrying about how I look and how others see me. Jennifer Evans, it's time to face up to the facts. It isn't important any more. You will never have a figure like Claudia Schiffer. I should have figured that one out when I stopped growing when I was twelve. It is all so irrelevant now. I quickly towel myself off, dress in my jeans and a black top and head over to Beck's. After all, we have work to do. I have to do something to take my mind off all of this. I have to try and keep it together.

I arrive at Beck's flat to find her looking like death warmed up. She mumbles something about having a chat with JC on the big white telephone all night. And it had obviously been a one way conversation. She looks bloody rough but she'll live to fight another year. She's lucky. Dustin is busy in the kitchen, crouched on the table helping himself to Beck's discarded bowl of cereal. The smell of stale sick hangs in the air. On entering the lounge, I open the window...wide.

Last night, after a heavy bout of drinking, we'd decided that we would hold up the local branch of Lloyds TSB in Ealing, to obtain funds to finance the next few days. I do realise that in the cold light of day this sounds like a totally ludicrous idea. But after several minutes, we'd validated the idea by assuring each other that we'd only be stealing the interest that the bank is making on the customer's money. So like latter day Robin Hood's we'd be stealing from the rich, and giving to the poor…us.

I also have an ulterior motive for hitting that particular bank in Ealing. It's my bank. The bank manager there has turned down my requests for bank loans time and time again. Not even three weeks ago, he'd yet again declined to extend my overdraft limit. He'd said in his whining little patronising voice, "I'm so sorry, Miss Evans. But your credit rating isn't as it should be, is it…hmmm? I am afraid that at this particular juncture in the financial year, we are unable to offer you the basic overdraft extension facility." Why hadn't he just said, sorry but no? Too easy I suppose. So now because of him, I am incurring a monthly penalty on my overdraft. Well, he can shove it up his arse from now on because he's not going to get another penny out of me.

The Bonnie to my Clyde decided that we needed to dress inconspicuously and should both wear facial disguises. So she too has on her jeans and a black top. I have to say even in my drunken state, I had my doubts about doing this. But Beck seemed to be quite excited about it all. So I went along with the planning. I mean, we wouldn't actually go through with it now, would we?

So I ask her. "What's your plan Bonnie?" We're both flaked out in the lounge.

Beck pauses momentarily before saying, "Right when we get in there, I'll whisper to the assistant that we are robbing the bank. I'll tell them to hand over the money sharpish." She continues, "Now we have to look as if we mean business." We spend the next hour searching Beck's flat, turning out every drawer and cupboard, looking for suitably shaped possible armaments. Back into the lounge we deposit our potential arsenal onto the coffee table. "So, what have we got then, Jen?" she says plopping herself down on to the floor next to the table.

I look over to her. I really don't know how I'd cope without her. She's so strong. Right now she is the scaffolding holding my derelict life together, when really it should be falling apart. God, I am going to miss her. I wish I'd been a better friend. You know, more reliable. I wish she knew how much I am going to miss her, how much I value her, and love her. I won't hold back any more, I can't. "I do love you Beck, you know," I blurt out as the tears start to well up yet again. I want to say so much more, perhaps share some of my pain, but what right do I have?

"Oh mate, you know I love you too," she stresses. "Now, don't set me off here. We have a mission to execute, remember," she tries to laugh. The stronger one of us wipes her runny nose on her Christian Dior cardigan, clears her throat and changes the subject. "So, let's see what we have got to choose from." Two vibrators, a 10" Black Mamba or vibrating 6" Rib Tickler, a mini hairdryer and used mastic gun, from when she 'had a man in' to tile the bathroom. I didn't know she had a vibrator, let alone two. It's funny you know, you think you know someone...

Of course it has to be the Black Mamba for me, with foreskin effect. And for Beck, the deluxe Rabbit, "Just in case I get bored on the bus on the way to the bank," she giggles! We've decided to use the bus as our heist vehicle, basically because it stops right outside the bank and one comes along every five minutes.

So, here we are. It had all sounded so ridiculously plausible last night. We both look decidedly the worse for wear as we adjust and tie our respective pair of tights to form rather fetching facial disguises. With disguises and weapons concealed about our persons, we walk to the bus stop. The bus is late as usual. It is late 'on time' every day. We only have to wait for five minutes. As it turns the corner, I stick my hand out and flag it down. It's one of those buses where you pay the driver as you get on. So Beck gets on ahead of me to lay claim to one of the last remaining seats, while I queue for the tickets. "Two returns to Ealing Broadway, please," I mumble in my infamously crap Australian accent, trying to be as inconspicuous as possible.

"Sure Jennifer. That'll be £3.70 please. There you go, my love." Uh? I recognise that voice. I look up to face the driver as he pushes the two ticket stubs towards me.

Oh bugger its Uncle Bob. "Oh, hi Uncle Bob, thanks." Bob Truman is an old friend of the family and my godfather. His wife Sue has been like a second mother to me. Mum and Dad had made him a god parent because he'd driven Mum to the hospital when she went into labour with me. If I'd been a boy they said they'd have called me Robert in honour of him. As far back as I can remember, he'd always been Uncle Bob to me. I should have remembered that this was his patch. Shit! While I'm talking to Uncle Bob, Beck has found a seat towards the back of the bus. It is already three-quarters full with shoppers heading for the mid-summer sales.

"Will you say hello to your parents for me, Jennifer?" he asks. Uncle Bob's lively blue eyes peer fondly at me from behind his thug-proof screen. He's due to retire at the end of the year. With a wink he hands me back my change.

"Thanks. Of course I'll say hello. I'm going home in a few days so I'll do it then. It's nice to see you, Uncle Bob. Give my love to Auntie Sue for me won't you." I turn to walk away, then catch myself turning back. The woman queuing behind me looks on impatiently, 'tutting' under her breath. Well, she can 'tut' all she likes and bloody well wait a bit longer. I have something to say. "Uncle Bob…I…just wanted to say I…I do love you, Uncle Bob," I stutter. I've never told him that before but I've always loved him.

Uncle Bob looks up in surprise and then chuckles, "Go on away with you now, Jennifer girl! You're holding up the queue. I love you too. Now off you go you silly bugger. See you again soon." A big smile spreads across his face. He has a lovely smile.

I pocket the change and start to make my way to the back of the bus. The bus pulls away. Suddenly without warning, it veers and brakes sharply to avoid what appears to be a suicidal cyclist. Instinctively I reach out to save myself and make a grab for the handrail. Unfortunately by doing so, I have to let go of my bag. It falls from my grasp. As if in slow motion, my lethal weapon escapes from the confines of my bag and rolls lazily down the central aisle of the bus. Oh my God no…!

It comes to a halt with a bump against the foot of an elderly gentleman, four rows from the front of the bus. He looks down to see what has knocked his foot, then looks back up at me. With a great deal of effort, he bends down and picks up the vibrator. With a look of bewilderment in his eyes, he switches it from one hand to the other as if it's a hot potato.

I hastily make my way back towards him and extend my hand towards the Mamba to take it from him. I notice that he has small dribbles of spit running from the corners of his mouth. His eyes are open, but there is definitely no one at home. Without warning he jumps to his feet and starts shouting, "May the force be with you. Vader… prepare to meet thy maker!"

He starts to make a whirring noise, as he regresses into a world all of his own. The Mamba's no longer an innocent vibrator. Oh no, now it's a fucking Star Wars light sabre! Bloody hell. And I thought I had problems.

By now, Uncle Bob has noticed that there's a bit of a commotion in the middle of the bus. He steers the bus into the next lay-by, flips the security catch and comes out from behind his protective Perspex wall and approaches Luke Skywalker. He spreads his arms out wide. I think it's to assure Luke Skywalker that he is unarmed and not a threat to intergalactic peace. "All right, Reg. Calm down mate. What have you got there then? Come on now give it to me, there's a good lad" he says in a soothing voice. Reg, on seeing the approaching enemy, hugs the Mamba to his chest and starts to rock back and forth, babbling incoherently. Uncle Bob tries another approach. "Luke my son, give me the light sabre. You don't want to make me 'use the force' do you?" Uncle Bob is doing a fabulous impression of Darth Vader, even down to the heavy breathing. I didn't know he had it in him.

Well it seems to do the trick. Uncle Bob relieves Luke Skywalker of his light sabre and gently sits him back down into his seat. Reg continues to mumble under his breath about the dark side and the force. By now I have returned to the seat next to Beck, who is crossing her legs, unable to speak for laughing. "Sshh. For God's sake don't say anything Beck, please," I whisper to her.

Uncle Bob has hold of the Mamba. He has it between two fingers and is holding it at arm's length. "Does this belong to anyone here?" he inquires in an unnecessarily loud voice. He holds it above his head. For a moment he resembles the Statue of Liberty. A few gasps and giggles escape from the captured audience. One mother covers her daughter's eyes with her hand, and pretends to look disgusted.

I decide that it's probably best to keep quiet. I mean, I can hardly shout out, "Oh, Uncle Bob, over here. Thank God. Yes, it's mine. You see I've been going through a bit of a dry spell on the man front recently, so once a week I clear the cobwebs away with my super duper vibrating dust buster, if you get my drift. Wouldn't do to heal up now, would it?" Oh the shame of it all...

There's a tense silence from the other passengers. All of them craning their necks to see who is going to lay claim to and admit to owning the black love implement, in Uncle Bob's hand. Beck is struggling desperately to control herself. "Any takers? Going once, going twice..."

"It's mine. Over here." Hang on a minute that's my pleasure tool. Who the hell do they think they are? I crane my neck to see whom the voice belongs to. It belongs to a rather large lady with lank greasy hair, a British bulldog tattoo on her forearm, and a perverse smirk on her face. Oh my God, she's licking her lips. I am going to gag. At this point Beck loses it completely and is officially out of control.

"Really?" says Uncle Bob. "Well, there you are Delores. I'd give it a bit of a wash before you use it again if I were you," he quips as he gingerly hands it over. Delores takes the Mamba from him with both hands. Well it is a good ten inches. She wipes it on her leggings and places it into her well-worn Tesco carrier bag. God, I dread to think what she's going to do with it when she gets it home.

"Now what are we going to do, Jen?" Beck is laughing so hard that there's a danger that she will have an accident. We hastily get off the bus at the next stop, to re-evaluate the situation and give ourselves time to think. We walk for a few minutes and then stop off at the grocers next to the bank. It is a West Indian green grocer's, which sells a fine array of appropriately sized and shaped produce. Decisions, decisions…I decide on a plantain, pistol size. She has regained her composure. She informs me that, "You know, I think I've dribbled in my knickers." Well thanks for sharing that my friend. I show her my new 'gun'. It fits perfectly in to my jacket pocket.

"So, are we all set then?" asks Beck. "How do we look?" We stand outside the green grocer's and check out our reflections in the shop window. After several Charlie's Angels poses and a poor impression of Bosley from me, we pull ourselves together and get serious.

"Should we really be doing this Beck?" I ask. I'm still not sure that this is such a good idea. Well, I know it's not a good thing to do, but it would be nice to have some cash to spend. And all bar one of my credit cards are charged up to the hilt, so I can't even resort to using them.

"What have you got to lose Jen?" is her response. She's right of course. She's always right. "If we get caught, we simply claim diminished responsibility with mitigating circumstances. And you know me," she adds, "I'm up for anything. It must be my hippie mentality." She laughs for a moment then pretends to put on a serious face. Linking her arm through mine, we start to walk.

Outside the Bank, there's time for one last check. "Are you sure you're sure about this?" I ask one more time.

"Of course dummy, I just said so didn't I? I'm ready when you are mate," she says with a wicked smile on her face. "Let's just get in there and get out as quick as we can."

"I can't believe we're actually going to go through with this." I'm still not convinced.

"Right I'm going in." Beck pulls her disguise over head. Then with a thumb's up and her rib tickling love toy metaphorically speaking, cocked, under the jacket draped over her arm, she goes in. Shit, there's no turning back now. I'm to give her a minute then follow her in.

Exactly sixty seconds later, I pull my fishnets into place and push through the double doors into the bank. In hindsight, I think maybe the fishnets were a bad choice. On entering the lobby, I bump into Mrs Gladstone who lives in the flat below mine. "Morning Jennifer," she chirps as she pushes past me. She's got one of those lethal granny bags on wheels in tow. Thankfully she's obviously not got time to chat. She's past me and out of sight in seconds.

I whisper a "Good morning Mrs G, lovely day isn't it" after her. If I don't she'll soon make a noise about it. Mrs G had lived in the flat below mine for years. In the past she had owned the whole house with her husband Reg. When he died, she had half of it sectioned off and put it up for sale. And bought a cat called Paddington for company. The day I moved in there was a knock on my door. When I opened it, there was nobody there, just a tin and an envelope placed on my new B and Q doormat. The note read, 'Welcome to your new home. I am your new neighbour. I go to bed early on a Sunday, so please be quiet after 9pm. Apart from that, I am a fairly tolerant person. I have baked you a cake. Hope you like chocolate. It's in the tin. If you need anything, just knock on my door. Please return the tin when you've finished. Sincerely, Beryl Gladstone

I would have to make my apologies later for not stopping to have a proper chat. As I enter the bank, I make a conscious effort not to look at the CCTV cameras and head for the nearest available counter. I look over to Beck. She is already in place at counter one. I mouth over after three, one...two...three. Beck raises her coat and points her concealed weapon at the assistant. "This is a raid. Hand over the money," she demands menacingly. "Don't even attempt to sound the alarm." She looks over triumphantly, with her completely wicked smile still intact and a glint in her eye as if to say, there that wasn't so hard was it?

Now it's my turn. I cough to clear my throat then rest my lethal weapon, still cunningly concealed in my jacket pocket, on to the counter. "Yeah, everybody on the floor, this is a raid. You, hand over the money right now." The assistant just stares. It's as if she's slipped into a catatonic state. I tap the glass to get her attention. "Hello?" I shout. She snaps back.

"How do you want it?" she whispers in a very shaky voice. She is petrified. Her eyes start to well up and her whole body is trembling.

Oh no don't cry. "Look anything, just hurry up please," I whisper.

They start piling the money onto their respective counters. A hush has descended upon the bank. Shit. Where am I going to put it? In my haste I've neglected to bring a bag. I'm just not cut out to be a criminal. I lack the criminal instinct for detail. I knew this was a bad idea. I look over towards Beck. Please say you have a bag concealed somewhere about your person. She mouths back, "I forgot to bring one too." Oh hell. I look around for a suitable bag.

I squat down next to the woman directly behind me. She is lying face down, along with the rest of the customers in the now horizontal queue. They'd all hit the ground when I'd walked in. It was probably something I said. Oh well the damage is done now. There's no turning back. "Excuse me luv," I say. "Can I borrow your bag? Sorry to be such a pain, but we haven't done this sort of thing before. And this is a one off, honest. You do believe me, don't you?" I ask her. She nods her head in agreement or is it just to appease me? Bless her, she's petrified. I take her purse and personal belongings out of the bag and place them by the side of her head. "Thanks ever so much. I'll get your bag back to you." I kneel down even closer to whisper in her ear. I tell her not to worry, and tell her she is completely safe and that we're not really 'real' bank robbers. I somehow don't think she believes me.

Beck has heard me chatting and rolls her eyes in disbelief. "Jesus, get a grip Jen...Pen! I mean Pen...Penelope." I stare back at her in disbelief. She slaps her hand over her mouth. Oh, just a minor glitch then!

Without warning, the uneasy silence is shattered. Somebody has triggered the alarm. I turn just in time to see the bank manager bringing his right arm back up in to the air, along side his left. For a moment I forget myself and point my organic gun at the bank manager. Why did he have to do that? I have taken on the persona of Ronnie Biggs. I am an armed robber minus a train. And at this precise moment in time, have a surging violent tendency towards him. "Please, please, don't shoot." He places his pasty little hands onto the top of his head.

"Why did you do that?" I scream at him. "You've spoilt everything now."

Beck is busily stuffing the money into the shoulder bag. "Come on Pen, let's split man," she grunts. I think it's a bit late to attempt a cover up mate. And what sort of accent is that?

With phase one of our mission accomplished, we back out of the bank. God I hope the bus is there. In unison we turn as we reach the doors and run from the bank, pulling off the fishnets as we hit the street. In complete hysterics, we scramble onto the bus just as it's pulling away. The journey home is uneventful, unlike the bus ride in. Fortunately, there's no sign of Uncle Bob either. Safely ensconced back inside Beck's flat, I pour us both a large whisky while she empties the shoulder bags contents out on to the coffee table. After a large mouthful of whisky she starts to count out the money. We are both visibly shaking from the adrenaline rush.

It takes Beck just over an hour to count out the bootie. "Well that's… £5,750." The coffee table is awash with our ill-gotten gains. "Not bad for a day's work, mate," sighs Beck. "We can really start to have some fun now. We have to get rid of these clothes though, and quickly. You can borrow some of mine for now. Then you can trash these at the tip on the way home. You must make sure that they are pushed deep into the rubbish Jen okay? They can't be found. Can you do that? We can't have any evidence hanging around," she says firmly.

"Oh yes, good idea. I'll do that. No problem." I assure her that phase two the ditching of all incriminating evidence is in safe hands. I've already decided that I am not going to take them to the tip. It seems such a waste when there is a charity bin in the Tesco's car park, which is right next to the dump, and on the way home. Someone will definitely benefit from these clothes and if they go abroad to someone in need, surely that would be all right? I don't ask Beck for her opinion. I know what she will say.

Yawning loudly Beck takes a breath. "Flick the telly on, Jen. The remote's on that chair you're sitting on. It's probably slipped down the side. Got it? Good. Let's see if we've made the news." Beck sits back against the sofa and takes a slurp of her drink. I put the bag to one side and make a mental note to return it to the lady on the address label over the next day or so.

There's nothing on telly. We sit for an hour or so, channel hopping and nothing. We watch The Tweenies, then Blue Peter. Blue Peter just isn't the same any more. I reckon it all went wrong when Valerie Singleton and John Noakes left the programme. And whatever happened to Magpie? "Another drink, Jen?" Beck eases herself up onto the chair and again yawns loudly, stretching and bending.

"Um, please Beck." By now, the aching in my back has risen to a conscious pain threshold, and I shift in the armchair trying to make myself more comfortable. It's the six o'clock news. "Look it's Moira Stewart. Oh, I do like her. You know she's only tiny? My Dad saw her once in town on Oxford Street and…" Beck cuts me dead mid-sentence.

"Shush, listen…" she hisses at me, a bit too sharply for my liking.

"...Made off with a substantial amount of money. The robbers were caught on CCTV cameras inside the bank. One of the robbers referred to her accomplice as Jen or Pen? Do you recognise them? Do you know who, Jen or Pen, could be? Did you see the robbers leaving the bank at 10.30am this morning? Our reporter Anthony Hopkins is outside the bank. Anthony, what's the latest on this story?"

"Thank you, Moira. Well I'm here with Anthea Jones, one of the counter assistants who was threatened during the hold up. Ms Jones, it was obviously a very disturbing incident for you. Is there anything in particular that stood out, that was different about the robbers?" questions Anthony turning away from the camera, to face the assistant. I recognise her as the one I'd demanded the cash from.

"Well, it was definitely a woman. The size of her...her behind gave it away," she blurts. She could talk the bitch. She was obviously upset, but had still managed to apply several coats of mascara and purple lipstick to her ugly mug for the sake of the camera. Well, you can put lipstick on a pig, but a pig is always going to be a pig...

The CCTV footage shows us entering the bank and captures the whole sequence of events, up to our hasty exit from the building. We both sit in complete silence throughout the bulletin. "If you can help or have any information then please call now on 0208 345 7584. Your call will be treated in the strictest confidence, and you may be eligible for a Community Action Trust Reward. Do not approach them. They are thought to be armed and dangerous. This is Anthony Hopkins, BBC news, in Ealing Broadway."

Becky flicks the TV off, with the remote control. We sit for several minutes in silent disbelief. "Bloody hell Jen, we did it," she eventually says.

"Yeah, I know. I can't believe it." It was surprisingly easy. Beck's face is twisted, in deep thought. I chuckle, "Look relax, we're in the clear mate, trust me."

Beck shakes her head. "No...no it's not that," she says.

"Then what is it?" I ask, yawning loudly at the same time.

"I reckon that bloke fancied me," she says deep in thought.

"What?" What on earth is she twittering on about?

"You know, the bank clerk? God, I would happily hold him up anytime. And I mean that in a completely sexual and unadulterated way," she finally blurts out, rubbing her hands on her thighs in a very Reeves and Mortimer fashion. Unbelievably, even in the most awkward, unusual situations she manages to pull.

Admittedly, the footage did seem to suggest that her counter clerk was more interested in her figure than her counter side manner. "Well just be careful," I warn her. "Give it a few days for it all to calm down if you are going to make a move on him. You are a complete nutter, you know that!" I throw one of the cushions at her.

"And your point is?" she retorts, laughing hysterically as she launches a cushion counter attack.

Eventually a cease-fire is declared. We bag up our disguises and apportion the stash. Initially, Beck doesn't want any of the cash but when I mention that Christian Dior has just opened a new store, next to the Westbury Hotel opposite Versace, she gracefully accepts her share.

"Right I'm off then," I sigh wearily. I'm tired and want to go to bed now. "I'll get rid of the clothes on the way home. And Beck thanks for today. You know, for helping me, standing by me. I wouldn't have done it without you. For a brief period of time today I actually forgot about all this shit. You're one in a million, you know." I pick up my coat that I've hung up on the floor by the front door, then open the door. I turn give her a big cuddle and add, "I don't know what I'd do without you." I mean it too.

Beck buries her head into my shoulder and says something but it comes out all muffled. "What was that?" I pull away and hold her at arm's length. She's crying. "Oh don't cry now," I say, trying to be strong for her.

"I don't know what I'm going to do without you, Jen. Sorry, I don't mean to be sad in front of you. It won't happen again, I promise. It's just..." her voice breaks, racked with emotion.

"Look, don't worry," I say trying to comfort her. "I'll call you later, OK? Go have another large whisky for me, eh? And I'll talk to you later my old lovely." I struggle to the car with the two bin liners of clothes and cash, give a final wave in the general direction of Beck's lounge window in case she's looking out, start the car and set off home. God I'm so tired. Doctor Gibson said I would become increasingly tired and slightly disorientated as the days pass by. I can't imagine being able to feel any more tired than I do right now. And what's with the stabbing pains in my head. I can't wait for my next dose. Six hours has passed and I need it.

On the way back to the flat, I drop the clothes into the Third World Charity bin in Tesco's car park. While I'm in the vicinity I call into the store and buy a bottle of Jamesons and a few other essential items, then head for home.

A note on the doormat tells me that I have missed Drusilla Mackenzie. The note says to call her in the morning. I am completely shattered. I tick off the day's task on the list Beck and I'd created last night. I must have pinned it to the fridge in my drunken stupor. I pour myself a large whisky and head for the bedroom. Flopping down onto the bed I drift off. When I wake it's already dark. I check the alarm clock. It is just before midnight. I have slept soundly for six hours. I pull the curtains, get undressed and curl up again. What a day…I can't believe we just did that.

Thursday 13th August... Albert and the free spirit

Again, just for a change, I wake up with my brain rattling around inside my head, like the silver ball in an over used pinball machine. This waking up feeling completely shitty every morning has become a habit. The sun shines it's obnoxious beams through the chink in the curtains straight onto the bed where I'm lying, as if just to spite me. I've been meaning to fix those damn curtains so that they close properly, since the day I put them up. But, I'd just never got round to it that's all. Like so many things.

I swing my legs out of bed, wait for the room to stop spinning and stagger over to the window. As I pass the dressing table I pull on my Ray Bans. Boy, do I feel like I could pebble dash the bathroom and redecorate the living room, all in one hit. A wave of nausea sneaks up on me. For a second or two I have to hold onto the bedpost, and again swear to the Almighty that I will never drink again. On second thoughts, forget that one. What's the point?

I regain my composure, and throw a couple of Diazepam down my throat in a last ditch attempt to control the rising panic. After several minutes of tugging at the curtains and cursing, it is obvious that the buggers just aren't going to meet. With a final tug, I resign myself to ill-fitting curtains and make a beeline for the bathroom to take my pills.

On the hall table, the answer phone's green light winks spasmodically at me. Whoever has left a message will have to wait. Tide and time and my bladder waits for no man. I flush the loo and go back into the bedroom. When I'd got home last night I'd stashed the money under the bed. Original no, but at that time of night and after the day I'd had, it was the best I could do. Kneeling down I grab the bag and heave it out and up onto the bed. Odd, it doesn't feel as heavy as I remember. I struggle with the granny knot. Sod it. I've broken a nail. I'll have to try and remember to stick a new one on before I go out. I grab the nail scissors from the dressing table and stab the bag. Only then to my utter horror and disbelief I realise what I've done. I've dumped the wrong bag. I've dumped the bag of money in the Third World Appeal bin, instead of the bloody bag of clothes.

In a blind panic, I throw on my jeans and make a dash to Tesco's. Skidding round the corner into the car park, I'm forced to take evasive action. Where the hell did that come from? The oncoming collection lorry screeches around the corner, and just manages to clip my wing mirror. The driver mouths a few choice words at me on his way past. Let's just say, I don't think he is telling me to have a nice day. So I mouth back, "May your sacs shrivel up and fuck you too, buster!"

Slamming on the breaks, I come to an abrupt halt in front of the bins and jump out of the car. "No!" I scream. They're empty. They're all empty. I start kicking at the sides of the bins, cursing and wailing to myself. Well, I thought it was to myself. I realise after several minutes that I have attracted a good-sized audience that is now watching my impression of an untrained fire-walker dancing on hot coals, with some interest. I must look a sight. I'd pulled on my jeans as I left the house but that was all. I just have on my jeans and a crop top sports bra, which I always wore in bed. I'd read somewhere that by wearing one at night, it can help to delay the droopy boob syndrome that is the curse of all women by the time they reach their forties. I've even forgotten to put my shoes on.

I have to think fast. I turn to my captivated audience, and put my hands together and bow. "Thank you for watching my demonstration of the ancient Chinese art of Tai Chi. If you would like to take up this ancient form of martial art, then please pick up a leaflet in the lobby at Tesco. Thank you again. Go Hey Fet Choi." It's the only oriental phrase I know, and means Happy New Year in Chinese. Well it's something like that anyway. It seems to do the trick. They all start clapping. And one old man even bows back to me. After much handshaking and more Go Hey Fet Choi's, I get into the car and head back to the flat, on the way cursing and gesticulating at every passing motorist as if it's their fault.

Once back in the flat I make a cup of tea, with just a dash of whisky in it. Sitting at the kitchen table sipping the brew, I study the wish list. The light on the answer phone is still flashing. It is starting to annoy me. You know what it's like, you're trying to concentrate and just on the peripheral of your vision something distracts you. I stomp into the hall and hit the playback button.

BEEP… "Jenny, its Mum. Are you still coming over next Wednesday? Your Father needs to know how big a roasting joint to buy. And do you prefer beef or lamb? Let me know love…I hate these machines…bye love"…BEEP. I love my Mum so much. I feel a muscle twinge in my chest. The lump in my throat is hard to swallow.

BEEP… "Jen it's Simon. Have you got my Oasis CD? If you have, I want…"

BEEP. What an arsehole. As if I'd have a copy of an Oasis album in my flat! And if I did have it, then I'd be using it to scrape the excess ice from the inside of the freezer compartment. Well, he can wait until hell freezes over. I would never be able to forgive him for his cutting remarks about my sanity, or lack of it.

There is definitely something wrong with this damn machine. I've only had it about six months. It started missing out parts of the messages a few days ago. But I'd been able to get the gist of them so far. Mmm... I'd have a look later. I rewind the tape, reset it and then shuffle back into the warm kitchen. The kitchen faces south, so benefits from the sun for the whole day during the summer months. Summer is my favourite season. Everything about it makes me feel so alive, the sun, lush green leaves on the trees and the intoxicating smell of rapeseed in the fields. Sitting back I shut my eyes for a moment and feel the warm sun rays on my face. I love my kitchen too. It's only small but it's like a haven within the madness that is my life. God I'm going to miss this. I have to force myself to concentrate on the list in front of me.

Usually at this time on a Thursday, I'd be sitting right here at the kitchen table doing the accounts for my small business, aptly named JCE Secretarial Services. I hadn't given it a second thought since Monday. Well, there's no need for me to do the books now, is there. It had taken me three years to build up a small client base, which provided me with a regular income. It was only secretarial work but it paid the bills and financed my busy social life nicely. But there's no point now.

I turn the card with Drusilla Mackenzie's details on over and over between my fingers for a moment. Should I call? I should call and apologise really. I was a bit off the other day. I'm going to call her. I fetch the hands free phone from the bedside table and dial the number. It's ringing.

"Drusilla Mackenzie" says the soft and mellow voice on the other end of the line.

"Oh hi," I stammer. "My name's Jennifer Evans. We...uh...met on Monday?"

"Oh yes, hi there Jenny. I'm glad you've called. I called round to your flat on the off chance yesterday but there was no answer" she says.

"Yeah, I'm sorry about that I was out and got held up?" Well the bank did anyway. I have to swallow a snigger. It's not even funny.

"That's fine really, no problem," she assures me. "Will you be in today, if I call round, say in an hour?" she asks.

"Well I have to go out this morning, but I can hang on." I have no idea what to expect from her, but I don't want to make her too welcome. I don't want her to think I'm needy or anything, because I'm not. She can come round, have a cup of tea and then go. As I say, I have things to do today. She assures me that she won't stay long and will see me in an hour.

I've decided that today I am going to do something that I have always wanted to do, but like so many things in my life, I hadn't done for one reason or another. Why? Because I didn't want to be a disappointment to my parents. Well, now my morals and standards seem to have gone right out of the window. Today, I've decided to enlist the services of a tattooist and body piercer, to fulfil my long time desire for a tattoo. I know it's hardly something to write home about but already I have a tingle in my tummy and feel quite unnecessary and aroused at the thought of it. I've always fancied getting my belly button pierced too. But they'd have to find it first. So, maybe not. Perhaps we'll give that one a miss.

I have wanted a tattoo for as long as I can remember. My unhealthy desire for Harley Davidson's and biker boys as a teenager possibly had something to do with it. So as soon as I was old enough I'd decided to get one. But each time I got to Frankie's Tattoo Parlour in Windsor, I couldn't bring myself to go through with it. Each time the image of my Father wagging his finger at me forced its way to the front of my mind and said, "If you want to look like a clown, buy a wig and a big red nose but don't desecrate your body." Well, sorry Daddy-o but today this girl is gonna get herself a tat. No more Miss Perfect Daughter, slave to the conformists of this world. I have nothing to lose. And if I don't like it, I won't have to live with it for long, will I? And Dad need never know.

I finish my tea and toast, and add the dirty dishes to the pile in the sink. The sun has made me feel sleepy. So a quick cold shower later and I'm awake again and nearly ready for the off. I've taken my Diamorphine and a Maxalon. I contemplate taking another couple of Diazepam, but decide against it. They do make me a little dozy and I have to drive to Windsor and back. I pack some essential items into my rucksack.

So now I just have to wait for Drusilla. I flick on the telly. Not even ten minutes pass and the front doorbell goes. I buzz her up. A soft knock on my front door and a lively "Hello it's only me, Drusilla Mackenzie" through the letterbox, confirms her arrival. Oh well here goes.

I feign a smile and open the door. "Hello Mrs Mackenzie, please come in." Stepping backwards, I beckon her through to the lounge.

"Hi Jenny. Lovely day isn't it?" she makes polite conversation. I offer tea or coffee. "Oh would love a coffee please," she oozes. How can she be so damn chirpy all the time? She goes into the lounge while I busy myself in the kitchen and have a sneaky fag.

"So, how you feeling? Have you started your medication yet?" she calls out. But before I can reply she adds, "You know the sooner you start it the sooner your body will respond." God knows what she's doing in there. I take one more drag on my fag and throw the butt out of the window. Waving my arms, I try to dissipate the cloud of smoke that has developed.

I hear her behind me. Embarrassed, I apologise for the smoke. "Just find it helps at the moment." As if I have to validate my actions to her.

"Oh not at all," she chuckles. I turn to see her with a cigarette in her hand. "You don't mind if I do, do you?" I have to smile. She looks like she is lost in time. Her unkempt hair and multicoloured T-shirt makes her look anything but like a nurse. She sits down uninvited at the kitchen table, lights the cigarette, sits back and inhales.

Placing the coffee cups onto the space between us I sit down opposite her. She has her eyes closed and is sitting right in the path of the sunshine streaming through the window. "This is lovely," she mutters then sighs.

I let her enjoy the moment and only speak when she has opened her eyes. "Mm... thanks for that." She picks up her cup and takes a sip. "Now for starters, let's get something straight here," she says. "Please call me Drusilla or Dru or Silla, I'm not really fussed, call me what you like. But not Mrs Mackenzie, if you don't mind." With that she pulls a face. She explains that, "It reminds me of when I was married. What a bastard he was."

I can't help but like this woman. I think she means well. "OK, Silla." For a moment I remember the little boy in the pharmacy in the hospital that day. The next thing I know she is resting her arms on the table and is staring right at me. "Sorry did I miss something?" I ask.

She laughs, "Blimey you were well away for a second there. Anywhere nice?" she probes.

"Oh no, not really," I say. I have to think for a moment as to why I asked her over here in the first place, and then I remember. "Look I'm sorry I was so rude to you that day. I was so angry." I look down at my hands. Unwittingly I seem to have curled them up tightly into fists.

"Don't apologise really. Under the circumstances I think we can let it pass don't you?" There's that smile again. Even her eyes appear to be smiling. "You still angry huh?" she asks. Well ask a fucking stupid question.

"Of course I'm fucking angry," I retort violently. "Wouldn't you be just that little bit pissed off if you'd been told that you have two weeks to live?" It's a rhetorical question and I'm not expecting an answer. But I get one anyway.

"It's good for you to get angry Jenny. And yes I'd be fucking pissed off as you so eloquently put it." She's smiling.

"Don't you ever stop smiling?" I snap unnecessarily. How can someone with a job like she's got, be so damn happy? When I look up her face is dead straight. I feel guilty now. I shouldn't have snapped. She's only trying to help right.

She takes a breath. I'm in for it now. "Not really" she replies, cradling her face into her hands. "You see, I reckon I'm lucky. I love my job. I have a home and I get to meet interesting people day in and day out. And you know the best thing about it? I get to help people. And as weird as it may sound, I get my kicks out of being useful."

So what does she want a medal? Before I can formulate another apology she continues, "My husband used to hit me you know. He used to say that I was as useful as a leaking bucket." Her laughter tinged with sarcasm, "He'd say I was a nobody."

"I'm sorry," I start to back track, but she just holds her hand up to silence me.

"So after one back hander too many, I left him. I said to myself, I'll show the useless bastard what I'm made of and enrolled at college and studied to become a nurse." She sits back in her chair again and shuts her eyes. "Since I left him, what six years ago now, I suppose no I haven't stopped smiling."

Looking at her I would never have guessed anything like that. I thought she was just one of those annoying people, do-gooders who always want you to think that they are so nice. Opening her eyes for a moment she sees my look of guilt. Patting my hand she re-assures me that it's OK. "I'm fine now Jenny. So that's why I need to feel wanted, to feel like I'm doing something worthwhile, in my life."

"Do you fancy a real drink?" I murmur, barely audible. But she hears me.

"Well you know I shouldn't, but hey why not. We can have a chat and discuss a few things civilly" she replies.

I wasn't expecting her to say yes. She laughs, "Hey, I may smile a lot and love my job but we all need our little vices right?" She winks. "Now where do you keep the glasses?" she inquires getting to her feet.

I pour us both a stiff Jameson and we retire to the lounge. Sitting back into the cushions she asks again, "So how are you doing? Do you want to tell me how you are feeling?"

I take a dram of whisky and allow myself to savour the taste in my mouth for a few seconds before swallowing. I stare deeply into my glass. What can I say? What am I supposed to say? So I just open my mouth and let it all out. "I feel numb and empty if you must know. And, I'm so angry it hurts inside. It's not as if I'm a bad person or anything. I pay my taxes, I love my family, and I'm kind to strangers, kids and animals. So I have to wonder, why me?" Still staring at my glass I raise it to my lips and drain the contents. I jump up and go get a top up, bringing the bottle back into the room with me. I hold it out towards her, but she shakes her head and gestures that she's fine for the minute. "What could I have possibly done to deserve this?" I say more to myself than her. "It's not fair."

"Mmm, good questions Jenny. But I can't answer any of them for you. Nobody can. You see, as I am sure you have seen at times during your life, sometimes it's not fair." She too drains her glass and holds it out towards me for a top up.

My face feels like its losing control and my bottom lip is shaking. I'm going to cry. She looks back towards me, and leans over. Patting my leg, she assures me that the best thing to do is to have a good cry. I choke back a sob cum laugh and tell her, "I've been crying since Monday."

"I know you have Jenny," she says comfortingly. I look up at the pictures of Mum, Dad and Lizzie on the mantelpiece. How am I going to tell them?

"My chest hurts," I add. Then in a torrent, all of my anxieties break out from the confines of my safety net. "Do you think it's because I've done something wrong? How will I know when the time comes?" I have so many questions for her. "I'm not ready to die," I gasp, dropping my glass and burying my face in the cushions.

She calms me down in a matter of minutes. She is good. "Nobody is ever ready to die Jenny. But we are all going to one day, breathe a final breath. For you, it's different. But that's where I come in. You are not alone. At least you don't have to be. I can help you manage your time and help you make the most of it. The medication you are on will keep everything at an acceptable level. And as we approach the final days, I can help you and up the dosage should it be necessary."

This is all way out of my league. I need another drink. She continues, pretending not to notice the amount of Jamesons I am knocking back. "Sometimes it's hard to let family help. Some people find it hard to allow themselves be seen as invalid by their loved ones. Again that's where I come in."

I manage to nod my head to show that I am listening. I just can't seem to speak right now. "Will you promise me that you will call me, doesn't matter if it's day or night, if you need someone to talk to?" Again I nod my head to acknowledge that I have heard what she is saying. "Have you decided how and when you are going to tell them?" she asks, nodding her head towards the mantelpiece.

I shake my head. I don't want to think about that. "I can't right now," I tell her.

She says "I can help you Jenny, you just have to say the word and let me in," so softly. "Look I really have to go now." She stands up and straightens her T-shirt. Draining her glass, she walks back into the kitchen and places it in the sink. "Remember Ben?" she calls out from the sink. "I'm off to see him now and his Mum Mandy."

She walks back into the lounge wiping her hands on the t-towel. "He's got Leukaemia you know. He really is a smashing kid." She laughs. I look over to her, standing there in the doorway. "He's always smiling too."

She turns throws the towel onto the kitchen table. "You going to see me out then?" she shouts from the hallway.

I force myself to stand. I feel so weak and tired. Crying makes me so tired. But I'm thinking of Ben. Now that truly is unfair. The poor kid. Wiping my nose on my sleeve, I lift my head and walk towards her. I have to smile. She's smiling AGAIN. It's infectious. "That's the spirit Jenny, try and keep your chin up. I know under the circumstances its going to be tough. But we will manage right?" she says defiantly.

"OK Silla." I open the door for her. "So I can call you…" Before I can finish my sentence, she's nodding her head.

"Day or night Jenny, at anytime during the day or night," she says finishing it for me.

"Take care love. I'll pop back when you're ready to see me again. Give me a call."

With that she disappears down the stairs. I'm just closing the door, when her head pops back round the banister. "Oh Jenny, you go easy on the alcohol," she adds. "Too much will make you feel quite strange, mixed with the medication." I force a smile and nod then close the door. Yeah right, as if I'm going to spend the last days of my life sober. I think not.

You know I may just call her. In a couple of days I may need a few softly spoken words of comfort. And who else is there for me to talk to. I've only told Beck. I don't intend to tell anybody else. I can't tell Mum and Dad. And Lizzie wouldn't understand. I wouldn't know where to begin.

I shuffle back into the lounge and close the window. She has left a pile of leaflets and booklets on the sofa. On top of the pile is a list of help line numbers and associations. Great some light bedtime reading material, just what I need.

I still have stuff to do today. I throw them back onto the sofa, before heading to the bathroom. I wash my face with cold water. Now, do I need a jacket? No, I'll do without. With that final thought, I shut the front door behind me and deadlock it. I put the bag into the boot of my passion wagon. I call her my passion wagon because it sounds so much better to call her that than a battered heap of rust resembling a Ford Escort. I turn and look over my shoulder on hearing someone calling out my name. It's Mrs Gladstone.

"Morning, Jennifer. Isn't it a beautiful day?" she calls out. Mrs G is hanging out of her lounge window, cleaning the window ledge with a big yellow duster. Why she doesn't come out into the garden and do them from the outside, I don't know. The last time I suggested it to her she muttered something like, "Oh no, wouldn't be good for my perennials, dear."

"Hi there Mrs G" I shout back, giving her a big wave. "You be careful now, won't you. I said I'd do those sorts of jobs for you, didn't I? You only have to ask you know," I shout across to her.

"I know love. Thanks. But I've got to keep active you know. Anyway, are you going somewhere nice? It's such a lovely day, isn't it? It's far too nice for staying indoors." She stops rubbing the ledge, and wrings out the cloth onto the garden below. That's not going to do her perennials any good, surely?

"I'm going into Windsor actually. Is there anything you need bringing in?" I ask.

I can see her frowning for a second, deep in thought. Then she says "You wouldn't get me a pint of skimmed milk and packet of chocolate Hob Knobs, would you? You know the ones I like don't you? Of course you do. That'd save me having to go out later."

"No problem Mrs G. I'll be back around teatime. Is that all right? Not too late for you?" I ask just to make sure. "If not, I'll go and get them before I go."

"No, that's lovely. Thanks Jennifer. You are a good girl. You have a nice day now."

Mrs Gladstone has recently been linked up to cable TV and has become addicted to American soaps. She is so funny. Every now and then she slips into American slang.

"Oh Jennifer?" she calls after me again. I know what's coming.

So before she can ask I say, "That was Silla Mrs G. She's..." Now I'm stumped. What do I say? A momentary pause and I have it. "She's my new personal trainer." I am a genius. A totally plausible excuse! With a knowing nod of the head, she disappears back into her flat. Her curiosity dealt with admirably, though I say so myself. I write myself a quick note and stick it on the dashboard to remind me to get the milk and biscuits on the way home.

Windsor

I wish I had a sunroof. Even with all the windows open, it's bloody hot in here. I fan myself with the RAC Handbook. The sun is so bright. I'm sure that this year it's stronger than ever before. I've had my car for four years now. For the first three and a half years it had been a pleasurable partnership, unlike the many other kinds of partnerships I've managed to get myself involved in over the same period of time. It'd only been more recently that I'd begun to notice the chinks and cracks in our once perfect, trouble free relationship. Then one day BANG...first the alternator went, then the gear linkage ring snapped. Whatever the hell that is. Then the water pump sprang a leak. Well in several places actually. It had been one thing after another for the past six months. It'll never pass its MOT in October. Still, I don't have to worry about that now. Ironically, my car is on borrowed time too.

It takes me half an hour to get to Windsor along the M4 and then via the Wine Merchants and newsagents in Slough. I buy two cans of Red Bull, three individual miniature bottles of Vodka and twenty Marlboro's. I'd changed to menthol after the first scan. But I may as well smoke what I enjoy now, and that's the Reds. I buy the Daily Mail because out of all of the tabloids, it's the easiest to read. I've never been able to handle a broad sheet. I always seem to end up with pages all over the place. Plus my arms start to ache within minutes, trying to hold the paper up at eye level so that I can actually read the print. I want to see if we've made the papers with the robbery.

I park in the car park next to the Railway Bridge that straddles the River Thames. I take a moment to admire the view. It is a beautiful river. The willow trees lining the banks dip their branches into the wake of each passing holiday cruiser, as if to try and calm the disturbed waters. I could quite happily sit here for the rest of the day and treat myself to a totally self-indulgent afternoon of watching the world go by. But I can't. I've got things to do.

I'm not 'au fait' as to how long a tattoo takes to do, so I get a day ticket. The last thing I want is a parking ticket on top of everything else. From the car park it takes ten minutes to walk to Frankie's, through the High Street then down past The Crown. I should know. I've done the route so many times over the years. On the way I stop off at the bank and draw out every penny I have in my savings account. There's not much, £650 to last me the next few days. I'll manage. Then I call in at WH Smiths and get myself a 'Make your own Will' pack. Drusilla told me about them. She said that if I haven't made a will by the time I die, then the state is entitled to everything. I'm not sure if that's true or not. So over the next few days I have to sit down, read the booklet and make one. She said she'd help me fill it out, if I need her to. I shove the pack into my bag and continue on my quest. I've tried not to like her. I don't want anyone's pity or help. But I think maybe if what she says will happen happens, I'm going to need her. I'm going to need somebody.

I turn the corner and there it is past the Crown on my left, like an oasis in a sea of chaos, Frankie's Tattoo Parlour. It's sandwiched between the Windsor Laundrette and Henry's Antiques. Parked on the pavement right outside the shop is Frankie's Harley Davidson. It's a Fat Boy. God, those machines do things for me. I've always wanted one. But now, I'll have to make do with drooling over this one. Frankie's Harley has a purple petrol tank with orange flames stencilled on each side of it. The highly polished chrome gleams in the summer sun.

The Parlour door is wedged open with a wad of newspaper. An off white beaded blind hangs in the doorway in its place. My shirt is sticking to my back. A dull ache pulses in my head, just where Mr Darius said the tumour is. I don't know whether it's the heat or my nerves getting the better of me. We're in the midst of a heat wave. Thankfully, it doesn't feel as hot as the summer of '76. I wipe the back of my neck with a hankie, take a deep breath, part the beads and enter the Parlour.

The blast of cool air is refreshing once inside the shop. A fake brass fan drones over head, adding to the cacophony of strange noises that fill the shop. The walls are covered with hundreds of designs all safely secured behind sheets of Perspex. And in the corner, there is a small reception desk with an Elvira lookalike slouched behind it. The young woman has most of her face pierced, nose, ears, eyelids, lips, and septum. As she speaks she reveals a large silver bolt through her tongue. "Yes? Can I help you?" She lisps. She's looking at me and is probably thinking, great, here's another yuppie rebelling against society. "See anything that takes your fancy?" she asks before suggesting, "How about a nice little birdie or a rose?" Now I know she's taking the piss.

"No, I'm fine thanks. I know what I want." I say as I turn my back towards her and pretend to study the walls. Feeling slightly woozy, probably due to the Jennifer Evans special brew concoction, the images on the wall in front of me come to life. Dragons, butterflies, skulls, roses and dolphins all merge together to form a surreal animation. Wow, these walls are awesome. The buzzing sound eventually stops.

"There you go mate," bellows a voice from beyond. "Fuck me, that looks fucking amazing, though I say so myself." I imagine the owner of the voice stepping back, making a framework with his fingers and admiring his new masterpiece.

The voice continues, "Remember, look after it over the next few days, and it will be fine." With that, the beaded partition separating the shop area from the back room is dramatically swept aside. A huge scary looking mammoth of a man appears in the doorway. "Carol, that'll be £45 for Animal's tattoo, less the gang's discount of course. So, let's call it £30 for cash. That alright with you, Animal?" asks the voice. The owner of it still concealed behind the veil of beads.

"Thanks a lot Frankie, you're the fucking best, man." The scary mammoth slams the money down onto the counter in front of Elvira. I can honestly say I have never heard so many 'fuckings' in such a short space of time. With that, Animal hitches up his jeans, re-arranges his bits and starts to walk towards the shop door. As he passes me, a waft of stale sweat tickles my nose. Suddenly he stops, right there in front of me. I again pretend to study the walls. I can feel his hot breath on my left ear.

"Hello babe, you wanna meet Albert?" he makes a kissing noise with his lips right up close to my ear. Who? I have no idea what he's on about. Elvira, otherwise known as Carol, sniggers out loud. Actually it's more of a snort really. God, if you think that's funny luv, you should take a look in the mirror. Now that is funny.

Yet again, the beads to the back room are swept aside by a large pair of hairy hands. Using my great powers of deduction, I take it that this is the man I have come to see. This is the owner of the booming voice. This is Frankie. With long hair tied back into a ponytail, he also has one of those handle bar moustaches that you'd expect an old RAF pilot to have. Stretching his chunky arms up above him and throwing his head back, he yawns loudly. "See you at the rally on Sunday then. Three o'clock kick off isn't it, Animal?" he asks.

Thankful for small mercies, the sound of Frankie's voice makes Animal turn away from me. I think he's lost interest in this particular victim. So there really is a God after all. "S'right Frankie, and don't be fucking late man, alright. You bringing any pussy?" he inquires as he re-arranges his bits yet again. Charming! Oh no, he's looking at me again.

With a scratch of his bare belly, Frankie opens his eyes and for the first time notices me in the corner of the shop, where I have now started praying for the ground to open up and swallow me whole. "Well, hello there. What have we here? Mmm... fresh blood! Want to come to a rally with me?" he asks rubbing his hands together a little too enthusiastically for my liking. I still have time to run. Animal waves his heavily tattooed arm, belches loudly and disappears out of the doorway, lurching into the street.

"Oh, I'm just looking thanks. You know, looking for a friend," I reply. I sound pathetic. I cringe at my own poor excuse. What am I playing at? "No, sorry. Yes, it's for me," I finally admit to him.

"Make your mind up, love. My eyes are hurting and I think I'm getting a migraine. My vision goes all blurry when I get one." He pretends to feel his way around the shop arms outstretched, with his eyes shut. Oh, I suppose you think you're funny, do you?

Carol is steadily losing control. She's looking at me as if I'm a prize twat. At this rate, with one slap I could easily re-arrange her face for her. She's starting to bug me. Frankie opens his eyes and winks at me, "Don't mind Carol, she's only teasing and so am I. Look, come on through love and we can have a chat, eh?" He majestically sweeps the beads aside and gestures for me to go on through.

I force a smile, steady myself and follow him into the back room. The beads brush against my face and then I'm in there, the inner sanctum. I am in Frankie's lab. He gestures for me to take a seat. I sit down in what can only be described as a dentist's chair with stirrups. Pleasantly surprised, I notice through the haze, that everything around me appears to be spotlessly clean. A box of lightly dusted rubber gloves are conveniently placed next to the chair. Various antiseptic creams and hand soap dispenser's line the shelves in a glass-fronted cabinet over the sink. The actual tattoo gun looks like the type of gadget that they'd used when I'd had my ears pierced some years ago.

Dad had taken Beck and I to Selfridges in Oxford Street when we were ten to get them done. He had made a day of it. We had our ears pierced first, then went to MacDonalds for a burger. It had been a memorable day. I had pearl studs and Beck had gold ones. On the way home we called into the chemists for TCP and cotton buds. We kept saying to each other over and over again so that we wouldn't forget to do it, "Every morning three complete turns to the left then three complete turns to the right." The memory makes me smile for a moment.

"So, what's your name young lady and do you know what you want? How about a little Rose or perhaps a swallow? Where do you want it?" Frankie enquires. I'd decided ages ago to go for the Chinese symbol for a free spirit. I found out what it actually looks like by asking at the local Chinese takeaway. Yes I do realise that they could have told me anything and I could end up with the symbol for Chicken Chow Mein forever embossed on my body. Well, I'm not that stupid. I've been to at least a dozen other takeaways and they have all confirmed that the symbol to be tattooed on my person is indeed that for a free spirit.

I pull the sheet of paper with the design on it from my pocket and pass it to Frankie. "What do you think? Oh, and my name's Jennifer."

"Mmm...that's cool, very cool. So where do you want it? I reckon it would look great on your tit, Jennifer." He holds up the bit of paper by my boob, then squints his eyes, deep in imaginary mode.

Well thanks for that little gem, but I think not. "Actually," I say, "I'd like it on the top of my arm, my right arm and just in black ink please."

With a disappointed sigh he says, "Fair enough. Just take your top off and I'll get myself ready." I pull off my Ealing Rugby Club shirt and get comfy in the chair. While he's scrubbing up and getting the needle ready, it gives me a chance to check out his own collection of tattoos. Virtually all of his body that is visible is covered in ink. Individual masterpieces blended together to form a walking mural. He has on a leather waistcoat, and a scruffy pair of Levi's. I notice that he has several body piercing's too.

"Right, let's do it then," he says clapping his hands together, sending a cloud of fine powder into the air. "This is going to take about thirty-five minutes and may sting a bit. If you feel faint then just let me know. Most people do with their first one. If you do, just put your head between your legs and take a few deep breaths. There's a glass of water on the floor by the side of the chair. You ready then?" I nod my head. With that, he switches on the needle and starts.

It's not too bad actually. I had been expecting loads of pain, and possibly a little fainting episode. But no, I can handle this. It's like an incessant tapping on my skin. It's not painful at all, just a little irritating. After a few minutes the area around the tattoo goes numb. The sound of the electric needle starts to have a hypnotic effect on me. I relax back into the chair.

I feel great. In fact, I feel on top of the world. It's as though all of my troubles are insignificant, just for now. I'm in a drug and alcohol heaven, and getting myself a tattoo. God, Dad is going to kill me if he ever finds out. I giggle to myself, not realising that I'm actually giggling out loud. For the first time in what seems like years, I feel rebellious, naughty and alive.

"So who's Albert then, Frankie? That bloke who was in before me, asked if I'd like to meet Albert. Do you know who he's on about?" I think I may be slurring, but Frankie doesn't appear to notice. He has his tongue just poking out of the corner of his mouth, deep in concentration. You know what it's like, you have a couple of drinks and you know what you want to say but those tricky buggers...words...just won't come out right. They try and trip you up. The drink lulls you into a false sense of security then before you even realise it, you're acting like a complete tit and don't even know it.

He flicks the gun off, and rests it on his knee. He doesn't look up. He's just staring down at the floor in front of him. "I know Albert," he says quietly. "Very well. You could say he hangs out with me all of the time."

"Really. So who is he? I take it you both know him then?" I can feel my bra strap is slipping off my shoulder. Frankie looks up from the floor, notices the strap and gently pushes it back into place. "Oh thanks, they always do that," I slur.

He looks deeply into my eyes and takes a deep breath before saying, "Listen love, not everybody gets to meet Albert, but would you like to meet him? He's a little shy, but I'm sure he'd be pleased to meet you." Frankie's eyes are twinkling like two sapphires. They're lovely.

So maybe I have led a sheltered life but I'd like to think that I'm quite worldly wise. Frankie is about to confirm the former. "Oh I'd love to meet him, please. Call him in." I look round eagerly towards the doorway.

There's nobody there. A little puzzled I look back at Frankie. He stands up, places the gun on his seat and removes his protective gloves. Then slowly one by one he unbuttons his faded Levi's. Now, at this point you'd think I'd be screaming or reacting in some disgusted way and walk out, but I can't. My eyes are firmly fixed on his flies. I am mesmerised. With a swift tug, he whips it out. It's obscene! There is no other word for it. It's a python. And there at the end of it, dangling like a curtain ring, is a huge silver loop. I try to look away, but I can't. Jesus that must have really hurt.

With a raised eyebrow and a smirk on his face he speaks. "Jennifer, let me introduce you to my best friend. Jennifer this is Albert. Albert, I'd like you to meet our new friend, Jennifer." He starts to gently stroke his pet python seductively. Now I should have been disgusted, perhaps offended but I find myself becoming extremely horny. But what the hell, seize the moment.

"That's uh lovely Frankie." I smile. "No, really. So what does it do for you? Does it hurt, you know, when you have sex?" I ask as I lean forward to get a closer look, trying really hard to focus my eyes.

"No, not at all. It feels pretty good actually," he says with total conviction. "It's something I had done for an ex-girl friend of mine last year. I was told that it makes the female sexual experience completely mind blowing. So I thought what the hell and had it done. And I have to say, I've not had any complaints, if you know what I mean." He winks at me and a sneaky smile spreads across his face. He's not bad looking for a biker. Well I am feeling tipsy and my vision is a little shaky.

Yep, I know exactly what he means. By now Albert has risen to unnecessary heights. This man and his partner should be in a circus. I start to feel a little uncomfortable. Not in a threatened way, but I'm rather embarrassed to say, in a damp way. Albert has certainly intrigued me and set my juices flowing, so to speak. Beck will not believe this when I tell her.

Slowly he starts to walk towards me, casually throwing his leather waistcoat to the floor. By now his trousers are around his ankles and walking is down to a shuffle. For a fleeting moment, a concern crosses my mind...how the hell is something of that size going to fit? I'm only used to stubbies and pencil dicks. Not that I am an expert on the size of male genitalia or anything. I've only slept with three blokes in my entire life. Before I have time to share my concern with Frankie and Albert, they are upon me. Oh my good God! I am Cinderella, and it fits!

It doesn't last long. With a final triumphant cry of, "He shoots and...he ...SCORES!" from Frankie, it's all over. If I never have sex again, which considering the time constraint enforced upon me is highly likely, I will die happy and content in the sexual gratification department.

After 'the event', Frankie pulls his protective gloves back on and finishes off the tattoo. The atmosphere is a little awkward to say the least. The silence is deafening. Still, I'll never have to see him again, so who cares? I close my eyes, relax back and enjoy my moment of euphoria. Eventually the constant whirring noise from the gun stops.

"There you go love, one 'free-spirit' tattoo. What do you think? Do you like it?" he asks. With that he reaches down and produces a small mirror from underneath his stool.

"Bloody hell" I exclaim. It looks massive. It's just on the top of my right shoulder, and it's truly a work of art. He gazes proudly at his work.

"Frankie, that looks bloody fab. Thank you so much. You know, you've made my life" I manage to say, before choking with emotion. I really have to try and stop feeling so damn sorry for myself. He probably thinks I'm having a post-coital hormone rush, or am pre-menstrual or something.

"Hey babe, are you OK? No regrets?" he asks with a look of concern on his face. Now how do I know that he doesn't mean regrets about the tattoo? I just know. He stands up and takes my hand in his.

"No really, it was great. I mean, it looks great. I am so happy. Thank you. Thank you for the fantastic tattoo and um...for introducing me to Albert" I manage to say, before going all shy as the mental image of a glistening Albert flashes up onto the big screen in my head. "What do I owe you?" I ask. Reaching down I get my purse out of my rucksack.

He's standing at the sink washing his hands. He looks over his shoulder at me. "Jen, can I call you Jen? I would like you to have it, as a gift. You know a kind of thank you. Not that I feel I have to thank you for anything. No, that came out wrong. What I mean is... look, just thank you, okay?" How endearing, he's blushing!

Very carefully I slip my top back on. I don't want to disturb the cling film like dressing over my free spirit. "Frankie, thanks for the tattoo, and..."

"Yeah I know." He really does look quite cute when he's humble. Still, I'll never get the chance to get to know him now, will I? Plus Dad would have a baby if I ever took 'a Frankie' home. The image of me pulling up outside the family home in the 'burbs' astride a Harley with Frankie in tow is hysterical. Dad's face would be a picture.

I part the beads with a theatrical sweep of my arm, just as Animal had done so an hour previously. Carol is still slumped over the counter, chewing on her gum for England. "Carol that's a freebie for Jen," says Frankie as he follows me out of the back room. She gives a knowing look and just nods her head at Frankie. God, don't tell me he does this to every yuppie-looking client he takes a fancy to? And is Animal all part of the act? Is Animal Frankie's warm-up man before the main act takes to the stage?

Well, whatever! Who gives a shit? I have my tattoo, and as a bonus have gone the rounds with Albert. I admit it, I stagger out knowing that I will never have to face the wrath for my deeds today and make a beeline for the Three Feathers. After a large scotch, I amble my way back to the car park and collapse onto the back seat of my lovely warm car. I wake up at nine, it's still light but then it would be, wouldn't it? It's summer. It takes a minute or two for me to remember where the fuck I am and why I'm here, then it comes to me.

I leave Windsor and head for home. Good job I wrote myself a note reminding me to stop off at the corner shop to get Mrs G's bits. Silla suggested that I should try and get into the habit of writing things down from now on. She'd explained that over the next few days my memory would start to wander. I didn't tell her, but it's been wandering for weeks now. Thirty-five minutes later I'm back at the flat. I knock on Mrs G's front door, and leave the milk and biscuits on her mat. Once inside my flat, I flick on the hall light. I let my jacket drop on to the floor. The flat has a distinct chill about it and for the first time in ages, I long for the comfort, warmth and safety of Mum and Dad's house. My back is sore and my free spirit's very tender. This dying shit is complete and utter bollocks. I have such a headache too. I take a painkiller.

In the bedroom I pull the curtains, undress quickly and snuggle down under the duvet. Curling up into a ball I allow myself, just this once, to revert to an old habit and stick my thumb in my mouth. "Night, night Jen. Sleep tight, mind the bed bugs don't bite," I mumble to myself. Before I close my eyes, I pause for a moment and contemplate the power of prayer. But I figure it's a bit late to ask for any favours or suddenly re-discover my faith. That had gone out of the window when grandpa died. So I pass on that one and allow my eyes to close.

Tomorrow promises to be a wild day. I have agreed to spend it with Beck. We are going to spend the day tripping the light fantastic. I can't wait.

Friday 14th August…Showbiz, Showbiz, Showbiz!

I've always had a fascination with the film industry and the stars, and I don't mean the ones that Patrick Moore watches with such passion and enthusiasm. No, I mean the Brad Pitt's, Tom Cruise's and Patrick Swayze's of this world. So when Beck and I compiled the list of things I wanted to do before I…well one of the things I wanted to do was to spend some quality time with Tom or Brad. Now, obviously this is completely out of the realms of all possibilities. But Beck, being an imaginative girl, had an idea as to how we can address this particular predicament.

The Production Company that Beck works for is called Oh Yeah Productions. They are based just off Dean Street, deep in the heart of Soho. The company specialises in commercials, pop promos, and the odd TV drama. Beck is the Company Secretary/PA and has been for about three years now. The majority of the time she works out of the W1 office. However sometimes, just sometimes, she is let loose on the set of a production, filling in as the Production Assistant. This only happens though, when Tarquin Farquison, the company's in-house Production Assistant, doesn't show for work. Tarquin has the odd day off here and there depending on which international social function his family has been invited to attend.

Tarquin's father Henry Farquison, the world-renowned film director, completed his latest project four months ago. And today is the day for the world premiere of his new movie, The Lion's Roar. From what Beck has said about it, The Lion's Roar is a love story set in a war-torn South Africa before the abolition of apartheid. Nothing new there then. But it sounded like it could be a good Saturday night weepy, in front of the telly with the girls and a Domino Pizza. Ewan McGregor and Natasha Farquison had been cast in the lead roles. So good to see that nepotism rules and is still thriving in the entertainment industry.

So in Tarquin's absence, Beck is to be the Production Assistant for a couple of days on an ongoing six-week shoot, for a new comedy sitcom called Hedonistic Heaven. The six-part sitcom was being financed by Channel 5, as part of a new series of home grown sitcoms to be screened later on in the autumn. Hedonistic Heaven was going to be an up-to-date version of the Good Life. The completely gorgeous man of the moment Tom Pit was to be the nineties equivalent of Tom, the character played by the lovely Richard Briers. Today I am going to spend a day in Luvvy Land, more commonly referred to as the film industry.

I wake up at 5.45am. My back is sore but not really uncomfortable. I just don't feel the full 100%. On the way to the toilet, I hit the playback button on the answer phone, to listen to yesterday's messages. I sit down on the loo and listen... BEEP... "Jennifer, it's Mum. Call me about..."BEEP. Bloody machine. What's wrong with it? The fist that has gripped my heart, since the day they told me, flexes itself to remind me that it's there. The thought of leaving Mum crushes me. Despair and never before felt physical pains in my heart, momentarily leave me short of breath. I have to take several breaths to catch it again. Come on Jen, keep going. You have to keep going.

I flush the loo and go to investigate. In the hall I flip the lid of the tape deck on the answer phone. Ha, that'll be the problem then. The tape's chewed up. Bugger it. I try and pull it free. It snaps in my hands. Oh well. I make a note to get a tape deck cleaner and a new tape either today or tomorrow. No, on second thoughts, I'll have to wait 'til tomorrow or Sunday now. I'll catch up with Mum when I get in tonight. I can't speak to her at the moment. The way I'm feeling right now, I may lose control and tell her.

In the kitchen I throw the mangled tape in the bin and make a cuppa. Back into the bathroom, I put my tea on the toilet cistern and then have a totally self-indulgent shower, shaving my legs and armpits in the process. I remove the protective dressing from my shoulder and bathe my free spirit. I'd left the dressing on for twenty-four hours as instructed by Frankie. Out of the shower I dry off, and pull on some cotton trousers and a loose fitting shirt. Don't you just love that feeling of cotton on freshly shaved legs? They feel all silky and smooth. Oh, the little things in life. I throw a simple red dress into my rucksack, just in case we go out for dinner later on and I'm ready. Oh nearly forgot, tablets. I empty the daily dose from the dispenser, take one and put the other three in my bag. I slip a handful of Diazepam and a couple of Maxalon into the inside pocket of the bag too, for emergency use only of course.

It's going to be a hot day according to GMTV. My arm is sore, but the free spirit symbol looks bloody fantastic. Frankie assured me that the scab would fall off in a couple of days or so. I have to force myself and resist the urge to pick at the outer edge of the scab. Pausing for a moment, I recount my episode with Frankie and his mate Albert. Oh my God! Wait until Beck hears about this one. Mind you, she'll never believe me. Good old, reliably boring Jen. I wish I'd met an Albert earlier on in my prim and proper life.

Still, it's too late to dwell on all that now. It's time to make the most of the time that is left. I suppose in a weird way, I'm lucky because I know roughly when I'm going to die. Most people have no idea until it happens and therefore don't even think of seizing the moment or taking a risk, because they think that there's always going to be a tomorrow. But there is no guarantee that tomorrow will come, is there? If I hadn't had the scan and they'd not found the tumour, I would never have known. Probably would have just dropped dead without warning. With a squirt of Gio by Armani, inside elbows, behind ears, neck and a quick squirt up my top just in case, I drain my cup of tea laced with a drop of the Irish and set off for Beck's flat. It isn't far. It literally takes me twenty minutes to get over there.

When I arrive, Beck is waiting impatiently. She has the car keys in her hand ready and is tapping the face of her watch. "Come on, come on, we're going to be late" she urges. I can tell she's got her serious head on this morning. Work always makes her tense. But she loves it really. She calls it her legal adrenaline-inducing fix. She thrives on pressure, and excels when challenged. I, on the other hand, am totally the reverse. Give me any level of pressure and I just crack up. Some people have it, some people don't. Beck has it, I don't. It's as simple as that. She hustles me out of the door before I even have a chance to say good morning. I had learnt some time ago that when she's like this, it's best to keep quiet and wait 'til she's calmed down and relaxed. I throw my rucksack onto the back seat, settle back in the passenger seat of her convertible black Golf GTI, and pretend to concentrate on the radio.

It's tuned in to Capital Radio. It's Chris Tarrant. I like Chris Tarrant. As kids, Beck and I used to love watching him on Tiswas on a Saturday morning. Beck would come over to our house because the commune, where she lived, didn't have a telly. She'd really missed out as a kid. She hadn't spoken to her parents or her brother Joshua for years now. I think she's still so embarrassed by their choice of lifestyle and blamed them for her mainly unhappy childhood. I can't imagine not talking to Mum or Dad for a day, let alone nearly ten years. Blimey, has it really been that long? Bless her. Beck had substituted her paternal family with a material family. She'd filled her flat with every modern day electrical appliance known to man. She doesn't use half of the stuff but I think in a funny sort of way it makes her feel real and part of a bigger picture. Does that make any sense?

We arrive at Dean Street just before 7.30am. Usually during the week, Beck gets the tube to work. She said it was much less stressful and easier on the wallet. But today we've had to drive in because Beck has to pick up some papers before we head out of town.

It turns out that we are going to be the only ones in the office today. Everyone else from the company will be either working on set, or taking an extended weekend depending on which end of the salary scale they are at. Beck silences the security alarm and disappears into a back room to make a jug of coffee. I can hear her making a couple of calls. A couple of minutes later she comes back out to me with the coffee and sits down.

I'm sitting in the extravagantly decorated reception area of Oh Yeah, watching the habitual human worker ants coursing through Dean Street. They're all tearing along at a ridiculous speed. I wonder whether any of them have the faintest idea, just how lucky they are? Do any of them ever pause for just a second and perhaps thinks sod it, and seize the moment? No, probably not. I never did, until now. It's not something you get round to thinking about really…not until it's too late anyway. "More coffee Jen?" Beck asks, hovering with the coffee jug poised ready to pour.

I shake my head and say, "Oh no, this is fine thanks love." She puts the jug back onto the tray and sits down again. "You feel well enough to go Jen?" Concern shows on her face. "Have you had your medication?"

"Of course," I assure her before quickly changing the subject. "Have you got what you've come for Beck?" I ask. "What's the plan of action for the day then?" Beck is busy shuffling papers and is deep in thought. A moment passes and then she runs through the day's schedule. She tells me what I'm allowed to do and what I'm not allowed to do, once we're on the set. I can't wait. I am so excited. Today is the day I get to fulfil my dream of spending some time in the film industry, and maybe get myself another shag. God, I'm turning into a nymphomaniac. And why not…

The filming schedule has a later start time today, which Beck referred to as the 'call time'. This was because filming was due to continue late into the evening. That's the only reason why we were still at the office at 7.45am. Ordinarily, the day would start with breakfast on location at 7.00am. Which meant the Assistant along with the Runner, would have to be on set for 6.00am.

From what I can gather from Beck, the Production Runner has the worst job on a shoot. The Runner is the office junior of the Production team. The Production Assistant isn't held in any higher regard either. But I know that doesn't bother Beck. She is so organised and in control that nothing fazes her. It will be good to see her in action, and actually see what I've been missing for all of these years. Filming is due to start at 10.00am.

Now as I mentioned before, the method in Beck's madness for this day of lights, camera and… ACTION is for me to meet Tom Pit, Hedonistic Heaven's leading character actor. He is playing the part of Tom the organic or orgasmic, as Beck had described him, farmer metaphorically ploughing through life's daily chores, running an organic farm. Sounded pretty boring but Beck has assured me that the story line is peppered with animalistic love scenes and punchy one-liners.

She described him as a blond tousled haired Luvvy, apparently hung like a stallion, how she knows that I don't know, with hazel eyes that could melt the clothes off any red-blooded woman. Oh, to bury my head in his organic hay! This man will not know what's hit him by the time I've finished with him. I really don't know what's the matter with me today. My hormones have been raging since yesterday afternoon. It's as if Frankie's Albert reached the parts that other appendages have never or could ever have physically reached before.

The location chosen for the series is a place called Deer Park Farm out towards Pinewood Studios. Exterior shots were going to be filmed on location at the Farm, and interior scenes shot at the studios, near Iver. We set off from Dean Street at 8.00am and head out for the A40 towards Pinewood. The traffic by now is pouring into town like a writhing snake with a belly full of irate motorist's, hell bent on causing as much mayhem as possible.

We leave London behind and head out towards Iver. It's already turning into a hot day. I intend to get hot and sticky today, preferably under Tom Pit. Ian McGaskill has predicted temperatures in excess of 29 degrees, with a high pollution level of seven. Looking back towards London, all I can see is a murky brown cloud of polluted air hanging over the city. I can't wait to get some fresh country air into my battered lungs.

At the junction for Maple Cross, we take the left-hand lane and veer off towards Iver. Bright orange flags tied under the official road signs direct us to the UNIT BASE. So, that's what those cryptic orange signs were for. I had often wondered what these mysterious fluorescent signs meant. They start off directing us to the UNIT BASE and then to LOCATION. As we get closer to our final destination they change again, this time to HEAVEN. Mmm…I hope it is going to be all the way to Heaven and then some.

We finally turn off the main road onto a dirt track. After about a mile we reach the end of it and are faced with a makeshift village consisting of mobile catering trucks, a double decker bus (Beck said that it's the dining bus), trailers and a marquee for the 'extras' that would be required during the day. People are scurrying about everywhere, all in hot pursuit of their own individual means to an end. We park up in the designated roped off area marked PARKING strangely enough, and make our way in to the hive of activity. I need the loo. Beck stops someone and asks where the honeywagon is? I'm about to say no I want a toilet, but then realise that, that's what they call it on location. God these people are weird.

By the time we reach the catering trucks, Hog's Location Caterers are well into the breakfast rush. We join the end of the queue and fill ourselves up with a full British breakfast. It's not as if I need to worry about my saturated fat intake anymore, or the dangers of heart disease and bunging up my arteries. Hell, I intend to eat whatever I want from now on. So, two sausages, two rashers of pig, beans, hash browns, toast, and a mug of tea later it is time to accomplish my mission. The mission being, well as soon as that little lot has gone down, is to have a bout of relentless unadulterated X-rated adult recreation, with the fabulous Tom Pit. I hope the beans don't prove to be a mistake later on in the day.

From our vantage position on the top deck of the dining bus, Beck and I look down on what is to be our home for the day. Beck begins pointing people out as they come into view. "Oh look," she cries. "No, over there! See? It's Felicity Kendall!"

"Is it her?" I ask her, completely under-whelmed. I have to say I'm not particularly impressed. I've always preferred Penelope Keith myself. I sip on my tea and scan the area in search of top totty.

"Doesn't she look fabulous for her age?" She says, still waffling on like a good 'un.

"Mmm...great" is all I can muster. Ha, now that's more like it! Tasty bloke exiting second trailer back on the right just before the honey wagons.

"Jen, are you listening to me?" She demands, shoving me hard in the ribs.

"Ouch! Well, I am now aren't I!" I manage to wheeze. She's winded me!

The look on her face indicates that she is descending into Grumpyville. "Sorry Beck." I hastily take up the commentary. "So, who's that bloke over there next to the fruit bowl?" I ask, pointing out of the bus window.

Beck looks to where I'm pointing. "That's my boss, Henry Whiteacre. He's directing the series," she says in her best stroppy voice.

"So what's he like?" I ask. I have to get her out of her mood quickly, or potentially it will ruin the day. From a distance the owner/director of Oh Yeah looks short and chubby, with a full head of white hair. I don't like short men. I've never liked them. Mum in her infinite wisdom had warned me as a child, never trust a short man...they have a chip the size of a small rain forest on their shoulder. It's because they feel inadequate, you know. Like many of these pearls of wisdom Mum had generously adorned on me during my adolescence, it hadn't really made much sense until I hit my terrible teens.

We put our empty plates into the washing up bowls of hot soapy water and make our way towards the set. As we pass Henry Whiteacre, Beck introduces me to him. "Henry, this is my best friend Jennifer Evans that I told you about. She's come down to spend the day with us. Jen, I'd like you to meet my boss, Henry Whiteacre."

I reluctantly take his outstretched hand and have to force out, through clenched teeth "Pleased to meet you I'm sure." I don't like the way he's looking at me at all. He's making my skin crawl.

Done with the pleasantries, he promptly asks me if I give good head, then throws back his head and laughs. "I beg your pardon?" I stammer. Surely I must be hearing things. He has succeeded where all others have failed. He has rendered me speechless. I look at Beck shocked and stunned. She looks back at me, shrugs her shoulders and smiles as if to say, that's men for you!

God, he must be a lonely man. I'd rather go down on Wayne Sleep, after a particularly energetic performance of Swan Lake, than go down on that. Some men, have no idea do they? Before I can get the remark out and tell him what I think of his lousy chat up techniques, Beck drags me away, frantically trying to restrain my flailing arms. She pushes me behind a nearby trailer and pins me to its side. "What the hell are you trying to do? You'll get me sacked you idiot," Beck hisses.

"Yeah, but did you hear what he said?" I protest loudly. "Let go of me Beck. Let me at him!" I begin to struggle again. My flailing left arm makes contact with something solid. I stop and turn to see who or what I've belted. The sound of a heavenly choral choir fills the air. I look around. It's obvious that nobody else can hear what I'm hearing. A vision of beauty, an angel, has landed slap-bang in front of me. If this is a taste of things to come in heaven, it's going to be a marvellous place. The man standing in front of me is a god on legs. A walking vaginal stimulator, no batteries required, primed ready to make any girl moist.

"Sorry, I...uh...I didn't see you there," I burble. Well that will be 'nil point' for originality for me then.

"Don't worry love, you missed everything of any importance," chuckles the heavenly apparition standing in front of me. He rubs his stomach.

"Hey it's Beck Monroe, long time no see babe. How you doing, girl?" he says as he leans forward towards Beck and kisses her on both cheeks. I've noticed that in the film industry people do the air kissy thing and the continental kissy thing at the drop of the hat. Now, that's all fine and dandy if you're being introduced to Tom Cruise or the lovely Brad. But on the downside, it gives the ugly bastards of the industry carte blanche to swap saliva with anyone they like and get away with it.

"Tom, honey. I'm good thanks, and you? Did you manage to get to Cannes in the end?" she asks. It's blatantly obvious that Beck has momentarily lost her self-control. I don't believe it. She's gone all starry eyed.

"Yeah, eventually got to go to Cannes" he replies, brushing a stray strand of tousled hair from out of his eyes. "Went along with Henry actually. We had a whale of a time. But enough about me...who do we have here then?" He nods his head in my general direction. Now call me old fashioned, but do I look like a deaf mute, unable to respond to a simple question like, what's your name then luv? If he tries to pat me on the head, I will not be held responsible for my actions.

Beck seems to have lost the use of her vocal chords and is staring deeply into Tom's eyes. I push her aside and offer my right hand. "Hi, I'm Jennifer Evans, Beck's best friend. But, please, call me Jen. My friends call me Jen. And you must be Tom?" He takes my hand in his and shakes it. How disappointing, he has the handshake of a dandy. I have to push Dad's advice on someone with a feeble handshake to the back of my mind, otherwise this love-god will never get to experience a little bit of the Evan's magic.

"I am so pleased to meet you, Jen. Yeah I'm Tom...Tom Pit. Beck Monroe, shame on you girl. Where have you been hiding her?" He looks me up and down very slowly. The man's a sleaze. He's undressing me with his eyes and doesn't seem at all bothered that he is making his intentions so blatantly obvious. But as Beck had assured me, this man is indeed completely gorgeous. His eyes are hypnotic and he obviously has the body of an Adonis tucked away beneath his well-worn jeans and denim shirt. He smells of CK for men, and has a silver Saint Christopher hanging around his neck. I come up to his chest. So he has to be at least six foot two. Still, shame about the handshake.

Beck regains the use of her vocal chords and rejoins us in the here and now. "Oh, Jen and I have been friends since primary school Tom. She's just had some bad news and well, she wanted to spend a day before...um...a day on a film set, to see what we do. So, here we are!" She holds her arms out wide, to push home the, here we are! Oh please, spare me the dramatics. I can honestly say I have never ever seen her lose control like this over a man before.

"Oh, I am sorry. Nothing too serious I hope? Is there anything I can do to help?" he offers. Mmm, not bad at all. That could actually pass for real concern? Perhaps I have underrated his acting abilities and misjudged his intentions.

"No, it's nothing really. I'll be fine in a few days," I mumble, looking anywhere but at Beck.

"Well, I'll catch up with you girls later then, yeah? It was nice to meet you, Jackie," he says, licking his lips in a seductive manner. Well, I'm sure he thinks it looks seductive. To me it looks like he's got sore lips and is licking them so that they won't chaff in the wind.

"Nice to meet you too Tom…and it's Jennifer not Jackie."

"Right, yes of course, Jennifer. Yep, coming Henry. I'll see you girls later. Oh and Jennifer? Like the tattoo a lot." With that and a wink and a swift double click of his tongue, the 'Walking Penis' saunters off towards the set. He brushes between us both and pats our bums before striding off towards the stable block. What a complete arsehole. Who does he think he is? But I am a woman on a mission. And I will ride this stallion like Frankie Dettori, if it's the last thing I do.

I turn back to look at Beck. She is staring at the free spirit in disbelief. "Is that for real?" she demands.

"Fraid so," I say with a big grin on my face.

Rolling her eyes, she mumbles under her breath, "I don't believe it! When?"

"Yesterday. It's a long story mate," I add. The very thought of my encounter makes me feel naughty but nice. I promise her that I'll tell her all about it later.

The day's filming gets under way right on schedule. Beck explained during the car journey that in the space of eight hours there would be about five minutes worth of actual 'screen time' shot and 'in the can'. Now in human speak that's five minutes of what the general public gets to see on the TV. It's a very slow process this filming malarkey.

Eventually, the set comes to life and starts to buzz. It becomes a hive of activity. Every now and then I catch a glimpse of Beck darting back and forth between the sets. It looks like organised chaos to me. She's left me with strict instructions, "Keep out of the way, and enjoy yourself."

Okay, I can do that. I find myself a quiet corner, settle back and observe in silence. There's a man shouting for blondes and redheads, "I want two redheads and a blonde and I want them NOW!" he demands. Another bloke walks past and shouts out, "Where's that bleeding dolly?" So maybe Beck has been understating the facts when she'd said that Hedonistic Heaven is peppered with animalistic love scenes. By the sounds of it, it's going to be a complete porno fest. I wait in anticipation.

To be honest after the first couple of hours, the day starts to drag on. It soon becomes apparent that blondes and redheads are types of lighting equipment and the dolly is a little trolley that the camera is mounted on for any moving shots. After the initial excitement of seeing the odd celebrity and the filming of a couple of scenes, it gets boring. And there's no sign of an animalistic love scene in sight. The time spent prattling around between takes, is painfully slow.

The crew breaks for lunch at 3.00pm. It passes with little drama. Henry Whiteacre made a grab for the makeup artist's breasts over one of the dining tables on the bus. In return for his efforts he received a swift kick in the bollocks. I had to stifle a cheer. That is girl power if ever I saw it. She in turn is removed from the set as swiftly as was her kick to Henry's bollocks. Two phone calls later, and Beck has sorted out the mess and has enlisted the services of another makeup artist. Whilst all this is going on, Tom Pit has simply surrounded himself with groupies and dribbling teenagers, all moist and gagging for a shag. He's loving every minute of it, acting like a complete pervert, fondling each one of them in turn.

The day's filming is due to finish or wrap as they refer to it in showbiz speak, at midnight. I look at my watch. It's only nine o'clock. I am completely knackered and aching all over. All the noise is making my head even worse, and the smoke from the fog machine is making my eyes sore. The night is humid and airless. The slacks and loose shirt had been a brilliant idea, but it is still uncomfortably hot. Unfortunately the beans are beginning to work their magic too. Damn it, I knew I should have had the tomatoes. The dull thudding in my head which has been with me, for what seems like forever, pounds away incessantly. I need a lie down for five minutes or so. And I need it now. I slip off when Beck isn't looking and find an empty trailer. Once safely inside I knock back a pill, snuggle down on one of the bunks and doze off.

Some time later, Beck wakes me with a prod in the ribs. "Hey sleeping beauty, wake up. We've just finished for the day." She looks tired but satisfied with her day's work.

"Oh right. Is it time to go home now then?" I croak, still half-asleep and yawning rather attractively I'm sure. I wipe some nearly dry dribble from my chin.

"You're joking. I told you I'd make this a day to remember for you, didn't I? Tom's just asked me if we'd like to go on to a club with him. I said we'd love to. He's waiting in his limo for us Jen. We're going to a Wrap Party mate. Here's your rucksack. Come on, get changed and meet me by the car in five, okay?" It was more of an order than a request.

"Do we have to?" I know I'm whining but…

Oh marvellous, bloody marvellous. The perfect end to the perfect day. Not only does this give Mr Personality, the perfect opportunity to have another paw at me, but now I have to go to a bloody Rap Party too. God…I really hate Rap music. And I have bad eggy wind. I know I should've had the tomatoes and not the baked beans. My tummy is bloated and my slacks are cutting into me. Oh bugger.

It's a wrap!

My protests fall on deaf ears. "But Beck, you know I hate Rap music. Can't we just call it a day and go home now? I'm knackered." I pop out the bottom lip, but she is choosing to ignore it.

Beck has got us invited to a Wrap Party not a Rap Party. She explains, "Now, in layman's terms a Wrap Party, that's Wrap with a 'W' not an 'R' Jen OK, is another name for a complete piss up, which takes place at the end of the making of a film. Basically any funds left over in the budget, gets used up on a big thank you party for the cast and crew. Are you with me on this now?" she asks.

"Oh, right! I'm with you now." I think I've got it anyway. This particular Wrap Party was being held to celebrate the successful completion of a film starring the up and coming all girl pop group, Devil's Own. Now according to Beck the lovely Tom was currently shagging the eldest member of the band, a twenty-year-old bimbo called Kelly. Beck said he had insisted that we escort him to the party. So, we pile into the back of the black limo that Oh Yeah are having to pay for, and set off towards the bright lights of the West End.

The traffic on the A40 is virtually non-existent as we cruise back into town. Tom is being the complete host, pouring the champagne and pawing both of us whenever he gets the chance. I have to say I'm rapidly going right off this potential shag-prospect. I'm beginning to think of more worthy things I should have put on my list of things to do. To shag a showbiz celebrity is one thing, but Tom Pit would never be my Tom or Brad. I'm just selling myself short here.

The bright lights of London are all around us within twenty minutes. We are heading for the Ten Room next to the China White Club, on Air Street. Apparently it's the latest 'in' club in the Capital, and the place to be seen. The limo cruises to a halt, bang in line with the red carpet. The paparazzi and a singular film crew are hanging around outside expectantly. Cameras poised ready to snap the stars as they arrive. It is coming up to half past midnight. Don't these people have beds to be in, homes to go to? I have to admit I feel a tingle of excitement in my stomach and start to giggle nervously. I reach for the door handle ready to climb out. Clumsily, Tom pulls me back and then proceeds to make a grab for my fanny as he clambers over me to greet his awaiting photo opportunity. "Oh sorry, babe." Yeah, I bet you are buster! Again, the annoying showbiz wink is unleashed. Who does he think he is?

By this time, Beck is well away. The beer and wine has been flowing constantly throughout the journey, and substantial amounts of illegal substances have been smoked and snorted. Now I've never been one for the weed, but I have to admit I did have a few toques, just to see what it was like. Of course, had I not been dying, I wouldn't have tried it. Or would I? Really, knowing that I am dying has given me a license to do whatever I want to do, and not have to face the consequences. In my hazy state, and at this precise moment in time, it feels as though there is perhaps a plus to this dying business. So let's party!

I clamber out of the limo after Tom and then turn back to help Beck. As we extract ourselves, without the assistance of Tom I might add, we find all of the awaiting cameras are pointing in our direction. I feel like a movie star. I raise my hand to give them my best Hollywood wave. Immediately the flash bulbs pop into life and shouts of "Over here girls, to the cameras," fill the air. For a split second, I am Claudia Schiffer. Nervously I link arms with Beck. Obviously not happy that he's no longer the centre of attention, Tom jogs his way back to us, pushes in between us, throws his hairy arms around our respective shoulders and marches us into the club.

"Good evening Mr Pit, and ladies. Welcome to the Ten Room, I hope you have a good evening," gushes the meet and greet bird. She shifts nervously in her sprayed on red leather hot pants, fumbling with her clipboard and pen.

"Yeah whatever, cheers babe," he says dismissing her with a flick of his hair.

A shiver runs down my spine, or is it? No, it's Tom making a grab for my left cheek, and I don't mean the one on my face. I've had enough of this. I wriggle free, and make a break for freedom up the winding staircase ahead of us. Unfortunately, due to my introduction and intake of cannabis resin, I manage three steps, lose co-ordination and fall up the rest. Oh bugger! Camera bulbs flash spontaneously into life behind me. Thank God for small mercies. I've got clean knickers on. Another one of Mum's little gems of advice. "ALWAYS wear clean knickers when you leave the house. You never know what's going to happen. What if you get admitted to hospital, or have an accident or something?"

I mumble a silent "Thanks Mum." Tom gallantly picks me up and ushers me up the next flight of stairs, round a corner out of the glare of the cameras. Beck is beside herself in complete hysterics and makes a feeble excuse, saying it's the weed and not the fact that I have made a complete tit of myself, that she has to go and powder her nose. She staggers off in the direction of the Ladies Rest Room.

Tom has me pinned up against the purple drapes, which are hanging regally from the walls. "You OK Jackie?" he slurs. "Want me to rub you better?" With his hand firmly clamped to my fanny, he starts rubbing me in an amateurish way, in a vain attempt to arouse me. I can feel his appendage straining against his chinos, as he rubs himself up against my thigh like a cat. Why aren't I having a good time here? Isn't this the opportunity I've been waiting for?

His breath smells of sick. You know that smell? That smell that all blokes smell of after about eighteen pints of lager, and have been belching all night. I try focusing on his face, which is particularly hard considering it's only inches away from mine. I push him away and focus. He on the other hand is obviously finding it very hard to focus on anything, let alone me. The blacks of his eyes are the size of ten pence pieces. I can hardly see any of the hazel that had been so eye-catching this morning.

"I have to pee, excuse me," I hiss between clenched teeth. With a final push, well yes maybe it was a little too hard, I slide out of his clutches and head in the direction that Beck had disappeared in. I turn to see two bouncers picking him up from the floor. "Oh and by the way TIM, it's Jennifer" I snap at him. What a waste and with those good looks and all. There's one bloke who will never have the pleasure.

In the safe haven of the Ladies Rest Room, I find an empty cubicle, lock the door behind me and sit down on the toilet. I'm actually dying for a wee. God, what a bloody relief. Niagara Falls has nothing on me when I am desperate to go. I take a Maxalon, because I feel a bit sick. Must be the Diamorphine. A scuffling sound alerts me to a Peeping Tom. Two hands and a head appear over the top of the toilet partition from the next cubicle. It's Beck. "Hello love." She is having a job to speak coherently. "You all right down there? Isn't he scrummy? You know, I think you're in there, you lucky cow!" Then suddenly with a squeal she loses her footing and disappears as quickly as she'd arrived.

"Bloody hell! Beck, are you there? Have you hurt yourself? Beck? Oh shit!" I pull my knickers up quickly and unbolt the cubicle door. I try her cubicle door. It's locked. I bang on the door with my fist. "Beck, open this door," I instruct her. Silence. "I mean it, open the bloody door now." I kneel down and peer under the door. She is leaning up against the toilet cistern. Her left foot is in the toilet bowl. Tears are streaming down her face. "You OK? Have you hurt yourself? Can you move your foot? Rebecca Monroe, for God's sake talk to me" I demand.

Between the sobs she tries to speak, "There's nothing wrong with my foot. It's my shoe. It's ruined. Fucking ruined, and they're bloody Gucci!" With that she lets out a wail worthy of any David Attenborough wildlife programme. With some coaxing and roughly fifteen minutes later, she shamefacedly opens the cubicle door. In her hand is the offending, dripping Gucci stiletto.

Whilst all this has been going on, a small crowd has gathered in the Rest Room. The Filipino wash room attendant seizes the opportunity and attempts to palm off her dodgy wares to the captivated onlookers. But they're all far too busy watching the unfolding drama. At the far end of the washroom, several women all of a similar age and appearance, bunnies in mini skirts, high heels, lip gloss and big earrings, are totally engrossed in their own particular form of entertainment. The showbiz babes are snorting coke.

I pull myself away from the Charlie Chasers, and back to accomplishing the task at hand. That being, to reassure Beck that having a soiled Gucci shoe, is better than not having a Gucci shoe at all. Five minutes under the hairdryer later and the shoe is nearly dry. It's a little discoloured and has a faint scent of pee about it. But we manage to get the shoe relatively clean, and indeed invest in several squirts of eau de something from the delighted wash room attendant.

"Thanks Jen. I love you." Beck is stoned and as pissed as a rat. Bless her. I'm going to miss her so much.

"Come on, let's go pull," I say. I take her by the hand, give it a squeeze and lead her through to the main party. The room is throbbing in time to the beat of the music. It's decked out in the same purple coloured drapes as in the lobby. A dense cloud of tobacco smoke hangs in the air. The atmosphere is heady and intoxicating. Secluded alcoves provide refuge for the so-called stars away from the prying eyes and main stream Wrap Party groupies. A tight-butted Spanish looking waiter approaches bearing a tray of champagne and glasses of red wine.

"Good evening ladies, champagne? Wine… red or white?" he asks in a broad East London accent. Go on and shatter a girl's Mediterranean fantasy, why don't you.

Beck instinctively grabs two glasses. "Cheers mate. Mmm…nice arse," she comments way too loudly. She's incorrigible. I thank him and help myself to a glass of red wine. He minces off in the direction of a group of silicone breasted babes. At least my 38B's are home grown, natural and all mine. God, I can be so bitter at times.

Everywhere I look there are recognisable faces from the television and film industry. I am in heaven. The film that has just wrapped as I said earlier starred Devil's Own, a new all girl pop band. I use the term pop band in the loosest of terms because none of them can actually play any sort of instrument at all. Beck points them out to me. They're all busting their skinny little arses, circulating with the so-called in people. All four of them air kissing their way around the room, giggling and batting their false eyelashes at all and sundry. When they reach Tom, Kelly his current shag gives him a lingering tonsil tennis kiss. For a moment it threatens to suck in all of those standing within a six-foot radius. I could quite easily say welcome back to the Hog's Caterers' teatime special of rich chocolate gateaux with optional squirty cream that I had annihilated some eight hours earlier. Thank God for the creator of Maxalon.

Before I have time to share my feelings with Beck, she grabs my arm and steers me onto the impromptu dance floor. A live band is playing but I don't recognise them. All very nice but not quite all there, if you know what I mean. So we sway for a song or two and then as I'm about to mention that home is perhaps a viable option at this particular juncture of the evening, the room suddenly falls silent. Thank God for that. It must be the end of the party. "Beck, can we go home now?" I ask. I turn around. She is staring at the stage with her mouth wide open.

I look towards the stage to see what all the fuss is about. And then I see why. A slight figure dressed in leather trousers, denim shirt and a leather waistcoat is climbing the steps up on to the stage. It is Nina Hendrix, legendary rock chick, and inspiration to womankind. I don't believe it. Now, you've got your Chrissie Hynde's and Melissa Etheridge's and Bonnie Raitt's, but Nina Hendrix... in the same room as us mere mortals? Beck has started to sway precariously. "Fuck me, isn't that Nina Hendrix? Oh my God! I am seriously not worthy. Jen, look it's Nina Hendrix" she gasps.

"Hey mind the tattoo!" I shriek as she grips my arm way too tightly.

As you've probably gathered, Beck is star struck. I too feel a certain amount of 'I'm not worthy', but I can live with it. I gently push Beck's jaw back into place so that she doesn't look like she is trying to catch flies, or before someone gets the notion to fill it with something. The room erupts into rapturous applause, as Nina welcomes the crowd. Her blonde shoulder length hair, which had been covering her face, falls back to reveal her features. She looks out at the crowd. She's beautiful. Her jawbone is to die for and her eyes are even from such a distance, hypnotic. The band fires up and music fills the air. Her voice is like that of an angel. If ever a woman could fancy another woman, she would have to be the one.

Wow, stop right there young lady! Rewind…Did I just think that? Hang on a minute? What am I thinking? I turn away and concentrate on my dance moves and on keeping Beck away from the undesirable leeches on the dance floor. The majority of them seem to have already hitched a ride on the big, shiny, psychedelic bus to oblivion. Beck metaphorically speaking is thumbing a lift down the same road with gusto.

We're really giving it some welly, when I glance across at the stage. To my horror, Nina is gesticulating to me. Or is she? I look around at my fellow groovers, but no one's paying attention. They are all concentrating way too hard on staying upright. Nope, she's definitely gesturing to Beck or me. Well, it has to be Beck then. Beck always pulls the girls as well as the boys. I tap Beck on the shoulder and try and shout above the din, "Is she pointing at me?"

"WHAT?" Beck cups her hand to her ear, as if that's going to help in here!

"IS SHE POINTING AT ME?" I try to enunciate the words so that she can understand me.

A smile breaks out on Beck's face, "Oh right. Yeah I want to be a tree too, mate." With that she starts flinging her arms about and making a whooshing noise. Oh whatever.

I continue to shake my bits and pieces on down in time to the music, but Nina Hendrix is still pointing. Is it me she's pointing at? I decide to have another quick look around me and scan the room, and again as before, no one else is paying any attention. OK, so it has to be me then. But why me? Oh fuck, fuck, fuck! My little red Wallis dress is neatly tucked into my size 12-14 hipster knickers. Shit, I must have done it in my haste to check that Beck hadn't hurt herself when she fell in the loos. I have been dancing and shaking my little white bootie without due care and attention for God knows how long. I deftly tug the dress free from the constraints of my knickers waistband, mouth an "Oh thanks" to Nina Hendrix and pray for the floor to swallow me up whole. I really want to go home now.

By now Beck has caught sight of my embarrassing predicament and finds it highly amusing to say the least. That's what friends are for, right? Wrong. I'll make the bitch suffer before my time is up. After several songs, Nina thanks the adoring crowd and introduces Devil's Own, and their backing tape. She jumps off the front of the stage and is immediately swallowed up by her adoring crowd.

Beck and I sidle off towards the bar, where the alcoholic refreshments are still flowing, oh so freely. We pick up yet another freebie and find an empty alcove from where we can do some people watching. Well, where I, can do some people watching from anyway. Beck has finally peaked. Her eyes are like piss holes in the snow. She falls into the corner of the alcove. It's going to take some cajoling to move her before the end of the night. I sip at my drink and take in my surroundings.

A voice interrupts my thoughts. "Hi there. Sorry about before" it says.

Wow, that cannabis I tried in the limo must have been bloody strong. I could swear that Nina Hendrix is standing right there in front of me, talking to me. I scrunch my eyes shut and then open them again slowly. Nope. Unless I'm hallucinating, Nina Hendrix is definitely standing there, in the flesh, in front of me and is definitely talking to me. Must be experiencing one of those hallucinogenic episodes. So I'm not supposed to drink much with my medication because of the side effects. But this isn't so bad. It's really quite freaky actually.

I look at Beck but she is well gone, away with the fairies. I turn back and Nina Hendrix is still standing there. I reach out to disperse the image with my hand. It makes contact with the image. It's solid. Oh shit. Now what do I do, what do I say? Be cool Jen, be cool. "Sorry. I thought I was seeing things. You are talking to me? Right! Hi, uh thanks for pointing out my dress. I'd been in a bit of a hurry and, well..." I'm stammering. Oh God, how embarrassing.

She laughs. "No problem, really. I'm Nina Hendrix. And you are?" She holds her hand out towards me.

I concentrate hard and reach out to try and catch hold of it. "Oh, sorry, how rude of me. I'm Jennifer Evans, Jen to my friends. Please, call me Jen, Ms Hendrix. It's a real pleasure to meet you, really." Her handshake is firm and cool.

"Pleased to meet you, Jen. Call me Nina please. Do you mind if I join you...and your friend? It's getting a bit too crowded in here for me," she says.

"No, of course not, please join us...Nina." I smile like a star-struck teenager. Pathetic!

I shift along deeper into the booth to let Nina join us. I say us in the loosest of terms, as by now Beck is lying comatose on the opposite banquette. She is dribbling slightly from the corner of her mouth. I reach across and wipe it away with a tissue. I introduce her. "That's my best friend, Beck. She's had a long day and she's…tired?" She is going to be so rough in the morning. And she's missing all the excitement too.

"So, what did you do on the film?" she asks. I still can't quite believe that she is sitting next to me, and that I am having a conversation with, the Nina Hendrix. I'd have to get her autograph for my sister. Lizzie is a massive fan of hers. She loves her music.

"Oh no, nothing like that. I'm not in this business. I run a small secretarial firm. It's much less glamorous I'm afraid. Beck my dribbling companion over there, works for Oh Yeah and dragged me along with Tom Pit." I gesture towards the heap that is my best friend. "To be honest with you, how can I put it? She's as pissed as a rat, and stoned out of her brains." I find myself laughing nervously.

Nina looked deep into my eyes. It's as if her deep brown eyes are searching out my soul. I feel a little uncomfortable. I don't know why. Surely, I should be feeling flattered that a huge star like Nina Hendrix is chatting to me? A big neon warning light is flashing in my head. Oh I remember now, I have read somewhere that she's gay. So is she chatting to me or is she chatting me up? Now hand on heart, I have never ever thought or fantasised about being with or even kissing another woman. I'm completely clear and confident about my sexuality. But for some strange reason I feel this irrational urge to see what it would be like, to kiss this one. It has to be due to that fact that I have nothing to lose and that she is indeed a very famous and incredibly attractive woman. Or maybe it's just a drug induced momentary mental glitch. Anyway, as if someone as gorgeous as her would fancy a Plain Jane like me. God, I must be really pissed.

"Would you like to, then?" Nina is talking to me again. Oh God, I've drifted off into what if land again.

"Sorry, what was that?" I ask. "Would I like to what?"

"I said would you like to come to one of my gigs at the London Arena next week? I can arrange for you to watch from the wings or back stage, if you like. Bring your friend too. That's if she's recovered by then." Nina points towards Beck and laughs. Poor old Beck, she's missing everything.

"That would be great, thanks for asking." Even in the drunken state that I find myself in, reality hits home like a good dousing with a bucket of cold water. Oh no, not the tears again. "But, I don't think I'll be here," I choke back.

"Oh, I'm sorry. Look if you're out of town next week there'll be another time I'm sure. Perhaps you could come to another show." Nina rests her hand on my leg. Her fingers are long and well manicured. She smells of Gio by Georgio Armani. The same perfume as I'm wearing. I have to take a deep breath and look her in the face. I wriggle free mumbling, "Excuse me please" and head for the Ladies Room. Tears blur my vision. I have to get out of here.

Henry Whiteacre is busy gyrating his massive being on the dance floor. He sees me out of the corner of his eye and makes a beeline towards me, blocking my path. "Well, hello there, sexy. Aren't you the one who gives good head? Oh yeah, baby yeah!" He attempts a sexy pelvic thrust. It's about as sexy as a sweaty WWF wrestler. The layer of fat on his vast being takes on a life of its own, and ripples into an unsightly frantic flab frenzy.

I snap. I've had enough now. Tired and confused, I jab my finger into his face and snarl, "Listen you fat fucker, I'd rather dance with the devil and have sex with Mr Blobby than with you. So piss right off!" I push past him, successfully embedding my fist into his flab as I pass.

I hear him shouting to his sidekicks, "She's gagging for it, I told you! I'm in there fellas." His gathered posse of knuckle dragging Neanderthals cheer and applaud his efforts.

I make it to the Ladies Rest Room with my composure in tact, just. I lock the cubicle door behind me, flip the lid down on the toilet and let them flow. I must have been sitting there for fifteen minutes or so, well until I ran out of toilet paper. With the last piece I wipe my nose, stand up and flush the loo.

The rest room is completely deserted. Even the Filipino rest room attendant has mysteriously vanished, leaving behind her bounty of dodgy toiletries unguarded. I shuffle over to the sink and splash cold water onto my swollen red eyes. My feet are hurting and I really want to go home. I think I'll go back in, get Beck and call a cab. I've had enough excitement for one day. The sound of the door opening behind me brings me back to the here and now. I fumble about in the direction where I think the paper towel dispenser is. I vaguely remember that it's somewhere on the wall at the end of the row of sinks. The sound of someone pulling a paper towel free breaks the silence.

"Here." I recognise the voice immediately. It's her.

"Thanks." I've managed to stop crying but rather attractively keep sniffing. I pat my eyes dry and try focusing on the human paper towel dispenser.

"Here, sit down, take your time and get yourself together. Can I get you anything?" She guides me to a nearby chair and kneels down in front of me. "You know Jen, you have such beautiful eyes. Specially when you've been crying." Her warm sincere smile is a welcome sight to my tired eyes.

"No, I'm fine thanks. Probably just too pissed. You know what it's like, too much booze, sleepless nights. Please don't mind me, go back and enjoy the party. I'll be fine, really" I assure her.

What's she doing? Nina strokes my face with her hand and looks deep into my eyes. Her cool hands help to disperse some of the rising heat in my cheeks. Now in hindsight, it has to be said I am in a vulnerable state at this precise moment in time. I mean, she's just being friendly right? I look at her in my most 'heterosexual' way. I hate to say this but her touch feels nice, comforting even. I notice that her lips are the type that every woman on the planet would die for. I wish my lips looked like that. They are full and lightly moistened with a neutral lipstick. I never thought I would ever think this, but if she kisses me now I won't be offended. Just to see what it would be like, you understand. But no, it isn't right. This is all very wrong. I pull myself together as best I can and attempt to get up. Dizziness pushes me back into the chair. Oh, I hate it when that happens. Fucking tumour...

"Hey, take it easy Jen, take your time." She holds my shoulders for a second until I regain my balance then says, "So what's all this about anyway? You know it's not worth getting upset over a fat wanker like Henry Whiteacre. Was it him who upset you? He's nobody. Shall I have him thrown out?" I can tell by the tone in her voice that she's not joking.

"No, really, I'm fine. It's not him. I'm just so tired that's all," I sigh. I'm so tired. At this point I don't know why but I feel that I have to tell her the truth. I have to tell someone else apart from Beck. I take a deep breath and confess. "That's not true. You see the truth is I have a brain tumour. I only found out four days ago. It's all been a bit sudden really. I'm dying you see. According to the doctors I have oh six, maybe ten days to live. I don't know what to do. I'm just not ready to die." With that, I bury my head into my hands. "I just want to sleep, then wake up and realise that it's all been a bad dream or a mistake."

Her soft cool hands gently pull my hands away from my face. "I am so sorry Jen. Fucking hell, I don't know what I'd do or what to say to you for that matter," she whispers hoarsely. "You are so brave." This is embarrassing. Not because I must look a complete mess, but because I feel comfortable with her and like the way she's making me feel. Is this the penalty one has to pay for smoking illegal substances?

Then it happens. I confess I don't pull away, I go with the moment. She kisses me. She kisses me as I have always tried to kiss, with softness and feeling. That feels really weird. There's no stubble. Her lips part slightly then she pulls away. She continues to cradle my face in her hands, and with her thumb she starts to stroke the edge of my mouth. Now I am confused. I have never been kissed with such tenderness before. And I enjoyed it. Does this make me a lesbian? But I like men. This is so weird.

"Come on, let's get out of here," she says firmly. "Do you fancy a night-cap? Just a drink back at the hotel, that's all. Don't worry, my intentions are completely honourable. Bring your friend too, if you like." I can tell that she is being sincere.

Well, why not? I've got nothing to lose. I have just broken all the rules by kissing her, haven't I? Why not talk some more, get to know her and have a night-cap? I admit it I like her. And if I go, I can get that autograph for Lizzie. She says she's staying at the Ritz. I mumble a quiet "Alright." I can't meet her gaze. I feel foolish and embarrassed.

Reassuringly she pats my shoulder and tells me, "I'll meet you and your friend outside the club. It's probably best that we're not seen leaving together. The papers will have a field day if they see me leaving with two women. My driver, Damien will be waiting for you in the lobby. He'll be the Man Mountain that looks like Lennox Lewis, the boxer. You know who I mean?" she asks.

"Yeah, I know who you mean." I know the bloke she's talking about. I accidentally bumped into him near the bar earlier on in the evening. He didn't even notice that I'd walked into him. I'd just bounced straight off.

I get to my feet and go in search of Beck. Are people looking at me? God, did anyone see Nina kissing me? Beck hasn't budged an inch. "Beck, wake up mate." I shake her by the shoulder. "We're off. Come on. I've sorted out a lift. Don't mind if we stop off for one more drink on the way home, do you?" Beck starts to mumble incoherently, which I take as a yes.

With help from Nina's driver Damien, we carry Beck down to the waiting limo. The paparazzi don't bat an eyelid. But why should they? To them we are just two drunken party animals trying to get home. Nina is already safely tucked away in the corner of the back seat as we pour Beck into the car. I jump in after her. I make her as comfortable as I can and put my arm around her so that she doesn't fall. Apart from Beck's mumbling and sporadic snoring, the drive to the Ritz passes in silence. I peer out of the window. What am I doing?

We enter the hotel separately so as not to cause a stir or raise any awkward questions at a later date. Damien carries Beck to the lift then into Nina's penthouse suite. Once inside the suite, he disappears through some double doors with Beck in his arms.

"Hey now wait a minute, buster. Stop right there," I shout after him. "Where the hell do you think you're going with my mate?" I demand. "If you lay one finger on her, I swear I'll...I'll...I'll batter you."

"Hey Jen, take it easy," says Nina, obviously startled by my reaction. "Damien is just going to put your friend to bed. I don't think she is going to wake up 'til morning, do you? She is in safe hands, trust me."

I have to make sure. This is my best friend we're talking about here. "Well, I'll just make sure she's okay myself, if you don't mind," I snap unnecessarily. With that I follow Damien and watch carefully as he gently places her on to the bed. I take her shoes off and unclip her earrings. She's completely out for the count. I tuck the cover around her, whisper a goodnight and kiss her on the forehead. The headstrong, ball breaker known as Beck Monroe, now looking so vulnerable and small on the Queen sized bed. I quietly close the bedroom door behind me and slowly make my way back to the lounge. The penthouse suite is awesome. How the other half lives. In each room a chandelier hangs from the ceiling. It is just as I had imagined the inside of a king's palace to be as a child.

Damien has drawn the curtains, turned on some music and is pouring Nina a drink when I get back to the lounge. "Anything else, Miss Hendrix?" he asks, standing with his arms neatly crossed in front of him.

Nina is relaxing back on a massive sofa, surrounded by little designer cushions. Her discarded boots are tucked neatly under the smoked glass coffee table. "No thank you that will be all. Wake me at the usual time. Oh, and hold my calls...Goodnight Damien."

With a "Have a nice evening, Ms Hendrix" and a courteous bow in my direction, he leaves the room. We are alone.

"Please, come and sit down. Make yourself at home. Kick back and relax," she says. "You must be feeling drained. I noticed you were drinking a whisky at the club. I hope you don't mind but I had Damien pour you a Chivas Regal. Is that all right for you? Or would you like something else?"

No, that's fine. Thanks." I take the crystal cut glass tumbler from her and sit down on the edge of one of the chairs. I wonder if I can still get a cab at this time of night and manage to get Beck home on my own? I still have time.

Nina pats the cushion next to her on the sofa, "Come sit over here, Jen. I won't bite you know. Well, not unless you want me to." Oh my God she is going to jump me after all. I must have a look of sheer terror on my face when I look up. She starts to laugh. "Relax, I'm just kidding!"

"Right I'm leaving. I don't like having the piss taken out of me. I don't like being laughed at, not by you, or by anyone. I don't need it right now. So if you don't mind, I'll just say goodnight." I slam my glass down onto the coffee table, and start towards the door. "Oh, and thanks for the drink."

Nina reaches out and grabs my arm as I pass by the end of the sofa. "Jen, please don't go. I'm sorry, I couldn't resist. Look, don't go. I just want to get to know you... just talk if you like. I'm not in the habit of bringing virtual strangers back to my hotel room. I've been on my own for a long time now. I've got used to being on my own. But when I saw you tonight on the dance floor...I thought you looked like the kinda person I'd like to get to know, to be friends with. I just feel a certain affinity with you. Do you know what I mean Jen? Do you? Please say you'll stay?" She looks pleadingly into my eyes.

She releases her grip. It's my call. What should I do? I can't leave Beck now, can I? I sit back down on the edge of the sofa and pick up my glass. In one mouthful I drain its contents. Her hand on my shoulder gently pulls me back into the soft cushioning. "I'll stay." I concede.

"I'm sorry. Forgive me?" she says quietly.

"Forget about it. I probably just over-reacted. I'm not used to feeling like this, that's all." I settle back and try to relax. I really need some sleep now. A loud yawn escapes me.

"Feeling like what?" she asks tentatively.

"Forget it. I'm just tired and I'm not ready to die yet." I tell her. I catch a glimpse of my reflection in the mirrored cocktail bar door. I look like shit. My hair is a mess, my skin pale and... I'm really dying. I cradle my head in my hands. It feels as though it's ready to burst.

Nina gently moves my hands away from my head and kisses them, first one then the other. The weird thing is I don't feel that any minute now I'm going to be jumped on, groped or used like a blow up dolly, then discarded in the morning. I lean into her shoulder and began to relax for the first time in days. Nina takes my glass from me and stands up. She is holding her hand out to me. Should I take it? I hesitate for a second, then take her hand in mine.

"Can't we just sit and talk, Nina? I'd like to stay. But I'd like to just, you know cuddle up? I don't want to 'spend the night' with… a woman. I just can't get my head round the fact that I want to spend some time with you. And that I am attracted to you in some sort of way. I can't explain it. It's all way out of my sense of reasoning. I'm sorry."

"No, don't be sorry. That sounds good to me too. Anything you say. It'll be good just to hold someone again. I'm so glad I've met you tonight. You're inspirational you know that. I want you to know that you don't have to deal with your problems on your own. I'm here if you need me. Come on, let's go and lie down…just to sleep and cuddle up. I'd love to wake up with you, if you'll let me." She smiles down at me.

I want to let her. I have sobered up enough to know what I am doing. I look at her, and can see the concern in her face. She has no alterior motive whatsoever. She cares. Suddenly I feel vulnerable. I need someone to care about me. I need someone to cuddle me, that's all. Nina leads me into the master bedroom and gently closes the door behind us, so as not to wake Beck. I just want to sleep forever and ever and never wake up.

Saturday 15th August... The morning after the night before

Where the bloody hell am I? OK, I'm still fully clothed. That's good. I'm on a huge bed. There's a chandelier hanging from the ceiling. It's starting to come back to me slowly. There's an arm draped over me. I look to my left and see Beck's head. She's still out for the count, snoring on every intake of breath. Her head's poking out from under the duvet, just as I'd left her last night. She's fast asleep. I don't have to be Sherlock Holmes to deduce that the arm doesn't belong to her then. I trawl back through the events of last night, scrabbling for clues as to where I am. I move slowly around to my right to get a better look at the owner of the arm.

"Good morning." The husky voice confirms what I already know, but don't want to believe. I have spent the night with Nina Hendrix. Oh bloody hell. "How are you feeling? Did you sleep well?" she asks. "You went out like a light last night." She reaches across and strokes a stray strand of hair away from my face. Her face is void of make up. She looks stunning. Why can't I look like that in the mornings?

Instinctively I pull away and turn back towards Beck. I don't want to look at her. I can't. "I'm sorry. I can't do this," I murmur.

"You can't do what, Jen?" she asks sounding puzzled. "I'm just saying good morning, that's all. Please look at me." I turn and look at her over my shoulder. For a brief moment a look of hurt flickers into her eyes. "You don't have to do anything or say anything for that matter. As I said last night, I just wanted to wake up with you. And for that, I thank you. I feel almost human again. I've been on my own for so long. I think I mentioned that last night, didn't I?" She smiles wryly. When she smiles her eyes light up the room. If only she were a bloke. She continues to speak, "You have nothing to be ashamed of. We just slept together, that's all. We just cuddled. We shared a little human compassion." With that she removes her hand from my face, and goes to climb off the bed. "It's what human beings do for comfort, to feel safe."

Of course, she is right. I grab her arm, "No wait. I'm sorry Nina. I didn't mean to be so hurtful. I really do like you...a lot. And its not because you're famous or anything like that. I mean I hardly know you, do I? Yet in a funny kind of way, I feel so comfortable and at ease with you, like I've known you for years. But you have to understand all this is way out of my league. I've never ever had the urge to be close to a woman like this before. Right now, it's scaring the hell out of me. I'm not gay and don't want to be either," I say rather feebly.

"Wow, now you just hold your horses a minute." Her tone of voice changes to a slightly aggressive mode. "Just because you've slept in the same bed as another woman, well two to be precise, doesn't make you a lesbian. When I look at you Jen, I want to kiss you, hold you and love you. Now that's being a lesbian. I want to make love to you Jen, but I know you're not ready and may never be ready. I can handle that. I came out years ago, and yes, at the time it was a shock to everybody that knew me. But they still love me, and love me because of who I am not what I am. Do you understand what I am getting at?" she asks.

The slightly aggressive mode reverts to the kind and softly spoken mode. Before I can dig myself out of the pit I've fallen into, she's off again. "Having feelings for someone of the same sex is not a bad thing or something to be ashamed of. It's just different, that's all. People that can't admit to themselves that they are unsure or scared of their own sexuality, are the ones who should be ashamed." With that she gently lifts my hand from her arm and lays it gently back down on to my stomach, leans forward and kisses my forehead.

Well, that told me then. Hell, Nina Hendrix likes me and not in a heterosexual way. It's not a surprise, I know that already. Boy, I need a drink. And I need one now. I very carefully climb down off the bed, so as not to wake Beck. In the lounge I walk over to the drink's cabinet and pour myself a large whisky. I know it's early in the morning but I feel the need for an injection of the liquid anaesthetic. Nina is standing in silence by the bay window looking out over Green Park, cradling a mug of something hot.

I'm not really sure what to say. So I just go for the safe option, "Nina, I'm sorry. I didn't mean to be offensive. If I was, I'm sorry. I'm just tired. I have a lot on my plate at the moment."

"I know you have" she says, but doesn't turn around. "If I could take away your tumour, I would give away all that I have right now." She pauses to take a sip from her mug then continues. "And as I told you last night, you're not alone. At least, you don't have to be. Whether you like me or 'like me' makes no difference to the way I feel about you. We can at least be friends, can't we?" she asks with hope in her voice.

What can I say? No, I'm afraid that is totally out of the question. Up until last night I had been one of those people who thought that being gay was a sickness. And now, I have no idea what it's all about. So I just nod and say "Yeah sure. We can definitely be friends." I walk over and join her by the window. The world looks glorious today. The sun is shining and the early morning joggers seem to have a definite spring in their step. I put my arm around Nina's shoulder. She in turn lowers her head and rests it on my hand. We stand in silence for a moment then eventually I say, "And thanks Nina, you know for everything. Maybe in another life, under different circumstances, who knows?"

"We'll never know will we?" With that Nina turns and put her arms around me. She has tears in her eyes. She makes me feel so comfortable and safe. Who knows, maybe in my next life? Where the hell did that come from? I think it's time we were leaving. I break away from the embrace and go to wake Beck.

"Beck, come on, wake up. We have to go now," I say as gently as I can. I don't want to make her jump unnecessarily. There's no response. In fact, if anything the snoring goes up by a few decibels. So I shout "BECK, WAKE UP!" There, that's done the trick.

Beck opens one eye, tries to focus and then mutters, "Where am I?" I don't think now is the right time to tell her that she is in Nina Hendrix's boudoir, do you?

"You're at the Ritz baby!" I say in my best Posh Spice accent. "Come on, we have to go home now."

Beck rolls towards the edge of the bed, misjudges the distance and crashes to the floor. "Ouch. I think I've broken something," she moans.

I do a quick check for breakages and spend the next five minutes convincing her that she is OK. "Jen, who do we know that can afford to stay at the Ritz?" she asks quizzically.

"Don't you remember?" Thank God, it's obvious that she has no recollection of last night's activities whatsoever. So I start to paint a pretty picture for her that I know she'll love, of the last 12 hours or so... "Well, we left the club. We all came back here, had a few sherbets, and then passed out."

Beck interrupts my flow, "Um...who exactly is 'we'?"

"Blimey you're joking right? You seriously don't remember?" I pretend to be shocked at her short-term memory loss. "We've only been partying with the one and only Nina Hendrix!" I try to put as much excitement into my voice as possible.

"NO!" Beck's bottom jaw drops in disbelief. "You're kidding me, right? Jen please say you're winding me up here?" she pleads.

I have to assure her that she had a fab time, didn't make a fool of herself (that had been my job) and that she'd made such an impression on Nina Hendrix that now it's official, she is great mates with a rock star. "Wow, that is awesome!" she says finally. "Bugger... I wish I could remember. Is she still here?"

I nod. "Come on, she's just ordering breakfast for us." Beck's face lights up with excitement. We go back into the lounge and I re-introduce my best friend to Nina. Nina in turn plays the perfect host and orders coffee and croissants and makes polite conversation with her newly recruited No.1 Fan. Half an hour or so later, we bid each other a very formal goodbye in front of Beck. Not that she would have noticed anything other than that. She's still drunk. Her eyes are open...just. But her body has flipped to autopilot. When her hangover kicks in, she is going to be so rough.

Piccadilly is virtually deserted as we leave the Ritz. Damien has the limo waiting for us by the side entrance. We drop Beck off first, then continue on over to my neck of the woods. I get Damien to drop me off at the end of the road. I don't want him to know exactly where I live. Mid-way through helping me out of the car he stops, reaches into his top pocket, and hands me a card. With another bow, he climbs back into the car and drives off. I stand and watch until the limo disappears out of sight, then look down at the card in my hand. It has Nina's personal details and personal mobile phone number on it. On the back of it she's hand written, 'If you need anything... Nina xxx'. Well at least I've got an autograph for Lizzie out of the evening. I'll give her the card when I see her on Wednesday. She'll be thrilled.

So I've spent the night with rock legend Nina Hendrix, a woman and enjoyed myself. That is until I woke up anyway. Not that we actually did anything other than cuddle. But still, it's a bit of a shock to the system. I'm attracted to her but it's a different sort of attraction. It's not a sexual attraction. I think it's more to do with who she is and her personality rather than what sex she is, that attracts me. But then there was the kiss. That'd been quite enjoyable. Oh well, so I've kissed a woman. What the hell, it's just another experience I can add to the list of things I have done.

Whilst in deep conversation with myself, I have walked straight past the paper shop. Bugger it. I do a quick about turn and jog back for the Sunday paper. I buy a Mail on Sunday and a packet of Marlboro Reds and then head for home. An involuntary shiver shudders through my body as I imagine the headline for The News of the World next Sunday – 'Rock chick Nina attracts yet another fan...ny!'

I've picked up a Sunday Mirror for Mrs G too and leave it on her door mat. My flat has a definite chill to it when I open the front door. I step over the mail and close the world out. I pop the kettle on, make a cup of tea and run a bath. The flat is looking decidedly dishevelled. The pots are beginning to pile up in the kitchen sink and the washing basket in the bedroom is now too full for the lid to close properly. I wander from room to room, waiting for the bath to fill up. There just doesn't seem to be any point in tidying up anymore. The wise one Mum always said, "A tidy house is a tidy mind." It figures. The flat looks like a bomb's gone off and it's official, I am losing my marbles.

I lower myself into the hot bath and sink back into the bubbles. The mirror and bath tiles slowly steam up. With a shaky hand I rub the steam away, and peer into the mirrored tiles surrounding the bath. I stare back at the reflection of the stranger that is me. Is it really fair that I'm dying? No, it's not fair. But then when is life ever really fair? You're luckier than most you know. At least you've had nearly thirty years of living. And you still have time to make some of the wrongs right, and make peace with yourself. You still have some time... The tiles steam up again. I don't rub it away again. I don't want to look at the stranger anymore, not while she's crying and feeling so damn sorry for herself.

I drag my body out of the bath because my fingers have gone pruney, and force myself to get dressed. It would be so much easier to just give up now. Then I could mope around the flat for the next few days, berating myself for leading such an unhealthy lifestyle. Alternatively, I can get my arse into gear, sort my life out and try and make the most of the time that I have left. I can try and make my leaving a little less painful for those who love me and who will be left behind. I look at my reflection in the mirror and say out loud, "Come on Evans, live a little...you're going to be a long time dead."

Before I leave the flat, I tick off another day on the wish list. I take my tablet. The headache has well and truly kicked in. I have to somehow get into a routine of taking the medication at the right time each day. I decide to write myself a note and pin it to the front door, so I won't forget in future.

For a moment I lean against the door, and try and calm my breathing. With each passing day I can feel the darkness closing in on me, surrounding me like a heavy sea mist. With each passing day, the panic inside of me is slowly rising. I have to keep my mind occupied as best as I can. Get a grip Jen. But that's easier said than done. I walk out to the car, slamming the front door unnecessarily hard. I mouth a "Sorry Mrs G," in the general direction of her lounge window and head for the M3 and the coast.

Sam I love you…yes I'm sober!

First, let me start with a question. Have you ever loved someone so unconditionally, so completely that the thought of living without him or her would actually be an unimaginable nightmare? In fact, life wouldn't be worth living at all? Well, I have. I knew that Samuel Benjamin Truman was the only man for me the moment I set eyes on him. From the crowds pouring through the college gates he emerged. To a cinematic fanfare in my head, he walked into my life striding like a Wild West hero with an attitude the size of Mount Everest. With a penchant for camouflage trousers, trench coats and a radical haircut, he was perfection. A perfect ten out of ten on the Evan's Totty-o-meter. He wasn't your stereotypical hunk of manhood but he certainly worked wonders for my recently discovered and ignited erogenous zones.

The relationship started out quite innocently, with the odd date here and there. We'd spent our time looking but not touching with every few words being said, until one cold Thursday night in November, at the Sub Zero night-club. At the end of the evening, ten to two in the morning, the customary slow dances kicked in, guaranteed to send any single teenager home, horny and frustrated. Sounds corny I know, but our eyes met across the crowded dance floor, and that was it. I had never slow danced with anyone in such a way until that night.

It felt as though I had found my other half. For the first time in my life I felt whole, complete. He was the Ying to my Yang. I can remember to this day some thirteen years on, the euphoria I'd felt that cannot be described with words. It's a deep gut wrenching feeling that if you've had it, then you'll know exactly what I'm talking about. If you haven't, then the day your moment of euphoria hits you…the moment you have an inexplicable rush of emotions …the moment when every inch of your body tingles for no apparent reason…the moment that your whole world suddenly becomes perfect…the moment you feel as though your heart in your throat… enjoy it and savour the moment. Because I can honestly say that since that one singular moment in time, I have never ever experienced anything remotely like it. It was so special. It was magical.

Then disaster struck at the beginning of the second year of college. Sam's parents split up and his mother moved to the south coast. With her divorce settlement, she bought a guesthouse and called it Ocean View. She took Sam and his sister Rose with her. I don't know what happened to his father or how I survived the final year at college. It was torture. By now Beck was working full time as an office junior in a production company in town. I think it was somewhere along Garrett Street. Anyway, she rallied round and tried to get me out and about at least a couple of nights a week.

Six months passed and it was clear that I couldn't live without him. Little things would act as a trigger and catapult his face to the forefront of my mind. Reminding me of the way he held me, the way he made me feel. The churning warm sensation I used to get inside. The fear of losing all that we had, left me wallowing in desolation and despair.

So with plenty of misgivings of my own and warnings from Beck, I caught the train to Southsea and moved in with Sam. The honeymoon period was fantastic. Our lives revolved around running the guesthouse for his mother, taking long romantic walks along the beach, jumping into bed at the drop of a hat and generally loving each other to death.

And it could easily have ended in death. You see, when we were in love, there was nothing like it. Likewise when we argued, it was advisable to take cover so as not to get caught in the crossfire. The relationship was passionate to the extreme. We loved each other and we hated each other at regular intervals. The arguments were never violent but got close on several occasions. It soon became apparent that we couldn't go on like this. The arguments became too regular. It had been a bugbear of mine from day one that Sam, on the odd occasion dabbled in recreational drugs, like Ecstasy and Speed. I thought I could accept it or that perhaps he'd change, but it wasn't meant to be.

So I left. Just like that. One morning I looked at him as he slept by my side and knew that if I didn't leave now, then one of us would be attending a funeral sooner rather than later. It was the hardest decision I have ever had to make to this day. I loved him so much that it hurt like hell. I left him sleeping, packed my few belongings, phoned for a cab and caught the 10.40am train back to London. I arrived on Mum's doorstep, crumpled and lifeless. Somehow she seemed to know. She poured me a drink, ran a bath and told me that everything would be okay. I didn't believe her.

I spent the next four years getting over him. Each day I willed the phone to ring and for it to be Sam, begging me to go back saying he'd changed and couldn't live without me. It didn't happen. I think that's what added so much hurt to my already aching heart. He hadn't loved me as much as I had loved him. It was as simple as that. I began to question my existence and whether it really was worth sticking around. Mum became my psychiatrist and over a period of several months nurtured me back to an acceptable level of sanity. I truly thought I was dying. My heart and my chest ached constantly, and I imagined that each night when I went to sleep, that I wouldn't wake up. I saw no future, just blackness. They say that time heals all wounds. Well, the old cynic in me always thought that such a statement was a load of crap. But it's true. With each passing month I began to live again, and find reasons to stick around.

I have to confess that I have made many late night calls to him over the years, since the break up. Each time whilst as drunk as a skunk, I'd convince myself that by making the call I would lay this particular ghost to rest once and for all. I tortured myself with images of our good times together and reminisced about the good old days with anyone that would listen. Thank God for the inventor of 141. His mother would definitely have tried to have me certified insane had she been able to trace the silent caller. You see when I called I'd never quite been able to pluck up the courage to actually say anything. It had been enough just to hear his voice.

As far as I know, Sam is still running his mother's guesthouse in Southsea. So, with six days to live and consciously counting, I'm on the road, on my way to lay this ghost, one more time... if I'm lucky.

I pull up outside the Victorian terraced guesthouse on the sea front opposite the pier. I look at my watch. It's 9.00am. The kiosks at the entrance to the pier are already open. The smell of doughnuts cooking and chips and vinegar tinge the air. The 'Vacancies' sign outside the guesthouse, gently moves in the breeze, caressed by the warm sea air. It looks like they've repainted the woodwork since I left. The window frames now emerald green, with a white stripe running around about an inch from the actual glass. It is, as a seaside guesthouse should look, pretty and welcoming. I turn and look out across the Solent and take a deep breath of sea air. Several yachts in full sail, tack their way through the choppy waters that separates the Isle of Wight from the mainland. It's already a beautiful day. It's going to be a scorcher.

So the mission ahead is for me to tell Sam that I still hold a torch for him and that I will always love him. And that I wish things had been different. I'm not going to tell him my news. Why torment him anymore? He's been receiving late night heavy breathing calls for the past two years. I adjust the rear view mirror to check my face and hair. They will have to do. The panda eyes I can't do much about. I look tired and a little pale. With shaky hands I pinch my cheeks a couple of times to try and encourage some colour back into them. My eyes look so sad and seem to have lost their sparkle. I put on my Ray Bans. Eyes give so much away. They really are the windows to a person's soul. Right now, I don't want anyone seeing into my soul. Each day my will to live is slowly slipping away.

Christ I have to get a grip. For a couple of days now, I've been having this two-sided conversation going on in my head. One minute the good side is telling me to go with Beck's advice and fight this damn thing with all of my being. Make the most of the time and make it worthwhile. And then the bad half of my psyche tells me to fold the hand of cards I have been dealt and give up. Am I cracking up here?

On this particular occasion the fight 'til the end option is victorious. So, it's back to the job at hand. I just have enough time for a quick rehearsal of my opening line... 'Sam! Hi there. I was just passing and...God you look so well. Tea? Yes I'd love one, thanks'. That'll have to do for starters. Not original I know, but what the hell. I haven't come all this way for an in depth discussion. I slam the door of my rusty passion wagon behind me, dislodging yet another chunk of rust from some unseen area of the bodywork.

Squatting down next to the car, I look to see where the rust has come from. I don't want to kneel down on the gravel just in case I ladder my tights. They were new on this morning. I swivel round when I hear a child gurgling and chuckling and a manly 'coo, coo' coming from behind me. It's Sam. In his arms he is holding what can only be described as a miniature Sam. Oh shit, this is not how it is supposed to be. Not Sam standing there with a baby in his arms.

Retreat, retreat, run away, run away! I quickly turn back towards the car and fumbling with the car keys, try to unlock the door. Why is it that whenever you want to unlock a door quickly, you always choose the wrong key or can't quite get the bloody thing in the keyhole? Come on, get in you bugger. Fumbling with the keys I start to panic. Then as if in slow motion the keys fall from my grasp, bounce once and tumble down the drain that I've inadvertently parked over. Shit, fuck, shitty, fuck, bollocks.

"Hey, can I help you love? You need any help?" inquires a gorgeously rich male voice. It still has a hint of a London accent to it. Of course, it's Sam still being the perfect gentleman.

"No, I'm fine thanks. I have a spare set in here somewhere." I mutter under my breath. I keep my face towards the car. This isn't how it's supposed to be happening. Where did I put those bloody the spare keys? I always keep a spare set in the 'secret pocket' in my handbag. Funny, I could have sworn I'd put them in there. Then the realisation that perhaps, maybe I have the wrong bag hits me like a cricket bat to the head. This is the brown handbag, right? Shit, fuck, shitty fuck, bollocks! They are in my black bag, which at this precise moment in time is slung over the chair in my lovely south-facing homely kitchen back in London. Marvellous, bloody marvellous.

"Jen, Jennifer Evans? Is that you? It is you! It's me Sam, Sam Truman. Surely you remember me?" He shifts position to get a better look at my face. No time to run now Jen.

I turn, blushing like a frustrated teenager and smile. For the second time in my life, words fail me. Sam is still as drop dead gorgeous, as he had been the day we had split up. His chestnut brown eyes, like molasses sweet and totally irresistible, and his black hair unkempt as always. Sam had lived in shorts whilst we were together and today was no exception. Two completely gorgeously tanned legs sprout out from a tatty pair of cut-off jeans. He's rounded off his little ensemble with a Stranglers T-shirt and a huge smile. Sam had been blessed with a smile that lit up a sizeable area around him, wherever he went. When he smiles, I have seen that total strangers can't help but smile too.

"God, it is you! How are you?" he gushes. "You look terrific. I'd have to say you look the picture of health. Here, meet Sam Junior. He's my son. Obviously! Sam this is one of Daddy's friends. Say hello to Jenny." He runs his spare fingers through his dishevelled hair. How I used to love the way he did that.

"Blimey, Sam? Sam Truman isn't it?" Go on girl play the nonchalant game, do the 'do I know you?' routine. "What a surprise. Well, well, fancy bumping into you here." Still fumbling with my handbag, I proceed to empty the contents out onto the pavement. "Shit, fuck, shit, fuck, bollocks," I shout and stamp my foot.

Sam bursts out laughing. "Yes, that's my Jen! Here, let me help you." With Junior expertly balanced on his hip he bends down and starts picking up the contents of my bag. "Look why don't you come inside and use the phone. Are you still in the AA, or was it the RAC? Give us a chance to catch up while you're waiting for them. What do you say?" he asks.

Sam holds the last few bits that he's picked up from the floor out towards me, two extra long Tampax, one packet of Clorets and a used tissue. "Sure, that'll be great thanks. I'm with the RAC now." I ram everything back into my handbag and follow him into Ocean View. I leave my sunglasses on and when he asks me why I just say, "Got a bit of a hangover that's all." He nods his head knowingly. He obviously believes me and accepts my explanation. He knows me so well.

It's lovely and cool in the hallway inside Ocean View, with the smell of sweet peas hanging in the air. I love the smell of sweet peas. My grandfather used to grow them especially for me when I was a child. Every summer Lizzie and I would go and stay with him for a week or so in the school holidays, and Grandpa would cut them fresh every other day for the vase between our twin beds. The smell has a habit of sending me back on an adolescent journey to reminisce. Memories of long hot summer days, barbecues in the back garden and picking raspberries, still fresh in my mind to this day. But now, ever since Grandpa's death, I feel such a heavy weight on my heart. Whenever I see sweet peas in the window of Florrie's Florists on the High Street or at Mum and Dads, I get a lump in my throat. Dad retired last year and took up gardening to keep himself in trim. He now grows raspberries and sweet peas.

"Jen, I said would you like a drink, tea, coffee, or something cold?" he asks. I must have been miles away, just drifting aimlessly amongst my memories. I follow him into the kitchen.

"Um, tea would be great, thanks." I say, somewhat distracted. He still has such a fine arse.

"The phone's in the front room by the window. But you know that already, don't you. Silly me. Go help yourself and I'll put the kettle on." Sam seats Junior in the high chair next to the scrubbed kitchen table, and turns to the sink to fill the kettle. His arse is as pert as ever. Each one of his cheeks a good handful. I wonder if he still has those edible dimples?

In the lounge I call the RAC and relay my predicament. "Don't worry Ms Evans, one of our chaps will be with you shortly. It's 9.30am now. Your patrolman will be Steve and he will be with you within the hour." An hour, I have an hour. Will that be long enough? It'll have to be. I wander back towards the kitchen, peeking into the other rooms along the way, just to be nosy. Sam is leaning back against the sink unit, crunching on an apple.

"So how have you been?" he asks. "It's been a long time. What, it must be four years? Still living in London or have you seen sense and finally decided to give your lungs a chance?" Strange, he's asking probing questions? He hated London.

"Yep. Life is fantastic actually," I say over enthusiastically. "Couldn't be better. I'm still in London. So, what about you then? I see you've been busy." I nod towards Sam Junior. Junior has the remnants of regurgitated milk down the front of his bib and from the look and colour of his face, is also preparing a little present in his nappy for daddy.

"Oh you mean Sam Junior? Yes, he's a sweetie isn't he? He'll be one in October. We are so proud of him. Rose has already put him down for Twyford Prep School, near Winchester. Apparently it's the best in Hampshire. She'll be home soon. They popped out to the shops about an hour ago." Rose is Sam's sibling. She would get involved wouldn't she. She'd be in if she fell in. Can't leave him to get on with his own life. She was always interfering. From day one the conniving cow had done her damnedest to split Sam and I up. No doubt she'd been like the cat that had got the cream and the mouse, when I left him that morning.

"Mm... he's lovely. He has your eyes." I lean across the table and take his little hand in mine. "Hello little man, and how are you, yes how are you!" I coo in my best Play School voice. Junior drags my hand up to his mouth and is sick all over it. "Oh dear...I've got sicky wicky on my handy wandy now, haven't I." The little shit!

Sam proffers a piece of kitchen roll and says, "Sorry about that. Don't worry its only milk sick. He's still breast feeding." He smiles and returns to his leaning position up against the sink unit.

Oh...well that's all right then! For a moment there I thought he was on solids. "No, don't worry. What's a smear of sick between old friends?" I manage to force a laugh through clenched teeth, as I wipe the stinking spew from between my fingers. "So are you happy, Sam? I mean, really happy?" I ask, praying for him to say no and then go on to tell me how much he misses me.

Sam takes a deep breath. "You know for once in my life Jen, I have everything. I am so happy. I have my little empire here." He gestures to his surroundings. "I have the son I've always longed for." Well since when? That's news to me. You always said you hated kids. "I have a partner who thinks the sun shines out of my arse, and a family who supports me. So yes, I have to say that I am fantastically happy." The look of contentment in his eyes says it all.

Mmm, well that'll be a yes then. Where had he learnt to pontificate so profoundly? Where is the old Sam? So much for the, "God Jen, I've missed you. You look so good." Then being swept off my feet, carried to the bedroom for an aperitif of cunnilingus, followed by a rampant main course of unadulterated sex. No sex on the menu today then. No chance of a shag, you know for old times sake? I really hate it when a plan doesn't come together.

A key turns in the front door and girlie laughter fills the hallway. I run my fingers through my hair and prepare for the onslaught. Like a mini tornado, they burst into the kitchen, out of breath and with a healthy seaside glow in their cheeks. I recognise Rose immediately. She looks like she's put on a few pounds...fantastic! So the day hasn't been a complete disaster. The person with her though, how can I compare? She is stunning, tall, slim and blonde. I REALLY hate it when a plan doesn't come together. I look at my watch. Still 45 minutes to go until the RAC man is due to arrive. Oh hell.

Rose's face freezes mid-cackle, the moment she sees me. "What the fuck are you doing here?" she demands. I see that she hasn't lost her flawless command of the English language. "Sam, why is she here? What's going on?" she snaps, as she stands with her hands on her oh so ample hips. Thank you God!

"Well, you see, I was taking Junior for a stroll and I ran into Jen on the seafront. She's lost her car keys, and so I..." he's talking fast, burbling under the pressure of interrogation. As if he has to justify my being here, to that miserable witch.

Hello, I'm still in the room bitch! "It's so 'nice' to see you again, Rose. Sam kindly invited me in to call the RAC. And you must be Sam Junior's mother. Hi, I'm Jen, Sam's ex. He may have mentioned me?" I extend my hand towards the leggy blonde, but she chokes back a laugh and chooses to ignore it. So, you want to play hard ball do you? Well that's fine. I turn and offer my outstretched hand to the gorgeous looking man who has appeared in the doorway behind them. He takes it and smiles shyly. How on earth did Rose manage to pull you?

The blonde looks like she's on a mission. She walks straight over to Sam Junior and plucks him out of his high chair. Kicking a chair out from under the table she sits down hitches up her virtually non-existent crop top, and proceeds to breast-feed him. Looking up she makes eye contact for the first time and replies, "Pleased to meet you, I'm sure. And no, Sam hasn't mentioned you but Rose has told me all about you." I bet she has the bitch. God I hate her with a passion. Rose had taken a dislike to me from day one. I think it was pure jealousy. When I came into Sam's life, she was no longer the focus of his or her mother's attention. Her father leaving had seriously disturbed her and I think she resented me for that too.

The uneasy silence is only marred by the Junior's suckling. I avert my eyes and concentrate on the wallpaper, to give her some level of intimacy with her child. "Damn it. Pass me some kitchen roll will you, Sam" she asks. "I've got a leak from my left one. That's unless you fancy a suck, babe?" she adds.

What? I don't believe what I'm hearing. Is he going to take her up on her offer? I really don't want to see this, thanks very much. Sam is laughing hard. He pulls a couple of sheets of tissue from the kitchen roll dispenser above the sink and dabs at his eyes. It's a conspiracy! How can he torment me like this? The male totty in the doorway shifts awkwardly from one foot to another, then about turns and disappears.

Rose shrugs off her leather jacket, walks over and sits down next to her. With a sneering look towards me she leans forward, cups her left breast in one hand and with the other begins guiding it to her lips. Fucking hell! My obvious embarrassment has become apparent to all in the room. My bright blood red cheeks give me away, yet again.

"You mean, you're not...and Rose?" I stammer. "You mean you're together in the gay type sense of the word? Then Sam, what on earth, I mean...?" My mind is racing. I'm at a loss for words.

"It's simple really Jennifer," sneers Rose with a gleam in her eye. "Joey and I wanted a child and Sam obliged. It was as simple as that really. You know the scenario, a couple of porno magazines, a Tupperware box, and a turkey baster..."

So Sam is simply a sperm donor and not her partner after all. So if she's not with Sam? Hey, maybe it's not too late after all. I could still be in with a chance here. Erotic images make your way to the front of the queue again, please! Maybe there's time to repair some of the damage and spend the last few days of my life in a climatic heaven. Finally I say, "Oh right, I see. That is so brotherly of you, Sam. You were always so giving. For a moment there, I thought you and Joey were the, you know, the item!" I laugh, embarrassed at my blatant misunderstanding of the situation.

Sam is still laughing. Joey is laughing. Rose is cackling. What's the joke? And why does it feel like it's on me? They're all laughing, cackling like the three witches in MacBeth. Sam takes a deep breath, and manages to stop laughing long enough to say, "Joey's not really my type, Jen," then cracks up again. This isn't funny. I don't think I like the new Sam anymore. Forget the possibility of carnal pleasures. I look at my watch for the millionth time, 25 minutes and counting.

The two women stagger out of the kitchen, pausing briefly in front of me to indulge in a tongue twisting passionate kiss, taking Sam Junior with them, mumbling something about having an afternoon nap. Once they're out of the kitchen, Sam sits down opposite me and reaches across the table, placing his manly hands over mine. "I'm so sorry Jen. But you know what Rose is like. She can get a little out of hand at times. I'm sorry for laughing at you, but your face...it was a picture!" He squeezes my hands. "Forgive me? I should have said earlier."

What can I say? Sam can hardly be held accountable for his retard of a sister, can he? So I tell him, "Sure Sam. It was just a shock that's all. So what about you? You say you're happy with your partner?" I cross everything and will him to say no.

"Jen, I have something to tell you. I'm not the old Sam that you used to know. I've changed," he says nervously fiddling with the salt and pepper pots.

"Me too," I say eagerly. Not too eagerly though, of course. This is obviously a big moment for Sam. God, I hope he's not going to tell me he's getting married or something. That would definitely put a damper on things.

"Jen, when we split up, I did a lot of soul searching and thinking. I went away for a while. I needed time to get my head together." Again he runs his fingers through his hair.

"Me too," I nod my head in agreement. Well, if you can count two weeks in Gran Canaria on the lash with the girls soul searching.

"We made a mistake, you and me. Jen, I realised back then that..." he pauses.
Go on and say those words I want to hear baby. I miss you Jen, take me back! Then get your clothes off and let's get ready to rumble. I hold my breath. Sam is looking straight at me, peering into my eyes...oh those eyes..."Jenny, I like men."

"Me too!" I say without pausing for breath. No, hang on a minute. What does he mean? It's my turn to look him straight in the eyes. "What do you mean, you like men?" I say slowly. "In what way exactly?" I don't like the sound of this at all. From the look in his eyes I don't think he means it in the biblically brotherly way either. His hands no longer felt manly over mine. I slide them away, and then he says it.

"Jen, I'm gay." He lets out a big sigh. "Like Rose, I bat for the wrong team too. Funny really, both a sister and brother turning out gay. Poor old mum didn't know which way to turn when we came out. But she's getting used to it now. The guy that was with the girls, that's my boyfriend Sascha. He's from Germany. And it's love Jen. It's the real thing this time. I've never been so happy." He looks sad yet relieved as if he's finally unburdened himself.

"But that's a girls name," Is all I can blurt out defensively.

Sam smiles and says, "Sascha is definitely a man Jen." Well, whoopee do for you mate! Just take a girl as high as you can, then drop her as hard as you can, why don't you.

What is there left to say? "I don't really know what to say, Sam. I suppose I'm happy for you, somehow. I hope you'll be really happy. No, really.

You deserve to be loved unconditionally," I say it and I mean it. "Let's face it, I couldn't, could I? And I'm glad I know now. Thanks. God, look at the time. The RAC man should be here any minute now." I look down at my watch. I'm so glad I've kept my sunglasses on.

Right on cue, a beep on a car horn lets us know that the RAC man has finally arrived. Thank God. "Right then, thanks for the tea Sam. It's been lovely to see you again. No really, it has. I'd better go. I can see myself out." I'm already on my feet.

"Please don't leave like this. I'm sorry you had to find out like this, Jen," he calls out after me.

I stop in the doorway and look back at him. He looks so vulnerable, so small. Where did my big strapping sexy Sam go? I smile and say, "Forget it mate. That's life isn't it. Seriously, as long as you're happy, I'm happy for you. He's gorgeous too…Sascha I mean."

Sam nods his head and the glint in his eye returns for an instant. "Yes he is, isn't he" he purrs.

Oh please! I ignore the shiver that tickles the full length of my spine. "You know you're a good person Sam. I wish you all the luck and love in the world. You only live once, so make the most of it. Look, I've really do have to go now." I pretend to look at my watch again.

"Thanks for not going completely crazy Jen. I thought you might have guessed though. The male porn magazines I used to buy for you were a bit of a give-away, weren't they?" he asks, as if I should have guessed. I'd just thought he was being liberal. "Look, can we still be friends Jen? Please?" he begs. I notice for the first time how effeminate he has become.

"Of course we can silly," I assure him, playfully slapping him on the arm. "Come on Sam, this is the nineties after all. I'm not that narrow minded." Not if the events of last night are anything to go by. I feel sick to the pit of my stomach. But let's be honest here, I'm hardly one to pass moral judgement on homosexuality now, am I? I turn and continue to make my hasty retreat along the hallway to the front door.

"I knew you'd understand, you know," he says smugly. "Rose was so wrong about you, Jen." What had that bitch said? "By the way, why did you come back to here? Was there something you wanted to see me specifically about, or was it purely coincidental that we bumped into each other?" Sam inquiries as he opens the front door for me, forever the gentleman.

Momentarily I consider telling him. But no, why tell him now? There's no more to be said. "No, really, I was just passing and thought I'd park off the promenade to avoid paying the parking fee. You know me, tight as a fag's arse." I wince at my faux pas. Size four and a half, straight into my big mouth. "No sorry I mean, look it's been great seeing you again, really. Congratulations on Sam Junior too. You must be so proud. He's the spitting image of you."

Standing by the car is Steve, the RAC patrolman. He is well built with big blue eyes, an earring in one ear and a rather endearing beer belly. Sam is still smiling as the patrolman unlocks the car door and gives me a spare key. I'm not sure who he's smiling at, Steve or me. I turn and give Sam a hug. For a split second, I will myself to feel the way he used to make me feel when he held me all those years ago. But it's gone. I drive off, giving a hearty wave until I'm out of sight. Then my digit configuration changes to the two-fingered salute.

I don't get very far before I have to pull over into one of the car parks on the seafront. I switch the engine off and just sit, staring out at the untamed ocean gently stroking the shore. I wind the window down and take a deep breath. My view is blurred. At last, I can take off my sunglasses now.

Sam seems so happy now. He has so much life in his eyes. So much more than he ever had when he was with me. If only fate had taken a different twist or turn, then who knows, Sam Junior could have been my child. But I'll never have children of my own now. For the first time in my life, it hits me. I will never be a mother. Damn it, surprisingly enough that actually hurts. I'd always sworn that I would never have children, agreeing with Beck and my other friends that stretch marks, morning sickness, abstinence from sex for the final months, were too high a price to pay for sleepless nights, shitty nappies, colic and financial difficulties.

And now I don't have a say in the matter. It's not just the fact that I will never have children that hurts, it's that my right to choose whether I have children or not, has been taken away from me. A lump in my throat pre-empts the tears of sadness. Or are they tears of self-pity? I will never experience the feeling of having another human being growing inside me. I will never get the chance to hold and comfort a part of me. Someone I've actually given life to. I will never have the chance to make up for my own inadequacies with lots of love, affection and cuddles. I will never hear my child calling out for me. I will never be the best Mum in the world. God, that really hurts. I've never really thought about it before.

And Mum and Dad, they've come to rely on me for the obligatory grandchildren too. Lizzie is never going to be in the position to sustain a meaningful relationship, let alone have a family of her own. So it has always been down to me to provide. And now I am going to deny them all. If only I could have another chance. But what ifs' just don't count anymore. There are no maybes, there are only when's. I only have a few days to make peace with myself. I start the car and back out of the parking space. This is probably the last time I will see the sea too. I take one more look. If only…

Sunday 16th August...A Night at Her Majesty's Pleasure

Yes, I know. This is a bit of a strange one. I mean, most people do their utmost to avoid getting into any sort of trouble or having any contact with the law, don't they? But it reality, most do. Whether it's for under-age drinking, gate crashing concerts, not paying to go on the tube, or speeding. Well, not me, and certainly not an Evans. Since I've been old enough to be held responsible for my actions, I have been a complete goodie two shoes, always being good so that Mum and Dad will be proud of me. Never once stepping outside the barriers that Dad had erected, when we were kids. I think the fear of not being able to sit down for a week, due to a beaten backside, probably had something to do with that though.

When Beck and I had been compiling the wish list of things that I still wanted to do and achieve before I have to go, I just happened to mention that for once in my life I wanted to be naughty. Nothing really bad, just on the cusp of unacceptable behaviour. I'd always said that if I'd been more generously endowed, I certainly would have been tempted to streak at a rugby match. All those lovely rugby player's legs. I had a thing for muscular legs. When Erica Roe streaked at Twickenham back in the seventies, I remember the looks on the player's faces. Billy Beaumont had been the captain. Bless him, he had no chance of getting through to any of the team while she was on the pitch. People called her an attention seeker. I just thought, God I'd love to do that. She was my hero. Well, I was only ten at the time.

So you see, I've always wanted to do a streak. It must be the suppressed rebel or something inside me. Plausible enough reason, I suppose. Beck thought I was off my rocker when I'd mentioned it, but had humoured me as we'd mulled over a few possible ideas. She'd just said it's your life mate. Thanks for reminding me.

After much deliberation, several large beverages and a spliff later, it had been decided. I would flash my breasts from the steps leading up to the Eros statue in Piccadilly Circus. I'm finding the prospect quite exciting. I've always been a bit of a closet exhibitionist really. I love walking round naked in the privacy of my own flat. I'd always fancied one of those naturist holidays too. But it would have had to be an 18-30 year old holiday. Couldn't be doing with too many wrinklies walking around, sagging all over the place. All in need of a good ironing, to sort out their creases.

I get up bright and early, have a long soak in the bath with a cuppa within easy reach, and listen to the radio. The DJ on Capital Radio, I can't remember his name for the life of me, is reading out the gig guide for next week. "And at Wembley Arena for three nights, legendary rock icon Nina Hendrix will be kicking off her European tour."

It's still hard to believe that I have met 'the' Nina Hendrix and that we'd got on so well. A world famous rock star and me. A sense of sadness and some confusion washes over me. Thank God I don't have to try and justify to myself the feelings that I have for her. They hadn't been sexual, but I'd felt so comfortable with her. It doesn't make any sense. All I know is that I am going to miss her. I wish I could see her perform live again...but there isn't the time.

DJ 'Nameless' interrupts my thoughts by announcing, "For all you Nina Hendrix fans out there that haven't been able to get tickets for the Wembley gigs, we here at 95.8FM Capital Radio, London's number one radio station, have a world exclusive for you. Yes, Nina Hendrix will be performing live and unplugged here on Capital Radio during the evening session on Wednesday night at 9.00pm."

I don't believe it. She didn't say anything about a radio gig? But then why should she? Who am I, her mother? And what is the date today? Will I still be here? DJ 'Nameless' continues in his fabulously pop-tastic tones, "So call in with your questions for Nina or e-mail us at the usual address. And now here's a sneak preview of what you can expect from Nina's new album to be released at the beginning of September. This is the first single 'Everything I have is yours', taken from the album, 'Take it to the limit'."

So I will get to hear her voice again. I climb out of the bath, towel myself off and change into my outfit for the day. I tie my hair back into two little pigtails to round off my little ensemble. Into the lounge, I draw back the curtains and invite the daylight in. The apple tree in Mrs G's garden is laden with fruit. I don't know what sort they are but they taste so good. During the summer months Mrs G always leaves me a bag of them on my doormat once a week. And has done since the summer I moved in. I love apples. I'm not too keen on those French ones that make you suck in your cheeks and make the muscles in the side of your face ache. But the red ones from the tree in the garden were to die for.

Brushing the happy memories to the back of my mind, I opt for a little liquid Dutch courage, pour myself a large whisky and take my daily dose. On the way out I make a mental note to remember to pick up a tape for the answer phone today, if I get the chance. I should write it down really, but I have to keep trying to keep my memory intact.

I catch the bus outside Florrie's Florists to the tube station and hop onto the next train into town. I'd told Beck the plan of action for the day. She'd laughed non-stop for about five minutes, then made some comment about taking a bag of ice cubes with me to ensure 'nipplus erectus'! I didn't have the balls to tell that I'd actually already thought about doing that. It would only validate her opinion that, I am truly insane.

The sun is shining and Michael Fish has again predicted temperatures in excess of 28 degrees. To be fair he has got better since his little faux pas in '87, when he'd stated that, "No there's not going to be a hurricane." I catch a glimpse of my reflection in the dry cleaners window, at the entrance to the tube station. I am dressed to kill. That is as in, dressed to kill anyone with fashion sense and style. I choose an empty carriage and make myself comfy. It only takes twenty-five minutes to get to Piccadilly. Again I check out my reflection in the train window. Um not bad...not bad at all. Pink crop top, black mini skirt and stilettos. Yes, you've guessed it, white stilettos. I've tried to go for the Cynthia Payne look. But if I'm honest with myself, I look more like a St Trinian's schoolgirl. All I need is a lacrosse stick and I'll be there.

The tube comes to a juddering halt. The sign on the station wall tells me I have arrived at my destination. I don Ray Bans and climb the steps up out of the tube station. Several cars and a rusty white transit beep their horns as I cross over the road at the pedestrian crossing. I feel great. I gave them all a big wave. I'm not too steady on the heels (I usually wear loafers or trainers) but remember what Beck said, "Head up, don't look down, and you'll be alright"...oh and "Work it baby!"

I make it across the road to Eros without any major hitches. The kerb tries to trip me up, but Beck's training saves me from any real embarrassment. At the bottom of the statue I look up. Poor old Eros looks a little the worse for wear. Eros the God of Love, covered in pigeon shit and with dried-on crusty vomit all over his laurels. It seems only fair really. What does he know about love, anyway? If my experiences of love and romance are anything to go by, then I have to say his accuracy with a bow and arrow leaves a lot to be desired. I climb the steps surrounding the monument. There are the usual punks, alchies's and down and outs sprinkled on the peripherals sipping Special Brew, barely noticing the additional freak joining their menagerie.

Well, here goes nothing...and after three...one...two...and...THREE! I grab the edge of my crop top and expose my mammaries for all and sundry to see. Oh, the joys of feeling the sun's summer rays caress my nubile bits. Completely liberating? No, highly embarrassing actually. As if on cue, an inebriated elderly gentleman sidles over to me and asks if I do draught and if so, from which pump. A sense of deja vue catapults its way to the forefront of my mind. Sam's sister, Rose. I still can't believe she did that yesterday. Still, the unexpected shiver makes my nipples stand out nicely. Thankful for small mercies, I thrust my chest projectiles out to their full extent.

'Mayday, mayday, mayday, bogey at two o'clock and closing rapidly'. Here we go. The cavalry has arrived. Strapping Adonis-like figure approaching from the Piccadilly end. How I love a man in uniform. He speaks. "Come on now, luv. Pop your top down. You're making a spectacle of yourself. And you can move along there Freddie. There's...um...nothing to see here." Freddie moves off shuffling his feet and mumbling away to himself.

Truncheon man steps in front of me in an attempt to protect my so-called modesty. Is he blushing? That is so endearing. I have to say he is the most adorable looking policeman I have ever laid eyes on. He must be well over six-feet tall. And from my vantage point on the steps, I notice his eyes are the colour of a perfect Caribbean Sea, azure, with the depth of the Atlantic Ocean. His smile is slightly lopsided but that just adds to the overall perfection rating that I have already subconsciously awarded him. A very commendable nine point five on the Evans Totty-o-meter.

"Come on now luv," he says again. "As good as they look, let's save them for the privacy of your own home, shall we?" He's struggling not to laugh or look at my boobs, which is a bit tricky seeing as they're only a couple of inches from his face. The symphony of car horns, cheers and wolf whistles from the passing motorists is deafening. I really should cover up now. But what the hell, just a few more minutes, eh!

He shouts impatiently. "Pop 'em away, and we'll say no more about it." I ignore him and turn to address another section of my audience. When I look back, the endearing smile has disappeared. "He says angrily, "Look, if you carry on like this I am going to have to caution you...Miss...Mrs?" he stutters.

Before I can stop myself I blurt out, "The name's Rebecca Monroe...Miss. Beck to my friends." If Beck ever finds out about this she will never forgive me.

"Right, well Miss Monroe, I have to warn you..." By now, his obvious embarrassment is turning to irritation.

Just then a van with, Reagans Builders Ltd...it's what we do best, inscribed along the side of it, beeps its horn. The driver sticks his head out of the window and shouts, "Hey luv, fantastic tits, got anything else you'd like to show us?"

"Wouldn't you like to know, darlin!" I scream back at him. Distracted for a moment, I decide to give him a big hearty wave and jiggle my boobs in his general direction. My adoring crowd roars with appreciation. I lose my footing. Oh no, I'm falling. I reach out to save myself and make contact with something solid. There's a sickening crunch. I've hit him in the face. Oh no, not the nose! Blood starts pouring from Officer 254674's nostrils. The look of surprise on his face turns to anger.

"God, I'm so sorry" I gasp in disbelief. But it's too late. He pulls a pair of handcuffs from his belt and cuffs my wrists. Out of the corner of my eye I notice that my newly acquired fan base is starting to get restless. They have seen the handcuffs go on and are not happy about it.

Shouts of "Let her go..." "It's only a bit of fun..." "Bloody police brutality, that's what it is..." fill the air. In a matter of seconds the atmosphere changes from light hearted to dangerously tense.

"Miss Monroe, I am arresting you for a breach of the peace and for assaulting a police officer. You do not have to say anything. But anything you do say..." he shouts, still pinching his nose to try and stem the bleeding.

"There's a hankie in my bag, please take it. It's clean...ish." I swivel my hips so that he can reach into my handbag. He unzips the bag to reveal my hip flask nestling nicely on top of the rest of the contents of the bag. Looking up at me he just shakes his head. All I can manage is a sheepish smile. I think I'm in deep shit now. He grabs the corner of the hankie, pulls it out from beneath the flask, and zips up the bag again.

"Thanks," he mumbles. He sounds all nasally, if there is such a word. I've really caught him a cracker. Blood is pouring from his nose, and it doesn't look like it's going to stop for some time. "I still going to arrest you though" he snaps. With that, he grabs his two-way radio and shouts, "Immediate back up required."

Within minutes the wail of a police siren informs us that back up is imminent. The crowd starts booing. An unmarked police van screeches to a halt next to the gap in the railings. Pinkie and Perky, cunningly disguised as two police officers, emerge from the back of the van, and jog towards us. The dense crowd that now surrounds us, immediately closes ranks, in an attempt to block their way. But the brave pair draw their batons and in seconds, as if by magic, a pathway appears in front of them.

As they get closer, they notice the state of their bloodied colleague and draw their own conclusions. I try to explain what has happened, but they're not in the mood for listening. Unceremoniously the two of them drag me off towards the awaiting van. My protests fall on deaf ears. For a moment I forget Beck's wise words and look down to see where I am treading. I somehow misjudge my step. My heel catches on the tow bar of the van and catapults me into the back. With a roar from the crowd of punks, alcoholics and American tourists, who think it's all part of the London Experience tour they have signed up for, and a triumphant punch into the air from me, Officer 254674 climbs in after me and slams the door shut. Oh goodie, they've put the siren on.

In the confines of the van, an unnerving silence accompanies us to the police station. We're on the way to Charing Cross Police Station. Apparently that's the nearest one to Piccadilly Circus. No more than ten minutes later the van comes to a sudden halt, throwing me up against Pinkie and Perky with a jolt. Far too roughly, they push me back up to a sitting position. Charming. The driver opens the back doors to let us out. Pinkie and Perky shove me out of the van and drag me along the path, and through the police station's double doors.

Inside the station's reception area, it is hot and sticky. It smells of old sweat and unwashed bodies, like stale digestive biscuits. The fans hang motionless from the ceiling. Why aren't they on? It has to be at least eighty-five degrees in here. Is it because of the recent government cutbacks or just because they don't want the 'guests' to the station to get too comfortable? As soon as we've entered the building, Officer 254674 removes the handcuffs from my wrists and disappears through an unmarked door. He looks terrible. The bruising is already coming through. Definite panda eyes by the morning. His once perfectly starched white shirt now splattered with copious amounts of blood. He looks like an extra from the Texas Chainsaw Massacre.

I find myself being shoved again, this time in front of a large desk with what looks like Satan's wife sitting behind it. To say she's ugly would be understating the facts. Imagine the actress in the Life and Loves of a She-Devil. Well her twin is sitting in front of me right now. Even down to the growth on her upper lip. "Name and address?" she snaps, obviously really happy to be here on a Sunday afternoon…not. From the sign on the desk in front of me, I take it that WPC Janet Land - Duty Officer, is addressing me.

"Please!" I say in my best slapper accent, chewing on my non-existent chewing gum. "Manners maketh man, you know!"

"Just answer the question, Miss." She says, spitting out the words. WPC Land doesn't raise her gaze from the sheet of paper in front of her. How rude is that? The sweat stains emerging from her armpits are particularly unattractive. Thank God there is a desk separating us. I bet she hums.

I feel it's time to hurry along the proceedings, so I say, "My name is Rebecca Monroe." I give her Beck's address. Beck really will kill me if she finds out about this. "Look, I am sorry for hitting your Officer...Officer Hilton, I think that's his name. But, well I didn't mean to. You see I was just waving and I lost my balance and..."

From somewhere beneath the desk, WPC Land extracts a tray and slams it down on the desk between us. She's obviously not the slightest bit interested in any explanation that I have to offer. "Personal belongings, jewellery, and that disgusting belt in the tray now. For some reason, Officer Hilton has decided not to press charges, so you can cool off in the cells for an hour or so. That will teach you a lesson or two, young lady." With a wave of her hand as if to dismiss me, she grabs another form and shouts "NEXT!"

I can't get the image of Beck losing it big time out of my head, if she ever finds out that I've lied to the police and pretended to be her. A moment of righteousness overcomes me. I have to tell the truth here. "Look I'm sorry," I say and start to explain, "My real name is Jennifer Evans. I don't know what came over me just then to lie."

"Oh right, love," says WPC Land in a sarcastic voice. She leans across the desk and rests her ample bosom on to the surface. "And I suppose then you're going to tell me that your real name is Penelope Pitstop, and the Anthill Mob will be along soon to post bail for you?" Is she taking the piss? Wit certainly does not become her. God you try to do the right thing...

By now my tattoo is starting to itch, my back is throbbing and I am getting jogger's nipple from my Miss Selfridges crop top. My eyes are tired and I feel a bit sick. Probably cos I haven't eaten today. Both of my ankles have blisters and one has started to bleed. I am shoeless too. I must have left them in the back of the van.

I retort, "Wit certainly isn't your forte is it? Or looks for that matter." I am here to tell the truth, right?

Beefy Janet Land is not amused. "I have to caution you Ms Evans, if that is your real name," she spits. "If you continue with this sort of behaviour, I will have no alternative but to detain you here overnight."

"Janet, can I call you Janet? No? Okay well how about Moby Dick then? Have you ever been mistakenly harpooned? Ever been swimming in the sea, and turned to see that you're being followed by men in a rowing boat with spears?" I sense someone behind me and turn to see that Officer Hilton has re-joined the party. He manages a small discreet smile in my direction.

He's changed into a clean shirt. His nose is red and he has pieces of cotton wool up each nostril. I have to suppress a giggle. He reminds me of Michael Palin in a Fish called Wanda, when Kevin Kline sticks chips up his nose.

Something tells me that Janet has just about had enough now. She screams "Right, that's it. Put her in the cells, Officer Hilton. I don't have to listen to this. Get her out of my sight right now!" Perspiration has broken out across her upper lip. Her left eye has begun to twitch too.

I protest weakly as Officer Hilton leads me away towards a door that's marked 'Cells'. I have to get just one more remark in for the She-Devil, "Harpoon that whale, Mr Christian!" I shout over my shoulder. Her face is thunderous. With the one eye twitching, she grabs my tray of belongings and throws it under the desk. "Oi, be careful. If you've broken anything, I'll sue!" I add angrily.

Officer Hilton pushes me through the door and kicks it shut behind him. "Sorry about all this. You shouldn't have wound her up though, you know. Mind you, you're not wrong! Somebody certainly tapped her with the ugly stick when she was born!" With a throaty laugh, Officer Hilton gently guides me towards a door marked Cell Number 5. Oh, my lucky number. I don't know how I could have been so wrong earlier. This man is definitely a ten out of ten. He shakes his head and smiles..."Moby Dick!" His laughter is infectious and I find myself laughing along with him. When he laughs, I can't help but notice that he's got lovely lips and pearly white teeth.

"So what's your first name Officer Hilton or 254674? I mean, all those numbers..." I ask bashfully.

He says, "We're not encouraged to give out that sort of information, Miss Evans. But, for your information, my name's Andy. And I have to say, thanks for making my day. You've been a great source of entertainment. Oh and by the way, you do have great breasts." He winks.

He has such a naughty smile! "Well, thanks for that, Andy," I say coyly. God I am being such a girl! "Nice name too. Look I'm sorry about the nose. I hope it doesn't hurt too much, does it? Is it broken?" I ask, gazing up at him. His smile causes an involuntary muscular movement in my nether regions. Behave yourself Evan's!

"No, it's fine really. I've broken it so many times over the years playing rugby, a knock like that hardly hurts at all. They're just messy." He gently rests his hand on my arm. Oh deep joy! He is a rugby player too. I pause briefly to imagine his perfectly toned thighs...Mmm.

"Now in you go. If you behave yourself, WPC Land may release you in an hour or so. You really pissed her off though. Oh, and should you decide to drop me in the shit at a later date, I shall of course deny all knowledge of this conversation."

I turn too quickly and lose my balance. He reaches out to steady me. I assure him that "Of course I won't drop you in the shit. And really, I'm so sorry for the nose business. I do hope you can forgive me?" He obviously thinks I'm barking mad, completely crazy. If only we'd met earlier and under different circumstances. With another cheeky wink and a sorry, Andy Hilton shuts the cell door with a bang.

So this is one of Her Majesty's smaller guestrooms. I turn to face my surroundings. The walls are covered in graffiti and there is a strong smell of disinfectant in the air. The smell of disinfectant always makes me feel sick. It brings back memories of a particularly sickly childhood followed by an irresponsible adolescence filled with alcohol and late nights. There's a small window way out of my reach that looks like it's been painted shut, which is letting in next to no light. A fluorescent tube gives some light to the dreariness. The room is roughly twelve average steps by ten. Within this space there's a stainless steel toilet with a pack of Izal toilet paper on the cistern and a bed with a thin mattress, which looks as if it's home to a variety of creepy crawlies. It's baking hot too. This is definitely not like Dixon of Dock Green. Thoughts of a friendly police officer handing over a nice hot cuppa, sharing his fags and a bit of light-hearted banter, go right out of the proverbial barred window.

As the sun moves round to the west, the cell is thrown into shadow. It starts to get quite cold. So I wrap the skanky blanket that was rolled up at the end of the bed around my shoulders. I perch on the edge of the mattress. It looks so dirty that I really don't want to sit on it properly, let alone lie on it later. God, this place is small and there's no window to open. I'm sure to run out of air soon. I can feel the anxiety rising. Ladies and gentleman, let's all put our hands together again and say a big hello and welcome back to... 'Claustrophobia'!

It feels as though the walls are closing in on me. Momentarily I lose control and start shouting hysterically, "Please, let me out. I'm sorry. I didn't mean it, you know, what I said. Please. I can't breathe in here." By now I'm pounding on the cell door, screaming. My pleas echo around the cell. Seconds later a small middle section of the door clanks open. It's Andy.

"Sshh, now calm down Jennifer," he urges in a whisper. "You'll attract the attention of WPC Land. She's still really pissed off with you. I think you hit a nerve when you referred to Moby Dick. You know she has the authority to strip search you, so keep it down, right? Look, take some deep breaths, you'll get used to it. And it won't be for long now" he assures me. "You can go in a couple of hours."

"What's the time now?" I have to ask. I had been stripped of all belongings, my watch, earrings and leather belt. The panic is still rising.

He looks down at his watch. "It's nearly eight o'clock," he says. "Look, it's against regulations but I'll get you a cuppa if you'll calm down. Here, take this." Andy reaches through the opening in the door and holds out his handkerchief. "Are you cold? I'll try and get you another blanket. Hang in there Jen. I'll be back in a mo." With that he closes the little hatch in the door.

"Thanks." I manage to get out, between the girlie sobs. I listen to his footsteps as they fade into nothingness. He called me Jen. I love the way he said that.

A few minutes later, Andy is back with a Styrofoam cup of tea. "Here you are. I put some sugar in it, for the shock. Careful it's hot. Oh and here's an extra blanket. If anyone asks, just tell them that there were two blankets in the cell when you got here. I'm going off duty now. Oh and by the way, WPC Land has just said you are to be detained over night after all. You've seriously pissed her off. But don't worry, I'll come and see you in the morning. Try and get some sleep, yeah?" With that he gently re-seals my tomb. "Goodnight Jennifer Evans" he says. I can tell that he is smiling by the tone of his voice. The cell is getting colder and I can feel the onset of fatigue. Again I listen until the sound of his footsteps are no more.

I pull the extra blanket over the top of the one I've already got wrapped around me. Doctor Gibson said that I would become increasingly tired as the days passed by and boy do I feel drained. I have days to go and now here I am sitting in a shitty police cell, just because I had a pang of conscience at the wrong time. I can rob a bank but can't bloody tell a little white lie when face to face with authority. Pathetic! The buzzing from the fluorescent tube mars the quietness that surrounds me.

And...cue the tears. So much for trying not to feel sorry for myself. I lean back on the bed, forgetting how bad it is and turn to face the wall. The tea has done something to re-balance my erratic behaviour, but I'm so tired now. I look down at the dirty hankie scrunched up in my hand. It has initials in one corner, AAH. I wonder what the middle 'A' stands for, Adam...Anthony...Albert? Don't go there, Jen. I shove the visual of Frankie's 'Albert' to the little recess in my brain, which houses all of the dodgy yet enjoyable memories from the past week or so. Instead I focus my attention on the little anecdotes etched on the once whitewashed walls.

'That fat fucker WPC Land, may she rot in hell!' I can go with that sentiment. She probably gets off on being a bitch.

'I'm in my prime, and committed a crime… and I don't give a fuck, signed Mel C – 24/7/98…xx' No, surely not? Probably won't be short-listed for a literary prize.

I had for the time being forgotten about my claustrophobia, and edged my way along the wall. As I get closer to the dirty stinking toilet at the bottom of the bed, the writing also takes on a filthier tone.

'Here I sit feeling bored, playing with my Tampax cord.' Mandy - 2/4/1999

'If you sprinkle while you tinkle, be a sweetie and wipe the seatie.'

'I luv Officer Hilton – I'd do anything to have a go on his pogo stick.' This particular gem is signed, 'bored and bleeding horny!' Mmm, I can relate to that one too.

Andy Hilton is gorgeous. The feelings he has stirred up inside me help to re-endorse the fact that I am indeed a complete heterosexual. Thank God for that. That 'thing' with Nina Hendrix had been how should I put it, an experience? Again, I push the memory back to the little compartment in my brain along with Albert.

I wish I hadn't had that tea now. I really need a wee. And I need one pretty soon. I take a closer look at the toilet. On closer inspection it looks like the public toilets that they used to have in Covent Garden, when Mum and Dad took us there as kids. Both grim and look as though they are home to every sexually transmitted disease known to man. I know they say that you can't get a STD from a toilet seat, but I'm not prepared to take the risk. I pull out several reams of Izal toilet paper and cover the entire rim. The actual seat had obviously gone walkabout some time ago. I look around just to make sure no one is looking through any of the cracks around the cell door. When I've finished I flush the loo, and climb back onto the bed. The guest in the next cell, is obviously several sheets to the wind. They're singing at the top of their voice, a slightly wobbly rendition of 'Oh Danny Boy'. That is one of Mum's favourites. I wish you were here with me now Mum. What would she think of me if she could see me now? I must look a right state. You know, I just can't quite get my head round the fact that I'm not going to be here, in what, maybe a week's time. Do I tell you or not? What do I do?

Subconsciously, I find myself singing along to her favourite song. When we've finished, silence follows. Then a slurring Irish voice asks, "So, got some Irish in you, my love?" I wait for the obvious next line, 'No? Well would you like some, darling?' But it never comes. Instead the voice introduces itself, "My name's Vincent by the way. I'm from Galway. Where's your family from, love? I'll take a guess now, Connemara?"

How does he know my family originated from Ireland? I call back, "They're from Monaghan actually, just south of the border. What are you in for, Vincent? By the way, my name's Jennifer," I add.

"I'm very pleased to meet you, Jennifer. Why am I in here? Well, I was going about my business today as usual with my mate Freddie. We were watching the world go by from beneath the statue of Eros, when some young upstart flashed her tits right there in front of us. Well, Freddie couldn't contain himself and went over to her to get a better look, if you know what I mean. I was beside myself. You see I've been on the streets for a long time now, and it's not every day you get to see such a beautiful sight. Sort of makes your day, you know. I had to celebrate." He pauses, takes a breath before adding, "Well, one can of Special Brew led to another, and it all got out of hand. Then police came and took the wee girl away, God bless her. It all got a bit fraught after that. A fight broke out, more police arrived and then they arrested me for being drunk and disorderly. Still, it was a fine sight indeed. Well worth it. She was a lovely looking girl, indeed she was." Vincent immediately goes up in my estimation from drunken bum to a connoisseur of good-looking women. The man has taste.

"She was pretty then, was she?" I fish for more compliments but Vincent has started singing again. I listen to his rendition of The Fields of Athenry, before curling up on my bug-ridden pit. I still have to lie on my right shoulder. My free spirit is healing nicely, but it's still a little tender. I gently stroke it and drop off to sleep.

Suddenly with a loud bang, the cell door is violently flung open. I turn over to face the door, shielding my eyes from the harshness of the corridor lights. Standing dramatically in the doorway, with the corridor light acting as her spotlight, is WPC Janet Land.

"On you're feet, Evans, if that really is your name. No matter anyway," she barks. "It's pay-back time, you miserable slut." I then realise what she's on about. I think it's the rubber gloves that give it away. She is going to get her own back by strip searching me. No fucking way! The sweat stains radiating from her armpits now reach the waistband of her regulation A-line skirt, which is obviously several sizes too small.

I scream at the top of my voice, but nobody comes. She gently pulls the cell door to behind her. "Strip girlie." She is coming at me, rubbing her hands together and licking her lips. "I am going to enjoy this more than you'll ever know. I'm gonna find every crack, hole and crevice to poke, that you don't even know you've got!" she snarls. She throws her head back and lets out a demonic laugh. I back up to the end of the bed, balancing precariously on the edge of the rickety frame. She's got me cornered.

"No please!" I plead desperately. "Look I'm sorry. I didn't mean what I said. I think you're actually quite nice looking (with my eyes closed) really. No don't…please…!"

I wake up in a sweat, lying on the cold dirty floor next to the bed. The room is in darkness. The electricity supply to the naked fluorescent tube has been switched off. I have been dreaming. I pick myself up and climb back onto the bed. I hug the blankets tightly around me, and push my back to within a couple of inches of the cold wall. Trying not to breathe in the blankets musty aroma, I close my eyes. I say a quick prayer and silently thank Officer Andy Hilton for his kindness. I struggle to sleep, willing the morning to arrive sooner rather than later. Just the sound of the toilet cistern and the odd creak from the next cell keeps me company. It's going to be a long night.

Monday 17th August...Revenge is sweet, my dear

There is something crawling over my shaky hand. Reluctantly I open my eyes and have a look to see what it is. It's an earwig. Instinct makes me shake it to the floor and stamp on it repeatedly until my foot hurts. It's dead. It's been a long cold night. The recollection of my nightmarish encounter with WPC Moby Dick, sends a shiver through my entire being. God, that'd been scary. Vincent finally stopped singing after another four Irish folk songs, including one of my all time favourites, The Wild Rover. All in all, it has been a pretty shitty night. I need my medication now. I feel stiff and shaky. And true to form the headache is coming back. I need my medication.

I have to say that pissing into a rancid toilet with the potential of catching all sorts from the rim and having to use crispy toilet paper, is not quite what I'd expected. This cell is nothing like the ones they have on The Bill. And as for sleeping on what can only be described as a housing estate of fleas, mites and other insect minorities, I feel like a walking tower block of infestation. First job when I get home? Long, hot soak in the bath. A full body detox to the extreme has to be first up on the menu. I raise each arm in turn and do the quick sniff test. They're not too bad at all. A faint aroma of body odour but as long as I keep my arms firmly to my sides no one will ever know. I run my fingers through my hair and wipe the sleepy dust from the corners of my eyes.

True to his word, Officer Andy Hilton arrives at about 7.30am with a steaming cup of coffee, in a real mug too and a couple of custard creams. He opens the cell door and steps over the threshold. "Morning Jen...Miss Evans" he says cheekily. "Here you go, I thought you might be in need of a little sustenance."

"Boy, am I glad to see you," I say with a sigh of relief. I give him one of my broadest smiles. "Oh, you brought coffee...great...thanks a lot." Mmm...it actually tastes quite good, for a dispensing machine cup of coffee anyway.

He looks at me in silence as I take another sip of coffee and then says, "Wasn't too bad last night, was it? The night duty officer said that your neighbour in the next cell had his singing head on all night. Did you manage to get any sleep at all?" he inquires.

"Oh no, it was fine really. Vincent...that was his name, we introduced ourselves. He was lovely. I fell asleep after The Wild Rover." I laugh nervously. Why does this man have such an effect on me? He is so, I don't know, so natural. I hand the empty mug back to him. "Thanks ever so much. That was lovely. Do you know, I haven't had custard creams for years." I make a mental note to buy a packet on the way home.

"Come on then, let's get you signed out of here." He places a hand in the small of my back and starts guiding me out of the cell. I think I must have flinched because he immediately takes his hand away and apologises. "Oh sorry. This way please...Miss Evans," he says so formerly.

Sod it. I only flinched because he'd caught the edge of the plaster covering the stitches. Go on please put your hand back, please. He leads me back to the desk in the reception area, to hand over my belongings and to sign the release forms. For the first time I notice the board on the wall behind the desk. It has a few public notices pinned to it, lost cat appeals, and there it, slap-bang in the middle of the board, a 'Wanted' poster. And there's a reward...for information that will lead to the arrest and conviction of the Ealing Two. Beck and I are the Ealing Two! She'll be so proud, or not as the case may be. I take a closer look whilst Andy is bending down behind the desk to retrieve the tray containing my possessions. I didn't look too bad actually. It's quite a good photo. Distracted for a moment by Andy's bum as he bends down...definitely edible dimples in those pants...I manage to draw my eyes back up to face level just in time, as he returns to a standing position.

"There you are, Miss Evans" he says formally. "One watch, two bracelets, a silver ring, and one leather belt, with Harley Davidson buckle and your purse." He slides the tray across the desk to me. He has two perfectly balanced black eyes with a really horrible yellow bruise trim around them.

"Thanks. Not just for that, but for being so kind to me last night. I'm really sorry for knocking your nose. I didn't mean to. It's just that, well, you see I HAD to do what I did and then I slipped. Trust me there was certain, if not warped method in my madness, for doing what I did. And here, thanks for the loan of the hankie." He looks down at the grolly-stained hankie in my hand and forces a sort of smile. "No, you're right, I'll give it a wash first before I give it back. I'll drop it back to the station over the next day or so, if that's OK?" I ask bashfully. Now there's a first for me, bashful?

"That's OK. Keep it," he says still smiling. "I have yours remember. So let's just call it quits, shall we?" He leans across the desk and whispers in a barely audible tone, "I'll meet you for a drink one night though, if you like. That's if you fancy it? I'd love to see you again, Jen." Our faces are inches apart. Wow, those lips are tempting. Taking a deep breath, I note that he's wearing CK for men. I love CK for men. It's my favourite. Mind you he could be wearing anything, and it would be my new favourite.

I would love to too. But I can't, can I? What's the point? A moment rears its ugly head, and I can feel the tear dispensers starting to crank themselves up, ready for action. I hastily arrange to meet him a week from today. It would be less painful this way. I wouldn't show. He'd think I wasn't fussed and move on.

With a, "Now you be a good girl and keep out of trouble. We don't want to be seeing you again, alright" and a sneaky wink, Andy sends me on my way. I turn the corner at the end of Agar Street and look back. He is still standing on the steps, leaning up against one of the pillars outside the police station. He really does have a fantastic smile. With a final wave I turn the corner. He is definitely a perfect ten. I'm freed from Charing Cross Police Station, on a gloriously sunny Monday morning at 8.00am.

For the first time in nearly a week, I don't have a hangover and I feel fan...bloody...tastic! But I have to take my medication. Maybe I do have a headache after all. I pause for a moment and yes it is there, just tapping away under the surface. Damn it. I rummage in my bag for the Pethedine. I keep a couple, just in case, in the inside pocket. Found them. I swallow one dry. Couldn't do that until all this started. Swallowing tablets without water always made me retch. But seeing as now everyday I feel sick just before I'm due the next dosage, it doesn't bother me.

I walk for about an hour, do some window shopping until the shops open, then pop into Rymans the stationers to get a tape deck cleaner and a new tape for the answer phone. At the top of Baker Street I buy a packet of Custard Creams from the Europa store then hail a cab and settle back into the seat for the journey home. I must have dozed off. The cabbie wakes me up by throwing an empty match box at me. Charming. I pay the man and climb out. I'm still shoeless. Still, no great loss, they were pretty dire.

Once inside the flat I call Beck straight away to tell her about the wanted poster and Andy. But she is out, so I leave her a message on her machine. "Hi, this is Beck Monroe, I'm not hear to take you call right now, so leave a message...thanks"...BEEP...

"Beck, it's me, Jen. You'll never believe what happened to me yesterday. I've met this bloke...he's a policeman...he's a perfect ten. No, really! Call me as soon as you get this message. Hope you're OK. Call me."

Of course, it's Monday. She'll be at work. As far as I know she is still working on location on Hedonistic Heaven. I am rapidly losing track of what day it is. All that I know is that after today, I have only days left. That's if the good doctor's calculations are accurate. In the shower, I scrub myself until I'm red raw. I hadn't stopped itching all the way home.

Feeling clean again, I drift into the bedroom, crawl under my 14-toggle duvet and pass out.

The sound of the rain wakes me as it pounds on my bedroom window, tapping out a message to all Arapaho Indians in the area that it's going to be wet today. The top window's open and the smell of the air is intoxicating. A fresh clean smell that can only be snorted and savoured during, and straight after a good downpour. Summer rain. There is nothing like it. I lay still for a while, listening to its melodic patter. I fancy a cup of tea but can't be bothered to get up just yet.

I'm going to miss the rain. Thinking about it, I'm going to miss lots of little things like that. I'm going to miss the sound of the wind and the sea. I'm going to miss the sound of the bird's early morning chorus. Contrary to popular belief, I have actually been awake early enough to hear it. I'm going to miss the smell of newly mown grass and freshly baked bread. I'm going to miss cuddling Mum and Dad and Lizzie. I'm going to miss having a girlie night in with my best friend. I'm going to miss the chance of getting to know Andy Hilton. I'm going to miss the chance of falling in love again. I can feel my throat closing up, as my tears begin to form an orderly queue again ready to fall. I'd do anything for another chance. I really would. I close my eyes and allow myself to grieve. I am grieving for myself and for my family and my best friend.

I cry until I fall asleep again. The next thing I know, it's midday. Come on now, no more tears. There are still things left to do. There's still time. I step over the mound of clothes on the floor next to the overflowing washing basket. I can't be bothered anymore. There's no need now. In the bathroom I run a bath. I know I only had a shower a couple of hours ago but this is going to be purely therapeutic. I need to calm down and relax. While it's filling up, I clean the answer phone with the tape cleaner and insert the new tape. I do a few dummy run throughs, then record the new message... "Hi I'm not in right now, or otherwise detained. Leave a message after the beep and I'll get back to you before I...I'll get back to you." That'll have to do.

In the kitchen, I switch the kettle on and take my pills while I'm waiting for it to boil. I don't bother looking at the list. I know what I have to do today. I have to organise my funeral. Well, there's no one else to do it is there? Beck already has enough on her plate with work. I can't ask her. I know I've left it a little late, but I just haven't been able to face it until today. I've been putting it off and putting it off. But now I have to do it. I am running out of time. And at least if I do it myself, I will be able to ensure that I get a dignified send off. I'm hoping that after arranging my funeral, I will be able to pick myself up with some self-indulgent vengeful behaviour. But the way I feel at this precise moment, it's going to take more than that and a couple of drinks to pull me out of this downward spiral.

I take an extra Maxalon and wash it down with a mouthful of whisky. I flop into the bath and with pad and pen at the ready, start to think. The decision that has to be made is cremation or burial. Given the choice, what would you choose? I have to weigh up the pros and cons. It still all feels very remote. It's as if it is all happening to somebody else. But, it isn't, I know that. I'm not stupid. It's happening to me. And now I have to make some serious decisions.

Let us ponder the question, do we have any recollection or feelings as we pass to the other side? Indeed, is there such a place as the other side? As we are about to take our last breath, do we see a light and feel a sense of peace? Or do we cling to life by our fingernails, howling and screaming, kicking out at the grim reaper, telling him to piss off and go pick on somebody else? Yes, deep I know. But, just think about? If we do then, I have to think twice about the crematorium. My skin just has to see the sun and it blisters.

On the other hand, there's burial. I have suffered from claustrophobia since I had a disturbing experience as a child. I'd had been trapped from the waist down under a pile of adolescent bodies at a YMCA summer camp. The vivid image of my little sister Lizzie trying to push past the adults, to try and pull me free from the rabble was always there, close to the front of my mind. The look of desperation and fear in her eyes still haunts me to this day. Finally, when the bodies had been peeled from the heap one by one, she hugged me until I could hardly breathe. Whilst all around us people were far from concerned about my near death experience. No, their only concern was what treats their mother's had packed for them in their lunch boxes.

So, I think we can perhaps rule out burial. But then again, maybe I should be thinking of those who are going to be left behind. I've always thought that having a burial site or a shrine is so morbid, and only serves to prolong the period of mourning for relatives and friends. But Beck, having lost her grandmother some six months ago, actually said that it was very calming and soothing to go and place flowers on her grave once a month. I went with her to the cemetery one time and she sat down on the grass at the edge of the grave, took out a hip flask and proceeded to talk to her Gran about what had been happening over the past month. She'd shed a few tears at the end of her one-sided conversation with her Gran then stood up, wiped the headstone with her hankie, and poured the remains of the hip flask on to the grave. We had said goodbye, and then made our way home. I think it's probably the only time I have ever seen Beck anything but the headstrong, rock hard, businesswoman that she usually portrayed. She is human after all.

Burning in the fires of hell has to be the choice then. At least then I can request that my ashes be liberally cast out upon the open sea. Although I live in London, my heart has always been with the sea. The sense of calm, the feeling of being free has been with me since the trips to Skegness as a child. Sand in the gusset of my cossie had not deterred me. The odd pebble lodged in my crack, not a problem. The sound and power of the sea has had me entranced to this day. So the decision has been made. There, that wasn't so hard was it? Or maybe I should go for the burial option? I climb out of the now lukewarm bath water and pull on my fluffy blue and white striped dressing gown. I pick up the cordless phone and go into the lounge.

I look up the number for Bancrofts and Son in the Yellow Pages. They're the local funeral directors. 'Discretion and Dignity' is their motto. Fetch me a bucket, please! Their shop is on the High Street, two doors down from Florrie's Florists. Only the kosher butchers and the 'Everything for a Pound' shop separates them. Florrie cuts them a special deal on bouquets and wreaths, ensuring that she has a regular flow of orders. She is such a sharp old bird. The front of the funeral parlour has a fake marble plaque with the company name and that fantastic motto inscribed on it. It has an eerie creak to it when it sways. And to round the image off, there are the obligatory white plastic lilies in the window with the traditional crushed purple velvet as the backdrop. Tasteful? Not even with your eyes shut.

Beck and I had been at secondary school with the 'and Son' part of the business. As I remember, Edward was a stunner. He was the boy in the class that every girl and several of the boys fantasised about. His father owned the local funeral parlour, as his father and his father had done before him. The kids used to taunt him because they had a mortuary in the back garden. He'd had a hard time of it but just used to laugh along with the wise cracks.

I dial the number. Good, it's ringing. "Good morning, Bancrofts and Sons, Edward Bancrofts speaking, how can I help you? Hello?" he enquires. "Hello? Okay, I'm putting the phone down right now," he says firmly, trying to sound authoritative.

"No wait! Hi there. My name's Jennifer Evans. We went to Ealing Secondary together? Well, not together as such but at the same time. I sat behind you in Chemistry next to Beck Monroe, remember?" I ask.

He pretends to remember me and says, "Oh yes, Jennifer how lovely to hear you again," he says. He asks how I am, and what I am doing now and "Are you still in touch with the girl you used to sit next to...Rebecca, wasn't it?" Typical, bloody typical.

I describe my predicament and explain the unusual circumstances. He shows the customary remorse. But that's all. I can hear the silent 'cha ching' sound in his head. I imagine him sitting at a desk rubbing his hands together with glee. Like father like son. Dad always said Harry Bancrofts, Edward's Dad, was a gold digger feeding off other people's misery and sadness.

"I am so sorry to hear that, Jennifer" he oozes false remorse. All of a sudden, he's my best buddy in the whole wide world. "What we'll need you to do is to pop down and see us right away," he says.

"Can't we do all this over the phone?" I ask. "You see, I have so much to do between now and then. I'm really strapped for time. I sure you can understand that."

"The thing is Jennifer," he starts to explain, "When a person dies, you have to get a doctor's certificate as soon as possible. You need one of those so that the death can be registered. Then the Registrar who registers the death will exchange the death certificate for a certificate for burial or cremation." He pauses and takes a deep breath then continues, "Only then, after the Registrar has handed the certificate to us the funeral directors, can we proceed with the burial or cremation. Unfortunately until we get the certificate our hands are tied, so to speak." As he finishes his explanation, I hear him exhale a sigh with relief. An uneasy silence follows. God, I didn't realise it was going to be such a palaver. Edward interrupts my thoughts. "Jennifer, are you still there?" he asks.

"Yes I'm here," I utter.

"Look I think it'll be so much easier for you if you come down and see us. Can you come today, this afternoon?" he asks. "Sorry to have to ask this but how long...how long have you been given?" he asks sombrely.

I tell him what Doctor Gibson had said. "But that's in a couple of days time," he exclaims. "This isn't a joke is it?" he demands. "You are joking, right?"

It takes me several minutes to persuade him that, "No this isn't a joke, but I really wish it was." His tone changes. He believes me. Is that true emotion I can hear in his voice? No, on second thoughts maybe not. He's probably sitting on the corner of a freshly completed casket, and has just trapped one of his testicles.

"Jennifer, if you're not joking and are completely serious, it has to be done now. If you want control over what happens to you when you die, then we have to get to work on the arrangements today. Do you understand? Jennifer, are you listening to me?" he asks.

"Well I..." I'm not sure what to say. I have plans for this afternoon. I have to keep to the schedule otherwise I'm not going to get everything done in time.

"Look if you want to do it properly, if you want to die with dignity..." he says patronisingly.

"Alright," I snap and cut him dead. I know I shouldn't be losing my temper with him but this is not going to plan at all. I'd thought a quick phone call, followed by a speedy electronic cash transaction and 'Bob's your Uncle', job done. I should have known that this dying shit wasn't going to be easy. "I'll be down this afternoon. What time do you close?" I ask.

"Six o'clock," he says. I can hear him whispering to someone in the background. "It's that fat bird that used to sit behind me in Chemistry," he whispers. "No, not the tasty dark-haired one. That was Rebecca something or other. No not that one, the other one, the blonde one. She's got a fucking brain tumour. Yeah seriously, straight up mate. She's dying and wants me to arrange her funeral."

"Well, seeing as I am such a fat bird" I interrupt sarcastically, "If I start walking now I should be with you before closing time. I mean, how far is it, about a mile?" That should shut the cheeky bastard up for a minute.

He starts to stammer an apology, "Oh no sorry, not you. I was talking about somebody else...really."

"Forget it," I spit. "I'll be round before six, if not first thing in the morning."

"Fine, no problem Jennifer. And please, let me just say on behalf of Bancrofts and Son, how sorry I am to hear of your misfortune. Don't you worry, you're in safe hands now," he says, attempting to do an impression of someone who cares.

I really can't face any more of that today. I force a "Thanks Edward," replace the receiver and let out a heavy sigh. I'm going to have to go down there and sort this out. And I'm going to have to do it today, if not first thing in the morning. It's not as if I don't have the time. I still have three days. I'll have to decide which way to go too, but not right now. If I think about it any more today, it will take more than the Diazepam to calm me down. I pour myself a large whisky and down two more Diazepams, just for the hell of it. I wrap my dressing gown around me and settle back into the sofa cushions.

I'm not a vindictive person. Well, that's not strictly true. I am. Well, maybe a bit anyway. During my life several people have really crapped on my family, or me, at one time or another. And now it's time to narrow down the list and put those chosen few through a brief yet intense period of living hell. A moment in time that they will never ever, be able to forget. I have decided to target the following fucking bastards. Okay, so I am bitter. But revenge is supposed to be sweet isn't it? Well bring it on. It's time to satisfy my sweet tooth.

About two weeks ago, three days before my little discovery, I had an unfortunate run in with a couple of beefy looking blokes in Greenford. What did they do the limey bastards? They only wheel-clamped my car. I'd pulled into the local pub car park at lunch time, under the pretence of having a drink, nipped to the bank and came back to find a bright yellow wheel clamp on my right front wheel. A well hidden, strategically placed sign warning of the possibilities of clamping was tucked behind a bush, at the far end of the car park.

A white transit with two identically dressed 'meat heads' propped up against it, was parked just to the left of the obscured sign. When challenged, the fatter of the two informed me, in his particularly sarcastic dulcet south London tones that, "It's gonna cost you £70 to remove that, luv. Didn't you see the signs?"

I'd been having real problems with my x-ray vision recently. I still can't quite see through solid objects, you arsehole.

He droned on. "Once it's on, we are not allowed to remove them without due payment. I...we see your predicament and suggest you pay in cash now and then request a refund in writing to our boss." With that he'd looked towards his skinny compatriot, pulled out his cigarettes and lit up a fag.

I turned and started to walk away. They were laughing at me. There is one thing that I cannot stand, and that is being laughed at. Nobody laughs at Jennifer Constance Evans and gets away with it. So totally pissed off, I returned to the bank and withdrew another £70. I paid them the cash and they promptly removed the clamp. They gave me their employee numbers, their main office address and then left the pub car park. So to cut a long story short, they didn't refund the money and I had about as much chance of getting a refund as pissing into the wind and not getting wet. I'd stormed into the pub, gave the barman some verbal abuse, gesticulated wildly for a few minutes, then left. I was so angry. They were lucky I hadn't been pre-menstrual, otherwise there would have been a blood bath. Complete bastards, the lot of them. I vowed never to drink in the pub again. I'd thought of things that I could do to get my own back on the clampers but had never followed through. Well, today it's pay back time.

I change quickly and leave the flat dressed in non-descript clothing, a black T-shirt, black jeans and a denim jacket. At a quick glance, I could be mistaken for a bloke. I drop in at the hardware shop and buy two dozen three-inch nails, one plastic petrol can and a Stanley knife. The clampers had been around at 12.30pm the previous week. I park in Tesco's car park, well away from the pub. It takes me five minutes to walk there. On entering the pub I order two pints of Guinness and a whisky chaser. I gulp back the two pints and wait. In the meantime, I sip the scotch and read the Greenford Observer. True to form, twenty minutes later I'm ready for a wee. I make my way to the ladies toilet with the petrol can in hand, swinging it casually by my side.

In the loo I check for squealers. The loos are empty. After some manoeuvring I manage to get most of the processed Guinness into the petrol can. Imagine the many times you've tried to get a urine sample into one of those stupid little plastic container's that the surgery gives you? Well in this instance, the size of the target area is bigger but the actual size of the container does prove to be a bit of a problem. Never try this one at home, kids. It entails acrobatic skills and great lip control. I wash my hands and practise my well hard face in the mirror.

With the deed done and in the can so to speak, I leave the pub at 12.25pm. Sure enough my old buddies, Fatty and Bastard are there propped up against their R reg'd transit van. You can see that they're twitching for a confrontation. Anybody, who has ever had to confront a wheel clamper, may have noticed that they always come in two's. And that one cannot function without the other. I think it's because they have to share that one brain cell. Suddenly, Fatty springs into action. He's seen an opportunity. Immediately Bastard is in hot pursuit. Now's my chance. I duck behind the van. I carefully place a small handful of three-inch nails behind each tyre.

By now the owner of the car, has returned. He starts arguing with them. I pour the re-processed Guinness into the petrol tank. Fatty starts pushing the businessman. Bastard looks on and starts to laugh. Oh, how they'll laugh on the other side of their faces when I've finished with them. With the Stanley knife I etch 'this is payback time' in the paintwork on the side of the van. I cross the street to a safe distance away and wait for the show to start. It's bound to kick off at any moment.

Businessman has started pushing Fatty back. Bastard's no longer laughing. He fumbles for his walkie-talkie, and frantically radio's for help. I'm laughing so much I drop my cigarette. My bladder twinges spasmodically to inform me that, yet again, I need the loo.

Bastard jumps into the van and backs it up for a quick getaway. All four tyres burst in unison, as he reverses over the strategically placed nails. The engine splutters and grinds to a halt. No amount of key turning is going to start that baby! They had taken the piss last week. Now I'm just returning the favour. Oh revenge is indeed, so sweet. I jog back to the car, chuckling away to myself. That was so much fun!

At home I change back into my dressing gown. The answer phone light is blinking. I press play as I pass by. BEEP..."Jennifer, it's Mum...call me luv when you get in. I hate these machines"...BEEP. I'll give her a call tomorrow.

BEEP... "Jen it's Silla. Call me if you need to. If not, I'm going to call round tomorrow afternoon if that's convenient with you"...BEEP.

The rest of the day I have planned to be one of pure telephonic pleasure. I have decided to torment my ex-accountant for screwing me on my VAT returns during my first year of business. I also have a few more people to torment should I have any time left on my hands after this little episode of fun. Today is the day to make the miserable bastards of this world pay.

I pour myself the last dregs from the bottom of the Jamesons bottle. I place it in the recycling bin along with the other five empty bottles. I feel slightly disturbed that I have consumed six bottles of Jamesons in a seven-day period. The bins are emptied once a week on a Thursday. But I do have good reason to drink, don't I. It's easier this way. I get another bottle from the cupboard, take it into the lounge with me and sit down on the sofa ready to review my list of calls to make. The shaky hand syndrome is getting worse.

I call Beck's flat again, and leave another message. It's weird. I thought she'd be over the moon at the news of our infamy. Thinking about it, I haven't spoken to her since the morning after the night at the Ritz. She's probably busy. What with work, regular retail therapy sessions and her already busy social life. It does seem strange though. We usually talk at least once a day, whether it was for a couple of minutes or an hour. I'll try her again later.

I turn the television on and watch the mid-afternoon news. We seem to have created quite a storm. The reward for the capture leading to conviction of the 'Ealing Two' now stands at £5,000. The police are still no closer to making an arrest. That's reassuring.

Bloody hell! It's Mrs Gladstone. She's on the London News. The reporter introduces her. "Mrs Gladstone was leaving the bank as one of the robbers was entering. Mrs Gladstone, was there anything in particular that stood out about this person? Would you recognise this person again?" he asks.

Mrs G is looking directly into the camera. She looks as though she is thoroughly enjoying her five minutes of fame. And is that a trace of make up I detect? Oh bless her. "Well, Matthew." Matthew Greening, anchorman for London News. "It was definitely a woman I think. She had brown eyes and spoke in an unusual accent, sort of Australian. I would definitely recognise those cruel brown eyes again." The cheeky cow. Anyway, my eyes are blue. What is she on about? With that and what looks like a twitch of the eye, the camera pans back to Matthew Greening who draws the interview to an end. Mrs G is so far out on her description of me. I wonder if she's got the onset of senile dementia or something. Well, what a turn up for the books seeing her on the TV like that, with the lovely Matthew Greening. I turn the volume down on the telly so that I can concentrate on the task at hand.

After some thought, I have come up with a couple of targets to aim my poisonous darts of vengeance. There's the obvious one, my ex-accountant. As a fresh faced first time businesswoman, Randall, Least and Partners a local accountancy firm had ripped me off big time. The perpetrator of the crime was Edward Least, one of the partners. At our first meeting, the lecherous beast had made a fumbled attempt to seduce me. Why is it that on the rare occasion when I do attract a man, he invariably turns out to be a suppressed homosexual, ugly or married? It must be just another one of my many hidden talents.

Anyway, after I'd rebuffed his advances he came over all professional and businesslike. A year later at the end of my first tax year, it came to my attention that the vindictive snake had not only doctored my books but had also charged me a monthly sum just for the pleasure of being a client of Randall and Least. What was a girl to do? When I confronted him, he informed me that he knew a lot of people and that I should take that as a warning, pay up and then piss off. Charming. I didn't have a leg to stand on. And being a good girl, I did as I was told. He had scared the shit out of me with his not so veiled threats.

Well, now it's pay back time. Edward Least lives in a large four-bedroom detached house in Bushey, with his wife Margot and their two dogs. He's obviously been very successful with the firm. They'd never had children.

Rumour had it that this was due to his low sperm count. So there is a God after all! Mum had been at school with Margot and said that she was a bit of a sappy mare, but had only married Edward Least for the money. She'd never really loved him. On one occasion, she'd said to Mum that the only thing she really loved about Edward, was his bank balance. She certainly sounded like a woman after my own heart. I have to make sure she doesn't get tangled up in my web of revenge. So first off I'm going to call the farm next to the dual carriageway, just off the A40 near Denham. I'd passed it many times on the way to the Italian restaurant in Denham Village. It was one of Beck's favourite eateries. When she got paid, on the 15th of the month, we'd often mark the occasion and treat ourselves with a nice meal at Gianni's.

"Afternoon, Sunnyvale Farm. How can I help you?" booms the farmer's voice. I quickly move the handset a few inches away from my ear. Don't really fancy a perforated eardrum on top of everything else.

"Hello there. Do you sell manure?" I ask.

"We certainly do. What sort are you looking for?" he asks. "We have a variety you see, here at Sunnyvale. We got cow, horse or pig. All completely organic, you know. None of your so-called chemicals pass through my animals. They produce the finest fertiliser in Hertfordshire. You know we supply Cilla Black with horse manure, for her roses. She has a trailer full delivered twice a year." He says, his voice brimming with pride.

"Oh how excellent," I chirp. That's possibly more information than I need right now but... "Yes, I need some for...my roses too. What do you recommend and how much do you think I'll need? I tell you what, what's good enough for Cilla, is good enough for me. Yes, it is quite a large garden. Yes, OK, let's say a trailer full then, shall we," I say.

"Where do you want it delivered then? Let me take your name and address my dearie," inquires the farmer. I give him Margot Least's name and address in Bushey, and say I will drop off a cheque first thing in the morning.

"Now I probably won't be home this afternoon," I explain. Margot plays Whist with Mum at the W.I. every Tuesday afternoon. "So just pop it inside the gates on the drive will you? Our gardener will distribute it from there. No don't worry about making a mess. It's quite runny is it? No that's fine. The runnier the better." I really don't want Margot to be home and have to face the 'shit' that is meant for that little shit of a husband of hers.

The farmer reads the address back to me and with a "Thank you Mrs Least," he rings off. The next thing to organise for the desirable Mr Least is also just a phone call away. I pause for a moment and pour myself another drink, and dial the number. Good it's ringing. This is going to be so much fun!

"Master Bates Fun House, Naomi Lovelace speaking. How can I help you?" The shrill high-pitched voice paints a mental picture in my head of its owner. I imagine a particularly well endowed young lady, probably with several bits of herself pierced, in a snug fitting T-shirt with, 'Get yer coat, you've pulled', emblazoned on the front of it. I see her probably sitting on the corner of a tatty desk filing her nails, in some smoky, windowless back room of one of the porno shops in Soho. So I have a vivid imagination!

Master Bates is a catalogue service for the confused man of the nineties. I hadn't realised at the time but Sam must have been a subscriber for years. It caters for the homosexual, transsexual, transvestite, adventurous hetro and the downright disgusting pervert. They sold everything from blow up sheep to Indian love beads. So that's where he'd got them. And the nipple clamps, which I'd refused to wear. I'd just like to state that for the record. For some reason Sam loved them. I have to say they looked better on him anyway. And as for the Indian love beads...!

When Dan, my best male friend at college told me what Indian love beads actually were and where they went, I'd felt my anal orifice spasm and clamp up immediately. At the time it had taken some serious self-control and several pints of Guinness to get the muscles to relax again. Even now at the thought of it, I feel a slight twinge in my 'back bottom' region!

"Oh hi. Yes, I'd like to order some stuff from you?" I purr in my best posh Essex girl accent, if there is such a thing as a posh one.

"Sorry Madam, we don't do snuff movies. We're a completely legit business here. My boss Mr Theodopolous said so." She lowers her voice and whispers, "But I do know someone who could possibly help you out. What sort are you looking for?" she furtively inquires.

"Bloody hell, I don't want a snuff movie! I said STUFF not SNUFF." I lose the accent momentarily.

"Oh right. For a minute there I thought you said snuff," she giggles at the other end of the phone. "An easy mistake to make. Well if you do need any snuff, give us a call back, luv. Ask for me Naomi Lovelace and I can sort you out, no problem. So back to business, what sort of STUFF are you looking for Madam?"

I hastily place my order for one blow up man, eight inches of Indian love beads (cue the twinge), six copies of Man on Man from the back catalogue and a complete maid's outfit, size XL.

"Lovely. And how would you like to pay for that, Madam?" she asks. "Card...Switch is fine. And where would you like the items to be sent to and addressed to whom?" Is it really Naomi Lovelace at the other end of the phone, or Eliza Doolittle? She is trying so hard to put on a more classy accent. I reach down to pick up my glass. It's empty. Tucking the phone under my chin, I pour myself another and wade into the Custard Creams.

"I'd like you to send them to Mr Edward Least of Randall, Least and Partners" I babble, spraying Custard Cream crumbs everywhere. I give her the company's office address. His secretary vets all of his mail daily and will have a field day when this little beauty arrives in the post and has to be signed for. It won't be long before the list of contents within the package is circulated around the local golf club and Institute of Chartered Accountants. I want to ruin the bastard. I want him to suffer like I had suffered two years ago. This will certainly do it.

I ring off and immediately collapse into a heap, laughing. Serves the lecherous, old git right. Master Bates runs a next day delivery service and Naomi had assured me that he would get his pressie's tomorrow. I drain my glass, and pour myself yet another. I get up to close the curtains and turn the volume back up on the telly.

I am satisfied. I have wanted to do this for so long now but just haven't had the nerve. Also, if either or both parties ever find out it's me behind their little mishaps, I will certainly be in for an uncomfortable time of it. But who gives a stuff, or even a snuff! Again the giggles turn into hysterics. I must be pissed. I'm laughing at my own jokes.

I had planned to make one more call today. I was going to call Sam's sister, Rose, pretending to be her partner Joey's new bit on the side. But you know, no matter how much I hate the bitch, it is hard enough in life to find someone to share the ups and downs with. Even she deserves to be loved unconditionally. And the one thing that I have regretted over the past week has been not having a partner to help me carry this weighty burden. To see any combination of human gender together and in love has to be something to be admired. I have no one. I can't bring myself to call her. That would be just too cruel.

I think about calling Silla, but it's late and anyway, she's bound to call me over the next day or so. I think she said she would. I can't quite remember. I sit back and fall asleep on the sofa surrounded by biscuit crumbs, with the

TV still on in the background. I sleep soundly. The half bottle of Jamesons and the medication probably has something to do with it.

Tuesday 18th August...Sex and the service

Hmm, today is the day I have been looking forward to the most. That is, if you can possibly look forward to wishing one of the last remaining days of your life away. I wake up on the sofa, cold and with a crick in my neck. I've got biscuit crumbs in my cleavage. Yesterday had been a good day in a funny sort of way. Revenge really is sweet and entirely satisfying to the vengeful palate. I allow myself a little smile. The look on the wheel clampers faces, I will happily take to my grave. And as for the Lecherous Least, I have no sympathy for him whatsoever. May he suffer at the hands of his peers, friends and especially Margot's lawyers. Mum said she'd been looking for a good enough excuse to divorce him, for years. When they've finished with him, he'll be ruined.

Having led a fairly sheltered life for twenty-nine years, I've decided that today I am going to unleash the wanton whore, find myself a willing participant and go 'at it' hell for leather! I'm going to pick my most intimate fantasies and live them. Compared to Beck I have led a fairly conservative life style. You could say I have all of the qualities needed to be a potential convent convert. Well, I did have up until seven days ago anyway.

However, before I do anything else today, I have to finalise the arrangements for the funeral. I look at the clock on the mantelpiece. It's nine thirty. The sun seems so much brighter than I can remember it ever being. I've got to get my skates on. I down my pills, grab my shades and dash out of the flat. By ten o'clock, I'm standing outside Bancrofts and Son. I feel surprisingly calm, thanks again to my recently acquired synthetic friends. They've been a godsend this week. I don't know how I'd have coped without them. I'm sure the pain would be unbearable had it not been for my daily dose. And each time I've felt the despair and self-pity spiralling out of control, a couple or three extra Diazepam and twenty minutes later, I feel calm and back in control. It's just the fuzzy lack of memory that is beginning to bug me.

The sun is lovely and warm on my back. It feels much better today. Not sore at all. The smell from the flowers on display outside Florrie's Florists, is intoxicating. Just then Florrie steps out of the doorway, gives me a big hearty wave and calls out "Morning Jennifer love. What a day, what a beautiful day!" She raises her arms skywards, smiling from ear to ear.

"Hi Florrie, yes it's a beauty, isn't it," I shout back. I bend down and pretend to re-tie my non-existent shoelace. I'm wearing slip-ons. I just don't want her to see me going into Bancrofts. I furtively look up through my fringe, and see her disappearing back into the shop. Now's my chance.

Two big steps and I'm through the front door of Bancrofts and Son, Funeral Directors. A large clanging bell attached to the door announces my arrival.

As if by magic, a man appears from behind a large black curtain, sombrely dressed in a black three-piece suit. It's Edward Bancrofts. With his hands clasped in front of him, he says "Good morning Madam, can I be of any assistance to you?"

I recognise him and just say "Hello Edward."

For a moment he has a look of confusion on his face, as if to say, do I know you?

Then he remembers me. "Oh my goodness, its Jennifer, isn't it?"

I force a smile and will him to call me fatty again, this time to my face. Swine! But he doesn't. He is at a loss for words. He even looks sorry for me. "Let's cut to the chase shall we, Edward" I say all businesslike. "I don't have all day."

With a cough he says, "Of course. Please come this way, will you?" He turns and pulls back the black curtain to reveal a small yet functional office. "Please take a seat, I'll be with you in a moment. Can I get you a tea or a coffee perhaps?" he asks.

"Tea will be fine." I sit down and turn to say thank you but he's disappeared again. I nervously tap my fingers on the edge of the desk in time to the softly piped music that fills the air. On the desk in front of me, there are several neatly arranged piles of paper. I do a quick check behind me to make sure that I'm still alone, then lean forward to have a sneaky nose. Oh that's interesting, 'WHAT TO DO… When you lose a loved one. A Helpful Guide To Duties When Arranging A Funeral…With The Compliments Of Bancrofts And Son, Your Family Owned Local Funeral Directors'. Mmm…nice. Next to the pile of, the essential guide to snuffing it booklets, there's a pad. I crane my head around to try and get a better look. I've never been any good at reading upside down. On closer inspection, it looks like a form of some sort, a bit like a questionnaire. I'm contemplating whether to get up and have a proper look when Edward appears again. I wish he'd stop skulking around like that. He'll give me a heart attack.

"Here you go, one tea," he says quietly, handing it to me, then going round to the other side of the desk and sitting down.

I take it from him and say, "Thanks." He leans forward and picks up a pen. Turning to a clean page on the pad he clears his throat and starts.

"So Jennifer…First let me say how sorry I am to hear your devastating news. It must have been quite a shock for you," he waffles on for several minutes until I can take no more.

"STOP!" I snap at him, holding my hand up in front of me. "Look, I know you mean well, but let's just get this over and done with shall we? Just tell me how much this is going to cost me and what I need to do, okay?" I say, struggling to control my rising temper.

"Sorry," he says blushing. There's that annoying cough again. He continues, "Have you decided whether you want to be buried or cremated?"

"Well, I'm thinking perhaps…" I start to say but am rudely interrupted.

"The thing is Jennifer, in this area, it being an urban area, burial space is not so easily available as it was some twenty years ago. Nowadays, roughly sixty percent of deaths are followed by cremation. I think that at this point it's probably a good time for me to mention that burial is more costly than cremation, too."

I leave him hanging for several seconds, before looking up and demanding sarcastically, "Have you finished?"

He's taken aback and gobsmacked by my sudden outburst. "Edward," I continue, attempting to harness the violent tendencies that are surging his way. "Why don't I tell you what I want, then you can tell me what's possible and what's not."

"Okay" he says, shrinking back into his chair and fiddling with his pen. He'd used to do that in Chemistry whenever Miss Longstaff told him off.

"Now to start with, I want to be buried, and if possible at St John's just off the Uxbridge Road." It has a lovely graveyard. It's where Beck's Grandma is buried too. "I want a standard coffin, with a purple material interior (my favourite colour). I want to be buried in the clothes that I die in, and with the items that will be surrounding me. I can give you a list, if you like?" I offer.

"Yes please," he mumbles sulkily.

"No problem, I'll do you one when we've finished," I assure him then continue, "I want one of those horse drawn hearses." He's looking at me as if I'm a woman possessed and just nods his head. "And a white limo, for my family to travel to and from the church." Again he nods his head.

I quickly run through the checklist in my head, ticking off the points that I've already covered. Ha yes...the headstone for the grave. "I'd like a marble headstone, with the usual name, dates, in loving memory etc. etc. Then I want engraved at the bottom, 'Now able to dream forever'. What do you think?" I ask him.

He's shocked by the sudden question. I think he switched to auto just after the hearse part of the conversation. That was about the time I noticed his eyes glazed over anyway. "That's... uh...very poignant?" he splutters hopefully.

"Now the service, can you arrange that too?" I enquire. Again he manages a nod of the head. "Right, I want something a little different. I don't want one of those services where everybody ends up wailing and sobbing. I want a light hearted affair with plenty of good tunes and a couple of jokes thrown in for good measure." I smile and take a moment to imagine the scenario.

"What do you have in mind?" he asks nervously, then leans forward ready to write down the details.

"I was thinking perhaps...I know this is a little unorthodox but I want 'We are the champions' by Queen played as I'm being carried into the church. Then after a few words from the Reverend, I don't want any hymns or anything like that. I'd like 'Seasons in the Sun' by Terry Jacks." I look up just in time to see Edward raise an eyebrow. "Something wrong, Edward?" I demand. "Do you have a problem with Terry Jacks?"

"No...no...no not at all. An excellent choice...really" he gushes so insincerely. No matter. Whose funeral is it, anyway?

I continue ignoring his putrid tones. "Then I want Rebecca Monroe, you know the dark-haired one, not the fat one?" I ask. He squirms under my gaze and starts fiddling with his pen yet again. "I want Beck to read out the eulogy and this poem." I take out a scrap of paper from my pocket and hand it over. He opens it out and reads it.

"Wow," he gasps. "Who's the poet?"

Hey hang on a minute, is that a compliment? "I wrote it actually," I say nonchalantly and shrug my shoulders. He seems impressed. His face takes on a whole new expression and he looks as though he's genuinely sorry that

I'm dying. He holds the piece of paper out in front of him and begins to recite its contents out loud.

Although I am gone,
I am still all around
And when you need me,
Here's where I'll be found

Look deep into your heart,
Go in search of me in your dreams
Close your eyes and call my name,
And I'll be there to mend the seams…

Of your heart, if it's been broken
And your pain is too much to bear
I'll stitch you back together
Because you know I'll always care

Whenever you feel lonely
Close your eyes and drift away
You'll find me there inside your heart
Every minute of every day

My body may be dead and gone
But my spirit will go on forever
For I will live on inside of you
We will always be together

His voice falters during the last line. "I'm sorry," he whispers. He looks up at me through glistening eyes. "This is for real, isn't it?" I nod my head. "Jesus, I am so sorry Jennifer" he says, his voice full of remorse.

I can only manage a "So am I, so am I," before a lump blocks my throat. Damn my tears. I draw on my last remaining fragment of composure and continue, "I'd like one hymn actually. I'd like Morning has broken, to be played as I'm being carried out of the church. I just want people to smile when they remember me. I want the grieving to stop by the end of the service. Grief hurts so much, doesn't it?" Memories of Grandpa fog my thoughts.

Then images of Mum and Lizzie both inconsolable and Dad standing there with his head held high, flash in front of my eyes. This is too much. Edward reaches into a drawer and after taking one for himself, he hands me the box of Kleenex. He blows his nose rather loudly.

"I think that about covers it all, don't you Edward?" I sigh. "I just want to settle up the bill and go home now, if that's all right with you."

"Of course. I'm sure we can accommodate all of your requests and I will personally make sure that your choice of music is adhered to," he says softly. He looks at me straight in the eyes and says determinedly, "I promise you."

"Thanks Edward. And I'm sorry for being so snappy earlier. I'm just finding it hard to cope at the moment," I say having to swallow a sob mid-sentence.

"No, I'm sorry," he adds. "I'm sorry I said you were fat too. I'm still such an insensitive bastard at times." He smiles apologetically. "You know, I think you've lost some since I last saw you."

"Yeah you are!" I say laughing. So finally I lose some weight and somebody notices. "So, let's get down to the nitty gritty, shall we. How much is all this going to cost me, Edward?"

He pulls a calculator out of the bottom draw of the desk and starts punching away at the keys. "That'll be…" concentration takes over his face…"£3,500, that's including VAT" he says finally.

"Right. Do you take Credit Cards as payment…Visa?" I query.

He nods his head. "That's fine Jennifer. We take Visa or Switch." I hand over my Visa card. That's it, no more credit left on any of them now. With a polite, "Excuse me for a moment," he stands up and leaves the room. A couple of minutes later he's back. He places the chit down on the desk in front of me and says "If you can just sign there for me, please." He points to where I have to sign.

I scrawl my signature and pass the pen back to him. "Thanks." I stand up and prepare to make a hasty retreat. Silly sod obviously hasn't cultivated any more brains cells since school. Oh, for credit cards. As if I'm going to have to worry about paying that one off now.

I've been spending money like it's going out of fashion. Following the slight hiccup after the bank job, I've virtually spent all of my savings and have now just used up the last credit on my credit card. I had thought about asking Beck for some of her share of the stash back, but she was probably having far too much fun, living it up on Bond Street. I'm still feeling particularly pissed off with my little mishap five days ago. Still, let's hope the sorters for the charity are more honest than I have been and when they find it, they will use the money wisely. Who am I trying to kid?

"Well, thanks again for your help, Edward," I say hurriedly. "I want to go home now."

"Of course," he says. We go back through into the front section of the shop and Edward opens the front door for me. I shake his hand, and smile up at him. He looks genuinely upset. "Don't be sad," I say earnestly. "You of all people should know that it comes to us all sooner or later." With a wink I say "See you in the next life, Edward!" and turn to start the walk home. I'm overwhelmed with a sense of relief.

Dream Date

By the time I get back to the flat it's gone midday. It's taken me over an hour to walk the mile or so home. I have to be honest I did dawdle. I walked back the long way through the park. It's such a beautiful day. There's not a cloud in the sky. The park had been pretty full with families picnicking and lovers canoodling. It's the perfect day for lovers. It's the perfect day for lust! Oh bugger, I forgot to leave the list with Edward. I'll have to go back, but not today. I notice a card tucked into the letterbox. Damn it, I've missed Silla. I'll give her a call later.

So today, seeing as I don't really have the time to create a meaningful relationship or nurture the non-existent one I have, I'm going to fuck with complete gay abandon. I am going to do everything I have ever wanted to do. And I mean that in the very heterosexual sense of the word. Let me just say that this is so out of character for me. No really, I'm doing things that I would never have dared to do before. I just don't see why I shouldn't anymore.

Anyway, I have decided after much thought, about ten minutes actually, to go for the safe option and book myself a male escort for the evening. Yes, I know I could quite easily go into any bar in the West End and pull a bloke. But I don't want to go out and pull a bloke who is absolutely drop-dead gorgeous when I've got my beer goggles on. Then end up taking him home with me, only to wake up in the morning with a lousy hangover and realise that I've been having sex with Quasimodo's twin all night. I want to be sober. I want to enjoy and savour every minute of it. So, the date has to be perfect. I want perfection. He has to be over six-foot tall, blond, with blue eyes, a good physique and a wicked smile. I prefer a tanned body, firm pecks, at least four out of the six pack defined...oh, and no facial hair. It gives me a rash. Oh, and not a stubby or a pencil dick. A happy medium will do very nicely thank you.

I flick through the Yellow Pages to E...Equestrian...Ergonomics...here we go, Escort Agencies (see Dating Agencies). Got it. Surprisingly enough, it's a very short list. The choices are AA Escorts, His and Hers Escorts, Oriental Girls, or The Perfect Dream Escort Agency. Well, we can rule out Oriental Girls and AA Escorts for starters. For one, Oriental Girls suggests to me that...it's all girls! And as for AA Escorts, any company that calls itself AA something or other, to ensure that they're at the top of the alphabetical listings, has to be crap. Through a process of elimination I decide to try The Dream Date Agency. I pour a drink and then dial out the number. Good, it's ringing.

"Good morning, Perfect Dream, Maureen speaking?" says a whining female voice at the other end of the line.

"Oh right yes, um...hello there. Do you do men?" I stutter. I successfully lose control of my tongue. I've never done anything like this before. So much for the brazen wanton whore!

There's a deadly silence... "Hello, is there anybody there?" I ask. Suddenly there's an ear-piercing whistle. "What the bloody hell was that for?" I scream. "Jesus, I only want to book an escort!" I shout down the phone defensively.

"Oh God, I'm so sorry, Madam," she gasps. "But we've been having a few perverted phone calls recently and I thought you might be one of them" she tries to explain.

I cut her short. "Listen, forget it. Can you help me or not? I'm looking for a good fu...friend, companion, a male escort. Do you have any available for this evening?" I ask.

Back in control and in her best business-like voice, she says "Yes we do. We have several gentlemen available this evening. Do you have any particular requirements?" she asks.

"Do you mean what am I looking for?" I ask. "Right. Well I'd like a nice tall chap, please. Oh the eyes, and physique? Well I'd like blue eyes, a good physique, and someone who's fun to be with." With extra anchovies please! God, it's like ordering a Pizza. "Sorry, I know it's short notice," I add apologetically.

"Not a problem at all, Madam," she gushes. "We have two gentlemen on our books that pretty much fit your criteria down to a tee. And both are available this evening. Can I tell you a little something about each of them?" she asks. "It might make it easier for you to make your decision."

Still with an annoying ringing sound in my ear I tell her to, "Please go ahead."

She takes a deep breath and starts. "First we have Adam. Adam is a thirty-year-old professional man. He is six foot two inches tall. He has blue eyes, mousey blonde hair and is terrific fun to be with. He loves music and playing sports and is our most popular escort at the moment," she adds with a theatrical flourish.

"If he's... If Adam is so popular, then why is he available tonight at such short notice?" I quiz Maureen, imagining I'm shining a Gestapo style flashlight in her face, trying to make her crack and tell the truth.

"His regular Tuesday evening has just called and cancelled. Between you and me, I think her husband's on to her," she gossips.

"And what about the other one?" I ask, choosing to ignore her gossip mongering.

"The other gentleman available this evening is called Scott. Scott has blue eyes and dark shoulder length hair. He too is very fit, attractive and a pleasure to be with."

She can scrub the Scott for starters. I wouldn't be seen dead with a Scott. So I'm a snob. It's going to be my perfect date so it has to be perfect in every way. "I'll take the Adam please. What does the date entail then?" I ask.

"How do you mean?" she asks.

Go on Evans spit it out. "I mean, what do I get for my money?"

She says "Oh right, I understand. Well, you can meet Adam at the restaurant or bar of your choice or he can escort you from your own home. He will take you wherever you wish to go, and will escort you home at the end of the evening, should you wish."

I think for a moment. I'll have to meet him at a bar. If he comes to the flat, Mrs G will have a field day. She doesn't miss a trick. So I tell her, "I'll meet him at The Chocolate Bar in Berkeley Square, at 9pm. And how will I recognise him?" I ask.

"He should be recognisable to you immediately, but to be on the safe side, we'll get Adam to carry a copy of The Evening Standard tucked under his left arm" she says.

"Right," I say.

"No left," she insists. "He'll have the paper under the LEFT arm, not the right" she stresses.

"Yes okay, I've got it, under the left arm." Oh please!

Well, I have to ask don't I? "Does he...does he do...would he...?" How do you say, will he take me to heaven and back? Will he ignite my fire with his flame-thrower?

Successfully reading between the lines she interrupts my descent into Hornyville. "Anything else Madam is between the client and the escort. We simply provide a legal escort service," she says firmly. She has that part of the script off to a tee.

"Good. Now how much is he... is Adam going to cost me for the evening?" I ask. I will have to get used to saying that name for tonight. It's all beginning to feel so secretive and deliciously naughty.

"Hold on a second, I just need to pull his rate card." I can hear her rustling through her papers. "There it is, got it. Right, for the first hour it's £150. And then for every hour after that it's £100. You will need to pay the initial £150 now to guarantee your booking. Then settle up with Adam at the end of the evening." Bloody hell this is going to be one expensive shag fest. Still, you only live once.

"That's fine. Do you take Switch?" I ask. We get the formalities out of the way. I pay up and ring off.

Beck had suggested that we go clubbing in the West End, then find a complete den of iniquity, and wake up in the morning in a strange unfamiliar place with a testosterone junkie. I can always rely on Beck. She is a complete party animal! Bless her. But I think it's a much safer option booking an escort rather than taking pot luck. We could still club it, but I want to make sure I have my man primed and ready for action at the end of the evening, yet still feel safe. It's really strange that she hasn't returned my calls. What's up with the miserable bitch? It's as if I've snuffed it already. I really need her tonight to help me out on this one. I need my friend around, just in case it all goes pear shaped.

As the days had passed and the ticks had one by one been crossed off on the wish list, Beck hadn't returned any of my calls or left a message on my machine. Although we were completely different and had morals at either end of the morality spectrum, we were made to be together. So why hadn't she called? I wonder if she'll agree to read out my eulogy? I'll have to ask her tonight.

I haven't really thought about how people are going to react at the funeral? I haven't up until now. I mean, it's not something that springs to mind when you're hanging over the fish finger freezer in Tesco on a Thursday's Singles night. The only funeral I've ever been to had been my Grandpas.

There had been a certain amount of wailing from various members of the congregation, plenty of nose blowing, and the odd chuckle at the content of the eulogy. I reacted in my own way. I thought about Grandpa, not even listening to the speeches or the service, just remembering him. His lovely smiling face, his funny moustache that I used to play with, and his unconditional love for me. I'd just sat there in silence with tears rolling down my cheeks.

Afterwards, relatives that hadn't seen me for years asked completely ludicrous questions like, "So how's school then?" and made comments like "My, haven't you grown." If only I'd had the license to tell them all to FUCK OFF and DIE. But it's just not the done thing to do when you're a kid, is it? Nobody was really interested in Grandpa. Most of them were only there for the after service drinks and the opportunity to look around his house, for something they could take... as a momento, of course. Thieving bastards. But as a child, what can you do?

I call Beck's again and leave yet another message. "Only me again. Come on you old tart, call me when you get in, please. I need your help today. Remember...on the list? It's the perfect date day. Look, just call me please." I whine.

It's getting on for six o'clock by the time I've ordered my date, and found something half-decent and clean enough to wear. She'll be home soon. I'll try her again in a couple of minutes. Christ, I've only got two hours to get ready. I flick through my CD's and put on Macy Gray's album. It's the perfect choice when getting ready for a night out on the tiles. I dance around the lounge doing a striptease to my imaginary date that is sitting on the sofa, pausing only to pull the curtains and to have a slurp of Jameson. Come on Beck phone me.

I pick up recently discarded clothes, and dump them on the floor next to the washing basket. I'm down to five pairs of knickers and four bras in my underwear drawer. I rummage around for a Bic, switch the shower on and dive in. Bugger! The phone's ringing. Whoever it is, I'll have to call them back. The answer phone clicks into life. Singing at the top of my voice, I shave all of my hairy bits including for the first time, my fanny. I manage to shave it into a sort of wonky heart shape. I've never shaved it before. Somebody said to me years ago, I can't for the life of me remember who it was said that if you shave your pubes they grow back twice as long, twice as wiry and completely out of control. And that you'll end up with a forest of pubic hair up to your belly button. Again, it's something I've always wanted to do but hadn't dared to. But now, why not? They won't have time to grow back now.

I dry off and apply various moisturisers, perfume and deodorant. The message light blinks at me from the top of the machine. I press play back...BEEP...It's me, Beck. "Hi Jen. Sorry I've not been in touch but...well...look I'm coming over, OK? You're probably in the shower or something. I'm sorry I've not got back to you but...anyway see you soon...bye"...BEEP.

That's strange. She sounds as though she's picked up a cold or something. That would explain why she's not returned my calls. I knew that there'd be a logical explanation. With another large whisky I return to the bedroom to finish getting ready. I apply the special cream to my free spirit that I have to say, looks fantastic. I have decided that tonight I am going to show it off to the world. I need to let the air get to it too. I pull on a black sleeveless T-shirt and a pair of black slacks. I suppose I should be semi smart.

There's the doorbell. It's probably Beck. She is going to get the full force of my wrath for not calling sooner, the tart. I press the buzzer to release the front door to let her in. A couple of seconds later, there's a knock on the inner door. I pull myself up to full height and with drink in hand open the door. "You cow, where have you been?" I demand. "I've been calling and calling...Beck?" I stop mid-sentence. She is standing there, just staring at the floor. "What's up? Have you been crying? Come in. Come on move your arse. Go and sit down and I'll get you a drink," I tell her. She still hasn't said a word and has avoided looking up. She shuffles past me mumbling and thrusts a bottle of wine into my hand. Great, she's going to be a bundle of fun tonight!

I pour her a glass of the wine and take it through into the lounge to her. She's crying. My anger dissolves into nothingness on hearing her sobs. I sit down next to her on the sofa and put my arm around her. "What's up mate?" I ask gently. A wave of déjà vu washes over me. This is like a re-run of that night. The night when I'd told her, except that now it's her who is doing all the crying. She finally, with some coaxing, looks up. Her nose is red raw and her eyes puffy and swollen. She looks as if she's been crying for days.

Between sobs she tries to speak. "Oh Jen, I don't want you to die" she pleads. "I need you around. I don't want to grow old on my own. You always promised me that we'd grow old together and ungraciously. Please don't leave me." She's crying uncontrollably. What can I do? What can I say to make it all better? There is nothing to say.

"Beck, don't cry," I whisper. "Sshh...even if I'm not physically here, you know I'll always be around you. I'll always be here to look after you." I rock her slowly until she stops crying.

"I can't believe it, Jen. Why is life so unfair? Why you?" She looks at me through her tears. "I feel so helpless."

"I don't know, Beck" I sigh. "I've asked myself a million times over, and nothing. I can't think of any reason why it should be me, but it is me." I just feel numb now and so sorry for my best friend. The strong one of us now vulnerable and the weaker one of us now forced to be strong. "I don't know what else I can say to you. I am resigned to the fact now. And the past seven days on the whole have been the most exciting few days of my life, thanks to you." I smile at her and tell her that, "Without you mate, I'd have given up days ago."

She turns and hugs me tightly, just like Lizzie had done all those years ago at the summer camp. I dread to think how Lizzie is going to react. But she's got Mum and Dad. Beck hasn't got anybody, except me.

"Come on," I say to her. "We still have a couple of days. Let's enjoy them together, eh? Now go and freshen up. I'll run you a bath shall I?" I offer.

"Please." She sniffs. I stand up and help her to her feet. She's unsteady on her legs to say the least. I run the bath and put some Radox Stress Buster bubbles in the water. I look out of the lounge window. The world seems smaller somehow. It feels as though it's all closing in on me, and there's nothing I can do about it. My heart aches so much. The invisible fist is squeezing the life out of me.

A noise behind me brings me back to reality. Beck has bathed and changed. As usual, she looks a million bucks. I love her like I love Lizzie. I have been so lucky having found a friend like her. "You look fab, girlie." I tell her. "Versace?" I ask smiling up at her.

She nods her head and tries to force a smile back, but it's hardly a smile. "Yeah, but my eyes are all puffy. I look a mess." She's still sniffling. The bath has done her some good, but boy she's going to have a bad time of it when I do eventually go.

"Come on," I say trying to sound chirpy. But trust me, it's just an act for my friend. "I'm so excited about tonight. Look, I phoned this agency and have booked myself a dream date. I knew you'd be able to pull whoever you want, so I just sorted myself out. You don't mind do you?"

"Really, that's fine Jen. I don't feel particularly on form tonight, but I will come along and keep an eye on you." She gives me a wink. She's trying so hard to act normally.

We order a cab into London and get to The Chocolate Bar at 9.00pm. It is the sort of place that to get in there, you have to be someone famous. I wouldn't have stood a chance had I not been with Beck. All the doormen at the top London clubs and bars know her through the many glittery showbiz parties that she's organised for Oh Yeah. On the way in she stops and speaks to the doorman to makes sure that he'll let Adam, the escort, in when he arrives. Good. Just enough time for a couple of shots of Dutch Courage.

Inside, the music is loud and the bar is starting to get busy. We buy ourselves a drink and sit down at one of the tables nearest to the doors. For the next fifteen minutes we scrutinise every bloke that comes in. Then I see him. I dig Beck in the side and hiss excitedly, "It's him!"

Beck looks over and checks him out from top to bottom. "Hey not bad Jen, not bad at all. But hang on a minute?" she pauses then looks at me. "Which arm is he supposed to have the paper tucked under again?" she queries.

"She said the left...or was it the right?" I plough back through the conversation I had with Maureen only a few hours ago. Did she say the left, or did she say the right? She'd got me so confused. I know I wrote it down somewhere...but where? Oh shit.

Whilst we're discussing the possibilities of it being the right arm or the left arm, Mr Gorgeous walks over to the bar and orders a drink. Before sitting down he scans the room. His eyes hover for a second when he sees us. He smiles. Well there's the wicked smile I ordered. "Beck it's him, I can feel it in my water" I giggle. "What should I do? Should I go over? What do you think?"

"Hey slow down there Juliet," she laughs. "If that's your Romeo then he can wait for a couple more minutes. You have to prepare yourself," she adds. She grabs my face between her hands and scans my features for any blemishes or imperfections. Satisfied she releases her grip and says, "You'll do!" then starts laughing again.

Oh no! It can't be? It is. There at the other end of the bar to Mr Gorgeous, is Andy Hilton. What the hell is he doing here? I grab the cocktail menu and hold it up in front of my face, much to the amusement of Beck.

"What on earth are you doing, Jen?" She's looking at me as if to say yep, you've finally lost it, mate!

"Look over there, the bloke in the denim shirt. It's him! It's the policeman that arrested me two days ago, when I..."

"Uh, stop right there young lady," she interrupts. "What the hell are you on about? You were what?" she exclaims in shock. Her face is a picture.

"I meant to tell you. I got arrested. I tried calling you, really I did. I left a message, several actually." I'm stumped for words. "Um...Look it doesn't matter. I'll fill you in later. God, he is absolutely gorgeous though, isn't he?" I gush.

Beck peeps around the corner of her cocktail menu. "Mmm, not bad at all. Are you interested or is it alright for me to go and chat him up?" she sleazes. At least something has momentarily made her forget her sadness.

"Bugger off. Sod the dream date. I'm going to cancel him. Wait here," I instruct her. I stand up, hitch up my bra straps and straighten my top.

Beck looks up towards the ceiling and smiles. "As if I'm going to go anywhere," she retorts innocently.

Making sure that I don't look in the direction of Andy, I hurriedly walk over to Mr Gorgeous. I clear my throat to get his attention. He turns and smiles. "Excuse me," I say. "I noticed the Evening Standard tucked under you arm? It is you, right?" I ask, shifting nervously.

"Well, hello there. And yes, I am definitely me," he says smiling, looking me up and down very slowly.

Thank God. "There's been a change of plan," I start to explain to him. "I'm really sorry but I 'm not going to need you this evening now. Something has come up."

He looks surprised and manages an, "Oh that's a shame." Do I detect a touch of disappointment? Well, what can you expect, he's only human.

I continue to say, "Look I'm really sorry about all of this. Will you take this for any expenses you've incurred getting here? It's the least I can do," I say apologetically and press fifty quid into his hand.

He looks at the money in his hand then looks back up at me. "Really there's no need," he argues.

"No, please take it," I insist, folding his fingers over the money.

"Well, if you're sure?" he says smiling and putting the money into his pocket. "Perhaps some other time then?" he adds. As I turn to go, he pats me on the arse.

I blush, and give him a final smile. "Yeah, maybe some other time," I say cheekily. Back at our table Beck is waiting patiently for me and has allowed herself to visually peruse the room for available totty.

"Right, I'm going in!" With that I hold my hand up to my mouth, do the breath check and run my fingers through my hair. Beck is in a world of her own, so I leave her to it.

I casually saunter over towards Andy, doing my best catwalk walk impression. Unfortunately, I don't notice the wet patch on the floor. I skid. My left leg goes straight out from under me and I end up on the floor, doing the half splits. Oh the shame, oh the pain!

"Are you okay there?" says a voice of concern. "Hang on a minute. I know you. It's you, isn't it? I hardly recognised you with your top on! It's Jennifer Evans." He kneels down beside me and takes hold of my arm. His smile lights up the bar. God, I've got it bad. "Come on, let me help you up. Do you think you can stand up?" he asks.

"Hello Andy" I sigh, and give him my best puppy dog eyes. "I think I'm okay." He helps me to my feet and sits me down on a chair to regain my balance.

"Can I get you a drink?" He asks. I just nod my head in affirmation. "What would you like? Whereabouts are you sitting?"

"I'm actually with a friend. We're sitting over there." I look towards the table where I've left Beck. She has her head in one hand and is banging her other hand on the table, laughing very loudly. It's good to see her laughing, even if it is at my expense.

Andy smiles and shakes his head at Beck. "Let me get you both a drink. I won't be intruding, will I? I'm sorry, how presumptuous of me. You're probably meeting someone, right?" he asks shyly. He seems a little distracted and looks down at his watch.

"No, please join us, that's as long as you have the time," I urge him.

"Hey I have all night. It looks like I've been stood up anyway," he says shrugging his shoulders. He looks a little embarrassed.

"Great, then I'll have a scotch on the rocks and the same for my friend please." With that he returns to the bar to get the drinks.

I slowly hobble back over to Beck, and collapse onto the chair next to her. "I'm so glad I'm a source of amusement to you," I mumble, rubbing my aching knee. "He's going to buy us a drink. And Beck, don't mention the escort business thing okay?" I plead.

"Okay," she chuckles, wiping a laughter tear from her eye. "You're so funny though Jen!" she adds.

He's coming over. He has on a denim shirt and a black pair of jeans. He looks smart yet casual. He looks divine. "There you are, ladies. Two scotch on the rocks." He gently places them on the table. "Hi, my name's Andy," he says directing it at Beck.

Beck holds out her hand, "I'm Rebecca Monroe, Jen's best friend. I'm so pleased to meet you. Do join us won't you?" she says invitingly.

Andy looks at me as if to say, can I? "Yes of course, please do Andy," I gush rather unnecessarily. "It's lovely to see you again." He sits down opposite me. I can't take my eyes off him. I feel like an awkward teenager again. The three of us make small talk for about an hour. Then unable resist the urge, Beck excuses herself, and glides effortlessly over to the bar to chat up one of the bartenders. That's my girl!

It is as if I have known Andy Hilton forever. Not since Sam, have I felt so completely knocked out by a man. We spend the rest of the evening comparing our childhood adventures and recounting the events of the day that we first met. Mid-way through the evening, he reaches over and takes my hand in his. My hand is the size of a child's compared to his. "I like the tattoo, Jen," he says nodding his head towards my free spirit. "What does it mean?" With his other hand he reaches up, and gently strokes my tattoo. His touch sends shock waves straight up my arm, in to my heart, then to the very tips of my toes. I can feel my heart pounding in my throat. I think I'm going to pass out.

"It's the Chinese symbol for Kung Po Chicken actually," I say offhandedly, desperately trying to control my breathing. "It's my favourite take away dish. I had it done so that when I order in future I just have to point to it." I only manage to hold my dead pan look for a moment. He looks up at me as if to say, you really are completely barking aren't you? I burst out laughing. "Sorry I couldn't resist. The look on your face...it's priceless!"

He smiles and shakes his head. "Oh right, and I suppose you're going to tell me that you've got the symbols for fried rice and prawn crackers elsewhere on your body, right?" He squeezes my hand in his. "Perhaps you'll show me sometime?" he says in a low, deep throaty voice.

Should I, shouldn't I? I don't want this evening to end. I have absolutely nothing to lose so here goes. "Do you fancy going for a coffee or something?" I ask dismissively. I don't want to make it sound like it's a big deal or anything.

"No I can't," he says hurriedly, releasing his grip on my hands.

"Oh right, no problem," I stutter. How embarrassed am I? I fiddle with my hair. It's a bad habit, but when I'm embarrassed, that's what I do.

"No, I mean I'd love to but I'm on duty in six hours, so I have to get home. Another time perhaps? How about next week sometime, to suit you, of course?" he says hopefully.

"Yeah, that would be great," I say dreamily. I can't stop looking into his eyes. He's got me, hook, line and sinker.

He gets up to leave, still holding onto my hand. I don't want to let go. He raises it to his mouth and gently kisses it. His eyes never leave mine. I'm in love or is that lust. Or is it both? He leans forward and kisses me on the lips. "I'll call you tomorrow," he whispers. "I'll get your number from your file at the station." He smiles cheekily.

"Okay, bye then," I say it, but I don't want it to be goodbye.

"Yeah, bye then" he says, still holding on to my hand.

He turns to walk away but then hesitates. Does this mean that we are going to have a coffee tonight, after all? He takes a deep breath. "Jen there's something I have to tell you. I'm here tonight not for pleasure, but for work."

"Oh right," I whisper and nod my head knowingly. "You're working undercover right?"

"No, I'm not working an undercover surveillance, or anything like that. You see I have a huge mortgage and I've been struggling to pay it, so I have a night job too. Jen, there's no easy way to say it. I'm an escort," he admits.

He carries on. "I'm here tonight because somebody booked me for the evening. And it looks like they haven't shown up. It was just for dinner and a drink. I don't do 'extras' or anything like that. And in about six months time I'll have earned enough not to have to do it anymore. I'm really sorry. But I don't want any secrets between us. Not if we're going to...You do understand don't you?" he begs.

OH MY GOD, he's kidding right? The look on his face indicates that he is completely serious. I suppress the urge to throw my head back and allow a full-blown belly laugh to erupt from within. "Oh right. I see. Well, it's always a struggle when you have a mortgage, isn't it," I nod understandingly. "You have to do what you have to do to make ends meet in this life. I can understand that. Thanks for telling me, for being so honest you know. So she stood you up then? It was a lady, wasn't it?"

"Of course it was," he retorts. "I'm not like that, Jen. I thought you'd probably gathered that by now. Can I still see you again?" he asks, looking up through his thick dark eyelashes. "I'll understand if you say no, and I won't bother you again." His eyes search my face for any signs of rejection. But all that he's faced with is my big beaming face. I hold back the giggles and tell him to still call me. Again he kisses me, this time on each corner of my mouth, then full on. He is excruciatingly sexy. "So, I'll call you tomorrow then?" he says.

"Absolutely," I reply dreamily. At the door he turns and winks in my direction. What a great wink...and such a fine arse!

When he's gone, Beck comes back over to the table. I have been laughing so much, I still have tears in my eyes. On seeing them, Beck's smile freezes then turns to thunder. "Did that bastard upset you?" she growls. She's bristling and ready for a fight.

"No, you daft cow," I manage to whisper. "He's just told me he's a male escort. Andy is Adam!" It takes a second or two for the cogs to click into gear in Beck's head.

"You mean..." With that she starts howling with laughter. "And did you tell him you were to be his punter and his, coffee mate? You mad tart!"

"Hang on a minute? That other bloke...my fifty quid!" I whine. Beck's face freezes.

She waits for my reaction. "Oh well," I sigh, pretending that I don't care and shrug my shoulders. "C'est la vie!" I can't hold it in any longer. I burst out laughing again.

We laugh until it hurts. It takes some time to get a cab. Nobody wants to stop because we're staggering around having to hold each other up for laughing. Finally an unmarked cab pulls over and we do a deal. He's a little chap so Beck and I take the risk. Anyway, in the frame of mind Beck's in she'll make mincemeat out of him if he tries anything. We get back to my flat at 3.00am, having called in at the 24-hour grocers for chocolate. By the time we've got back, we have eaten a box of Maltesers each. Both completely paralytic, we collapse fully clothed onto the bed and pass out. Didn't get a shag, but boy it was fun.

Wednesday 19th August... And now the end is near

Oh, how much can a head hurt? The sound of snoring rouses me from my slumber. Do you know, I can't remember if I pulled or not last night. What happened? No wait, hang on? I allow my brain a minute or so to get up to speed. I remember. I feel a smile take over my face and a tingle start to spread through my body. Mmm...Andy Hilton, that smile, those eyes, that kiss...coffee? Come on, come on, think girl, did he or did he not take you up on the offer? The fog finally lifts and the last part of the evening becomes crystal clear. No, he didn't. He said he had an early start. Oh bugger.

So if I'm awake and Andy hasn't taken me up on my veiled offer of coffee, then who the bloody hell is lying next to me, snoring like a trooper? Very slowly I roll over and lift up the corner of the duvet. Thank God and praise the Lord! It's only Beck. What's that brown stuff all over her face and on the sheets? The final piece of the jigsaw slots into place. We'd left the Chocolate Bar, caught a cab and stopped off at the 24-hour shop on the way home? A tidal wave of sickness washes over me as the Maltesers and the Jamesons from last night are churned violently by the, I told you so fairies, deep in the depths of my stomach. I'm so glad we hadn't stopped for a kebab (with the extra hot chilli sauce that always sounds so inviting if not essential after eight large whiskies) on the way home. Oh no, I'm going to have to make a dash for it. EMERGENCY...extremely unwell woman coming through.

I spend several minutes chatting to JC on the big white telephone, or was it Ralph or Hughie I'd been calling for? I then wake Beck up from her alcohol-induced coma. After much cajoling and offers of fresh coffee and a couple of headache tablets (extra strength of course), she manages to open one eye. Not only is she well hung over but also dehydrated from all of the crying she has been doing, for I don't know how long. I pour a Lucozade then a Red Bull down her throat (she doesn't notice that she hasn't had a coffee yet) and bundle her into a cab to take her home. I promise that I will call her tomorrow. But I know that I won't. I have so many things to do today. There isn't much time left. I feel as though I am running out of time here.

Today I have to say my final goodbyes and tie up any loose ends. If pale face and Doctor Gibson are anywhere close to being right, then there's only four or five days to go. I still don't really know what to do, what to say or how to feel. Sounds pretty final, doesn't it? I mean, how can a doctor be so specific and narrow down someone's life expectancy? Does he have a direct line to St Peter or something? And what about Mum? I don't want to leave Mum. I still can't work out whether I should tell her or not. What will she do without me? I know it sounds pretty stupid but being a premature baby has made our invisible cord, the one that the midwife cannot severe, totally unbreakable. She is always there for me and I'm always there for her. I wrote her a letter, explaining what was happening and why, just in case I couldn't get the words out today. But I screwed it up and threw it way. I have virtually made up my mind not to tell her. It will be better this way. Think about it, how do you tell your own Mother that you are going to die? It's not a question I'd ever dreamt I'd ever have to face.

I don't want to cry but the sense of despair overwhelms me. I don't want to be anywhere where she is not. I feel the panic rising. The truth is, she'll go to pieces without me. I love my Dad too, of course. A strong proud man, who has endured more of life's downs, than ups, and has over the past ten year's been the best Dad ever, but he isn't and could never be, Mum. Mum and I have been able to bare our souls to each other, ever since my early childhood. She truly is an incredible woman. We'd shared moments and thoughts that we would never ever talk about again, but would both always remember. Her taste in music however, left a lot to be desired. I mean, Englebert Humperdink?

I can't imagine not being able to just drop round at any time, call at some ridiculous hour, just to tell them that I love them. Today is going to be a bad day. Good old Jenny, always good for a laugh, now totally vulnerable and it could be said out of control. Yes, that is a fair assumption. A blubbering, shaking, miserable wreck. The big pink and green ticks on the list and the counting down of the days, makes it all so final. I am going to die. But I don't feel too bad, certainly not as if I am dying anyway. My back isn't sore anymore either. It just doesn't make sense. I throw my morning pill and a Maxalon down my sore throat and pour myself a small drink. I will be driving in an hour, so only a small one.

I take a long hot shower, my glass of whisky carefully balanced on the soap rack. Looking down at my belly I pat it affectionately. Not too hard though. I can't afford to be sick again today. So far this morning I think I've managed to pull every muscle in my stomach. I don't know why but I've always thought I was such a gargantuan tank of a girl and always wanted to be slim. True, my belly isn't a Claudia Schiffer but then again it isn't a Roseanne Barr either.

Let's take a moment and put things into perspective here. I've spent my whole life worrying about how I look. I've been given all the love and support I've ever needed and still my self-image has been such a mighty psychological cross for me to bear. How fucking sad is that? The way we look should be immaterial and what we have inside, should be what counts. In a perfect world this would be true. But we don't live in a perfect world, do we. We live in a world where, from the day we are born, obstacles and missiles are thrown in our way at any given opportunity. In hindsight I wish I'd had the rationality years ago to face up to this fact. Knowing that I am dying certainly has made the turbulent murky waters of my life suddenly settle and become crystal clear.

Damn the water's gone cold. I've only got a small water tank in the flat. Another thing I've been meaning to change but had never got round to. Bugger it. I jump out of the shower with fantastically erect nipples and towel dry myself off a.s.a.p. Back in the bedroom, I pause to check out my nipples. In the cold light of day, I see that I'm not fat, chubby maybe, but definitely not fat. I can honestly say, I've seen more meat on a heavily used butcher's pencil. And my boobs look fantastic. Stepping over the mountainous range of dirty clothing strewn on the floor around the laundry bin, I find a clean T-shirt and a pair of shorts in one of the open drawers, and change.

During the night at the police station I'd made a mental list in my head of the people I really want to say goodbye to. I pick up a pen from the bedside table, plonk down on the bed and begin to copy out the list onto the back of a used envelope.

For starters there's Mum, Dad and Mad Lizzie my younger sister. I must remember to give her Nina's autograph. Then, there's Beck my rock. I'd decided and then made her promise, to leave me alone for my final days. If I'm going to wallow in self-pity, then I want to do it on my own. Also, Grandma Ellen who wasn't quite all there and who if I said, "See you in the next life Nan," would say, "Alright dear, what time and where we shall meet?" And finally Daniel Reed my best friend from college, who has been a bit of a bastard over the years but then all men are bastards at times, aren't they. In his defence, he has always been there for me when I've really needed him.

Right a quick phone call and I'll be on my way. Good it's ringing. "Hi Silla, it's Jennifer Evans. Yes, I'm doing okay," I tell her. I want to ask her how am I going to tell Mum.

"Oh I'm glad you've called Jenny," she says. From the tone of her voice, I hazard a guess that she is smiling again. "I popped round yesterday, but missed you again. You sure you're okay? I just wanted to check in with you, to see how the medication is working."

I tell her that, "Surprisingly enough, I don't feel too bad." A little embarrassed, I add, "I'm having a few problems going to the loo though."

"Oh that's entirely to be expected Jenny," she reassures me. "I'll pop round later if you like?" I tell her I'm going out. "I'm going to say goodbye to Mum," I whisper. I try to swallow.

She talks soothingly to me, for what seems like forever, comforting words. But, they don't really help. God I'm dreading this. I tell her I have to go or I'll be late. "Take care Jenny love," she says. "Call me later if you need to" she adds. I put the phone down, and lean against the table for a moment, to pull myself together. Several deep breaths and a pep talk from the, fight 'til the end voice, and I'm as ready as I'll ever be.

My first port of call is to be Daniel's house. He doesn't live far from Mum and Dad. Still at home with his parents, Daniel has always been a year behind me in whatever we do. I pull up outside 27 St Mary's Road in Perivale. We had spent three years of our teenage lives at college, sharing ups and downs, dreams and ambitions. Daniel is a stunner. Some say he is a dead ringer for Keanu Reeves. I'd have to disagree. If he looked anything like Keanu, I'd have jumped his bones years ago. Wherever he went, girls swooned around him. Unfortunately for the female population of the planet, Daniel is very fussy when it comes to the opposite sex. His taste in women, how can I put this, is not quite the norm. He likes a bit of both really. He'd discovered this after a brief encounter with a particularly effeminate Drag Queen called Gloria that we met on a holiday in Tenerife, five years ago. He'd been so confused at the time. Gloria was a fantastic looking woman, who outside working hours, answered to the name of Georgio. These days Dan sticks to the fairer sex and is currently dating a secretary called Angela, who has a thing for being tied up, so he says.

I lock the car door and slowly walk up to the front door of No.27. Daniel opens the door before I have time to ring the bell. "Jen, you old slapper!" he exclaims, throwing his arms around me and messing up my hair. I pull away slightly when he touches my head but he doesn't seem to notice. "To what do I owe this honour? God I haven't seen you for ages. You never call me anymore either, you cow! Come on in...Mammy, Jen's here," he shouts over his shoulder.

I've always had a soft spot for Dan's mum. So like my own mother, kind, understanding and always there for Dan. She shuffled down the stairs towards me and gave me a kiss and a cuddle. As usual she has on a housecoat. For as long as I can remember, she'd always worn one. And it was either a blue checked one or two tone brown. Bless her. "Hello love, it's lovely to see you again" she smiles and affectionately rubs my arms. "Are you well? Now, how about a nice cup of tea?" There it is again, that question. A dismissive question that is thrown into virtually every conversation that we ever have.

I give Mrs Reed a big hug back. "I'm fine thanks, Mrs Reed. And I'd love a cuppa please. And you've had your hair done too. It looks great." I say and hold her at arm's length to have a proper look.

"Oh, do you think so?" she sounds thrilled that I've noticed. "I can always rely on you to notice. You don't think it's too short, do you?" she asks. "Danny and his Father haven't even noticed yet that I've had it cut. I had it done nearly a week ago too. I suppose that's men for you" she chuckles and then turns towards the mirror, patting her hair into shape, subconsciously posing for a second or two.

Dan starts to protest lamely saying he did notice, ACTUALLY. It was just that he'd forgotten to say anything at the time that's all. He punches my arm and mouths, "Arse licker" at me, as I make my way up the stairs to his bedroom. I stick my tongue out at him and punch him back. I flop down onto a beanbag by the window.

"So, why are you really here, darlin'? It's not like you to just pop in for a chat and a cuppa. Not anymore anyway, now you're a high flying career woman. So what's up babe? Men trouble?" he probes, sprawling like a 70's porn star on his bed and puffing on his cigarette.

How can I tell him the real reason I'm here? I can't. I turn and face the window, which looks out over the back garden. I take a deep breath, as if it's my last and say "Dan, it's... I don't know how to say this really. I'm, I'm going away." I can't look him in the face. If I do, he'll know I'm hiding something. He can read me like a book. He has a special talent for doing that to me.

"Where? Don't tell me, you've finally thrown caution to the wind and really are going to go for it and get out and see the world, Jen?" he asks.

I turn and look at him across the bedroom. He's lying opposite me, blowing smoke rings into the air, with not a care in the world. I can hardly say, "Oh, it's just that I am taking a trip to Heaven that's all. I'm gonna pop my clogs. Ride the escalators right up to the top floor," can I? So I say, "Yeah something like that. I'm going to stay with Ginger. Remember her? I met her on that cruise I went on after we finished our final year at college. She lives in the Caribbean?"

Dan looks puzzled then the penny drops and he says "Oh right, yeah, I remember now!"

I continue to say, "Well she has a two-bed condo overlooking Megan Bay. She's been going on at me for years at me to visit. So I'm going out for a few months, just to get my head together. You know, decide what to do with my life." Mmm, plausible enough, I suppose. Ginger has been saying for years to go over and stay for a holiday.

"Wow, you lucky old tart!" he says, his eyes sparkle with excitement. I can't tell him. I want to, I really do, but... "Wow, hang on a minute, I thought you knew what you wanted in life. You have your own business, your own flat. Jen you have everything. You have a life. What's going on here?" he demands, raising himself up on to his elbows. He's trying to make eye contact with me. I have to get out of here fast.

"Fucking hell, look at the time, Mum's expecting me for lunch today. I've got to be there by two. You know what Dad's like if I'm late. Listen Dan, take care of yourself won't you? I do love you, you old queen." I'm rambling and talking too fast. Oh no, not the tears again. My tear ducts have been working overtime for more than a week now. Oh no, the walls are closing in on me again. I have to get out of here otherwise he's going to cop the lot. I don't want another trauma victim on my hands. Beck's already one too many.

Dan bounds off the bed and crushes me with his trademark bear hug. "I love you too, you old tart. Don't cry or you'll set me off. Jen, are you sure there's nothing wrong? You know you can tell me anything?" he says now holding me at arm's length. His eyes scan my face for clues. "Are you cold, you're shaking?" I know that I can tell him anything but also know that I can't this time.

I nodded my head and manage a "No I'm fine really. Just a bit pre-menstrual you know, time of the month and all that." I pat my tummy and pull my, oh I've got cramps, face. I pull him back towards me and hold him tight.

"Oh right" he says knowingly, as if to say well that explains it. "Well, as long as you're sure. Anyway, I'll see you again soon enough. P'raps I'll come out to the Caribbean and see you, and try some dark meat eh! Now will you please let me go, you're strangling me" he laughs pretending to choke.

"Oh sorry Dan. Damn it, I've got some snot on your shoulder, sorry. Bye then, love you." I release him from my Vulcan death grip.

The walk to the car seems to take forever. I can barely see straight. My legs feel like jelly and I'm a little dizzy again. In the car I take a deep breath, turn the key and pull away from the kerb, waving wildly as I usually do but without looking back. I can't. The road ahead looks narrow and bleak. As if to mark the moment, the sun disappears behind the only cloud in the sky.

It literally takes fifteen minutes to get to Mum and Dad's from Dan's house. At the garage on the edge of the village, I nip into the toilets and wash my face. The cold water brings little relief to my sore gritty eyes. But I have to agree with Nina, I really do have the finest blue eyes after a good cry. Nina... it's her unplugged session tonight on Capital Radio. I think its at nine o'clock if I remember rightly. I should be home by then. The face looking back at me in the mirror looks tired and drawn.

Mum and Dad have been married for 42 years and have lived in the village for the majority of this time. Ten minutes later, I pull into Nevermore Avenue. "Morning, Alfie," I shout. "How are you? The garden's looking beautiful as always. That rose bush has really taken this year, hasn't it?" He is kneeling on a grovel pad in amongst the flowers. He lives next door to Mum and Dad. On hearing my voice, he looks up from his labour.

"Hello, my love" he says looking pleasantly surprised to see me. "Do you think so? It's coming on isn't it. I managed to shift the green fly this spring, so fingers crossed." Alfie's all smiles. He holds up a gnarled arthritic pair of fingers and crosses them. He looks back down and pulls a pair of rose cutters from his pocket. With a great deal of effort he cuts a single red rose from the nearest bush and holds it out towards me. "Here you are, young Jennifer. A rose for a rose," he proclaims. He's always had a knack of making me feel so special.

"Oh it's lovely, thank you Alfie. You know, you're still the only man who ever gives me flowers." I laugh, but it's true. No one ever buys me flowers.

"It's not as lovely as you though, Jennifer. My, you get more and more beautiful each time I see you." He has said this to me each time I've seen him over the years. He has a wicked twinkle in his eye for an octogenarian.

Alfred Hampton had watched me grow up over the years, in the Avenue where we'd lived for what seemed like forever. When I started college he'd always said, "If only I was forty years younger"... He was like the grandfather I didn't have. Both had left me before my thirteenth birthday. It is my belief that when you die, the ones that you have loved and lost will be waiting to welcome you to wherever it is that we all go. It's something I have to believe in. Hey, now there's something to look forward to. I'd soon be back in their company. Both Grandpas will certainly welcome me with lots of cuddles and love. Boy, I miss them. Will I really get to be with Grandpa George again? I have to believe it. Many people who have had near death experiences say it is peaceful and something to look forward to, when the time actually comes. I really hope that is the case.

"I'll come and say goodbye before I leave, Alfie. Gotta go. Dad will kill me if I'm late." I sniff the air and call back to him as I walk up the path. "Mmm...something smells good, doesn't it? See you later Alfie."

The back door to The Chestnuts is open as usual. Mum always leaves it propped open in the summer. The house is called The Chestnuts because of the conker trees in the garden. There are four. Two with pink blossom, and two with white blossom. During my primary school years I'd been crap at sports. I blame the bloody puppy fat for that! But each winter I managed to redeem myself. I was the school conker champ. I reigned supreme. We grew the best conkers in the village. In the evenings after I'd finished my homework, I'd bag up the conkers and sell them at school for ten pence a bag. I had developed my business sense at an early age.

The smell of fresh coffee and roast beef wafts towards me. It's seductive lures teasing me into the kitchen. Roger Whittaker is singing away merrily from the ghetto blaster next to the microwave. As a child I had hated listening to his dulcet tones EVERY Sunday morning. It was either Roger or Slim Whitman. Mum would boot up the old record player in the lounge and do the housework to it, singing along at the top of her voice. Both Lizzie and I had hated Sundays and would don headphones as soon as the first verses could be heard. Funny, but today it's comforting. On hearing *There's a ship lying waiting in the harbour...*, I know that I am home.

"Muuuummmm, Daaaaaad, I'm here" I shout at the top of my voice. The drone of the vacuum cleaner stops. Mum spends hours putting the lines back in the thick pile carpets that she insisted on having in the most used rooms in the house. To say she is house-proud would be an understatement. But rather that, than live in a shit hole eh? Her passion for all things domestic hadn't rubbed off on me at all. Well maybe it had a little. I did have a cleaner once. But she only lasted a week. The bitch had been stealing my jewellery. I couldn't bring myself to trust anyone after that. So once a week, I blitzed the flat. I could do the whole place in three hours. And that's including one fag and a coffee break.

The smell of the Sunday roast fills the kitchen. The sound of the roast potatoes cooking in the sizzling fat, fights to be heard above Roger. If eating equates to sex, then right now I'm seriously indulging in gastronomic foreplay. I am starving. Thinking about it, I haven't eaten properly for days. It hasn't really been high up on my agenda of things to do. Just then the kitchen door flies open. "Hello love!" It's Mum, rosy cheeked and with the most beautiful smile and eyes that have ever been bestowed upon a human being. "Oh, it's good to see you, Jenny. You look a bit tired though. Are you OK? Arthur...Lizzie...Jennifer's here." Oh, Mum what am I going to do without you?

Dad follows shortly after her into the hot kitchen. "Morning bleeder." He's always called me that. Copious amounts of kisses and cuddles follow. I don't want to let go of either of them.

"What's wrong, Jenny?" Mum asks. "You look a bit peaky. Is it your period, dear?" She holds me at arm's length, studying my features for the tell-tale signs. She is looking for a spot that usually appears just to the left of my mouth, two days before my period. Mum put everything down to the monthly curse. As a teenager, I'd prayed for an early menopause. Dad's gone quiet and busies himself at the cooker. He hates it when we talk about women's stuff, as he likes to call it. It's always a sure-fire way of shutting him up. You just have to mention the words period, cramps, ovaries, or blood and he's off.

Just then, there's a rumble on the stairs. This can only mean one thing, my little sister Elizabeth, fondly known as Titch, is home. Lizzie is a bundle of fun. She epitomises life, so full of energy and love. She is the best sister anyone could wish for. Although painfully thin and several inches shorter than me, she has the personality and enough love for a hundred people. Like a mini tornado, she tears into the kitchen.

"Hiya sibling, got me a pressie then?" she says before throwing herself at me. Lizzie is twenty-two and only sees the good in everyone. Faced with some learning difficulties, she excels in people skills. She still lives at home with Mum and Dad. She is the most likeable person I know. Yes so I'm biased, but hey, that's my prerogative as her sister, isn't it? I give her a big hug and a sloppy wet kiss because I know she hates that. "Urghh Jen. Stop it. That's gross!" She wipes her face on my T-shirt, and gently slaps me on the arm. I squeeze her so hard that she squeals and tickles me to let go. I have bought her a present, I always do. I've bought her the new Robbie Williams CD. She is mad for him.

"Oh thanks Jen. I love him. Have you heard Track Ten? That's my favourite one you know. Shall we go and listen to it upstairs?" Lizzie pulls on my arm. "Come on, please?"

"Hang on a minute, I've got something else for you." I instruct her to, "Close your eyes and hold out your hand." She holds out her hand but can't keep still. She is so excitable.

"What is it? What is it? Can I open my eyes yet?" she squeals. I place the card that Nina had instructed Damien to give to me into her hand.

I make her wait a second longer then say, "Okay, you can open them now!"

Lizzie opens her eyes, and looks down at her hand. "What is it?" she asks. She looks puzzled.

"Well, turn it over and have a look" I egg her on.

The moment is magical. She turns the card over and reads it. "Is this for real?" she gasps. "Is it?"

"Sure is. It's an autograph from the one and only Nina Hendrix! So what do you think of that then? Am I a cool sister or what?" I brag.

I'm suddenly bowled over onto the kitchen floor. In an instant Lizzie starts kissing me and laughing. "Thank you ever so much. Is it really real Jen, is it?" she keeps repeating.

"Yes it's really real!" I say for about the fourth time. "I met her the other day and got that for you." Well, it's just a little white lie.

"You are the best sister ever!" she squeals.

"No you're the best sister ever, and in the whole wide world," I argue. If I'm not here, who's going to watch out for her if anything happens to Mum and Dad? Oh God. Why is life so FUCKING unfair? I'm crying but pretend that it is because I'm laughing so hard. I look at Mum and give her a wink and whisper, "I'm fine Mum, don't worry about me."

What else can I say? How do you tell the most important people in your life that you're going to die before them? As children we try and prepare for the inevitable, imagine what's going to happen when they go. But, for a parent to lose a child...at this precise moment, I make the decision not to tell them. Why? How can I?

I change the subject by asking Dad, "Do we have time to go upstairs and listen to Lizzie's new CD before lunch? I've listened to the whole album. It's great Lizzie. Dad, have we got time?" I look over to him, standing by the cooker in his blue and white striped butcher's apron.

"Lunch will be about half an hour," he says over his shoulder. "I'll give you a shout when it's on the table." He turns towards us both and winks. His smile is so warm and loving. He's never been one to show his affections, but we have always known.

"Thanks Dad. Come on Lizzie, race you up stairs!" I shove past her to try and get a head start. From past experience I know I'll never beat her in a fair race, so I have to resort to dirty tactics.

"Oh Jenny," Dad has followed us out of the kitchen and shouts after us from the bottom of the stairs. "If you still feel rough tomorrow, well... just get it checked out, bleeder. Don't take any risks. We don't have private healthcare for fun, you know. There's probably a very reasonable explanation why you feel off colour."

"Alright Dad" I shout back. "Don't fuss. I'll go tomorrow, OK? It's probably just my ovaries playing up again." That should do it. True to form, Dad makes a hasty retreat back into his comfort zone, the kitchen. Oh bugger, Lizzie has taken full advantage of Dad calling me back and is standing triumphant on the top of the bed. "That is so unfair, I demand a re-run!" I pause in the doorway gasping for air. Don't know why I'm so out of breath these days.

Lizzie bounces off the bed over to the stereo, and puts the CD on. As the first notes blast out of the speakers she starts to dance around the room. She still has Nina's card firmly gripped between her fingers. She looks so content. To her life is always good. She's always in a good mood and has time for anybody at any time. I can't believe that, after today, I'm not going to see her again. I can't handle this. I lay down on the bed and close my eyes.

"Shove over then, let me on too." Lizzie digs me in the ribs to move me over.

"Hey steady, that hurt." It didn't really but it makes her laugh.

"Did not! Wasn't hard enough." Lizzie climbs on to bed and we both lay there, on our backs, staring at the ceiling. After a few minutes she says, "I can see an elephant, can you see it too Jen?"

Now I know what you're thinking, she's a nutter, right? Let me explain. It was a game we had played as kids. The artexing on the ceiling, if you squint your eyes, you can see all sorts in the patterns and shapes. I open my eyes and look up at the ceiling. "Oh yeah, I can. I can see a hot air balloon there...see it?"

After a couple more minutes Lizzie breaks the silence again. "Um...Jen, can I ask you something?" she says, scratching her head, looking at me with a puzzled look on her face.

"What's up Titch?" I ask. We'd always called her Titch because she had been such a small baby when she was born. My heart feels as though it's breaking. I have to look away.

"Are you poorly Jen? You look a funny colour. You know, if you are poorly, I'll always look after you" she says, with total conviction and belief that she could look after me, come what may. God how I wish you could Lizzie.

"No of course not, silly. I'm just tired, that's all," I sigh and pretend to stifle a make believe yawn. "Hey want to see something?" I ask her in an attempt to change the subject. "You must promise never to tell Dad though?" The free spirit tattoo will distract her from her line of questioning. I could at least share that secret with her.

"Oh what? Tell me...tell me please...promise not to tell Dad, cross my heart and hope to die" she says. The look of innocence and excitement on her face steals a breath from me, and crushes my chest.

"Well..." I pull up my shirtsleeve to reveal the masterpiece that is my free spirit tattoo. "So, what do you think of that?" I ask. Her eyes open as wide as is physically possible.

"WOW! Is that real? Not one of those sticky ones you can get at the corner shop, in with the bubble gum strips?" She leans forward and licks her finger, then gently rubs it to see if it will smudge.

"It's real, trust me" I assure her. "So what do you think? Remember, you promised not to tell Dad" I remind her.

"Oh I promise. It's great. Can I get one done too? Will you take me? I'd have one just like you then. Will you take me please Jen, please?" she begs.

So I say, "Maybe, OK. I'll think about it, we'll see."

"Yippee!" With that she starts jumping on top of me, kissing and hugging me again. "You're simply the best, better than all the rest..." she sings at the top of her voice, drowning out the Robbie William's CD. I grab a pillow and start a pillow fight. What can I say? I love her so much that the thought of leaving her hurts like hell. I feel like my insides are being torn apart.

A shrill wolf whistle stops us in mid-fight. Lunch is ready. It was the only way Dad could ever make us hear him whenever we had any music on.

"Coming," we shout in unison.

Clambering off the bed, Lizzie turns and offers her hand. She pulls me up off the bed.

"Thanks Titch" I say.

"That's all right Jen," she says. "You're the best sister anyone could ever have. You won't forget about the t.a.t.t.o.o. Will you?" She spells it out. So cute.

"No I won't. Come on, Dad will be in a mood if we don't shift our arses." I push her towards the door. "I love you Titch."

"God, you're so soppy sometimes!" She pushes me backwards back onto the bed, and bolts out of the room and disappears. I wipe my eyes on my sleeve. Just then a head appears around the door, it's Lizzie. She's out of breath, but manages to say, "Okay, I love you too, Jen. You really are the best sister ever. Now come on …we're coming Dad!" She's off again.

Lunch proves to be the hardest few hours I have ever had to endure in my twenty-nine years on this planet. The roast beef is succulent, but sticks in my throat. The Côte du Rhone is smooth, yet burns my mouth. I go along with the plans for the summer holiday to Portugal. We are going to go back to Carviero. I mean, they are going to be going back to Carviero. I notice a new photo on the sideboard. It's a picture of the four of us from last Easter. A complete and happy family.

I can't stand it any more. I have to tell them. I want to say, "Look, don't be upset, but I have a tumour and only have a little while to live." How selfish would that be? Panic's starting to rear its ugly head again. I need air.

"Jen, my girl, you make sure you make that doctor's appointment tomorrow," says Dad after he's swallowed his last mouthful of food. "You're looking pasty," he adds looking closely at me. I can't meet his gaze.

"I will Dad, promise. I went last week too. I…I…uh…I went for my regular scrape. You now, the sm.…" We always mouth the last part of the word.

He coughs and mutters, "Oh right."

"Old Sanjeev sends his regards Mum," I say. I pop the last mouthful of food into my mouth and place the cutlery together, just like Dad had taught us to do as children. I have to wash it down with a gulp of wine.

"He's a lovely man, isn't he," oozes Mum. If only she knew. "So, when do you get the results?" she asks. Mum, I'm dying, sod the smear. I'm dying. Nope I just can't quite get those words out.

"About a week I think he said. Listen, thanks for lunch. It was lovely as usual, Dad. I'd better hit the road. You know things to do and all that. Give us a kiss then. Line up," I try to joke, but am finding it hard to keep it together. I feel like screaming.

Dad first... "I love you Dad. Look after Mum and Lizzie, and yourself, of course."

"When will you come and see us again?" he asks. "Your Mother is running up the fattest phone bill ever." I hug him so tightly. I can't bear the thought of not cuddling my Daddy ever again.

Mum next... "Bye Mum. I love you more than life itself. I'm going to miss you so much." I nearly choke on a sob.

"You silly cow," she chuckles in her own special way. "I'm not going anywhere." She too has tears in her eyes. She always cries when I'm leaving after a visit. How can I possibly tell her? "Come and see us soon. Phone when you get home, to let us know that you're safe."
"Sure. Don't I always?" I say.

"Lizzie, I'm going now." Lizzie had excused herself from the table and gone back upstairs. She still has her music on so loud. The house is shaking slightly, in time to Natalie Imbruglia. "LIZZIE!" She can't hear me shouting. Dad whistles.

Within a matter of seconds thunderous footsteps, again, pound the stairs. "Bye, bye sis. See if you can get the tickets for the Bee Gees concert next month, will you? Pull a few strings, eh! Thanks for my CD and the autograph. You're the best sister ever. Oh and don't forget the t.a.t.t.o.o." she whispers the t.a.t.t.o.o. bit, in my ear. It tickles.

I wrap my arms around her small frame and bury my face in her Motley Crue T-shirt. "I love you Lizzie. Look after Mum and Dad for me. And don't forget our secret, you promised."

"Don't be silly," she says. "You know that's your job, to look after us. Not mine. Oh and you can rely on me, Mums the word!" She taps the side of her nose and winks at me.

"Bye then." For the last time I take in the image of my family. Their smiling faces, the look of love and togetherness in their eyes. They stand together at the end of the path and wave goodbye until I'm out of sight. My heart is breaking. I struggle to breathe. Never have I felt so alone. Never have I had such a deep feeling of grief. Never have I wanted to live so much. I get home, curl up in my bed and cry without tears. I would do anything to have another chance.

I wake up just in time for Neighbours. I'll have to leave the call to Grandma Ellen, until after Neighbours and Countdown. She loves Richard Whitely. We'd noticed a touch of dementia had crept into her life about a year ago. I mean, you'd have to be a little touched, to fancy Richard Whitely.

I decide on a White Musk bubble bath, and for a change, a large G and T on the side. It has a drop more of the G than the T in it. I pop the stereo on. I have a true passion for music. The first record I ever bought was Bang, Bang by B A Robertson. I think I mentioned that already. With the passing of time, my tastes have changed noticeably for the better. I lay in the bath until the water goes lukewarm, and the bubbles have dispersed. Wrapped in my fluffy dressing gown, I dial Nan's number. It's ringing. Slumping back onto the sofa, I shove my spare hand deep into my pocket. Oh how gross. I gingerly pull out the offending object. It's a fluff covered, mangy Custard Cream.

"Hello, who's speaking please?" says the gentle voice at the other end of the line that belongs to Grandma Ellen.

"Nan it's me, Jennifer. How are you, love?" I say. I have to shout a bit because she has selective hearing.

"Oh, hello me duck" she says. "I'm not so dusty, thanks. And you, how are you doing? Is college alright?" Bless her. She really is stuck in a time warp, roughly ten years in the past.

I stifle a giggle and say, "Yeah, it's fine thanks. Nan, I'm calling to let you know that I'm going away for awhile."

"Anywhere nice, dear?" she asks. "Skegness is lovely at this time of year you know, and so reasonable" she assures me.

"Yeah? Well, I may just go there on the way. I can't chat for long, but I just wanted to tell you that I love you."

"You silly bugger. I know that" she chuckles. "So when are you picking me up to go to Skegness?" she asks. She has no grasp on reality. What a fantastic way to live life. I tell her I'll pick her up at the weekend. What else can I say? Nan, I'm dying? And she'd say, "Oh that's nice dear, when?"

I draw the call to an end. There is no point. I put the phone down. The stereo is still playing away to itself in the bedroom. Who wants to live forever...? Why me? This doesn't feel like a game anymore. It's real. I'm dying and no amount of gay abandon can change or rectify this. I still have so much left to do. It's taken a couple of days but I now realise that I have so much to live for. It's too late.

Ten days of pent up anger and emotion, that I thought I'd actually vented throughout the week, erupts into a violent rage. I lose control completely and go berserk. Storming into the kitchen I rip the list from the fridge door. I smash every piece of crockery that I can lay my hands on. Minutes later, the list lies in shreds on the kitchen floor, and there are pieces of broken crockery everywhere. I slump down to the floor and lean up against the fridge exhausted. My head is aching and my back is throbbing in time with my heartbeat.

Another night with Nina!

I admit it I'm a mess. Shit...it's nearly nine. I have to drag myself up off the floor and struggle to walk to the bedroom. The answer phone is winking at me again. As I pass the hall table I push it to the floor. Fuck 'em...Fuck 'em all. I don't want to speak to anyone. I just want to drift off to sleep tonight and not wake up in the morning. I've had enough. I want to lie down fall asleep and exhale my last breath dreaming of whatever or whomever. I can't take anymore.

I collapse onto the unmade bed. It's still light. Well, it's only nine o'clock isn't it. Clothes are strewn all over the room. All of the drawers are half out, and the washing basket is threatening to burst. The ashtray by the bed is overflowing and there's an empty Jameson bottle tucked under the pillow. I'm a slob, and it's official. I clear a space on the bed, pull a nearly new bottle of Jameson from the bedside table, flop down and take a swig. Fuck being ladylike.

"Welcome to the evening session with me, John Watts, here on 95.8 Capital Radio. We have a real treat in store for you tonight...Nina Hendrix live in the Unplugged Studio. Nina welcome..."

"Hi John, it's good to be back in the UK." Nina's husky voice resonates out of the stereo speakers. For some reason it gives me goose bumps. Memories from Friday night come flooding back.

"So, you have a new album out at the end of the month and are going to do a couple of gigs here in the Capital this week. Two nights at the Arena, right?" he asks. John Watts has been with Capital Radio since it's launch some years ago. He is a top DJ, a true professional. But you can tell from his voice that even he is in awe of, the Nina Hendrix.

"That's right, John," says the familiar husky voice. "I'm at Wembley Arena this weekend. I hope you all out there in the Capital will come and join me for a night," she purrs invitingly. The select crowd ripples a response, with a couple of wolf whistles thrown in for good measure.

"Absolutely Nina. And of course Capital Radio will be covering the concert live from the Arena on both nights. So Nina, what are you going to start with tonight?" he asks.

I'm feeling a bit affected actually, I have to confess. I'm lying on my bed with a bottle of Jameson for company. I'm settled back and ready to listen to a woman, an incredibly famous woman that I've slept in the same bed with but not technically slept with, sing live and unplugged. Wow, the world is seriously looking strange through my alcohol and drug tainted, rose coloured glasses tonight.

I relax back and take a swig from the bottle. Nina starts with a couple of acoustic tracks from the new album. Billy Samson is accompanying her on bass. Just as I'm getting comfy, the third track finishes. The select few gathered within the Unplugged Studio go berserk and start clapping and whistling again in appreciation. Nina speaks, "Thank you, thank you very much. This next song isn't on the album. In fact, I only wrote it at the weekend. So it's a bit rough but I want to play it, if that's okay with you all? I wrote it for a very good friend of mine. I haven't known her long, but what an amazing human being she is," she says quietly.

I sit bolt up right… She continues, "You see, she's dying, and boy I wish I'd met her before last week. This song is for my friend, Jen. She has a brain tumour and is dying. Makes you think doesn't it?" The silence from the studio audience is deafening.

"So Jen, if you're listening, this is for you. If you need me, I'm here for you. You know where I am. This song is for you and it's called Running out of Time. Take it away Billy."

I have to concentrate on the words…

So many things still left to do
So many things still left to say
Time is passing by so silently
I can feel my life just slipping away

Unlike the ticking of a clock
A human heart's been made to stop
No chance of living for ever more
No time to even up the score

So when the chance is there…then take it
Don't push too hard in case… you break it
Live for the moment, living for the day
Cos for all of us, time is slipping away

We're all running out of time
No need for tears, no need to cry
Thinking what might have been
Living life as a lie
You have to ask the question why?
We're all running out of time

So with every breath that is exhaled
Take another one for the man who has failed
Because in life there is no full stop
This existence we live...will stop

Unlike the ticking of a clock...

I can't believe I have any left to cry. Tears stream from my eyes, and roll down my face. I didn't think I had any left in me. My tear ducts seem to have gone into overdrive. She's summed up my feelings in just a few words. Nina pauses, while Billy does an acoustic guitar solo, then...

This is a no win situation
We're all just grains of sand in the wind
There can be no ever after
We've got to face up to our sins

So when the chance is there...then take it...

There's another chorus, a final flurry of acoustic 12-string magic, then silence. The radio goes dead. Shit, I must have lost the signal. As I'm about to stand up, applause breaks the silence. "Wow Nina, powerful song. Let's hear it for Nina Hendrix folks." John Watts can barely speak. Now there's a first.

"Thanks John. Jen, that was for you." Nina's voice betrays her. I can tell that she's hurting. It must be obvious to everyone listening that she's crying. John Watts hastily lines up another record.

Why me? With all the strength I can muster, I throw the bottle of whisky at the far wall. It smashes into a million pieces. I roll over and bury my sore head into the pillow. Please let me die. Please don't let me wake up in the morning. You've had your fun God, now please let me die.

Thursday 20th August...So this is it then

I look at the illuminous face on the alarm clock. It's 3am. I need a wee and a drink. Shuffling to the bathroom, I do my business and get a glass of water. Downing it in one, I pour myself another before shuffling back into the bedroom. I open the curtains. It's a lovely night. The sky is so clear. I look up at the stars and try to spot the handful of constellations that Grandpa had taught me when I was a child. There's the Bear, and the Plough, and there amongst them all, the brightest star in the sky. A few nights after Grandpa had died, Dad had come upstairs to tuck Lizzie and I into bed and found me crying into my pillow. He'd plucked me out of my bed, and carried me over to the window.

"Look Jenny, you see that big bright star up there?" he'd said, pointing up towards the night sky. "Well, whenever you feel sad and are thinking about Grandpa, you just have to look up and find the brightest star. Because you know Jenny, that's Grandpa's star. And as long as you can see it in the sky, you know Grandpa is watching you and thinking about you...wherever he may be."

I'd believed him. And now I find myself having to believe in him again. I look up and smile at Grandpa's star. I'll be with you soon, Grandpa. I can't wait to cuddle you again. I leave the curtains open so that I can see his star from my bed.

Chris Tarrant wakes me at 8am by shouting, "Get up, you sleepy head, you'll be late for work!" God, why does he always have to shout so loud? I roll over, reach down and pull the plug on him. Rolling back over, I lay staring at the ceiling. Any day now if Doctor Gibson is right, the only people who are going to see me in all my glory are Bancrofts and Son, the Funeral Directors. I can admit it now but I've never told Beck, I really fancied Edward at school. I'd had about as much chance of snogging Edward as hell freezing over. Still that hadn't curbed the cranial fantasises I'd allowed myself to indulge in on a regular basis. The best one was set in the mortuary in his back garden. It had me rolling around on top of one of the slabs with him. And not just lying there with my mouth sewn shut, pumped full of formaldehyde and alcohol (well, with some alcohol but not a total transfusion), eyelids glued, and with my legs firmly clamped together. It's funny really, but after meeting him again after all those years, I think I'd prefer the latter option, mouth sewn shut, and definitely with my legs firmly clamped together.

It really stinks of whisky in here this morning. There's broken glass all over the floor. Strange, how did that happen? I get up and open all of the windows in the flat. Padding from one room to the next, I am ashamed to say it, but this place is a complete shit hole. I flick on GMTV then spend the next hour picking up bits of paper, chocolate bar wrappers, empty Jameson bottles and try to raise the level of squalor to just about acceptable. The kitchen will have to wait 'til I get back. Last night in my fit of rage, I've succeeded in breaking everything that is breakable and then some items that were supposedly unbreakable.

In the bedroom I bag up the dirty clothes surrounding the wash basket. On the dressing table is the Make Your Own Will kit that I picked up from WH Smiths, in Windsor. I have a quick look through. It looks straightforward enough. I have to get it written up today. I know what I want to leave and to whom, and I need to make sure that everybody knows that the funeral is organised and paid for. I'll do it when I get back from the shops. I've got a few bits to pick up before I settle down for the rest of the day. I must phone Beck today too. In my rage last night, I forgot to call her. Well, I didn't forget. Just couldn't bring myself to call her.

I leave all of the windows open and head for the High Street. I'm not going to be long. I'm sure they'll be fine, left open for half an hour or so. The flat really needs a good airing. Paddington slinks over to me as soon as I step out of the front door. "Hello mate," I say gently. He's been a bit timid, since the bin lorry hit him last year. I make that sucking between your teeth sound... "Puss, puss, puss." He brushes up against my bare leg. His body is lovely and warm from the sun.

"Well I can't stop, Paddington. I've got things to do today. You be careful now. See you later," I whisper to him. He meows back at me as if to say, see you later Jenny. It takes me fifteen minutes to walk to Florrie's. It's more of a jog than a walk really. I've got to get back and make that Will. Before I even get to the shop, the smell of the flowers brings a smile to my face. I take in a lung full of pollen and enter the shop. It's deserted. A voice from the back room shouts, "I'll be with you in a minute Jenny."

"No rush, Florrie," I shout back. I look around the shop for a hidden camera. Florrie always knew who was in the shop, without even looking up or peering round the door from the back room. It was uncanny.

Eventually she bustles in. "Morning Jenny, how's life treating you? Have you got rid of that dodgy boyfriend yet?" she asks with a big grin on her face. Which one does she mean? There'd been several since I'd moved into the flat.

"Not bad thanks, Florrie. Actually I've got a cracking bloke now. He's a policeman. I just love that uniform don't you?" I say dreamily, leaning on the edge of the counter cradling my face in my hands.

"Mmm, our local one always calls in on a Wednesday afternoon and buys a big bunch of chrysanths for his Mother. He's a lovely chap...very firm...very authoritative." Florrie pauses for a moment, and then snaps back to now. "Sorry Jenny, I was miles away then. Now, what can I get you my love?" she says changing the subject rapidly. She's blushing! "I've got some lovely peach coloured roses in today. I haven't had time to put them out yet. There the best I've seen this year."

"I'm actually after some sweet peas and some lilies, if you have any in, Florrie?" I ask trying to sound all casual.

"Oh no, there not for a funeral are they? Nobody's died, I hope?" Florrie enquires so innocently. If only she knew.

"No, I'm just feeling maudlin today, that's all." I dismiss her concern and convince her that, "It's just my memories getting the better of me at the moment. Buying flowers helps me to cope with Grandpa's death, and you know other things. Sounds mad I know, but do you know what I mean?" I ask.

"Oh love, I know exactly what you mean," she says nodding her head in agreement. "My Henry left me some ten years ago now, yet sometimes I still get so down. A bunch of gladioli's always helps to pick me up again though."

I pick up my flowers that Florrie has wrapped so carefully, whilst we've been chatting. I say my good byes, and hurriedly exit the shop. Florrie shouts out after me, "You keep your chin up Jenny, do you hear me?"

I turn and give her a wave and a big smile. "Bye Florrie," I say but the words are barely audible. She'll know soon enough. I nip into the, Everything for a Pound shop, and buy a pack of three Glade Plug-ins. I want the flat to smell nice. Then I pop the list that I'd promised Edward Bancrofts the day before yesterday, through their letterbox.

I get back to the flat in time for Trisha. The hallway looks as though a bomb's gone off in it. I kick the door closed behind me and put the flowers in the kitchen. Back in the hall, I pick up the answer phone and put it back on the hall table. Surprisingly enough, it's still working. The post that's accumulated over the past week looks like a patchwork rug on the hall carpet. I bend down and pick it all up, and place it in a neat pile on the table. A quick scan through backs up my assumption that they're all bills and junk mail.

In the bathroom, I run the bath and add plenty of Radox Stress Buster Bubbles. I'm a bit generous with the measure. Well, you can't take it with you can you. But wouldn't it be great if you could. You know, pack a suitably sized suitcase of things like, M & S undies, a personal CD player and the latest book by Jackie Collins. Plus the other necessities, a toothbrush, a selection of CD's, Gio by Armani... and sanitary towels? Now there's a good point. Do women still get periods in Heaven and Hell? I suppose in Heaven you probably don't. Because let's face it, periods are Satan's work. They have to be. I conclude that Satan has to be a bloke.

I lower myself into the bubbles and let out a big sigh. I really thought I'd feel different by now. I don't feel particularly sad or depressed. Quite the opposite in fact. I feel calm, even content. I feel ready. They say that an animal knows when it is going to die, and spends its last remaining hours looking for a place of peace and calm. A final resting place, away from the crowds. I suppose that unwittingly, that's what I am doing today. I am preparing to die. I have a few final tasks to complete, and then I intend to get completely plastered, take a couple of extra Diamorphine tablets just in case, then hopefully fall asleep and not wake up again. I don't want to spend the next few days degenerating at a rapid pace and end up like Grandpa did.

On reflection, I don't think I've done anything really bad, have I? Sure, the bank robbery was quite bad, but nobody got hurt and we only stole money from the bank. And anyway I never got to spend any of it. So technically I only removed it from the bank. I never actually used any of it. I'm glad I got my tattoo done, too. My only regret on that one being, that I hadn't had it done earlier on in my life. It makes me feel like a harmless rebel. It's provided a real buzz. And as for Frankie...Frankie and Albert...now there's a notion! And I still can't quite believe that Sam is an uphill gardener. Who'd have believed it? And then there was the little liaison with Nina Hendrix. I've met Nina Hendrix and she fancied me. Oh my God! And last, but by no means least, Officer Andy Hilton. That has to be my biggest regret. I knew the moment I laid eyes on him, that we would've been perfect for each other. Damn it. Why did we have to meet now? It's too late.

On reflection, I have to say that yesterday was the hardest day of my life. Even now, my heart feels as though it's going to stop at any second, as if it's going to break. How am I going to manage without them? I know I'm being selfish but I can't help it. Take a reality check, Evans. I angrily brush a singular tear away. How do you think they're going to react when you die? Sometimes you can be such a victim. Yes, I've had ten days of pain and heartache. But they are going to have to live with the loss for the rest of their lives. Having to spend the next God knows how long beating themselves up, continually asking the question, why? I swallow the lump in my throat. That told me then.

I can see through the mist, from the bathroom into the kitchen. It's a disgrace. The list is still in shreds on the floor. I really have to clean up in there. But I'm starting to feel tired now. I haul myself out of the bath, swathe myself in body lotion then wrap myself up in my dressing gown. For the first time in what seems like ages, I pull the scales into the middle of the floor. I've put on half a stone. Oh well. I push them slowly back into place under the sink. It dawns on me that I haven't been to the loo for a couple of days now. It must be the Maxalon. Silla said it would make me constipated. That would explain why my stomach looks so bloated too.

From the doorway into the kitchen I survey the damage. Not quite sure where to start I brush the broken crockery off the table on to the floor and sit down at the kitchen table. The heavenly scent of my Body Shop White Musk moisturiser wafts around me like an additional layer to my aura. I know it's early, but the Jamesons' is already out. I pick up a plastic measuring jug from the floor. I might as well go out happy. It doesn't take that long to clear it all up. I even do the washing up. I don't know how I let it get so bad.

I flick the radio on and root around in the cupboard under the sink for suitable vases. I arrange the sweet peas and take some into the lounge and some into the bedroom. The lilies, I arrange in the tall blue glass vase that Mum gave to me last Christmas. I thought I'd put them on the hall table. I call Beck's flat, but there's no reply. So I leave a message, "Beck don't call me back. I'm just going to go to sleep now. Just wanted to say..." I sniff and take a breath, "Thank you for being there for me. I'd have given up you know. So, shit how do you say goodbye?" The machine cuts off. I raise my eyes and mutter a "Thank you for that."

Damn it. I've still got to write to Mum. I have to explain all of this to her myself. She deserves that at least. I need her to know that I have accepted my circumstances and that I have sorted everything out, i.e. the funeral, and that I am going to miss her. She needs to know that I haven't suffered and that I am at peace with myself. Now, I've got some writing paper somewhere in here. I rummage in the dressing tables drawers. There it is. It's some old stuff I'd had when I was at college. I used to write loads of letters by hand back then. But since I got the computer, I've become lazy and now they're all typed. The paper has Winnie the Pooh and Tigger on the bottom right hand corner.

I head for the kitchen, pausing briefly in the hall for a pen. The sun is shining brightly. Even with the window wide open, it's gloriously hot. I make a brew and then start.

Dear Mum,
I'm dying...

Nope, that's crap. I rip the page from the pad and throw it in the general direction of the bin. Now try again. Imagine what you'd want to be reading if you were in Mum's shoes when she receives this. I pause for a moment then pick up my pen again and start to write.

Dear Mum,
I don't really know where to start. So as somebody once said, 'let's start at the very beginning'. By the time you receive this letter, I will be gone. I know it's easy for me to say but try not to feel sorry for me. I just want you to know what's been going on, straight from the horse's mouth, so to speak. About a month ago I found a lump on my back. I dismissed it, and just thought it was a bruise from where I banged it whilst rearranging the furniture in the lounge. Remember? You said the sofa would look much better opposite the fireplace? As usual, Mum you were dead right! Well, anyway on Monday 3rd August, Doctor Singh sent me to Hammersmith Hospital to see a specialist. To cut a long story short...it was benign Mum. But then they said they wanted to me to have another MRI scan like the one I had a few months ago, because of my headaches. They found a tumour in my brain. It's inoperable. So I have known for the past ten days that I am going to die. Seeing you all last Wednesday nearly killed me. I thought my heart was going to stop. I really wanted to tell you Mum, but I couldn't. Anyway, I need you to know that I have arranged and paid for the funeral. Bancrofts and Son on the High Street have made all of the arrangements and the contact there is Edward, the son.

I am appointing Beck as the Executor of my Will. Yes, I have finally got round to doing it. Better late than never, eh. I haven't asked Beck yet. So if I don't get to speak to her again, will you ask her for me please? Basically everything goes to you, Dad and Lizzie. I will leave the Will on the mantelpiece in the lounge.

I know it's a daft thing to ask but please try not to be sad. I've put myself through the emotional mangle so many times these past few days. I've cried enough tears to supply the south of England during a drought. And now I have accepted the eventuality. I have just about done everything I've ever wanted to do over the past ten days. Some you will not be happy about, but then I hope you can forgive me. I am at peace with myself and am ready to go.

However the thought of leaving you Mum is unbearable. I have to keep saying to myself, that one day we will be together again. Remember what Dad used to say about Grandpa's star? Well, when you look into the night's sky and see the brightest star, think of me and smile. I'll always be keeping an eye on you. So you behave yourself now.

I think that's it. My heart is breaking Mum, and nothing can fix it. I don't know what I'm going to do without you. I love you Mum, more than you will ever know. So until we can be together again...I'll always love you Mum, it'll just have to be from afar now. So for the time being...

Lots and lots of love always and forever and a day...

Your Jen xxxxx

I grip my chest as my shoulders start shaking uncontrollably. The pain is immense. This is it. This really is happening. Oh God...Mum. There are no more tears. There is only pain. This is the most pain that I have ever felt in my twenty-nine years on this planet. I shakily write the envelope and stick a first class stamp on the front. I rest my head on the table.

When I eventually raise it again and look at my watch, it's nearly midday. Instinctively, I go to wipe away the tears, but there aren't any. I feel so drained. But you still have things to do, Jennifer Evans. Come on look sharp. Something makes me stand up and I wander into the hall. I'm on autopilot. I have to get changed.

When they find me, I want to look good. I want to be found looking like a million bucks. Clean undies and dressed to kill, or die in these circumstances. I decide to wear a dress that I know is Mum's favourite on me. She always says I look like a princess in it. It's blue and has flowers embroidered on the hem. It's a real summer in the sixties style dress. Oh Mum.

It's weird, but I can honestly say I've never felt better. I haven't felt much pain thank god. Silla has certainly helped manage that side of this unfolding nightmare. Damn these drugs are good. The only pain I have felt is in my heart. But that's more pain than I can cope with right now.

I busy myself and tidy the rest of the flat. I bag up the rubbish and take it down to the bins by the front gate, pausing only to say, "Hey" to Paddington again. From the step at the front door, I look out into the street. A plane flies over. They seem to be getting lower and lower these days. I can make out the Virgin symbol on the tail. This is it then. I step into the cool hallway and close the door for the final time.

Dragging my feet I start the ascent to my flat. I get half way up the stairs, when she calls up to me. "Oh Jen, hang on a minute love." It's Mrs G of course. I stop dead in my tracks and lean over the banister so that I can see her.

"What's up, Mrs G?" I shout back down to her.

She sticks her head round the banister and looks up. "I have to tell you Jenny, those fish net tights did absolutely nothing for you last week." With a sly smile and a little wink, she disappears out of sight.

I don't believe it. She knew all along that it'd been me at the bank. And yet she hadn't turned me in. I manage a smile, and haul myself up the last few steps. Good old reliable Mrs G. I have to laugh, so that's why she gave such a dodgy description to Matthew Greening. On my doormat is a Tesco carrier bag. I untie the knot in the top of the bag and investigate. Great, some more apples from Mrs G's tree. On entering the flat I notice the light flashing on the answer phone.

BEEP..."Jen, if you're there, please pick up...Jen...this is serious. Jen, I'm at the police station in Ealing. I've been arrested. You've got to help me...Jen..." BEEP. The pips sound and she's cut off. She's joking right?

BEEP..."Jen, I had to tell them. They said they'd cut me a deal. Well, you won't be around so it doesn't matter does it? Jen, please come down here and back me up on this one...or I'm in deep shit"...BEEP. This is not good.

BEEP..."Hi only me. Andy, that is. Just to say I'm so glad we ran into each other the other night at the Chocolate Bar. Can I see you tomorrow night? Give me a call on 0208 849 7453 and let me know either way. I look forward to seeing you again, Jennifer Evans. Bye"...BEEP. He won't want to know me, when he finds out what I've been up to.

BEEP..."Hi, it's Nina. I just wanted to see how you're doing. If you need to talk, call me Jen."...BEEP. A little chat with Nina, is the last thing I need right now.

BEEP..."Jenny it's Silla. Give me a call so we can arrange a time for me to call in." Yeah maybe later eh.

I pour myself a large drink into my plastic jug. That'll do for starters. The scent of sweet peas fills the flat. I wander into the lounge in a daze and put the telly on. I throw open all of the windows again. The news is on. It's Moira again. Does she ever have time off? I collapse back on to the sofa.

"One woman has been arrested and is in custody in connection with the Ealing bank robbery which took place last week. Rebecca Moonshine Monroe of Finsbury Park, North London returned to the bank and was identified by Roger Branford, one of the counter assistants, who was threatened during the robbery. Investigations are under way to track down her accomplice, also believed to be a woman. The police have taken the unusual step of releasing the name of the suspect as Jennifer Evans. If you know the whereabouts of Jennifer Evans, then please contact Ealing Police Station. The suspect is not thought to be of any danger to the public. According to police sources the Ealing Two, if convicted, could face up to eight years in prison for the robbery even though they were technically unarmed."

Well that's it then. I'm finished. Not only do I have days to live but it also looks like I'm going to spend them behind bars. And what was that dizzy tart Monroe doing returning to the scene of the crime? I told her to leave it for a few days. I bet she went back to chat up that bloke. Men are going to be her downfall, trust me. Obviously the Moonshine magic hadn't worked this time. This is serious. I get up and dead lock the flat door, and push the bolts across. I am now officially a fugitive. I have robbed a bank, threatened people, made malicious telephone calls, slept with a woman, met the man of my dreams, and had a tattoo. Dad is going to kill me. There is no way I am going back into a police cell. There's no way Andy is going to want to know me now. I pour myself another quarter of a pint. I really would be better off dead.

The Storm

No please, I didn't mean it, I swear. It's all been a big mistake. It wasn't a real gun. It was a plantain for God's sake. You can't do this to me. I'm screaming, struggling frantically to free myself from the police officer's vice like grip. He's pushing me in the direction of a door marked Cells. His teeth are all yellow and his breath smells of cheap cigarettes.

The sound of Mrs G hoovering in her flat below, releases me from my tormentor. I've been having another nightmare. I stare up at the ceiling and try to catch my breath. My T-shirt is wringing wet with sweat and my heart is racing. I also dreamt that Beck and I had been sentenced to eight years for the bank job. Dad, of all people, was the sentencing Judge. As he slammed the gavel down and passed sentence, he looked at me and said, "You're supposed to be an Evans, girl! Your Mother will be so disappointed in you."

Then, I'd protested that lenience should be shown, as I have only days to live. Everybody in the courtroom started laughing. They were all laughing at me. I'd urgently scanned the gallery of observers, looking for Mum. There she was. She's waving her hankie at me and smiling. She didn't look upset at all. And there was Lizzie, asleep next to her. Next thing I know, I was in a prison somewhere. I don't know where. Andy was one of the prison officers and WPC Land was the prison governor. Nina Hendrix was there too. She was the top dog on the block. Everywhere I looked the other inmates were cackling, laughing and pointing at me. "Not such a free-spirit now are you!" they were all chanting. Nina had just looked at me and winked seductively. Oh my God, she'd had her arm around Beck too.

A shudder racks my body. I jump out of bed and throw the curtains open to let some of the sun's warmth in. It's another glorious day. I collapse back down on to the edge of the bed and take some deep breaths. I can't focus my eyes. Oh hell. What am I going to do? I run my fingers through my hair. It's stuck to my head with perspiration. I spent most of the night ploughing through the images that I've stored up in my head from over the past ten days. I mulled over the good things I'd done and the not so good things that I'd done. It hadn't taken me long to suss out the score. It hadn't taken me long to realise that the odds are well and truly stacked against me. I am in deep shit. I'm dying and to top it all off, it looks as though the police are only a matter of hours away.

With sweaty palms and gasping for breath, I scrabble around in the bedside drawer for my Diazepam. Bloody childproof lids. I wrestle with it for a second, willing the bastard to come off. Suddenly the lid comes away and the contents fall to the floor. I drop to my knees and with shaky hands collect up three.

The letter! I'd posted Mum's letter before I saw the Doctor yesterday. She'll get it this morning. Oh no. My legs are shaky but I manage to make it through to the kitchen without falling over. I lower myself down onto a chair. I'm so out of breath. Habit forces me to pour a large Jamesons into my plastic measuring jug. I wash down the tablets, then drain the remainder in one hit, and pour another. I still haven't made my Will yet either. And I think I said in Mum's letter, that I'd leave it on the mantelpiece. Oh God, why did I post that damned letter.

Staring into space, I try and fathom out what to do next. Beck has been arrested and it's only a matter of time before they'll come for me. I lean back on my chair and check to make sure that the front door is bolted. It is. I remember I got up in the night and did it. With a sigh of relief I lower the legs of the chair back down on to the floor. What am I going to do? The doorbell distracts me, buzzing like a trapped irate bee. That'll be someone at the door then. I get up slowly and take a few steps down the hallway towards the front door. "Who is it?" I shout out furtively.

"It's only me Jenny," says the voice. It's Mrs G.

Thank God. I let out a sigh of relief and hurry to the door. Pulling back the bolts, I pause for a moment and ask her, "Are you alone, Mrs G?"

"Yes Jen, I'm on my own," she calls back.

I open the front door a crack and peep through. I quickly scan the hall. She's on her own. I open the door and usher her in, immediately closing it behind her as soon as she's crossed over the threshold. "So, how are you this morning Mrs G? Beautiful day isn't it?" I say trying to sound cheery. "Oh, and thanks for the apples yesterday" I add.

"That's all right," she says and smiles. She looks up at me. Her eyes look sad. I hope that's not pity I detect in her expression. It better not be for me. The last thing I need right now is pity. "So what can I do for you this fine day?" I ask her. I beckon for her to follow me back into the kitchen. "Fancy a drink of something?" I offer. I pull out a chair for her to sit on.

She notices the measuring jug and Jameson bottle on the table. "It's a bit early for me, thanks love," she says tactfully.

I sit back down and gesture for her to take a seat. We sit opposite each other. An uneasy silence follows. I can't bear it. "So don't you think we're having a perfect summer, Mrs G? I don't think I can remember ever seeing the apple tree so full." I try and make conversation.

Mrs G has her arms resting on the table and is peering down at her hands. I've never really had the chance to have a look close up look at Mrs G before. Her face is a mass of wrinkles. She looks up at me. Her eyes are a pale blue and a little rheumy. I've always thought she was about the same age as Alfie, Mum and Dad's neighbour. But she must be in her mid-eighties, at least.

She takes a deep breath. "Jenny, the police called round about an hour ago. I said you'd popped to the shops and would be back around two-ish. Since they called, I've noticed that there's a blue car parked outside No 43, with two fellas in it. I think they're waiting for you, Jenny," she sighs sadly.

Oh God. I jump to my feet and start pacing. "That's it then, I'm finished," I babble.

"Keep away from the window Jenny," she says urgently. "As long as they think you're out, you're safe in here. You've got to decide what you want to do, and be quick about it. You're running out of time, Jenny. It's nearly two o'clock."

I drop to the floor and hug my knees to my chest. "What am I going to do, what am I going to do?" I say more to myself than to anyone else. There's a good chance that I'm going to start crying, any second now.

With a great deal of effort, Mrs G heaves herself up off the chair and shuffles over to where I am cowering by the fridge. "Now, now, don't you cry Jenny. It can't be all that bad," she says sympathetically. She pulls a lace hankie from up her sleeve and stuffs it in my hand. "Here."

"Thanks," I manage to mumble between gasps for air.

Mrs G is staring down at me. I feel like a child again. I feel vulnerable. "Why did you do it, Jenny?" she asks. "If you needed money I could have lent you some, you know." She gently pats me on the head and smiles.

Looking up at her, I sigh. I tell her, "It's a very long story. Trust me, you really don't want to know." I blow my nose again in to the delicate hankie.

Easing herself back down into the chair that I'd been sitting in, she reaches across the table and picks up the measuring jug. Turning back to face me she says defiantly, "Try me." I take the jug from her extended hand.

"Well, you see I found this lump..." Over the next half-hour, I tell Mrs G all about the past ten days, well most of it any way. I leave out a few minor details like Frankie, the Wrap Party and the phone calls. Every now and then she nods or shakes her head knowingly. She is so easy to talk to. The odd gasp escapes from her as the story unfolds. "So you see, I'm in deep shit Mrs G, excuse the French. I really don't know what to do. I don't want to spend my last few days in police custody." I look at my watch, "And Mum will have got the letter I posted to her by now." I rub my face with my hands. I can feel a tension headache coming on. "Do you know, I've even arranged my own funeral this week," I say laughing like a lunatic.

Mrs G unscrews the top off the whisky bottle and pours a hearty measure into my jug. "Thanks." I take a slug and feel its warmth, as it sinks down into my stomach. I force a smile, and say, "I've stumped you, haven't I? I don't suppose you've got any advice for a dying fugitive on the run have you?"

She looks at me and shakes her head. "My, you are in a pickle aren't you." She says re-arranging her pearls, obviously deep in concentration. I'm sure, if I listen hard enough I'll be able to hear the cogs turning in her brain.

"If you think about it" I start to say, "It's ironic really. One day I'm told that I'm dying, begging for just one more chance to live. Now if feel as though dying is my only option. It's my only way out of all of this. And sooner rather than later."

All of a sudden Mrs G claps her hands together and shouts, "I've got it!" The sudden noise makes me jolt and spill my drink.

"Oh sorry love, did I make you jump?" she asks. Her eyes are sparkling, radiating a glimmer of hope. I must look so desperate to her. "There, there now Jen," she reassures me. "I'm sure we can come up with something."

"What do you mean?" I ask eagerly. "Mrs G, do you have a plan?" Just then the phone rings. I try to stand but I'm feeling a little tipsy. I giggle and start hiccupping. By the time I've dragged myself up to a standing position, the answer phone kicks in.

BEEP... "You bitch. I'm going to have you, you miserable bitch. You think you're clever? Well I know it was you. You've made a big mistake messing with me. Well it's pay back time, Ms Evans. Have a pleasant evening. It may well be your last"...BEEP. I recognise the snarling voice immediately. Oh my God, it's Edward Least. He knows. How did he find out?

The strength in my legs deserts me. I drop back down to the floor. The look on Mrs G's face says it all. She looks disturbed by the threatening phone call. She opens her mouth to speak. I hold my hand up, shake my head and just say, "Don't ask Mrs G, don't ask."

We sit in silence. There's just the sound of the kitchen clock ticking away and the hum from the fridge, disturbing the silence. Mrs G sighs loudly before saying, "I was going to suggest that maybe you could dress in some of my things and make a break for it. But now, I don't know. They're bound to have alerted the airports by now. And that phone call sounded particularly nasty, Jen. I dread to think what else you've got yourself mixed up in. I think you should give yourself up," she says firmly. "I'm sure the police will take into account the unusual circumstances. And they can at least protect you from whoever that was." She waves her hand in the direction of the phone. "This is very serious, Jenny."

"I know. I think I just need some time to think, you know be on my own for a while." I pray that she'll take the hint. I've come to the conclusion that no amount of talking is going to help me. I don't think she has really grasped the reality of the situation.

"Well, I'll leave you be then, Jenny." Mrs G slowly gets to her feet and starts shuffling along the hallway to the front door. "You just bang on the floor if you need me, you hear," she calls back to me.

"Wait, let me see you out." I call after her. I really hope she says no. I don't think I can get up again. I feel quite pissed actually.

"No need, Jenny. You stay where you are. And remember, as long as they don't see you in the window, you have some time." She opens the front door and looks back at me. She must think I'm an idiot. Flaked out on the kitchen floor, up to my eyeballs in trouble and getting pissed. With a wave of her hand, she starts to close the door behind her.

"Mrs G?" I shout out after her.

"What is it, Jenny love?" she asks, turning to look back at me.

"Thanks a lot for listening Beryl." I raise my hand to my mouth and blow her a kiss. Hopefully it'll find the real one out of the three Mrs G's I can see. I've never called her Beryl before. It hadn't seemed right before now.

A big loving smile fills her face. "You're welcome love," she says and closes the door to behind her. Those damned American soaps.

I sip on my whisky and bask in the sun's rays. I have this niggling feeling that I should make a Will sooner rather than later. So I may as well do it now before the police arrive, and I'm too bladdered to write. You know, strike while the iron's hot and all that. I've just got to get motivated, or should I say up off the floor. Come on Evans, on your feet girl. It takes me several minutes to stand up. But once I'm up, I'm fine. I stumble back into the bedroom, drop to my knees and go commando style past the window to the dressing table. I allow myself to slip into imaginary mode and pretend I'm infiltrating enemy territory. I reach up and scrabble around for the kit. There it is. I drag it to the edge of the dressing table top and let it fall to the ground. Clenching it between my teeth I crawl back, keeping low to avoid sniper fire, to the doorway before standing up again. A quick flick of the invisible switch and I'm back in reality mode. I wipe the saliva off the front of the pack onto the front of my T-shirt and go back into the kitchen. It's already lovely and warm and cosy in here. I'm tempted to try and open the window. But they're bound to spot me.

Now how do I do this? I break the cellophane wrapper and spend the next half-hour reading through the guide. Basically, as long as I am of sound mind and not a minor, I can make a Will right now. It says that, if there's no Will, on your death, the law of intestacy will apply to the disposal of your estate. Which I suppose in plain English means, if I had a partner or was divorced then the partner would have no claim to my estate. That is totally irrelevant to me, so onto the next paragraph.

It's pretty straightforward really. I can hand write it. And as long as the contents are clear comprehensive and concise, I don't need to engage the services of a solicitor. There is a Form in the pack, so I don't even need to hand write it. I just complete, sign and date it. First off, I need to list my assets. That shouldn't take too long! I've got this place, my passion wagon, I have that Life Insurance thing I signed for without realising what I'd signed for when I left college, SERPS or something like that and I have all the flat's contents.

I pull the forms out of the pocket of the Make your Own Will Kit. Bloody hell. It's a bit complicated. I'm just about to give up on the using a form idea when I notice, tucked at the back of the pack there are several layouts and types of form to choose from. There are four different styles of Statutory Will Forms. I flick through and choose Form 2. Form 2 has been designed for, 'those of you who wish to give all of your possessions to someone without having to identify all of the possessions'. A Will designed just for me, quick and easy. I start to fill in and tick all of the necessary fields.

I leave everything to Mum. She can then distribute everything as she sees fit. I appoint Rebecca Moonshine Monroe as the executor of the Will. I request that she deal with the outstanding debts, so that Mum doesn't have to get involved. I state that I have arranged and paid for my funeral, and that should a hospital require any of my organs, then they're welcome to them. I'd stay away from the liver though. It's already pickled. I sign and date the Form, and the deed is done. If I'd have known that it was this easy to make a Will, I'd have done one year's ago. Reading back through, it's a bit untidy but I've got a shaky hand, so it's bound to be.

Well, I think I need to do some serious thinking. Jennifer Evans you are in the poo, big time. So watcha gonna do about it? I seem to have temporarily lost the use of my legs again, so I have to crawl back into the bedroom. Propping myself up against the bed, I survey my surrounds. I spot a half-empty bottle of Jamesons under the bed and one of my red Totes socks that I thought I'd lost last week. I scoop up another couple of Diazepam, just for the hell of it. I'm feeling tipsy, but surprisingly calm. Wow, the room's going all fuzzy. I think I must have bent down too quickly. I'll just rest here a while and gather my senses.

Sometime later

Mmm...I need a drink. Who broke in while I was asleep, and filled my mouth with sawdust? I wipe away a string of dribble that stretches from the floor to the corner of my mouth. From the position of the sun, it has to be late afternoon. The bedroom is in shade. It's gone nice and cool. I rub my eyes and push myself back up to a sitting position. I must have fallen asleep. I know what I need. I need a bath. It in doubt, if in a quandary, have a bath. That's what'll do. I'll have a bath. I climb up the side of the bed and flop down on to the top of the duvet. When the room has stopped spinning, I tentatively stand. I check the ground to make sure it feels solid under foot. There's nothing worse than walking on a wobbly floor. It passes the foot stomping test, so it's onwards to the bathroom.

I turn the taps on full and add a generous measure of White Musk Bubbles. Whistling away, I wander back into the kitchen and have a quick slurp. God, I'm hungry. I open the fridge door to reveal that the cupboard is bare, apart from three Dairylea triangles, half a box of Maltesers and a cheese and onion slice. It's a proverbial banquet. I prepare my little feast and take it back into the bathroom with me. On the way through, I notice that the answer phone light is flashing. I put my plate of goodies down on the top of the toilet cistern. I wonder who called. I take a wild stab in the dark and try and hit one of the three buttons I see before my eyes. Hey, good shot.

BEEP... "Jenny, it's Mum. Pick up the phone, Jenny. I got your letter this morning. What's going on? Jenny, are you there? Pick up the phone. You're scaring me. I just want to talk to you. Call me as soon as you get this. No on second thoughts, we're on our way over"...BEEP.

"No! Don't do that," I shout out loudly. I snatch up the phone and shout into the receiver, "Mum, its me. Mum...hello?" The dialling tone purrs back at me. Duh, it was a message, stupid. I knew that. Now what do I do? Dad will kill me. Wondering what to do, I dead lock the front door and slide the bolts across again. I know what I need. I need to put some music on. Now what's it going to be Barry White or Culture Club? In the lounge I blow a kiss to Mum, dad and Lizzie on the mantelpiece. Culture Club it is then. "Give me time, to realise my crime, let me love and steal..." I chuckle at the lyrics. How apt. With a Boy George hop skip and a jump, I bounce erratically back into the bathroom. Oh bugger. The bath is overflowing. I turn the taps off and throw a couple of towels down on to the floor, to mop up the spillage.

I must have turned round too quickly. The next thing I know, I'm skidding on the water and crash to the floor. Ouch, my arm. Shit, I can't move it. I look down to see if there is any obvious damage. Nope, the skin's unbroken but the pain is making me dizzy. I feel a bit sick actually. Pain killers? I scrabble in the cupboard and throw back a couple of Pethedine, for a quick hit. On second thoughts, maybe two won't be enough. I pop another one for good measure.

I stagger to the bedroom, pausing in the doorway. I think I'm going to pass out. I have to lean up against the doorframe, and wait until the nausea passes. With one final effort, I fall forward towards the bed. The pain in my arm is excruciating. I think I may have broken it. Bloody marvellous. I wonder if and when my day is going to start getting any better. I lie back on the bed and search the artexing for images, while they take the desired affect.

Surprisingly enough, during the time it takes Boy George to sing Karma Chameleon and Church of the Poison Mind, the pain has gone. Now, what was I going to do? I rack my brain. I know I was going to have a bath. As carefully as I can, I head for the kitchen to grab the whisky, and then back to the bathroom. My left arm hangs limply by my side. I reach across and stroke my tattoo. It looks fabulous. The thought of Frankie brings a brief rush of warmth to my nether regions. It quickly dissipates at the thought of Dad's reaction if he ever sees it.

Mmm...the sweet peas smell lovely. I look in the bathroom mirror and look at the smiley face staring back at me. "Oh you are in a bit of bother now, aren't you Jen?" I say out loud, wagging my finger at my reflection. "You'd be better off dead now wouldn't you eh? You're in the shitty shit, Jennifer Evans. Daddy's going to kill you, if the tumour doesn't get you first," I sing.

It takes me a while but I eventually manage to get my T-shirt off. Oh God, Mrs G will think I'm a complete mess. I've got one of those, 'Welcome to Barbados, have a nice day' T-shirts on. And it's covered in chocolate stains. Dan bought it back from there about three months ago. He did one of those all-inclusive holidays with the sadomasochistic woman he's going out with. You know the one who likes to be tied up, Angela.

I tilt the blinds at the window, because the sun is really strong. That's better. With everything within easy reach of my right hand, I climb into the bath. Oh, it's just right. It's just the right temperature. It's not too hot, just hot enough. Boy George serenades me with my favourite Culture Club track, Victims. What more could a girl ask for? A lovely soothing bath, a nice drop of the Irish within easy reach, a cheese and onion Dairylea-topped slice and for afters, the piece de resistance, a nearly full box of Maltesers.

I pop a handful of Maltesers into my mouth and let them melt, followed up by a swig of Jamesons to wash it all down. I am in a food and alcohol heaven. Settling back, I allow myself once more, to drift back over the events of the last week. Given the circumstances leading up to my ten days of social, physical and verbal vandalism, you'd be lying to say that you would have done anything different. Imagine being told, "Oh by the way you know you were healthy and full of life yesterday, well sorry but from today you've only got two weeks to live. Yep, that's right, you're dying...sorry." It's unimaginable isn't it? So perhaps you can see why I've done all the things I've done. But it shouldn't take something like that to give you the will to push the barriers down, exercise some insanity and live a little, should it? But they'll never understand will they.

My fingers have already turned pruney in the water. I take a sip from my jug. It floats in the water now, so I don't have to hold it. It looks like a Spanish galleon, bobbing on a sea of bubbles. The miracle of science! I think they call it Archimedes Principle or something. If I have to go to prison for my final days, it's going to be communal showers, and "Would you like me to wash your front for you, luv?" Oh God no. I can't go there. There's no way I'm going to spend the last few days of my life in prison. And what about Mum, dear old Mum? Mum my soul mate, my real best friend, even more so than Beck. She will be so ashamed of me.

My moment of tranquillity is shattered. "Jennifer Evans, we know you're in there," shouts a voice. God that made me jump. Who the bloody hell is shouting their mouth off out there? As if by magic or by the power of telekinesis, my question is answered. "This is the police, we have you surrounded. Give yourself up and you will come to no harm." The policeman's voice resonates around the tiled walls. Well that's that then. How do they know I'm in here? Did Mrs G tell them? Nah, she'd never do that, bless her. The blinds! You pulled the blinds. Oh you silly cow, Evans. What did she say? DON'T go near the windows. Will I ever learn? Am I that much of a hopeless case?

"Piss off, I'm not here," I shout out at the top of my voice. It comes out a bit croaky. I've got one helluva sore throat for some reason or other.

"You've got five minutes to give yourself up Jennifer, and then we're coming in," shouts the big mouth with the megaphone.

I think, Jenny my lover, you are in the shit big time. I sip at my drink and try to think what to do. It's bloody hard because it all keeps going fuzzy in my head. Right, let's try and rationalise this. Rationalise? Who swallowed a dictionary then? I start laughing and slip from my wedged-in position. I usually have to wedge my big toe by the cold tap to stay above the waterline. After choking momentarily on my White Musk Bubbles, I re-take my position.

Now what about Mum and Dad? Dad will definitely disown me. He's sure to. What with me bringing disgrace to the Evans name, and all that. It's not as if I've been to a school disco at the village hall, got pissed and at the end of the evening got tangled up in a fight. He'd forgiven me for that one. Well he did after a severe beating, anyway. But this is a way bigger an offence to consider. And what about Mum? I feel a smile take over my face. I know she'll forgive me. She'd forgive me, even if I committed a murder. I'd still be her Jenny. But can I really justify putting her through visits to a filthy stinking police cell. She's never been into a police station before, let alone a cell. I can't put her through that.

I chew intently on my cheese and onion Dairylea topped slice. I brush the floating crumbs to the tap end of the bath. I never put my head at the tap end. Even when I'm sharing, I have to have the smooth end. If I sit the tap end the chain always seems to get in my crack. I stifle a snigger but still manage to spray pastry crumbs into the water. God that had been funny…Sam and I always used to share a bath. On one particular occasion, for some reason I was at the plug end. I must have been bad and felt that I owed him or something. Anyway, I was trying to get comfy and a sharp bit of chain scratched my bum something rotten. It really hurt. But all was well a little while later. It had taken Sam three hours to rub in the antiseptic cream. Or was that the baby oil? Oh Sam, dear old loveable Sam, such a waste.

"WILL YOU STOP SHOUTING?" I have to scream. The big mouth in the street is at it again. Whoever he is, he's really starting to bug me now. Can't a girl reminisce and have a rest in peace? R.I.P…now that's funny!

"Ms Evans, you have three minutes. If not, we will have no alternative…we will break the door down," he shouts. A loud click cuts him off. Then there's another click.

"Jenny, Jenny can you hear me? It's Silla." Oh God that's the last thing I need. "Jenny come on out love, we can sort this mess out," she shouts, which causes the megaphone to emit an eardrum shattering whistle. "Jenny they are going to break in if you don't let them in voluntarily," she adds, having lowered her voice somewhat.

Well, do what you like, is all I can say. If you think I'm just going to stand up and walk out to spend my last dying days in a cell, you've got another thing coming. I shift my weight and try and get more comfortable. My arm is floating like a dead thing on the water. It doesn't hurt, but I think it's definitely broken. It's going a funny colour too, just there above the wrist. How strange, it's gone purple.

Purple...purple drapes...the Ten Room. What a complete tosser he turned out to be. Tom Pit a heavenly being on the outside, personality and actual inner beauty, demonic. Wow, one day he is going to wake up and be so disappointed. And I can't believe I actually danced, for God knows how long, with my dress tucked into my knickers! Now that was funny.

That's weird, it's starting to get dark. But it can't be. It's not even 5pm. The sun must have gone behind a cloud or something. I close my eyes and try and keep up with Boy George. There's a knock on the front door. Well, when I say a knock, it sounds more like someone's banging seven bales of shit out of it. Well let them. "Bugger off the lot of you," I scream but it comes out as a whisper. Oh well.

It's strange but I feel so happy. I've just about done everything I've always wanted to do in the past few days. If I die now, then I won't mind. I'll miss Mum still. But weighing up the pro's and con's of living, the con's far outweigh the pro's. It's like three pro's, Mum, Dad and Lizzie to five con's, police custody, the shame, the debts, my business has gone to pot, Dad's anger. That's not five. I hold up my good hand and count them. It's really handy, cos I can see at least ten fingers, so I don't need to use my poorly hand. One, two...wait a minute...one, two...Doh, they keep moving. I give up trying to count them out. Anyway, I know that there are more con's than pro's.

Shit, hang on a minute, what about Lizzie? When Mum and Dad die, who's going to look after her? Oh God no, they'll put her in to residential care home or sheltered accommodation. She'll never manage in this big bad world without me. I've always promised Mum that I'll never allow that to happen. She's going to need me. I can't leave her like this. She'll never understand. It's no good I can't allow myself to fall asleep here. You've got to think of someone else for a change, Jennifer. She's going to need me. You can't be that selfish. But I'm going to die anyway, so what difference does it make? Boy I'm getting confused here.

With my good arm, I try and lift myself up. Bugger. It must be the extra half a stone I've put on. I splash back down into the bath, banging my poorly arm on the way down. Doesn't hurt though, those Pethedine things have really done the trick. It tingles a bit, that's all. I reach out for my jug but it's floated out of arms reach, down to the plug hole end of the bath. I've really done it now, haven't I? I can't seem to open my eyes. It's all gone very dark in here. Somewhere far away, I can hear a dull thudding sound. I try really hard to force my eyelids open.

I manage to open my eyes and after a second or two focus them. "Hey, what the bloody hell do you think you're doing?" I shout indignantly.

There's a bloke standing by the bathroom window, facing out into the street. He's waving to them. Bloody police, they have no respect for a woman's privacy. "And you can shut those blinds again too. I closed them for a reason you know," I snap. The sun has obviously decided to come out of hiding from behind the clouds. The bathroom is filled with brilliant light. The water is going cold, but the sun seems to be keeping me warm. The man by the window chuckles. "Oh, so you think it's funny, do you?" I say angrily. "Well let me tell you buster, when I get out of this bath I'm going to knock that chuckle right out of you." I'm a little confused, but I know what I mean.

Still he doesn't say a word. "Who are you?" I demand in my best authoritative voice. At least I think it's authoritative. I can't actually hear my own voice. I must have got some bubbles in my ears, when I slipped under the water a minute ago. I reach up and wiggle my finger in my ear to try and re-gain some level of hearing. He's starting to unnerve me now. "Come on, turn round. I demand to see your police credentials."

Finally, the man at the window turns around to face me. He has a brown corduroy jacket and brown trousers on. He raises his head and looks at me. He has a big smile on his face and is still chuckling away to himself. He's holding out his hand towards me. At last, someone is going to help me get out of this damn bath. That's funny, he has a moustache a bit like the one Grandpa used to have. No hang on a minute. A feeling of complete well being washes over me. The man speaks. I can hear him. He's not a policeman at all. "Come on Jenny, time we got you out of this mess, eh?" he's saying in a soft and gentle voice.

I can feel a big smile spreading across my face. I don't feel heavy anymore. I hold out my good hand towards him, and take his outstretched hand in mine. "Hello Grandpa. Boy, am I glad to see you. I've really missed you, you know." He pulls me up out of the water and cuddles me...

Is this heaven or hell?

"Oh I've missed you so much too Jenny," he whispers. We cuddle for what seems like an eternity. The silence is then broken. Grandpa sighs and says, "Sorry peanut, its not you're time now after all. HE has spoken. So that's that, I'm afraid."

"But Grandpa, you have to take me with you," I plead. "I don't want to stay here anymore. I'm so tired you know Grandpa." He looks at me in the way that he always used to. His moustache, as ever, is perfectly preened and his big toothy smile threatens to take over his face. He winks.

"I know you're tired Jenny, but them's the rules, and what HE says goes," he says with a shrug of the shoulders and an apologetic sigh. "Look, I'll come back for you another day, I promise. Then you can see Granny and Uncle Arthur again."

I look up into his loving eyes. I am a child again. He leans down and strokes my face, wiping a tear from the end of my nose. I lean my cheek into his warm hand. I always felt so safe, loved and wanted when he did that. What I would give to walk into the bright light with him. I can just make out the faint outline of people in the centre of it. They look like they're waving to me or beckoning me towards them. I think its Granny. I try to shout out, but it's no good. Not a sound comes from my mouth.

"Don't go Grandpa, please!" I beg silently. But it's no use. He straightens up. He looks so tall, taller than I ever remember him being.

"I do love you Jenny, and I miss you, you know. I'll say hi to Granny for you, OK?" He turns slowly and starts to walk away from me, towards the light. I think I can hear voices. I try to wave and run after him, but my legs don't want to work. They feel like lead. I feel dizzy. What's happening to me?

"Oh don't cry Jenny," he calls back over his shoulder. "I'll be back some other day. Be good for your mother, won't you?" Oh no, it's going dark again.

"Jennifer? Jennifer love, can you hear me?" calls a voice from the distance.

Oh no...

I'm gagging. Now there are two possible reasons as to why this is happening. One, I've mastered the fine art of performing fellatio in my sleep, or two someone is trying to kill me. I arrive back into the here and now, choking. A bolt of pain ricochets around inside my body, like a stray sniper's bullet. My throat feels as though I've swallowed a packet of razor blades. This is not looking good. Nope, this is not looking good at all.

"It's alright Jennifer love, try to stay still now," says an unfamiliar sounding voice. "There, that's it. There's a good girl. I'm just taking the NT tube out of your throat. We have had to pump out the contents of your stomach. Was it just the Diamorphine and the Maxalon, and the whisky you've taken, Jennifer love?" it asks softly. "Or have you taken the Pethedine too?"

Oh my god, I've failed. I've bloody failed. The memories claw their way back across the murky quagmire that is my hazy reality. I vaguely remember the Jamesons, and oh no the pills, the bath and then I couldn't get out of it. But hang on a minute, I'd changed my mind. But it'd been too late. I couldn't lift myself out of the bath. Not even to save my life, so to speak. So it wasn't really my fault after all. I hadn't really wanted to go through with it? So it's not so bad, is it?

"Jennifer love, can you here me? God, I think we're losing her. I need help in here people, NOW," shouts the voice as it fades into nothingness.

The memories of the past few weeks' flash back in a blur, on the big screen inside my head. To torment me even more, they are projected in wide screen, with DVD surround sound. I remember I'd found a lump on my back. A biopsy and then the MRI scan. They'd told me, a brain tumour. They said I am dying and have ten, maybe fourteen days to live. The pain of seeing Sam my ex and Satan's spawn, more commonly known as his sister Rose. God I've screwed up. Not just a bit but a huge gargantuan amount. In anyone's book, it is safe to say that I've fucked up big time.

"Jennifer love? Don't panic people, she's back," sighs the softly spoken voice with relief. The owner of the syrupy, butter wouldn't melt in my mouth voice, is starting to grate on me. "You'll just feel a little scratch on the back of your hand, pet. We're going to let you sleep for a while now. The nice policewoman will have to wait for awhile, if she wants to speak to you."

The police? Why? Oh what a bloody mess. I go to wipe my eyes. I still can't open them. They're so heavy. My eyelashes feel like they're stuck together with sleepy dust. A dull ache in my arm thuds away incessantly. I remember, I broke it didn't I. What will mum say? She'll never forgive me for this one. I wish I were dead. I am so tired. I wish I'd never woken up. I should have gone with Grandpa.

Coming round

The sunlight streams into the room through the chink in the curtain. I've really got to fix those bloody things so that they shut. I've been meaning to do it for ages, but you know how it is. Yet again, the sun wakes me from my slumber by angling its demonic rays directly onto the part of my bed, where I've just happen to be flaked out. I reach out to turn off the alarm clock on the bedside table. The beeping is driving me crazy. That's weird, my arm won't move. I manage to force one eyelid open. Where the hell am I?

I attempt to focus. Momentarily, reality-check man pokes my closed eyelid. He looks a bit like Mr Ben. So it's not a dream then. I'm in trouble and can't quite remember all the reasons why, but it's serious. Finally focusing, I scan the room for clues. Hanging up at the window are some dirty looking vertical blinds. You know the type that never quite works properly, so that one end is always higher than the other end? A little more in focus by the bed, there's a small table with a bowl of fruit on it. It must be a hospital room then. I mean let's be honest, how many households have a bowl of fruit by the bed? Personally, it's more likely to be a bottle of Jamesons, the alarm clock and a half empty pack of Marlboro by mine. The regular beeping noise draws my attention away from the array of fresh fruits, round to the other side of the bed. It's a monitor, like the ones they have on Casualty. It's reading 96 beats per minute. Oh no, those bloody curtains again.

"Well Dr Watson, I surmise that we are indeed in a hospital room."

"By Jove Holmes, amazing deduction, just amazing! Brilliant."

So I'm alive then. Well, hoo-bloody-ray. Roll out the red carpet and hang out the flags. Hang on, the door's opening. It's a policewoman. I turn my head to see who has taken hold of my hand. Thank God, it's Mum. She pats my arm reassuringly.

"Jenny Caroline Evans?" spits the policewoman.

"Yes" I manage to croak.

"Jenny Caroline Evans, I am arresting you for the armed robbery at Lloyds TSB in Ealing, on Tuesday 11th August 2000. You have the right to remain silent. Anything you say will be taken down and may be used in evidence..."

Mum interrupts crossly, "It's Jennifer, not Jenny. And her second name is Constance." Yeah, you tell her Mum! Bless her, always right there by my side in my hour of need.

The policewoman leans forward and picks up the clipboard, hanging at the end of the bed. A puzzled look crosses her face and she taps the front of it. "Well, it says Jenny Caroline Evans on here." First she looks at Mum then she looks at me. "You've got a one year old daughter right?"

"Er, no!" I say, my voice tinged with insolence. Do these hips really look like child-bearing hips to you? On second thoughts, let's not go there.

"Wait here," she barks, disappearing out of the room. Oh as if I'm gonna be able to get up and do a runner in my present state.

"What's going on Jenny love?" asks Mum, her eyes searching mine for answers. I wish I knew. I don't quite remember. I only manage to shake my head in response. God, that hurts. I need some painkillers. We sit in silence for what seems like ages. We wait for nearly two hours. I pretend to sleep. I just can't face any more questions right now.

Finally the door opens. It's the policewoman accompanied by a Doctor, who is fiddling with his stethoscope. Funny how doctor's always seem to be fiddling with something. "So...?" I ask wearily. My throat is really sore from that damn tube they'd shoved down it.

He sighs and then looks at me full on. "Somehow you're medical records have been mixed up with another patients." With a sharp intake of breath he adds, "Jenny Caroline Evans died three days ago from a Grade 4 Glioma, a brain tumour. We need to re-run some tests on you Miss Evans, and take another MRI scan. But, if what I think what has happened has happened, then you are no more dying than any one of us in this room," he says waving his arm and smiling.

"You mean..."...but I had pains, I really did. I could feel that something was there. I felt it. No, it was definitely there. I shake my head.

He carries on, "That's right, I think we'll find that you are in the clear," nodding his head enthusiastically. "You are going to be all right Jennifer." If he starts clapping and cheering, I swear I'll floor him.

"But, but...the pains, they were there. Look my hands are still shaking. I still feel sick..." I struggle to validate my symptoms.

"Well I am sure that you do think the pains were real. Under the circumstances, it's quite natural that you would feel some ghost pains. But I can assure you, that they were purely a figment of your imagination. We call them psychosomatic pains."

I look at Dad. His eyes are closed. Mr Big Gob, who appears to have swallowed a medical journal, is on a roll. "Let me explain, psychosomatic or ghost pains are…"

"Shh!" is as much as I dare utter. I hold my good hand up and signal for him to stop.

A nasty smile spreads across the policewoman's face. Mum grabs my hand and kisses it in relief. It's only then that I notice Dad is staring at me from the far corner of the room. He's not looking happy. Nope, he's not looking happy at all.

Oh no, and you know Beck is really going to kill me now. Hell hath no fury like a best friend scorned.

Oh dear…

**A time to live
A time to die
A time to ask the question why
A time to reflect when we are full grown
A time to reap the many seeds
That have been sown**

About the Author

Rachael is somewhat eccentric, yet saner than your average fruitcake! In 1998 she finally settled down to work in the film industry. Writing has been her passion for many years. Starting off with poetry and song lyrics, she began to write Running out of Time in 1998, without a clue where to start or how to do it. There have been a few knock backs, but faint heart never won a book deal. She has written three children's stories, as well as completing four commissioned work's for a children's publishers. Rachael now lives on her beautiful narrowboat in Buckinghamshire, with a cosy wood/coal burning stove and a decanter of Jameson.

The song Running out of Time has been recorded and a demo is available. If you would like to hear it, send your request to: rachaelconisbee@yahoo.co.uk

If you like the book and want to read more, please check out her webpage on the Trafford Publisher's website: www.trafford.com

Also as yet to be published:

Adult:
The Sequel to Running out of time
The Beachwalker
These Four Walls

Children's (Shorty's Tall Stories):
Gilbert
The People in the Clouds
The Christmas's Holiday
Pootle Perkins, the cat who lost her purr
The Old Clay Pipe
The Eddie Craze Mysteries (series)
The Keeper of the Smells (series)

All by Rachael Elizabeth Conisbee (Shorty) ©2004

Front and back cover photography by Rachael Elizabeth Conisbee©2004